J.H. Riddel

Susan Drummond

a novel

J.H. Riddel

Susan Drummond
a novel

ISBN/EAN: 9783744745840

Printed in Europe, USA, Canada, Australia, Japan

Cover: Foto ©Andreas Hilbeck / pixelio.de

More available books at **www.hansebooks.com**

SUSAN DRUMMOND.

A Novel.

BY

MRS. J. H. RIDDELL,

AUTHOR OF "GEORGE GEITH OF FEN COURT," "THE MYSTERY IN
PALACE GARDENS," ETC.

LONDON:

RICHARD BENTLEY AND SON,

Publishers in Ordinary to her Majesty the Queen.

1885.

CONTENTS.

CHAP.		PAGE
I. AN OFF DAY IN THE PARK		1
II. SIR GEOFFREY CHELSTON		12
III. GAYRE, DELONE, EYLES, AND GAYRE		25
IV. MR. GAYRE'S BROTHER-IN-LAW		34
V. A POSSIBLE SAMARITAN		45
VI. ELIZA JUBBINS		53
VII. WILL HE PROPOSE?		64
VIII. FATHER, DAUGHTER, UNCLE		75
IX. SUSAN		82
X. MR. SUDLOW IS ADVISED FOR HIS GOOD		94
XI. "SHOULD AULD ACQUAINTANCE BE FORGOT?"		102
XII. HIGH FESTIVAL		112
XIII. SIR GEOFFREY'S OPINIONS		128
XIV. ON THE WAY HOME		141
XV. SIR GEOFFREY'S TACTICS		149
XVI. LANDED		159
XVII. BETWEEN WIND AND WATER		169
XVIII. THE BLACKNESS OF NIGHT		183
XIX. SIR GEOFFREY'S IDEA		195
XX. THE TRIAL		203
XXI. "EVENTS ARRANGE THEMSELVES"		216
XXII. THE WIDOWER		227
XXIII. A DOG IN THE MANGER		237
XXIV. A GREAT SURPRISE		251
XXV. WITHOUT FOILS		261
XXVI. BEYOND HIS STRENGTH		275
XXVII. "HOW MUCH ARE YOU SORRY?"		285

CONTENTS.

CHAP.		PAGE
XXVIII.	HIS PRICE	297
XXIX.	ON THE MARINE PARADE	306
XXX.	WHAT MR. GAYRE WISHED	316
XXXI.	"HAVE YOU EVER BEEN TO TOOTING?"	323
XXXII.	AWAKENING	338
XXXIII.	LUCKY AT CARDS, ETC.	348
XXXIV.	THE LESSER EVIL	358
XXXV.	"ALL FOR LOVE AND THE WORLD WELL LOST!"	369
XXXVI.	ANYTHING BUT PLEASANT	375
XXXVII.	MR. GAYRE THANKS HEAVEN	382
XXXVIII.	CONCLUSION	395

SUSAN DRUMMOND.

CHAPTER I.

AN OFF DAY IN THE PARK.

Down in the country the meadows were yellow with buttercups, the hawthorns were in full blossom; in the Hertfordshire woods, sweet-scented white and purple violets literally carpeted the turf; beside the meandering streams of Surrey wild flowers were spreading and blooming; but still the spring had been late and ungenial, the accustomed easterly winds had held a longer carnival than usual, vegetation, on the whole, was backward; and as a natural consequence, Hyde Park, which seems specially sensitive to the influence of weather, could not, in the May of 1874, be considered looking its very best, as is sometimes the case in that " merrie " month sacred to catarrh, rheumatism, and bronchitis.

The winter of 1873-1874 was what is generally called "singularly mild." It was singularly disagreeable, at all events : snow and frost held aloof, and bitter blasts and raw unwholesome mists and damps prevailed instead. That season will in one district of London be ever held memorable for a most dense and awful three days' fog, during which period a darkness like unto that of Egypt spread its pall over the whole of the East End.

On New Year's night 1874, indeed, it seemed as though the English climate had determined to turn over a fresh and satisfactory leaf. Such a fine evening was surely never known before on any 1st of January; so magnificent a moon rarely, even in August, has shone on fields where the grain was ripe for the reaper's sickle ; but, like too many good resolutions made that day, the promise of amendment led to no lasting improvement, and winter dragged itself into the lap of spring ; and the spring itself was late and dreary ; and in the May of that year Hyde Park was not looking its best.

B

Hyde Park is a place which appears to greatest advantage when seen in full dress, when the trees are full of leaf and the flowers in full bloom, and the Drive full of carriages and the Row full of riders, and the whole scene one of incessant motion, and constant change, and shimmering colour, and varying effects.

At some periods and under certain conditions it looks more mournful than a desolate heath or a wide expanse of lonely moorland. There is a sky under which its aspect is depressing in the extreme. Even in the "season" there are times when the very genius of desolation seems to be brooding over the grass, and the trees, and the mud-coloured Row, and the Drive whence the last carriage has departed.

It is then, plodding his lonely way homeward, the whole show over, with the sun setting behind him, and night coming on apace, the pedestrian who is not rich or fashionable or prosperous feels a fine despair oppressing him, and is inclined, as a comforting exercise, to recite aloud six verses taken from the ninth chapter of Ecclesiastes.

Judging from the face of a lady who was walking her horse along the Row, she had compassed this state of mind little more than an hour after noon on that specially dull May day in the prosperous year of grace eighteen hundred and seventy-four, when my story opens. Tittlebat Titmouse himself could not have looked more dissatisfied. Her expression was gloomy as the aspect of the heavens, which seemed to betoken rain; and her listless dejected attitude accentuated the desolation of the Park, which was almost empty.

A Drawing-room had drawn nearly all the rank and fashion in town off to St. James's; and the few who at an earlier period of the day graced the Row were now gone home for luncheon, leaving but one solitary rose to bloom, almost unseen, in a desert peopled apparently only by nursemaids, children of tender years, and Life-guardsmen.

And this was not a rose that liked to blush unseen. Solitudes were not places she would have affected of her own free will. She preferred to be amongst her kind, more especially when that kind included a considerable number of male admirers. A quiet life would certainly not have been her choice, and yet for the twenty years she had lived in this world a quiet life chanced to be her portion.

She was a very singular-looking girl to be riding in the Park,

apparently a total stranger. She seemed unknown, even by
sight, to those who had, earlier in the day, passed and repassed
her, and who now were gone away. Not a woman had spoken
a word to her, not a man raised his hat. She had walked and
cantered her horse round and round the Row, evincing a
curious tendency to "hug" the railings, instead of venturing
out into the middle of the ride. A gray-haired groom attended
upon her, keeping closer to his mistress than is the usual habit
of grooms ; and the discontent which clouded her face assumed
on his the proportions of absolute ill-humour.

Yet, if beauty count for anything, she was a lady most
grooms would have felt proud to follow !

As has been said, the Park was singularly empty. There
were not any equipages worth noticing ; the few equestrians
had gone away, either because they feared rain or were hungry ;
the usual loungers were elsewhere ; but still the young lady
rode up and down, and round and round, with the dull steady
persistence of a person on the treadmill.

That she was not enjoying herself in the least might have
been patent almost to a superficial observer ; the groom, who
was enjoying himself even less, knew wherefore, and wondered
why she did not end the ordeal and go home.

No fairer face was seen in the Row that season. One man,
leaning upon the railings, decided no fairer face ever could
have been seen anywhere. It was quite new to him. He had
not beheld it before, and, while he stood watching her as she
passed, he marvelled more and more who she could be, what
she was, and whence she came. He was a man of thirty, with
closely-cut light-brown hair, and rather starved moustache. He
had the look of a man about town ; and, while evidently captivated by the girl's appearance, he eyed her with a critical inves-
tigating glance, which spoke more for the coolness of his head
than the warmth of his heart.

He seemed to have no appointment to keep, or anything
particular to do, for he waited on and on, watching lady and
groom with a puzzled expression that certainly did not betray
the full extent of the admiration he felt.

To him, over the grass, there came, with a quiet but not
stealthy step, a man much his senior, who, saying, " Well,
Sudlow, as usual, admiring rank and beauty," took up a
position beside the person he so addressed.

" I do not know much about the rank," answered Mr. Sudlow, " but the beauty is undeniable ;" and he fastened a bolder

gaze than he had previously ventured upon the girl, who was passing at the moment.

She saw this and coloured, and yet there was a look in her eyes—a downcast, indefinable look—which told she did not feel wholly offended.

The new-comer followed her progress thoughtfully.

"She can't ride a bit," he remarked.

Mr. Sudlow made no answer, but he turned his head and stared hard and inquiringly at the speaker, who, though no question had been asked, replied, "I should say not," and then they both remained silent till after she passed again, which she did this time at the side of the Row furthest from where they stood.

"She is very beautiful," said Mr. Sudlow.

"No doubt, to those who admire that sort of thing."

"What sort of thing?" asked the younger man.

"If you can't see for yourself, it would be useless to try to explain," answered his friend, in a tone which had something annoying in its very calmness; "but the girl *is* good-looking —beautiful if you like."

"I wonder who she is? Did you never see her before?"

The other shook his head.

"Never; and it would not grieve me if I never saw her again. What have we here?" he added, as two persons, riding very fast indeed, came at a hard trot down the road leading across the Serpentine. "You'll get yourselves into trouble, my friends, if you don't mind what you are about," he added.

But apparently the pair knew very well what they were about, for, reining in their horses, they walked as quietly down the Row as if they had been riding lambs instead of powerful hunters, that looked ridiculously out of place in Hyde Park, and carrying such light weights.

There was a lovely flavour of the country about the new-comers. One, a lady, was mounted on the heavier of the animals—a roan with black legs, a grand chest and splendid action, well up to fifteen stone.

For a moment Mr. Sudlow's acquaintance wondered why she rode the roan instead of the magnificent bay, upon which he fastened an appreciative gaze, but his wonder was not of long continuance. Just as the horses were passing the spot where they stood, the bay took umbrage at the sight of a stone roller which lay at the side of the Row. If it had been a wild beast he could not have made more fuss about the matter; he shied almost across to the opposite railings; he got up on his hind legs, and reared as if he meant to fall right over on his back; then he put down his fore-legs and kicked, till Mr. Sudlow felt sure his rider's last hour was come; after that he tried to get his head and bolt; and when he was balked of this intention he seemed for a minute to lift all his four feet off the ground at once, and dance upon nothing in the air.

Meanwhile the gentleman sat the horse as if he had been part of him, and his companion looked on without evincing the slightest discomposure or anxiety.

"By Jove!" said the elder of the spectators under his breath, with an admiration which was as involuntary as it was genuine.

"People shouldn't bring such brutes into the Park," observed Mr. Sudlow, who had turned quite white, and who would, indeed, have speedily placed himself beyond all risk of danger had not his dread of ridicule been greater even than his cowardice.

Then the centaur patted his horse on the neck as if he had done something praiseworthy, and the bay and the roan proceeded peacefully on their way side by side.

At the same moment, the girl who had been for so long a time exercising herself on the Hyde Park treadmill, and who was just then retracing her way from Albert Gate, shrank past the pair, putting all the width of the ride between them.

No words could adequately describe the agony of terror into which the scene had thrown her. She had been coming on to meet the new-comers when the horse shied, and during his varied performances she sat with her eyes fastened on the rider, frightened almost to death, afraid to turn back, afraid the creature would rush madly upon her, afraid her own steed might next take alarm, suffering a thousand agonies in the space of about a minute, and for once in her life utterly unmindful of who might be looking at her, or how she looked. She had never even cast a glance at the roan, all her attention being concentrated on the bay, which she regarded in the light of a four-footed demon; nor, indeed, did the lady on the roan particularly regard her: but as they passed the groom a sudden light seemed to dawn upon her mind, and she looked back.

"Why, that must be Lavender!" she exclaimed; "and, yes—certainly—that is Margaret Chelston;" and without more ado she wheeled her horse round, and, riding after the girl, said as she got close up to her, "Who would have thought of our meeting here, Margaret?"

"That settles the matter," remarked Mr. Sudlow's companion to that gentleman; and Mr. Sudlow somewhat shakily answered, "Yes." Evidently there had been a doubt of some sort in the minds of both men which was now laid at rest.

"I wonder who she *can* be, Gayre?" said Mr. Sudlow. "Are you sure you have never seen her before?"

"Quite sure; and yet, oddly enough, her face seems familiar to me. O look! this is very funny."

It was rather funny. The girl on the hunter had put up a warning hand to keep her companion at a discreet distance, and then, placing the object of Mr. Sudlow's admiration in safety between herself and the railings, proceeded with her conversation, whilst the man who was thus debarred from the delights of feminine society philosophically fell back on Lavender, to the manifest discomfort of a groom who "knew his place" and "had been accustomed to what was fitting."

"It is long since I beheld so lovely a woman," observed Mr. Sudlow.

"I never did," answered Mr. Gayre.

"It is a pity you so seldom speak seriously."

"I fail to see the particular application of your remark."

"Why, it is not ten minutes since you said she might be very well for those who liked that sort of thing; now you declare she is lovely."

"O, I was talking of the other one."

"Pooh!" exclaimed Mr. Sudlow.

"There is no accounting for tastes," remarked Mr. Gayre.

"So it seems," was the curt reply.

"You need not be angry with me because I have not fallen in love with your beauty," said the elder man. "She is a very nice thing in girls, indeed. I should say she is not long from the country; but she will soon know her way about town. I daresay, Sudlow, you may meet her at some party or other before you are much older."

"Do you really think it likely?"

"I do, indeed. I should not mind buying that horse," he added, following the bay with the eyes of a person who understood horse-flesh.

"What a curious seat the fellow has!" observed Mr. Sudlow, trying to emulate his friend's critical manner.

"Do you know the reason?" asked Mr. Gayre, cruelly throwing him at once.

"No; do you?" retorted Mr. Sudlow.

"Of course; he has been accustomed to ride buck-jumpers."

"And what the deuce are buck-jumpers?"

"It is a pity your grandfather is not alive to tell you," observed Mr. Gayre; which was an extremely unkind cut, had Mr. Sudlow clearly understood the full meaning of his friend's remarks.

"What are you going to do with yourself this evening?" asked Mr. Gayre after a pause, which Mr. Sudlow had devoted to the consideration of that conundrum concerning his grandfather.

"I do not know—nothing."

"Come and dine with me, then."

The fashion of Mr. Sudlow's face instantly underwent a change. It lighted up with pleasure and surprise, and he answered heartily,

"I shall only be too glad. How very kind you are to me! I can't imagine why you should be so kind."

"Neither can I," was the answer. "You do not amuse and you do not instruct me. I have no daughter I want you to marry, and I have enough money of my own without trying to rob you of any of yours. Farewell, then, till eight. If in the mean time you discover why I am civil to you, tell me."

Left thus to follow his own devices, Mr. Sudlow, after a moment's hesitation, turned and walked after the lady who had attracted his admiration.

"I knew it," said Mr. Gayre, glancing back; and then, with a cynical smile curling his lip, he pursued his way, which happened to be Cityward. He was accounted a great man in the City; he was a great man anywhere, indeed, if money and greatness can be considered synonymous terms. If a stranger had asked any one of the many persons who touched hats to him, and waved hands at him, and made a point of stopping to say, "How d'ye do? how are you?"—as if their own existence depended upon hearing that the state of his health was satisfactory—who he was, the answer would have been,

"That, sir, is Mr. Gayre, the banker—Gayre, Delone, Eyles, and Gayre, Lombard Street."

Utterly ignorant of the wealth and wisdom they had passed by unheeded, the two young ladies rode slowly on, talking as they went.

"Who in the world, Susan, is that person you are with?"

It was Miss Chelston who asked this question the moment the "person" thus spoken of was relegated to the improving society of Mr. Lavender.

"He is my cousin," answered Susan.

"O, indeed! which of them?"

"Mrs. Arbery's son. He has just come back from Australia."

"Did he bring his steed with him?"

"No," said Susan, laughing; "that pretty creature and this," stroking the roan as she spoke, "belong to a neighbour, who lets us exercise them."

"Does he wish them exercised in the Row?" asked Miss Chelston; "because if he does, I will never venture into it again."

"No, it is too far for us," was the reply; "but we should not do any harm to any one if we did come. Are you as timid about riding as you used to be?"

The beauty shrugged her shoulders.

"I hate it," she answered.

"Why do you ride, then?" was the natural question.

"Why do we do a hundred and fifty things every day of our lives we would rather not do?" she retorted. "O Susan, pray keep your horse a little further off. He has not a nice expression of face at all. He looks as if he would bite. I can't think what could induce you to mount such a monster."

"He is tall," agreed the other indifferently; "but a hand or two does not much signify."

"And where have you been living since your uncle's death?" said Miss Chelston, giving two young men who met them at the moment a full view of her face turned towards her companion, and her eyes raised with a bewitching expression of interest and sympathy. "You dear old thing, it was hard for you to have to leave the Hall."

"It was not so hard for me to have to leave the Hall as for you to have to leave the Pleasaunce, Maggie," answered the other, with straightforward frankness and good sense. "I knew the day must come when it would be necessary for me to go; but you—O, I felt so sorry for you!"

"Yes; but, after all, I don't think things are much worse with us than ever they were. Indeed, I think on the whole they are better. As for you, it is simply dreadful—to be brought up as you were and then left without a sixpence. I call it disgraceful of your uncle."

"Don't say anything against uncle, please, to me," said Susan, involuntarily tightening her rein, and so causing the roan to spring forward, which movement elicited a little scream from Miss Chelston ; "and I am not left without sixpence," she added. "I have two thousand pounds saved from the wreck of my father's fortune. If uncle had known sooner that the great India house was going to fail, he would have arranged to leave me something ; but as it was—"

"I know," interrupted Miss Chelston ; "he always intended you to marry his son."

"Who came home with a wife and two children," added Susan. "Dear uncle—dear, kind uncle !"

"That is all very well," said Miss Chelston ; "but he might have left you some practical proof of his kindness. Even my father, who, as you know, is not remarkable for the interest he takes in the troubles of any one excepting himself, says it is a shame for you to be left out in the cold—a very, very shame;" and Miss Chelston nodded her pretty head to italicise the naughty words she would not utter in their native force and integrity.

'How is your father?" asked Susan ; then, without waiting for a reply, she added, "the first ride I ever had in my life was on his old horse, Wild Indian. Do you remember Wild Indian? It was my fourth birthday, and he took me all across the park and up the long beech avenue."

"And he has told me often enough since you were not frightened, and that you ought to have been his daughter instead of me. I wish with all my heart you had been."

They did not speak for a minute ; each apparently was busy with her own thoughts ; then Susan, looking at her old friend, said suddenly, and as if the fact had only just struck her,

"You are prettier than ever, Maggie."

"Do you think so?" answered Miss Chelston.

"Yes, I always thought you were the most beautiful creature in the world ; but you are more beautiful now than you used to be. It is London, I suppose, and dress."

"Dress improves every one," said the young lady, as a sort of general statement which she immediately applied to a particular case by asking,

"What could induce you to come out in that hat and habit?"

"What is the matter with them?" asked the other.

"Matter ! Why, they must be ten years old !'

"I daresay they are, or more ; they are not mine.   I tore my own habit to rags almost in Ireland."

"Have you been staying in Ireland?"

"Yes, with the Dudleys.   By the way, I wrote to you from their place, but I suppose you never got my letter.   The girls hunted, and of course I went with them."

"Of course you did.   Does Mrs. Arbery hunt?"

"Good gracious, no !   Why, she must be nearly sixty."

"I didn't know.   I only thought that might be her habit. Seriously, Susan, you must buy yourself something fit to wear."

"It is not worth while.   I shall not have the chance of riding even borrowed horses long."

"Dear me ! what will you do?'

"Do without."

"And you so fond of galloping about the country."

"A man may be very fond of champagne, and still find himself able to exist without it.   Will Arbery says where he is, out in the Bush they drink nothing but tea."

"Will Arbery is this latest cousin, I suppose ; any tenderness there?"

"Not the slightest.   He has come home for a wife, I may tell you, and that intended wife's name is not Susan Drummond."

"Most unfortunate Susan ! whose cousins won't marry her, and who, for all her knowledge of horseman—or rather, horse-womanship—has not, I see, yet learnt to hold her reins properly."

"Yes, is not it stupid of me ?   I have tried to break myself of that old trick ; but, do you know, I do not feel as if I had the slightest power over my horse when I take them the other way.   Where are you living now, Maggie?"

"We have only a friend's house for a short time," was the reply.   "When we are settled you must come and spend a long day"

"I shall be delighted," answered Miss Drummond.   "You know Mrs. Arbery's address, don't you?"

"Yes ; Enfield, is it not?"

"Enfield Highway," corrected the other.

"Good heavens ! have you ridden all that distance to-day?"

"It is not so very far," laughed Miss Drummond.

"And don't you want to get back before night?"

"There are many hours before night," answered Susan. "Still we ought to be making our way home.   Just let me

introduce Will to you. Sultan is perfectly quiet, I assure
you."

"Well, I don't know; however, if I am killed my death
will lie at your door. Your cousin won't come very near me,
will he?"

The introduction was effected without any mishap, Sultan
comporting himself during the ceremony as if he had never
stood on his hind legs or lifted his hind heels in his life. Then
adieux were exchanged, and Miss Drummond and her cousin,
having announced their intention of returning home *via* Camden Road, turned their horses' heads towards Stanhope Gate,
and were soon out of sight.

With a sigh of relief Miss Chelston pursued her way to the
Marble Arch, thinking pensively as she rode slowly along that
it was a pity Susan Drummond had not the slightest idea of
making herself fit to appear in decent society, and wishing she
felt as little afraid of horses as that young lady.

"Who do you think the girl is we saw in the Park to-day?"
Mr. Sudlow asked Mr. Gayre the same evening, as they sat
tête à tête over their wine.

"Which of them?" returned the banker.

"O, the one with the dark hair, and the dark-blue eyes, and
the long lashes, and the damask-rose complexion."

"Yes, go on; who is she?"

"Miss Chelston, the only daughter of Sir Geoffrey Chelston,
of the Pleasaunce, near Chelston."

"Of Sir Geoffrey Chelston!" repeated Mr. Gayre, setting
down his claret. "God bless me!"

"Why, do you know him?"

"I used to know him," was the unexpected reply. "*He
married my sister.*"

CHAPTER II.

SIR GEOFFREY CHELSTON.

THERE have been, since the institution of that order, all sorts
of baronets—even good. To the latter class, however, Miss
Chelston's father certainly did not belong. He said himself he
" was a good deal better than some, and not nearly so bad as
most ;" but, then, no one who was fortunate enough to be
acquainted with Sir Geoffrey attached much weight to any of
his statements. Had this estimate of himself been true—which
it was not—the moral condition of the rest of the world must
have been, indeed, regarded as lamentable in the extreme ; for
Sir Geoffrey had, since his boyhood, been in the habit of doing
those things which he ought not to have done ; whilst those
things which he ought to have done he did not.

Geoffrey is not a name which suggests a taste for the Turf,
a fondness for the society of jockeys, blacklegs, and gamblers ;
an almost inconceivable amount of ignorance, except on the
subject of "sport," horses, games of chance and skill—an abun-
dance of that disreputable lore which a man who has always
been knocking about the world's least desirable haunts cannot
fail to accumulate ; to say nothing concerning a distaste, which
almost amounted to hatred, for the pursuits, trammels, and
traditions of a decent and orderly life.

There was no shame about the man, and there was no hope
whatever of repentance—unless it might be a poor makeshift
death-bed repentance, with a wasted life stretching behind, and
an unknown eternity yawning in front. So long as a "chance
remained for him "—a chance, that is, of returning to the mud
in which he loved to wallow—remorse was not likely to fasten
its tooth upon him. His doings, his sayings, his sins, his short-
comings, were enough, in very truth, to have caused the scholarly ancestor from whom he inherited his name to rise from
the grave, sold by this degenerate descendant to strangers, and
return to see the ruin wrought by one man—one solitary man.

There had been spendthrifts aforetime amongst the Chelstons, but no spendthrift like unto this. There had been sinners—wicked, godless, graceless sinners; but either they died young. or, taking thought to their ways betimes, reformed and settled down ere age came upon them. There had been misers who grudged themselves food and the poor a farthing; but it was left for Sir Geoffrey to spend freely on his own pleasures, and rob both rich and poor of that which of right belonged to them. His inherited title—won by a certain Ralph Chelston on a battle-field, where the fate of the day was changed by a mere handful of gallant soldiers—he dragged like a worthless garment through the mire of the kennels; while his name, one of the oldest in the kingdom, had become a mock and a byword amongst the vilest of women and the worst of men.

He was not born to poverty like many another, who, with equally little satisfaction to himself or any other human being, has travelled the road to ruin. It was not necessity which first made him acquainted with strange bedfellows. No impulsive generosity. no desire to serve a friend, no boyish prodigality in the way of giving great entertainments. or wild desire to scatter gifts around, brought him into early contact with the Jews. If he had desired a father's help and counsel, he could, till he was nearly twenty-six, have obtained both from a parent wise as loving. So far as man could tell, there was not an excuse for the bad mad race on which he entered. Some said he "cast back" to a certain Elizabeth Hodwins, who was raised by a former baronet from the condition of a fisherman's daughter to the rank of Lady Chelston; but those best learned in the family lore shook their heads when they heard this theory; for Elizabeth, possessing for her dower as much sense as beauty, had proved the saviour both of her husband and his fortunes. When she married him he was, with other gay gallants of his time. running a muck; but she took her husband well in hand, and brought him out of the ordeal safe, though not unscathed. She wore her honours with a splendid meekness, winning respect rather than compelling it. She had. as one, who knew her well, chronicled, a "smile for the rich and a tear for the poor;" in all ways an exceptional woman, who once, it was recorded, saved a child's life at the peril of her own. Except as regards mere brute courage, Sir Geoffrey did not own a trait in common with his brave and beautiful ancestress; but he had one good quality—physically he was no coward.

People marvelled a man of such ancient lineage should play the pranks he did.

"Why, don't you know," said a farmer once in the village tap-room, "'the older the seed, the worse the crop.'"

Sir Geoffrey was an awful crop for any house to have to gather home within its records. With him the race seemed destined to die out. Slightly varying the words of James V. of Scotland, it might have been said of the wealth of the Chelstons that it had "come with a lassie," and that the name "would go with a lassie." The king who conferred the baronetage on Ralph the soldier added the hand of an heiress, who was nothing loth to wed the handsome hero. Since that time heiresses had come and gone, adding their fortunes to the Chelston coffers; but now the coffers were all empty, and Sir Geoffrey owned no lands, or houses, or money, or son, or anything, save one fair daughter and a pile of debts that never could be paid.

Well might men wonder where the money had gone. There was nothing whatever to show for it. Sir Ralph had bought the estate, adding to his own small patrimony many a broad acre and goodly manor; Sir Charles built the great rambling house, and laid out the quaint gardens, and planned the terraces from the west front to the river Chel; Sir Bruce built the stables and kennels, and then, when he tired of dogs and horses, purchased the pictures and statues which made the Pleasaunce a show-place. Then there was the Sir Ralph who entertained royalty; and Sir Geoffrey, who spent his life in collecting blackletter and rare editions, and who wrote a book full of useless learning, of which he printed but one hundred copies; and then came the saintly Sir Francis, who, after a youth of sin, devoted his old age and his money to ecclesiastical purposes, rearing and endowing one of the loveliest churches in the whole of England; then there was another Sir Charles, who performed great deeds at sea, and died an admiral; and a Sir James, who was a great politician, and rose to be a foremost man in the councils of the nation; and then there came Sir Cecil, with the scholarly tastes of his progenitor, Sir Geoffrey, which he entirely failed to bequeath to the son he named after that "lover of the best thoughts of older minds."

Never, surely, was there such a man for getting fortunes and wasting them as Sir Geoffrey the second. Before he was seven-and-twenty he came into possession of the Pleasaunce, a large sum in ready money, pictures, plate, horses, carriages, everything necessary to the establishment of a gentleman of rank and position. When he was thirty his mother, who had been an heiress, died, and he got her money. Two years later he married Miss Gayre, dowered with a fortune of thirty thousand pounds, which was so settled, the lawyers declared, that a coach-and-four could not be driven through it. When matters came to be investigated, however, it was found that if a coach-and-four had not scattered her fortune, Sir Geoffrey had burrowed a way into the money. Four years afterwards his grandmother left him a satisfactory sum in ready cash, and this legacy was soon after followed by one from his only uncle.

But all these legacies were mere drops in the ocean; Sir Geoffrey went through them at a hand-gallop; and when he finally sank in a very rough sea of well-nigh unlimited liability, there was not a thing left to show for the money that had sifted through his hands but piles on piles of writs, and lawyers' letters in sufficient quantity to have papered the walls of the new "thieves' kitchen" hard upon Temple Bar.

Everything saleable was sold; everything go-able was gone —books, pictures, statues, horses, lands, furniture, stock, timber. If he had been able to dispose of his title, that would have followed in wake of his other possessions. In less than thirty years from the time of his father's death he had not a rood of his own ground left, not even the family burying-place; not a roof to cover his head belonging to himself; not a chair to sit down on, or a table to dine at; not even old Chelston Pleasaunce with its moss-covered avenue, and its rusty gates, and its park, kept latterly like a meadow, and its garden, where the roses were trailing across the paths—to go down to, when London grew for him very hot indeed.

To say that in any one respect, whether personally or mentally, Sir Geoffrey even faintly resembled a gentleman, would be to libel a class not accustomed to flattering similes.

Of course when people heard he was a baronet, and had run through hundreds of thousands of pounds, they declared there was "something about him," that "blood would tell," and all the rest of it; but meeting him casually "knocking about," it never occurred to any human being to suspect he was other than some disreputable horsey individual who frequented racecourses and stables, who affected very tight trousers, who was a proficient in bad language, who wore his white hat a good deal on one side, who walked with his legs wider apart than is the custom of those who have not spent best part of their waking hours on horseback, and to whom no respectable landlady in her senses would have let her first floor, even if furnished with the best references and offered a month's payment in advance.

It had happened to Sir Geoffrey in his comparatively palmy days to be taken for what he looked like; and as he never afterwards hesitated to tell the story himself, there can be no harm in repeating it here.

One day wanting something in a hurry, he called at the shop of a saddler with whom he had never before had any dealings, was shown what he required, and marvellous to relate, laid down a sovereign in payment.

The price of the article was one pound precisely, but the shopkeeper handed him back two shillings.

"What's this for?" he asked.

"O, *we always allow ten per cent to grooms*," was the answer.

"Do you?" said Sir Geoffrey, coolly pocketing the two shillings. "I think I'll patronise you again."

Which, indeed, he did to some purpose; for when the final settlement of his bad debts came about, it so happened he owed that particular tradesman something like four hundred pounds.

It is delightful to think of the charming manner in which favoured persons can incur debts they know they will never be able to discharge, and how easy it is for any man with a handle to his name to cozen the British tradesman.

You and I, my friend, with a limited income, might wait a long time for a loaf of bread unless the B.T. were well assured the wherewithal to pay for it would be duly and truly forthcoming. But a baronet, or a knight, though he may not have a lucky penny to bless himself with, need not, even at this present incredulous period of the world's history, want any manner of earthly thing that is good.

As regards Sir Geoffrey Chelston, he was one of those men out of whom no created being seems able to make money. He had no steward or lawyer or agent, or mistress or boon companion, who waxed fat while he grew lean. He was not systematically robbed or persistently cheated. His tenants were harassed, his solicitors worried, his friends victimised, his servants' wages left unpaid, and, as has been said, at the end of it all there was nothing to show for the princely estate mortgaged, for the fortunes gone, for the pictures and the books and the jewelry and the timber, any more than might have been the case had the whole been swallowed up bodily on one disastrous night in the Goodwin Sands.

Nay more, misled by the Baronet's easy indifference, by his gross ignorance of matters with which most men are conversant, by his "devil-may-care" manner, by a certain fatalist warp of mind which had descended to him not from the fair Elizabeth, and by the impossibility of conceiving that it was absolutely necessary such wide estates and such an old title should "go down into the pit," many hopeful persons had tried whether "something could not be done."

Joyfully Sir Geoffrey surrendered the helm to each in succession : the credulity of any fresh fool concerning the future, meant ready money to him in the present. That it also meant loss to the fool did not affect the Baronet in the least.

"They speculated for a rise," he was wont to say laughingly, "and the stock fell—that was all."

The stock did fall indeed ; there is no quotation known on 'Change that could adequately represent the fall in the Chelston stock as it appeared eventually to those who had felt quite sure they would be able to make a good thing out of it.

If I had not to write this book about quite other people than Sir Geoffrey Chelston and his dupes, or rather the dupes of their own imagination and self-confidence, who, setting out to shear, came home shorn, an instructive history might be compiled for the benefit of solicitors, bankers, money-lenders, and others, who were each and all represented on the bankruptcy schedule when the Baronet went airily into Portugal Street with a rose in his buttonhole and a straw in his mouth to pass his examination. Liabilities scarcely to be recorded in figures : assets available for the benefit of the unsecured creditors—*nil*.

Take one pleasing instance as an illustration—but a poor illustration, it must be confessed, because it is sketched from a landscape over which the evening shadows were drawing rapidly down.

A smart young lawyer, who thought all the wisdom of his predecessors folly, bought a practice in the market-town of Chelston, near the Pleasaunce. There he heard a great deal about Sir Geoffrey, his debts, his recklessness, his rent-roll, his mortgaged acres, his embarrassments, his one daughter, till he got nearly beside himself with the magnitude and originality of the design he had conceived.

He possessed a few thousands; he believed he could

c

reckon on a few thousands more from his relations. He knew a man who was enormously rich and the father of an extremely plain daughter; the "oracle" might be worked, he considered; so without more to-do he set himself to work it.

Sir Geoffrey was not difficult of approach—bless you, not he! The young lawyer did not experience much trouble in boarding the good old ship Chelston, in enticing the Baronet into his pretty little parlour, in introducing that worthy to his blue-eyed wife, in walking down the street to the Golden Stag, where Sir Geoffrey put up; the talk between them being all the while as "pleasant and familiar as talk could be."

After a short acquaintance, he began dexterously to feel his way.

"Your affairs have been mismanaged, Sir Geoffrey, I am afraid," he suggested.

"They have, damnably," agreed Sir Geoffrey, with agreeable frankness; but he did not say by whom.

"It seems to me that all they require is a little systematic arrangement," observed the adventurous young man.

"That's all they ever wanted," answered Sir Geoffrey with another oath.

"If a person were to devote time and energy to the matter, they could soon be put in train," observed the lawyer tentatively.

"They might," replied the Baronet; but it is only justice to add his tone was dubious.

There was nothing more said then. They went, of course, into the Golden Stag, where Sir Geoffrey asked his new friend what he "would take;" and the wine which the landlord produced having been duly added to an already long score, the nominal owner of Chelston Pleasaunce got on his horse, and rode back to that place, leaving the lawyer well satisfied with the progress he had made.

Not a fortnight elapsed before he was installed as Sir Geoffrey's legal adviser, of whom that gentleman had already about a hundred. He was told just as much as the Baronet chose to tell him; he paid out a couple of small but very pressing executions; he wrote to several persons who had issued writs; and he began to find his affable client in "pocket-money."

That was Sir Geoffrey's lively way of putting the obligation, and you may be sure the young lawyer laughed loud and long at the pleasantry.

The Baronet wanted so much pocket-money, however—or, as he put the matter, "he had such a confoundedly big hole in his pocket"—that ere long his accommodating friend thought it might be better to expedite affairs a little ; so one day he went across to the Pleasaunce, where he found Sir Geoffrey seated in the library, the portrait of his scholarly ancestor surveying, from its frame above the mantelpiece, long lines of well-nigh empty book-shelves ; a small dog lying on the table, and a large one stretched on the hearth-rug ; brandy and soda-water on a tray beside him ; and a number of unopened letters littering the blotting pad.

"All duns," said the Baronet, sweeping them carelessly on one side. "Well, and what has blown you over? Some good wind, I am sure : for I was just wondering where I should get enough money to carry me to town."

The lawyer took a seat, and commenced, with diplomatic caution, to unfold his plan.

"You'd like to be rid of all this annoyance, Sir Geoffrey ?"

It was thus he opened his first parallel.

"Indeed, I should well like to be rid of it," answered the Baronet ; "and if any way out of the —— mess has occurred to you, I shall be only too glad to discuss it when I return from London."

He had gone through too many interviews of the same sort not to have learnt his best wisdom lay in deferring the final hour of explanation. Explanation, bitter experience had taught him, meant a sudden stop in the supplies.

"When do you suppose you will be back?" asked the lawyer.

"O, in a few days; a week at the farthest," said Sir Geoffrey ; "and I want to start this afternoon, if I can anyhow raise the funds."

"I have not much money with me," observed the lawyer.

"I can take your house on my way to the station," suggested his client.

"Before I leave I should like just to ask you one question," ventured the other.

"Ask away," said the Baronet graciously.

"Should you have any objection to resettle the estate ?"

Sir Geoffrey stared at him.

"How the deuce could I do that," he asked, "when it's as good as out of my hands altogether?"

"But if it were back in your hands ?"

"That's quite another matter. I'd do anything in reason, I'm sure, to get out of this blank blanked continual hot water. I can't see, however, where the good of resettling would be now. As you know, or as, perhaps, you don't know, there is not a male left to come into the title after me; and there was no remainder to females in the patent."

The Baronet took great credit to himself in that he never, in his later years, told his legal advisers a syllable he could not swear to. He did not count silence any falsehood. So long as they asked no questions he held his tongue; when they put a thing to him plainly, time had proved it was better to answer without equivocation. Then if they liked to go on deceiving themselves—which they generally did like—it was their own fault, not his.

For which reason he told this latest adviser a fact "any fool," to quote Sir Geoffrey, "could find out for himself from the Red Book in a minute." There was no heir to the title.

"I am aware of that; O, I am quite aware of that," answered the other.

"All I want is everything to be fair and above board," said the Baronet, with a genial frankness. "I don't know how you mean to help me; but I take it for granted you have some project maturing in your head, and all I can assure you is, you won't find me stop the way if you are able to find an outlet. Only don't ask me to listen to any details now; for it is of vital importance that I should get into town by the afternoon express."

Sir Geoffrey was detained so long in town by reason of what he called a "stroke of luck," that his new friend deemed it prudent to follow and "put matters in train."

He found the Baronet, who had won something considerable on the Turf, in the highest spirits. His talk was of a certain outsider who had come in first; and it proved somewhat difficult to get him to listen to all the other had to say.

Divested of verbiage, the lawyer's proposition was this:

He knew a gentleman who had made his money in trade—"never mind what trade," he said hesitatingly.

"That does not matter in the least," observed Sir Geoffrey, in a truly liberal spirit.

"If there were one thing this man adored beyond all other things, it was rank. He would, in a way of speaking," declared the lawyer, "part with all he possessed for a title."

"Well, that's odd too," commented the Baronet. "I'd

sell my title and"—but I need not particularise the other adjunct Sir Geoffrey offered to throw in as a mere makeweight —"for a few thousands, cash down."

"He has a daughter," went on the lawyer. "She is not handsome, certainly. I suppose, however, you would not allow that to influence you much."

"I always did prefer a pretty woman to a plain one; but what has she to do with all this? Her good or bad looks can't signify to me."

"I thought you would take a sensible view of the matter," observed the other. "Now, I believe—indeed, I know—a marriage might be arranged which would at once relieve you from your more pressing embarrassments, and induce my millionaire—"

"Stop a minute," said the Baronet. "Do you mean a marriage with *me?*"

"I could not mean one with anybody else," was the reply. "You see no objection, I hope?"

"There is only one objection; but I am afraid it is insurmountable, unless you are able to find a way out of the difficulty. We can't get rid of Lady Chelston."

"What Lady Chelston?"

"My wife."

"But you have not got a wife."

"Haven't I?"

"She died fourteen years ago."

"Did she?"

"You—you haven't married again, Sir Geoffrey, have you?"

"No, faith! One wife at a time is enough for any man."

"But you were left a widower fourteen years ago, when you came back from abroad with your little girl, dressed in deep mourning; and you said then, 'Poor Maggie has lost her mamma.'"

"So she had. When we were on the Continent my wife and I parted for ever. My daughter and I were in mourning, I remember; but it wasn't for Lady Chelston."

"And do you mean to tell me Lady Chelston is still alive?"

"And likely to live, so far as I know."

"And has there never been anything to enable you to get a divorce?"

"My good fellow, do not ask such ridiculous questions."

"And you are tied hand and foot matrimonially as well as pecuniarily?"

"Your statement of the position is painfully accurate."

"And how am I to get back the money I have advanced you?"

"If you advanced it in the expectation of being repaid on my marriage with your friend, who is, as you say, not handsome, I really have not an idea."

"But I can't lose my money because you happen to have a wife living when everybody thought she was dead."

"If you like to take your chance of hanging, you can get rid of her."

Then the lawyer broke out. Sir Geoffrey himself could scarcely have indulged in worse language, in more futile and frantic profanity.

He would expose the Baronet. England should ring with an account of the transaction. He had been swindled; he had been robbed; he had been dealt with most treacherously; his pocket had been picked by a person who called himself a gentleman, but who was in reality no better than a common thief and swindler.

"He goes on in this way because I won't commit bigamy." said Sir Geoffrey, addressing the imaginary jury the lawyer had summoned to sit in judgment on so heinous a criminal.

"But surely in common honesty you will pay me?" said this irate creditor.

"Pay you! how in the world am I to do that?"

"Why, you have won a lot of money, you say."

"O, but I want that for myself; besides, there is very little left. You talk about being deluded and disappointed. You have not been half so grossly deluded as I have been. What is your disappointment compared to mine? I made sure you had hatched some scheme for cheating the Jews and giving me my own again, and now the whole thing resolves itself into an impossible marriage. Gad, if I had been free I'd have got a rich wife for myself long ago! You may be very sure I never should have employed a lawyer to look one out for me."

Perhaps this matter hastened the end a little; but, under any circumstances, that end could not have been long deferred. There was a rush down to the Pleasaunce, a race as to which creditor should get his man into possession first; but they all got there too late. Sir Geoffrey had "taken the wind out of their sails" by begging a Jew to whom he owed a large sum of money to petition the court, and the court sent down a messenger, who was comfortably installed at the Pleasaunce when the representatives of the two chosen tribes of Israel, and various so-called Christians, who may have been, and very probably were, descended from the other ten sons of Jacob, put in an appearance there, only to be immediately turned out again.

There was wailing and gnashing of teeth amongst bailiffs and sheriff's officers, and lawyers and creditors; but the Baronet remained nobly serene.

"It was bound to come," he explained to the friends who offered him their condolences. "I don't really know that I can be much worse off than I was;" and seeing the resigned, not to say cheerful, manner in which Sir Geoffrey bore his misfortunes, people came to the conclusion there was something in the background, that he had prepared a feather bed to fall on, satisfied of which good management on the part of the Baronet, society refrained from giving him as cold a shoulder as it might have done had that amiable abstraction believed he was an honest man.

"I shall have to take a house in London," he remarked, not because at the moment he had the slightest intention of doing anything of the sort, but merely for the reason that he thought the statement sounded well; "a furnished house, till I can pull myself together a little."

Then upspake young Moreby, who had been causing the large fortune left by his papa, a great colliery proprietor, deceased, to disappear like dust before the wind, till his mother, the widow Moreby, who, though sometimes doubtful in her English, had a thorough knowledge of business, came to town, and, assuming the conduct of affairs, as she had a right to do, being not merely executrix, but part-owner of all the coal-pits whereout old Moreby had extracted his money, announced her intention of taking him abroad away from "all his vicious companions;" upspake this youth, who had not been blest with Sir Geoffrey's friendship for more than a few months, and said,

"My crib in the Regent's Park would be the very thing for you, Chelston;" and then there ensued a little chaff and various allusions to Mrs. Moreby and another very different sort of lady who had exercised the mind of the worthy widow in no slight degree, which need not be more particularly chronicled here; and Sir Geoffrey made himself very agreeable while these themes were in progress, and any one might have imagined the last thing he had in his thoughts was of the house in question, or of taking in young Moreby.

But somehow he just stepped into the "crib" as it stood—fully furnished—and, when he was fairly in residence, said quite calmly to his youthful friend,

"I do not know how to thank you sufficiently for lending me your house. It shall be taken good care of, I promise you."

Now young Moreby had never dreamt of lending Sir Geoffrey anything without being paid for it; but he found the Baronet's understanding so dense on the subject, he was forced to yield the point with such grace as was possible under the circumstances.

CHAPTER III.

THE Spirit of Improvement, taking a walk about the middle of the year 1857 down Lombard Street one day, bethought itself that the banking-house leased by Gayre and Co. from the gentleman whose fleshly tenement was temporarily occupied by the meddlesome sprite referred to, ought to be rebuilt.

Nothing less to the taste of the old firm could readily have been suggested. Ancient ways seemed good in their sight; spick and span new edifices savoured, according to their ideas, of shoddy companies, limited liability, tricks of trade, bankruptcy, and various other matters hateful to honest men.

More, to rebuild would cost much money, and Gayre and Co. did not like parting with even a little money, unless, like bread on the waters, it was sure to come back to them after many days with interest from date added. Rebuilding would inconvenience them, and that was even a more serious consideration than the pecuniary outlay; rebuilding was unprofitably laying down gold at some ridiculous rate per foot on the property of another man; and the fuss and bustle, the hoarding, the scaffolding, the masons and labourers, the mess and lime and confusion, and utter demoralisation of the integrity of their dear old dirty den, would prove annoying, not to say intolerable, to their clients, who were mostly slow-going people of title and old-fashioned City merchants, whose fathers and grandfathers had trusted their money to Gayres' keeping, and never found cause to repent of the confidence reposed.

If a bank, and all a bank's customers, dislike change, cleanliness, and convenience, it is evident that without great external pressure things are likely to remain in their original condition till the crack of doom; but when this pressure did come in the shape of an expiring lease, and a ground landlord who would not be diverted from his purpose even by the offer of money, old Mr. Gayre, who was then alive, and Mr. Edwin Gayre, his son, set their wits together to try how

little they could do in the way of making their bank look like
any other bank of recent date as possible.

It is only fair to say they succeeded in their endeavour.
Even to the present hour Gayres' is a model of what a counting-
house ought not to be. An old building at the back, which
chanced to be their own freehold, was left untouched, and in
a portion of that edifice the Gayre of to-day gives audience to
the few persons who ever ask to see him, and transacts the
little business it is necessary for him to attend to. Gayres'
have not gone on with the times; but they feel no desire to
do anything of the kind.

Banks have come and banks have gone, but Gayres' still
holds on the even tenor of its respectable way. Though the
main part of the bank abutting on Lombard Street was, as
has been stated, brand-new less than twenty-five years ago, it
has managed somehow to acquire during that period quite a
look of antiquity. For one thing, it was built on the old lines,
and kept rigidly free from any improvements of structure or
originality of design. It is as square as the shape of the
ground would permit; it has steps up to the door, apparently
with the intention of checking the ardour of any stranger who
might feel disposed to rush in and open an account; the exterior is utterly destitute of ornament, and the inside as plain as
Dissenting chapels used to be. It is badly lighted and not
ventilated at all. The way to the strong-room is encompassed
by as many traps and perils as those which beset Christian on
his road from the City of Destruction to the better land; and
there is a dark step down into Mr. Gayre's own especial
sanctum which has nearly ended the earthly career of more
than one intending client.

Any one who by some rare piece of good fortune gets a
cheque to present across Gayres' counter feels as the narrow
half-door swings behind him that he has stepped out of Lombard Street and the modern days of hansom cabs, railways, and
electric light, into the seventeenth century, and he half expects
when he steps out again to see the old signs which denoted
the goldsmiths' whereabouts in the days when Mr. Francis
Child, the first regular banker, married Martha, only daughter
of Robert Blanchard, citizen, and lived with his wife, business,
and twelve children in Fleet Street, where, to quote Pennant,
" the shop still continues in a state of the highest respectability."

The Gayres were goldsmiths also about the same period,
and had been notable people in the City even before the time

when their relation, Sir John Gayre, was Lord Mayor of London. No mushroom house this, eager to extend its credit by means of cut stone and ornamented pilasters, or to flaunt its wares in the face of the public through plate-glass windows, or reflect the faces of dupes in French polished mahogany counters and brass knobs and rails. It was quite enough satisfaction for any man to know himself in the books of the firm, without looking upon his own distorted likeness in shining furniture and glittering lacquer.

Gayres were by no means anxious to open accounts " on the usual terms;" indeed, their terms, according to modern ideas, were most unusual. They did not even care for the "best bills;" upon the whole they preferred that bills of all sorts and descriptions should be negotiated elsewhere, and he would have been a rash man who had ventured to ask Gayres' manager to discount even the finest mercantile paper.

Conservative in their ideas of trade, though following civic traditions, perhaps somewhat independent and radical in politics, Gayres' notion of banking was eminently primitive. According to the traditions of their house a banker was a man of substance and repute, who took care of money for his customers. Gayres professed to do little more than this. Like their predecessors the Lombards, they could, though rarely, be induced to accommodate a well-known customer; but the whole transaction was fenced about with such forms and ceremonies, prefaced by such details, and requiring such an expenditure of time, legal advice, and thought, that "the business" was, as a rule, transferred to some house accustomed to more rough-and-ready methods of procedure.

Time, to Messrs. Gayre, Delone, Eyles, and Gayre, might have represented eternity, to judge from the deliberation of their movements. To take, say, one hundred pounds in five notes over their old Spanish mahogany counter occupied more time than the cashing of ten thousand might at Glyn's.

But then Gayres' looked down on Glyn's, as it did on Child's. Gayres represented itself as being more respectable than any other banking-house in London.

" Nell Gwynne banked there, did she?" said a Gayre, long and long anterior to the date at which this story opens; " and Childs are proud of the fact, are they? I wouldn't have let the hussy set foot across our threshold."

Which remark may give the key to Gayres' policy. Respectable, decorous, sound; if you had wound Gayres up at any minute in the twenty-four hours, enough would have been forthcoming to satisfy everybody and leave a balance.

Yes, even in the year 1874, when the Gayre in whose veins flowed the blood of all the Gayres since 1647, to say nothing of many previous generations, laid down his claret, and astonished his guest by declaring his sister had married Sir Geoffrey Chelston.

As has been said, banks had come and banks had gone, and, it may be added, banks were going; but Gayres' knew no anxiety as regarded its financial position. The heads of the firm had not appropriated their customers' title-deeds—a favourite form of latter-day banking dishonesty; the security on which their good money lay at interest they had never found need to mortgage. All their business lives for a couple of centuries, at least, they had been quiet, honest, orderly people, living well within their income, owing no man more than they could conveniently pay, eschewing speculation, holding aloof from the railway and other manias, that beggared and crippled so many large houses in the years preceding the great show in Hyde Park.

And yet Gayres' was not what it had once been. It could not have counted down guineas with some of the great banks, as it might formerly. The principals had not gone on with the world; and so the world, which latterly has got into the habit of travelling very fast indeed, made no scruple about leaving Gayres' behind. Some even of their titled customers, finding the old bank allowed them no interest on balances, were contracting a nasty habit of transferring two or three thousand pounds at a time to the London and Westminster, or National Provincial, or any other great bank which had the knack of being more considerate. They kept their accounts still at the "old shop," which once hung out a tortoise for its sign; but even country squires and Tory noblemen were learning a few things their ancestors chanced to be ignorant of, and seemed as anxious and greedy to make a "tenner" as a lad to toss for tarts.

City wags occasionally suggested it would be the most fitting of all fitting things if Gayres' were to hunt up the old tortoise out of their cellars, and hang it in the sun. Scoffers declared "Gayres' was the slowest coach going in the City." They wondered why, if Gayres' would not amalgamate with a bank that "had some life in it," Gayres' did not shut up and cut the City altogether?

"And there is only this one fellow left, and he not married," was the remark generally made. "Why, he must be as rich as a Jew;" which did not happen to be the case. Mr. Gayre was well off, very well off, but he could not be called a millionaire for all that.

Nicholas Gayre came of a stock more famous for saving money than making it. To pitch thousands about, to see gold flung recklessly into this venture and that, would have seemed criminal in the eyes of men who esteemed riches a possession to be desired, more especially when accompanied by a good name. Thus, if they had lost little or nothing, they had not made fortunes in a day, like their neighbours up and down the street. They took few measures to extend their connection : and so it occasionally happened that, as the heads of a family died off, the younger branches carried their accounts elsewhere.

Banking, in a word, had changed its character, and as Gayres' refused to veer round at the bidding of the banking world the old house came gradually to be pushed up into a quiet business corner, like a dowager at a ball, "whose dancing days are over."

But it was while Jeremy Gayre and his son Joshua—whose name figured at the tail end of the firm—were the actual heads of a house in which Delone and Eyles had long ceased to be anything save sleeping partners, that a blow was dealt, sufficient to have destroyed a business built on any other foundation than the rock of honesty.

First, Delone elected to be paid out, and then Eyles. For long previously they had both been drawing the full share of the profits, and when the opportunity occurred they gladly said, paraphrasing the words of the Prodigal Son, "Give us the portion that falleth to us." Unlike the prodigal, however, they did not waste their money in riotous living; they bought estates, and went into mining and other speculations, and added to their store, and married heiresses, and took up their position among the first in the land, while Gayres' was left with a decreasing business and a reduced capital. Well was it for the bank that the then principal in the firm had always lived, not merely well within his income, but so as to save largely out of it. Jeremy Gayre was, indeed, one to have satisfied the author of *Banks and Banking*, who thus drew, in pen and ink, a type of a class now well-nigh extinct :

"He" (*i.e.* a banker of the old school) "bore little resemblance to his modern successor. He was a man of

serious manners, plain apparel, the steadiest conduct, and a
rigid observer of formalities. As you looked in his face you
could read, in intelligible characters, that the ruling maxim of
his life, the one to which he turned all his thoughts and by
which he shaped all his actions, was, that he who could be
trusted with the money of other men should look as if he
deserved the trust, and be an ostensible pattern to society of
probity, exactness, frugality, and decorum. He lived, if not
the whole of the year, at least the greater part of the year, at
his banking-house; was punctual to the hours of business, and
always to be found at his desk. The fashionable society at the
West-end of the town and the amusements of high life he never
dreamed of enjoying."

Times, even during the noonday of Mr. Jeremy Gayre's
existence, had changed so far that few merchants in a large way
of business resided on their City premises. The upper portions
of their houses could be utilised much more profitably, it had
been found, than as mere dwellings; and Mr. Gayre, who
understood the full import of that old Scotch saw which tells
how "many a pickle maks a mickle," when he married let off
part of the Lombard Street establishment, moved "west of
Temple Bar," and took up his abode in one of the old roomy
houses in Norfolk Street, Strand.

There was no Embankment then, or thought of one. At
high tide the water came lapping up to the railings at the
bottom of the street; and, save at the Strand end, there was
no exit. Cabs and vans did not go tearing and rattling over
the pavement, as is the case now; and the dwelling Mr. Gayre
bought was as quiet as though it had been situated in some
retired City court.

When in good course of time Joshua Gayre, the son, took
unto himself a wife, he set up housekeeping in Brunswick
Square, where four sons and one daughter were born and bred.
Of these four sons, Jeremy, the eldest, died before he came of
age. Edwin in due time went into the bank, in which, while
still young, he was associated as partner. John elected to take
orders; and, in compliance with the bent of the youngest son's
inclinations, a commission was bought for Nicholas in a cavalry
regiment.

The three were all good men and true. They sowed no
crops of wild oats for their father and themselves to reap.
Edwin took kindly to banking, John to the Church, Nicholas
to the army. The latter rose rapidly in the service; he went

through the Crimean campaign; and his regiment, crowned
with distinction, had just returned to England, when the Indian
Mutiny caused it to be again ordered off to the East.

Five years elapsed before young Gayre, who had fought his
way to the rank of colonel, saw his native country once more;
then he came back in obedience to a summons from his father.

Great trouble had fallen upon the head of the now elderly
banker. Edwin was dead, and Margaret had left her husband.
Mr. Gayre did not see how the Lombard Street business was to
be carried on without help, necessitated by the state of his own
broken health.

Should he take a partner, or amalgamate with some other
firm; or would Nicholas leave the army, and fill the place left
vacant by the death of his elder brother? Nicholas took a
week to consider, and then, to his father's infinite joy, signified
his willingness to devote himself to commerce.

With a clear head and a stout heart he set to work to
master the mysteries and intricacies of banking; and if Gayres'
had been a different establishment, one in which the energies
of an active man might have found full scope, there can be
little question he would in the commercial world have risen to
eminence.

But without changing entirely the lines on which the business had hitherto been conducted, he soon saw it would be vain
to attempt to make the old bank a monetary power in the City.
It might preserve its character for unspotted respectability,
and for a long time be made still to return a fair income; but
no great financial future could be hoped for a house which had
voluntarily dropped behind in the commercial race, and wilfully
shut its eyes to the great changes for good or for evil being
permanently wrought by steam, electricity, luxury, limited
liability, the destruction of old landmarks, the extravagance
of the Upper Ten, and, in the lower stratum of society, the
determination of Jack to be as good as his master.

All this did not trouble Mr. Nicholas Gayre to any very
great extent; and yet it would be idle to deny that it was a
disappointed man who, leaning over the railings in Hyde Park
on that May day when Mr. Arbery's bay mare indulged in such
wild antics, saw Susan Drummond for the first time. When he
unbuckled his sword and took up the pen, when he exchanged
the saddle for a seat in his father's office, there can be no question he relinquished a great deal; but till he tried the experiment he fancied he should be able to find sufficient excitement

in the heart of the City to compensate him, in part at least, for the career in which, when he abandoned it, he had so rapidly been rising to distinction.

By degrees he learnt he and his people were not made of the stuff out of which, at this time of the world's history, celebrated financiers are fashioned. The game was to be played, but not by him. Great things were possible, but not to Nicholas Gayre; and so, feeling he was out of the running, he stepped quietly aside and watched the mercantile game, where, as a rule, the stakes were power or poverty, wealth or bankruptcy, a baronetcy or outlawry, with a certain cynical pleasure he might not have derived from the contemplation of greater things.

Never, perhaps, in the history of the City of London was there a better time for observing the humours of commercial speculation than the years immediately following his introduction to business life.

The wild speculation, the reckless private expenditure, the sudden madness of all classes; the swamping of little men, the absorption of small concerns into large, the wholesale annexation of many Naboth's vineyards in order that the great houses might have even "larger gardens of herbs;" the pulling down and the rearing up; the pomp, the pride, the extravagance; the belief that the tide of apparent prosperity, then running so strong, would never turn—these things, and many more of the same kind, were for a time—only a short time, though—stopped by the collapse of '66.

In one minute, as it seemed, the Corner House tottered and crashed in; and for a while banks kept failing, firms stopping, old-established businesses tottering. Throughout the whole of England—from orphans who were left penniless, from widows stripped of their incomes, from country rectory and hall and cottage—arose an exceeding bitter cry of "mourning and desolation and woe."

"See the end of these men, Nicholas," said old Mr. Gayre to his son. The prosperity of many a mushroom concern had tried the banker's faith—indeed, it is not too much to say there were times when he felt he "had washed his hands in innocency in vain;" but now, as he looked at the commercial ruin hastened by the collapse of the Corner House, he shook his head gravely. "'I have seen the wicked in great power,'" he quoted, "'and spreading himself like a green bay-tree. Yet he passed away, and, lo, he was not: yea, I sought him, but he could not be found.' We have great cause for thankfulness," added Mr. Gayre, after a moment's pause ; and truly such was the case.

Weighed in the balance of that terrible panic, Gayres' was not found wanting. Every security was safe in the strong-room ; the bank needed no help—nay, it found itself able to give assistance ; through the ordeal it passed in quiet triumph ; and yet, eight years later, Mr. Nicholas Gayre could not be regarded as a perfectly contented man.

His being a nature which coveted success, it was scarcely to be expected he should feel satisfied with having merely com-passed safety. "And yet," as he himself remarked, "safety is a very good thing when it means the possession of a comfortable income."

CHAPTER IV

WALKING leisurely towards that "crib" hard by the Regent's Park which Sir Geoffrey Chelston had appropriated as coolly as the cuckoo does the hedge-sparrow's nest, Mr. Gayre employed his time in dissecting the motives which were taking him to North Bank. Love for his brother-in-law could certainly not be reckoned amongst them. In every capacity of life—as man, as gentleman, as baronet, as husband, father, friend, relative—Sir Geoffrey was distasteful to him. Only for one thing had Mr. Gayre ever felt grateful to the well-born sinner. Sir Geoffrey's life had been so openly shameful that it was vain for him ever to think of suing for a divorce. Lady Chelston was Lady Chelston still—living abroad in the strictest retirement on a pension duly paid to her every half-year by the solicitors of Messrs. Gayre and Co. The scandal, now an old story, was confined to the knowledge of a very few persons; it had never been a nine days' wonder or a case for the courts. Sir Geoffrey held his tongue about the woman who had made such a wreck of her life, and society did not trouble itself to ask whether the disreputable Baronet were married or a widower. It knew in either state he was not fit to associate with. Voluntarily he had placed himself outside the pale as well of intimacy as curiosity, and no one thought of being inquisitive concerning him. To the Gayres the Chelston connection had ever been a source of loss, annoyance, and disgrace, and it was not love for his brother-in-law that could be one of the reasons now drawing Mr. Gayre to the unaccustomed pastures of the Regent's Park.

Given to sarcastic analysis of the motives of others, no one could accuse Mr. Gayre of undue lenity towards his own. It was not as a censor he regarded the foibles of his fellows; on the contrary, his great failing happened to be that he looked on life—unconsciously, perhaps—as a bystander at a game. He knew all the moves and tricks and subterfuges, and he

watched the play with a cynical interest which even extended
to the working of his own heart.

Surprised perhaps at finding a human weakness in that
great citadel, he would trace its birth and career with a curious
and intelligent attention. As some persons have a mania for
the study of bodily disease, his craze was to watch the mani-
festation of mental sin and folly. Making due allowance for
original temperament, it might be said his nature had grown up
malformed by reason of two accidents in early life. There was
good in him and there was bad, and he would have assured any
questioner solemnly there was neither bad nor good, that he was
an utter negative; that he had no pleasure except in watching
a woman spin a web, and then invite some fly who thought
himself very clever to walk across and see what a beautiful web
it was, or, greater ecstasy still, noting the process by which
one big thief was robbed by a bigger. Finding so little to do
in Lombard Street he had turned his attention to these matters;
and having at length decided to go to North Bank, it was most
unlikely he would arrive there till he had ascertained why he
had decided to call.

"Given," he thought, "ten parts, there is one to form some
slight conjecture how my precious brother-in-law, without a
penny of visible income, without property, character, or friends,
manages to shuffle along. Shall we say one for that, or is it
too much? We'll say one. Two—because I really can look
no longer at my sister's child making such an exhibition of herself, and feel constrained to stretch out a hand which may save
her or—may not. Then there is Sudlow worrying me to death
to introduce him. We'll put a half for that—three and a half
out of ten; how much is that per cent, in City phrase? Never
mind; it leaves six and a half for the girl with the brown eyes,
and the wonderful hair, and the pure complexion; that is a
large proportion. Nicholas, my friend, you had better mind
what you are at. It's a case, I'm afraid, of either kill or cure;
you'll either find the first half dozen words you hear her speak
disenchant you totally, or else—you've met your fate. But I
haven't met her yet," he added more cheerfully—"only seen
her once with the breadth of the Row between us—and for that
matter, I may never meet her anywhere, or see her again."

Having arrived at which conclusion, he turned down North
Bank, and sought the residence of his kinsman.

Every one acquainted with North Bank knows exactly the
sort of house, secluded inside high walls, which obtains on the

preferable or canal side of the way; the mysterious postern-gate that, being opened, discloses three yards of gravelled path, a few evergreens, some trellis-work, and a peep of greensward and water beyond; houses small, it may be, but capable of being in their style made anything—which, indeed, they often are—save respectable.

Mr. Gayre smiled grimly as he recognised the type of dwelling, and asked the irreproachable Lavender, who, in striped waistcoat, without his coat, and in what he modestly called his "small clothes," answered the bell,

"Is Sir Geoffrey in?"

Lavender did not know in the least who the new-comer might be; but he looked at the erect carriage, the trim cut-away coat, not half an inch too wide, not a quarter of an inch too small; at the cropped head, the military moustache, the quiet tie, the trousers and waistcoat *en suite*, the command in the cold gray eye, and decided,

"Here at last is somebody decent come to see master."

"Well, sir," he answered, shocked at his *déshabillé* and the consciousness there was no one to do the honours, "Sir Geoffrey is in, but he's not up. He did not come home till late last night, and he has not yet rung his bell."

Which was, indeed, within the letter of truth; for Sir Geoffrey had not come home till so late last night that the water-carts were abroad before he made his appearance, and when he did come was so drunk Lavender had no expectation of hearing his bell till late in the afternoon.

"I ought to have taken that first check," said Mr. Gayre to himself in the days to come; but he did not, and went on, "Is Miss Chelston at home?"

"Yes, sir," answered Lavender; "but—"

"If you take in my card, she will see me," said Mr. Gayre; "I am her uncle."

"I knew it," affirmed Lavender, subsequently; "I knew it was somebody decent come to the house at last."

"If you'll walk in, sir, please," he observed to Mr. Gayre; and that gentleman was consequently shown into the morning-room of young Mr. Moreby's lady-love—that lady-love whose doings, and more especially whose spendings, had so distracted the soul of Mrs. Moreby, widow.

"Humph!" reflected Mr. Gayre, looking round the apartment, which was about eleven feet by seven; "a fool and his money are soon parted."

"If you will be pleased to walk this way, sir," repeated Lavender, who, having seized the opportunity of donning a coat, now felt himself quite a master of the ceremonies; then, flinging wide the drawing-room door, he announced "Mr. Gayre."

There was something so ludicrous about the whole business that Mr. Gayre could have laughed in his sleeve, had he not felt it was bad form on his niece's part to wait till he had crossed the small hall and entered the charming apartment overlooking the canal ere coming to make his acquaintance.

"She is not a duchess," he thought; "and, considering where I find her, she might be a little more natural. However—"

"And so at last I see my niece," he said aloud; and then Lavender discreetly closed the door, and Mr. Gayre found himself alone with a most lovely young woman, who, in the shyest manner, gave him her hand and timidly held up her face, so that he could kiss her if he liked.

Which he did, though with no very great good-will; and yet there were ten thousand young men in London, to say the least of it, who would have availed themselves of such a chance with effusion.

Well, well, thus runs the world away, and it is only natural that it should.

"And so at last I see my niece," Mr. Gayre repeated, which, for so usually ready an individual, seemed a needless waste of words. "Let me look at you in the light;" and, framing her cheeks between his hands, he drew her towards one of the windows. "If you are only as good as you are pretty," he said, releasing her.

"O, I don't think, uncle, I am so very bad," she answered, with delightful confusion.

"How far are you off your copybook days?" asked Mr. Gayre.

"What a funny question! Nine or ten, I suppose."

"Then you remember self-praise is no recommendation."

"O, how dreadful, uncle! I did not mean to praise myself. O no; I'm very, very sure of that, because—"

"What is your name, my dear?" he interrupted.

"Marguerite," she answered.

"And your mother was called Margaret. Well, perhaps better so."

They talked together in the house for a while; then they walked out on the sharply sloping lawn for a time longer, she with a dainty parasol over her wealth of dark brown hair, he bareheaded. Then they returned to the drawing room; and after she had drawn the blinds half down, they exhausted, as it seemed to Mr. Gayre, all topics of ordinary interest, and he was just racking his brain to think what he should say to her next, when the door opened, and Sir Geoffrey Chelston—clean, clothed, and in his right mind, and on his very, very best behaviour—entered the apartment.

"I take this very kind of you, Gayre." he said—"deucedly kind indeed," he added. And, soothed and cheered by these amenities, Mr. Gayre resumed his seat.

By dint of long endeavours to keep his hat on three hairs, Sir Geoffrey had contracted a habit of shaking his head, which caused many persons when first introduced to imagine (erroneously) he was afflicted with palsy or some other disease, which had somewhat impaired both his bodily and mental powers.

Under this impression they were wont to challenge him to play billiards and other games, to take his bets, and all that sort of thing, and come signally to grief.

If subsequently they departed cursing him, surely Sir Geoffrey was not to blame. It was only a habit; but some men's habits are useful, and his proved eminently so.

"This is your first introduction to your niece, isn't it?" observed Sir Geoffrey, after a few interesting remarks had been made about the weather and the locality. "Well, and what do you think of her?" he went on, with a knowing twitch of his head, when his brother-in-law had signified acquiescence with the previous proposition. "She's not so bad, is she?"

"I have already taken the liberty of remarking to her that if she is only as good as she is pretty—"

"Ay, that's the thing," interrupted Sir Geoffrey; as though he himself were such a paragon of virtue, the mere idea of naughtiness proved repugnant to his moral sense; "that's what I used to say to her and Susan, 'Beauty's only skin deep,' 'Handsome is as handsome does.' Haven't I told you so a hundred times over, Peggy, when you were going to fly at Susan and scratch the ten commandments over her face, because I said she was prettier than you?"

"I feel no doubt you have," answered Peggy, with a tender smile, which was somewhat belied by a look in her eyes that made Mr. Gayre fancy in her heart she desired nothing better at that moment than to grave some lines on Sir Geoffrey's sallow cheek.

"Who was Susan?" asked the banker. "I always thought you had never but the one daughter."

"That's right enough—no more I had. Who was Susan? why, the merriest little lass in the whole world, and fond of me, too—far fonder than my own child ever was. Lord! it seems no longer ago than yesterday when she used to come running across the lawn, and say to me, with both her little arms round my knees, 'Dive me a wide, papa Geoff.' Didn't she, Peg?"

"I have no doubt she did," Peg replied, with another smile.

"Doubt!" repeated Sir Geoffrey; "why, you know she did, just as well as you know what a nice passion you used to get into when anybody said she had a better complexion than you."

"I was only a child, papa," reminded Miss Chelston.

"Ay, only a child," agreed the Baronet, with another indescribable twitch; "and now you're a young woman, there's no need for you to be jealous of anybody, though I say it. And that brings us back to what your uncle remarked, that he hoped you were as good as you were pretty."

"Well, you are a strange pair," considered Mr. Gayre, contemplating parent and child with admiration.

"And this Miss Susan," he suggested—"is she not pretty now?"

"O yes, she is," said Sir Geoffrey, "but she's not as handsome as my girl there. Those very fair children somehow don't look so well at twenty as at six. I can't tell why. Susan's good, though, that she is."

Having dealt his daughter which back-handed compliment, and leaving both his hearers to take whatever meaning they pleased out of it, the Baronet proposed an adjournment to the next apartment.

"You must have a glass of claret, Gayre, after your walk," he declared, with the hospitable warmth of a man who gets his claret for nothing. Mr. Gayre did not want the wine, but he accepted the proffered civility, as he wished to speak to his brother-in-law alone.

"Now look here," exclaimed Sir Geoffrey, piloting the way to the dining-room, "take some champagne, do—claret's an un-English, ungenial sort of tipple, except when one can't get anything else. I have some first-rate champagne, as you'll say when you taste it, and I'm going to have some myself. Champagne and soda-water is the best 'pick up' I know, and, to tell you the truth, I feel I need a pick up of some sort.

We did keep the ball moving last night. I'd have been right enough if I'd never gone to bed; but now my head seems spinning round and round, like a coach-wheel. You'll have champagne? That's right, with just a dash of brandy in it. I always advise the brandy; champagne's cold without, and, some people find, absolutely unwholesome too."

Mr. Gayre said he would venture upon the champagne minus the brandy; and this point being amicably settled, Sir Geoffrey, to show he was not recommending what he feared to practise, followed up the first prescription he ordered for himself with that he advised for his brother-in-law; after which proceeding. regarded by Mr. Gayre with curiosity, not to say awe, the Baronet stated he felt much better—"fit for anything, in fact."

"You've dropped into a nice place here," said the banker, as he and Sir Geoffrey sauntered down the garden. "You might be a hundred miles in the country."

"Yes, it's quiet enough in all conscience," was the reply; "fact is, it's *too* quiet and out-of-the-way for me. Still, we can't have everything; and the little cottage costs me nothing. Moreby—capital young fellow—lent it to me."

"So I heard," remarked Mr. Gayre; and he might have added he had also heard how Mr. Moreby came to lend it.

"His mother took him abroad all in a hurry, and not an hour too soon," explained the new occupier, in the tone of a man who is paid for denouncing vice at the rate of about a guinea a word. "He was going a pace! Why, just look how this house is furnished! I only wish I had the money it must have cost him."

Really, to hear Sir Geoffrey talk, any one might have imagined he had never possessed a spare sixpence or been given a solitary chance in his life.

"It was too good an opportunity to let slip," he went on, finding his brother-in-law made no comment on the desire last expressed, "for I had not a roof to put my head under. Don't think that would have troubled *me*, though; I can live anywhere and on anything. I'd as soon sleep on the floor as not; and nobody ever heard me object to gin when I could not get Cliquot;" and having, in the contemplation of his own self-denial, almost dropped his hat, Sir Geoffrey shook it on again with the conscious rectitude of a person earning two pounds per week by hard labour, and contriving to save fifteen shillings out of it.

"But it was my daughter," he said, after a slight pause.
"I couldn't let the girl remain without a shelter, however
willing I might be to make shift myself."

"It was a difficult position, certainly," observed Mr. Gayre,
feeling this concession could not compromise him.

"Difficult! I believe you! Give you my word, I could
not sleep o' nights wondering what on earth I was to do with
her;" a statement which, as Sir Geoffrey very rarely slept of
nights, usually soundly reposing by day, meant less than it
might otherwise have done.

"You called her Marguerite, she tells me."

"Faith, that I did not, or anybody else, so far as I know,
except herself. Her right name is Margaret, of course, but
she thinks Marguerite fits her better, somehow; and if it
pleases her, I am sure it may please me."

"Has she many friends in London?" asked Mr. Gayre.

"Many!—not a soul; I don't know what to do with her,
or how to set about getting her acquaintances. Time slips
away; and I can't tell how long I shall be able to keep this
house. It's confoundedly awkward altogether, for something
ought to be doing."

"You want to get her married, I suppose?"

"If I can," answered Sir Geoffrey, breaking off a bay-leaf
and eating it with great apparent relish.

"You'll not compass your object, I'm afraid, by sending
her out in the Park."

"Have you seen her there, then?" said Sir Geoffrey,
reddening under his brother-in-law's steady gaze.

"Yes; that is how I knew you were in town. You had
better let her abandon equestrian exercise. In the first place,
she can't ride."

"No, indeed. she can't," groaned Sir Geoffrey; "if she
could she'd have been worth a fortune. in a way of speaking.
But she'll never be of any use to me—not the least in the
world; she hasn't a notion of making herself useful. Why,
with her appearance—"

"You will have to be careful what you are about," interposed Mr. Gayre, with decision. "You must get some lady of
position to introduce her."

"I don't know who that lady is to be, then," retorted Sir
Geoffrey. "If you can find her, I shall feel mightily obliged
to you. It's all very easy to talk, but I can tell you it's not so
easy to do. Why, there's my own second cousin on the

mother's side, Lady Digley. When I was a boy the old people
thought it would be a fine thing to make up a match between
us ; and she was brought down to the Pleasaunce on view.
But I couldn't stand her nose—too much of the Coriolanus,
Roman-senator-business, about that nose. However, as I was
saying. I wrote to her, telling her my daughter was in London,
and mentioning the girl's good looks, and so on, and in plain
words asking would she take her up."

"Well ?" inquired Mr. Gayre.

"The old hag sent an answer by return. Lady Digley
presented her compliments, and the rest of it, and Lady Digley
regretted to say circumstances over which she had no control
compelled her to decline the honour of making the acquaintance of Miss Chelston. Damn her !" added Sir Geoffrey, with
great fervour, referring to Lady Digley, and not to his own
daughter.

Mr. Gayre made no remark for a few minutes, but stood
looking thoughtfully down upon the canal.

The situation undoubtedly was awkward ; and it did not
seem as if any fresh revelation was likely to improve its aspect.

"Why did you bring her to town at all at present?" he
asked, after a pause, during which Sir Geoffrey, looking as
much unlike a dove as possible, plucked another leaf.

"Why?" repeated that gentleman ; "because I had no
other place to leave her. It seems to me, Gayre, you don't at
all understand how I am situated."

" I think I do." was the reply; "but had you *no* friends
near your old place with whom the girl could have stayed
for a while?"

"Deuce a friend." answered Sir Geoffrey. "Believe me,
my dear fellow, when a man has got to the bottom of the hill,
those who were civil to him at the top find it convenient to
forget the fact of his existence."

"But your daughter." urged Mr. Gayre ; "young people
form acquaintances for themselves, and, as a rule, the young
are not mercenary. Was there no single door held wide to
welcome my niece?"

"Not one "

"But think—for example, that Susan you were speaking of
just now, did she hang back ?"

"Susan Drummond? No, she did not hang back ; but she
had nothing in her power. You see, about the time that
things got to the worst with us her uncle died, and she had to

clear out. She wrote me as nice a letter as you could wish to read. She was always fond of me, poor Susan!" I know she thought a deal of me," added the Baronet almost sentimentally.

Mr. Gayre looked askance at Sir Geoffrey, and wondered what in the world any girl or woman could see personally or mentally to admire in the disreputable jockey and battered *roué*.

"There is no accounting for the caprices of the sex," he decided, and reverted to the original question.

"It will save us both a great deal of time if I am quite plain with you," he said, almost smiling as he spoke in Sir Geoffrey's slowly-lengthening face. "I don't mean you to dip deeper into my pocket than you have done; but as regards my niece, I should like her, at all events, to have a chance of making something better of life than an utter failure. For this reason I will see whether, amongst my own connection, I cannot find some one to chaperone her; you must do your part, however. Keep her in the background till she can come to the front properly. Could you not, meantime, get some lady to reside in the house, as governess or companion, eh?"

"Well, I'm afraid not," answered Sir Geoffrey. "We've tried that sort of thing before, and though I am sure I was always most courteous and careful, still, 'once give a dog a bad name,' you know; the respectable ones wouldn't stop, and—"

Mr. Gayre laughed outright. "We need scarcely pursue the other side of the question," he said, a decision which, on the whole, proved rather a relief to the Baronet.

"If your daughter had even some young friend stopping with her for a time," suggested Mr. Gayre. "Where is that Miss Drummond? wouldn't she come?"

"I daresay she would; she spent more than half her time at Chelston Pleasaunce. Yes, she'd come fast enough; but then, you see, I don't know where she is."

"But your daughter does, no doubt."

Sir Geoffrey shook his head dubiously. "I don't think so," he said.

"Ask her," advised Mr. Gayre; "there she is."

And, indeed, there Miss Chelston was, framed within an open window, to which her father at once advanced.

"Where is Susan Drummond now, do you know?" he asked; and Mr. Gayre, standing a step or two behind, watched her face as she answered,

"Susan Drummond, papa. I haven't an idea. She was in Ireland, staying with some people who live near Killarney."

"But you've an address where you can write to her?"

Miss Chelston lifted her beautiful eyes and looked at her father, as she answered, in the accents of utter truthfulness, "She did tell me where an aunt lived who would always forward on any letters; but I have mislaid the direction, and quite forget what it was."

"After that!" thought Mr. Gayre; and his meditations as he strolled through Regent's Park homeward, were of a more unpleasant character than those with which he had amused himself a couple of hours previously.

CHAPTER V.

IT is one thing to ask friends to "take up" a girl, and quite another to get them to do it.

This was Mr. Gayre's experience, at all events. He went very heartily into the business, in the first instance full of faith and hope, and later on with a species of desperation.

"Margaret's child!" repeated his brother, now a great dignitary of the Church, with a town house in Onslow Square, Rector of Little Fisherton, Canon of Worcester Cathedral, Chaplain to the Queen, and Heaven only knows what besides—"Margaret's child! Ask Matilda to invite her to this house and introduce her to our friends! My *dear* Nicholas, the thing is an utter impossibility. I would not for any consideration prefer such a petition to my wife."

"Why not?" demanded Mr. Gayre.

"It is a matter into which I really must decline entering. Your own usually excellent sense should tell you it is out of the question persons in our position could for a moment entertain the idea of bringing forward the child of our unfortunate sister, and the daughter of that most disreputable reprobate Sir Geoffrey Chelston. Our dear Fanny and sweet Julia are not aware even of the existence of such a cousin. And you say she is in London; what a dreadful misfortune!"

Every one was in the same story; the words might be different, but the sense proved the same. Sir Geoffrey rich might have managed to slip his daughter through a camel's eye into the social heaven presided over by Mrs. Grundy; but Sir Geoffrey without an acre of land, with no balance at his banker's, living on his wits, regarded by gentlemen of his own order as a very leper, had not a chance.

"I reckoned without mine host," said Mr. Gayre to the Baronet *Cagot*. "It is not to be done."

"I told you so at the beginning," answered Sir Geoffrey, who, if he had learned nothing else from experience, could not help knowing the sort of reception any creature belonging to him was likely to meet with from the fashionable world. "You meant it all kindly, Gayre, I know; but there is no use in trying to kick against the pricks. You had better stop in your own comfortable home, and not trouble about us out-at-elbow folks up here. If Margaret and I cannot swim together—and it seems we can neither of us do that—we must sink;" and the Baronet, as he concluded, regarded his brother-in-law furtively out of the corner of one knowing eye, for he was wondering what on earth this latest benefactor meant to do, if not for him, for his daughter.

"Confound him!" considered Sir Geoffrey, "why does he not adopt her? If he took her to Wimpole Street, and got some dashing widow to matronise her, and hinted he meant to give her a handsome *dot*, he might pick and choose a husband for her. Ah, if I had only in my power what he has in his, I'd soon bring the old dowagers who have sons about me, begging and praying for my daughter's company! But he's only a duffer, that's what he is, spite of his military achievements and the old bank at his back. Lord, how lucky some men are!" and Sir Geoffrey, with his hat more on one side of his head than ever, wended his virtuous way to pluck the latest pigeon good fortune had made him acquainted with.

"If Gayre were in my shoes he'd starve, that's what Gayre would do," he decided; and he walked along, thinking what a clever fellow Sir Geoffrey Chelston was, and what a fool Nicholas Gayre. "Still, I should like to know his notion about Peggy, because he has some notion, I'll swear."

Sir Geoffrey would have been very wrong in swearing anything of the kind. Mr. Gayre had no fixed notion whatever concerning the divine Marguerite. He wanted her to marry well; but he failed exactly to see how, weighted as she was, she could marry at all.

"I should say," was the result of Mr. Gayre's mental reflections, "that she is as awkward a girl to get 'settled' as ever I saw in my life. India would be the place for her; and yet I don't know. She might get a husband on the voyage out, most likely; but then it is not every husband that would suit her. If she could have been properly brought out in London—but I see that is not to be thought of."

There was one way this might have been accomplished— one way which would have suited Sir Geoffrey and his niece extremely well; but it is only justice to that excellent sense

Canon Gayre, in his suave voice and best pastoral manner, declared Nicholas possessed, to say the idea of adopting his niece had never once crossed the banker's mind.

Even had he taken to her, which indeed was not the case, he would have thought a long time ere installing himself as a parent to another man's child, and that man Geoffrey Chelston. About Nicholas Gayre there was nothing much stronger than his strong common sense—that sense which induced him, when he went down to war amongst the City Philistines, to drop the title of Colonel, and sink into simple Mr. Gayre.

"I've seen," he said, "vans going about the City with 'Dr. Hercules Smith, blood-manure manufacturer,' and 'Sir Reginald Jones & Co., patent stench-trap makers,' painted upon them. Thank you, nothing of that sort for me. I have no fancy to figure as Colonel Gayre, banker, like the fellow in the Volunteers who puts on his business-card, 'Major Robinson, waste-paper dealer.'"

Upon the whole, excessive virtue has a great deal to answer for. Its action, as regarded Margaret Chelston, had certainly the effect of making Mr. Gayre wonder whether, after all, there might not be some merit in vice.

"I need no man to remind me"—thus ran his thoughts—"what a black, disreputable, sinful old sheep Chelston is; but hang it! surely if John's religion has any reality, that ought to make him more anxious to help the girl. She is not answerable for her father's faults; and after all, she is Margaret's child."

During the course of the stormy correspondence which ensued on the Marguerite question between the Canon and his brother, the banker made some unpleasant remarks, which the Rev. John took as personal injuries, concerning the priest and the Levite who passed by on the other side, and left to a Samaritan their proper work of tending the man who had fallen among thieves.

Nicholas, being at the time not merely very angry, and greatly disappointed, but possessed by a gibing devil, which at times "rent," and caused him to foam at the mouth, ransacked the New and Old Testament for texts concerning the pride and worldliness of priests and Levites, to hurl at his brother's head. The Canon simply "ducked," and declined the contest; he would not argue, he said, with a man in so "unfit" a state of mind. He promised to remember him in prayer. He alluded to St. Paul's oft-quoted statement concerning evil communications corrupting good manners, and mildly hinted he feared communication with that evil thing Sir Geoffrey Chelston was corrupting the small amount of morality Nicholas had brought with him out of the army.

In good truth, John Gayre was as furious as a Christian and a canon of Worcester might be. In orders he had done remarkably well; yet, since the death of his eldest brother, he had often felt that, but for orders, he might have done much better. Further, he never really loved Nicholas; and Nicholas, on his part, had not fraternised with "canoness" Gayre and the minor canonesses Gayre as he ought to have done. When dear Julia published a song for the benefit of the Lambeth Shoe and Stocking Society, Nicholas suggested, first, it was brought out less to benefit bare-footed Lambeth than as a bid for a future primacy; and then offered to buy up the edition and sell it for waste-paper, on condition she forswore musical composition ever after; whilst he criticised so mercilessly some "angelic" hymns written by our sweet Fanny, that the Canon's favourite child, feeling all moderate Church views vanity, and meeting with a sympathetic "priest," was for some time in danger of going over to the Ritualists, which would indeed have proved a most grievous slap in the face for that party from whose hands Canon Gayre hoped some day to receive a mitre.

Altogether, a great division seemed imminent in the Gayre camp one morning, in the fine June following that late May when Mr. Sudlow, leaning over the rails in Hyde Park, admired rank and beauty as, embodied in Miss Chelston, it rode timidly along the Row.

Mr. Gayre, banker, walking Cityward, had left an extremely nasty letter behind him in Wimpole Street, emanating from Mr. Gayre, Canon. It went into money matters, always a fatal and terrible subject to select for family correspondence. It expressed quite plainly, grievances which had never before been more than hinted at. It referred to one topic, regarding which Nicholas desired forgetfulness; and it said a man who voluntarily permitted himself to become entangled for a second time with Sir Geoffrey Chelston could only be considered a fit candidate for the nearest lunatic asylum.

" Moderate," proceeded Canon Gayre, " as you must be too well aware, my means are, in comparison with what I expected, and had a right to expect, they would prove, I should not have hesitated joining you in settling a small annuity on the daughter of our unfortunate and erring sister; but to be exposed to your insolence because I refuse to disgrace my cloth by taking, as an inmate of my house and the associate of my wife and daughters, the child of a blackleg and a woman who forgot what was due to her name and her sex, is more almost than I can bear. Happily, however, I am not vindictive, and I shall earnestly pray you may never hereafter find some of the texts of that Scripture you now so painfully wrest, applicable to yourself.—Faithfully your sorrowing brother."

There was so much " excellent sense," common sense, worldly sense, plain useful sense, in this epistle, that it stung Nicholas to the quick. So far as money matters went, he felt himself blameless. He knew, if no one else did, his father had made a fair will, and left John as much or more in hard cash as the business would stand. He remembered the annuity paid to his sister came out of his own pocket ; he was aware that, had he not given up the profession to which he was devoted, John's large income would have been considerably smaller ; he understood perfectly what his brother wanted was a share in the bank, if not for himself, at least for one son-in-law, or perhaps two sons-in-law. It was not as regarding £ s. d. the letter irritated, though it hurt ; no arrow the Canon shot really found its mark, save that which criticised the prudence of his conduct regarding Margaret No. 2.

He was well aware he had acted on an impulse he was powerless to control, and Mr. Nicholas Gayre did not like to act on impulse.

Canon Gayre himself could not have looked with more disfavour on such a freak than the banker of Lombard Street.

" However," thought that gentleman, " I have gone in for my niece, and I shall try if I cannot ' see her through.' The materials are not promising ; nevertheless, I think something may be done. The world is not bounded by my own social horizon, and it is inhabited by a good many other people besides Canon John and Lady Digley—only who is going to play the part of good Samaritan ?"

A pertinent question, truly. Mr. Gayre had gone the round of his own friends, and met with " No," for answer in every tone and every form of words a negative could be uttered. It was clearly of no use expecting help from Sir Geoffrey ; and so far the young lady herself appeared either unable or unwilling to mention the name of any person with whom she could take up her abode, or who might be induced to enter the gates of North Bank as an honoured guest.

E.

"Still," considered Mr. Gayre, "the thing is to be done, and I must do it, if only to take the canoness 'down a peg;'" inspirited by which idea the banker mended his pace, and, walking briskly Cityward, reached Lombard Street just as the clock of St. Mary Woolnoth chimed half-past eleven.

On the top step of the three which at Gayres' afforded departing customers that number of chances for breaking a limb the banker beheld an apparition which filled him with ire. It took the bodily form of Lavender, but behind it Mr. Gayre knew stood the prompting figure of Sir Geoffrey. Now, he had told that worthy, in plain and unmistakable language, he must not ask him for money or appear at the bank. "Here is the first breach of our convention," he muttered, acknowledging with but scant courtesy Lavender's pleased and respectful greeting, and receiving the letter written by the Baronet's own hand in a somewhat ungracious manner.

"I took it to Wimpole Street, sir," explained the man, "but you had just left; and as Sir Geoffrey he wanted an answer very particular, I got on a bus, and came here as fast as I could."

"Don't stand there," answered Mr. Gayre testily. "I can't attend to you for a few minutes—wait inside till I am at leisure." And having thus successfully snubbed poor Lavender, and permitted the bank porter, and consequently every clerk in the establishment, to see there was "something up with the governor," he walked into his own room, still holding Sir Geoffrey's envelope unopened in his hand.

There was a pile of letters awaiting his attention, and to these—laying aside the Baronet's epistle, as though some serpent might be expected to crawl out of it—he first addressed himself.

Almost at the bottom of the heap he came upon a tinted envelope, with an imposing crest wrought in silver for seal. The banker smiled as he drew out the enclosure, and read :

"Brunswick Square, Wednesday.

"Dear Mr. Gayre,—*As usual*, I am in trouble, and also as usual I ask you to advise and help me.

"My poor little Ida is still ailing, and Dr. Tenby says I must get her out of town. He does not want her to go far away, as it will be necessary for him to see her frequently. He recommends me to take a house in the country, and yet near London ; for, sweet darling, she is so delicate, she requires every possible *home* comfort. There is a place to let near Chislehurst (furnished) which, from the description I have received of it, would, I think, suit her *exactly ;* but, alas ! I am chained to the sofa with a sprained ankle. There is no hope of my being able to walk for weeks ; and the agent writes that the house is sure to be snapped up immediately. What am I to do ? Have you any elderly and reliable clerk who could go down and bring back a faithful report of ' The Warren ' ?

" Of course, whatever expenses might be incurred I should only be too happy to pay. I am always encroaching on your kindness ; but I know you will forgive me. Is not the weather lovely now ? It does seem so *dreadful* to be pent indoors, with the sun shining and the birds singing.—Yours very sincerely,

" ELIZA JUBBINS."

"Eliza Jubbins will be the Good Samaritan." said Mr. Gayre aloud in triumph. " I wonder how I could be so stupid as never even to think of her ;" and, seizing a pen, he wrote back :

"Dear Mrs. Jubbins,—I will go to Chislehurst for you with much pleasure. Tell me to whom I must apply for an order. When I call with a full report I shall hope to find you and Ida much better.—Yours faithfully, NICHOLAS GAYRE."

"Now to see what Chelston wants. I wish he had not selected this particular time for beginning to worry me ;" and, seizing the Baronet's epistle, he tore it open with the air of a man determined to face the worst.

And behold, after all, there was nothing so very terrible—only a crossed cheque, with a good signature attached, which Sir Geoffrey wanted his brother-in-law to cash.

" For I have no banking account," he explained ; "and if I took it to any of the tradespeople I should perhaps be expected to leave most part of the change behind me."

Mr. Gayre pressed his bell.

"Spicer," he said, " send in the person who has been waiting for me, and tell Hartlet I want him."

Doubtful, perhaps, of the reception he might meet with, Lavender hung beside the door till the banker, with all his usual affable frankness when addressing those inferior to himself restored, bade him come forward ; and while Hartlet was absent getting fifteen ten-pound notes, the precise form Sir

Geoffrey had requested the change might take, asked how Miss
Chelston was, and remarked on the fineness of the weather,
and altogether relieved and satisfied the man.

"O, by the bye," said Mr. Gayre at last, "do you remember one day when you were in the Row seeing a gentleman's
horse shy at a stone-roller? It was a hunter—bay, with black
legs."

"Yes, sir, well; he was riding with Miss Drummond. I
don't know if you noticed her horse—a very handsome animal
too."

"It was the bay took my fancy," answered Mr. Gayre. "Do
you happen to know the rider's name?"

"No, sir, I never saw him before; but he was a free-spoken
sort of gentleman, not long back from the Colonies, as he gave
me to understand, and, if I remember right, he said he and
Miss Susan had ridden across from a place I think he called
Enfield Highway. I don't know if I am quite right in the
name."

"There is an Enfield Highway," remarked Mr. Gayre; and
then he put up the notes in an envelope, which he handed to
Lavender, smiling to think how far matters seemed to have
advanced in the course of a single morning.

"I'll see, my dear niece," he decided, "whether I cannot
ascertain Miss Drummond's address, which you say you have
forgotten."

CHAPTER VI.

ELIZA JUBBINS.

WHEN Colonel Gayre decided to exchange his sword for a pen, he took up his residence in Brunswick Square with old Mr. Gayre, who had long determined not to remove from that central and convenient locality till the time came for him to be carried to the Gayre vault in Highgate Cemetery.

The house was situated on the north, or quietest, side of the square. No fault could be found with the number or size of the rooms, the healthfulness of the situation, or the general air of comfort pervading the whole dwelling. Nevertheless, Mrs. John Gayre and her husband both professed themselves surprised at their father electing to stop in a house where he had known so much trouble. His wife and son both died in it; and there also he faced that bitter sorrow concerning his daughter.

John urged the old man to make his home with them, or, at least, to move further westward, and "away from all the sad memories which clustered around Brunswick Square;" but his parent asked in return, "Where could I go that it would be possible for me to forget my dead?"

Those were the days ere it had become a fixed belief of the English nation that happiness and health are to be compassed by eternal change of residence; but yet John Gayre felt it very unreasonable for any one to refuse the delights of constant clerical companionship and those intellectual pleasures only to be found in the more fashionable parts of London. He and his wife became more exercised in their minds than ever as to whether the sole-surviving member of the Gayres meant to take a certain "designing" manager into partnership. Long previously Mrs. John had settled future banking arrangements entirely to her own satisfaction. Her brother was to put in a certain amount of money; and then his son would marry dear Julia or Fanny, and so "preserve" Gayres for the family. John had been "pushed forward" in the Church in a truly "miraculous manner," but his wife wished him to be pushed forward a great deal more.

A most worldly and ambitious woman, she was constantly trying to manage an old gentleman who erred, perhaps, on the side of fancying that all his life he had contrived to manage exceedingly well for himself. Mr. Gayre, however, utterly declined to be managed. He got very tired, he said, of general society, and, resisting all attempts to induce him to change his abode, he " shut himself up," to quote Mrs. John Gayre's own words, " to question the justice of the Almighty." But in this statement she was quite wrong. Mr. Gayre was a much truer Christian than his daughter-in-law had ever been. He had lost, but he did not sorrow as one who has no hope ; disgrace had touched him, but he went among his fellow-men and transacted his business notwithstanding. As for other matters, he still maintained his custom of giving four formal dinner-parties each year; and if the guests who accepted his invitations seemed to Mrs. John " dreadful people," they suited the banker a vast deal better than the folks he met when seduced to an " at home " in Onslow Square.

They might not know much of Court or the " dear Queen," or dukes and duchesses, but some of them were acquainted with Baring and Rothschild ; and if they could not talk about the latest pieces of fashionable scandal, they were aware how stocks stood, and shook their heads mournfully over Jones's huge failure, and told how Smith had netted fifty thousand at one transaction. Further, at his dinner-table he delighted to see the clergyman from the church situate in Regent Square, just at the back of his own house, and any officer or civilian to whom Nicholas asked him to show a little attention.

There was plenty to eat in Brunswick Square, and of the best quality, Mr. Gayre's spreads differing in this respect from the Onslow Square parties, where, as once was said, a fellow never got anything except " water ices and iced water."

Mrs. John Gayre had, indeed, reduced gentility to a science. Her " social gatherings " finally became so eminently genteel, no one who could help it went to them twice. Mr. Gayre had reason when he objected to drive all that distance and stand " in a crowd " with nobody he knew near him, and get nothing in the way of food save a morsel of sandwich and a wine-glassful of claret-cup. What he enjoyed, and what really kept him in Brunswick Square, was the companionship of a few old friends, who liked their rubber and a bit of supper to follow, and something hot and comfortable in the way of punch as a genial good-night; all lights out by half-past eleven, and the whole household warmly asleep before twelve. Insomnia was not a thing Mr. Gayre knew much about, and he did not want to know about it.

"The modern manner of living," he was wont to declare, " brings all sorts of evil in its train ;" a sentiment his friends in Bedford and Russell Squares and Gower and Guildford Streets were quite willing to echo so long as old-fashioned customs presented so pleasant an aspect as they did in the hospitable banker's house.

Amongst the friends who for many a long year after Mrs. Gayre's death had helped to soothe the widower's loneliness by taking a hand at a rubber was a certain Mr. Jubbins, who, though not old in comparison with most of the worthies wont to assemble in the comfortable drawing-room, was certainly by no means youthful. His father had been a well-to-do oil-merchant in a very large way of business ; and Mr. Samuel Jubbins, devoting his attention to the same line of money-making, contrived, through some process, either chanced upon by himself or devised by another person, literally to turn oil into gold. Give him the dirtiest, thickest-looking stuff imaginable, and it came forth from his warehouse clear and beautiful, a thing to be admired. an article to be paid for.

This wonderful process seemed also to have produced a similar effect on Mr. Jubbins. All the oil of his nature was good and pleasant and genial. No better, or honester, or kinder man ever cut for deal. He was good to the poor swarming in the courts off Gray's Inn Lane, and other neighbourhoods adjacent to his house; and he bore the tyranny and the tantrums of an elderly maiden sister, whose bitter tongue was the terror of Bloomsbury, with a patience which should have secured him canonisation.

Amongst his many friends was a solicitor, who lived in great style at a corner house in Bedford Square, having offices in Bedford Row. This solicitor owned one child, a daughter ; and Mr. Jubbins had dandled this young lady when she was a baby, and won her childish heart with presents of fruit and cakes and confectionery. Her name was Eliza Higgs ; and it may safely be said, as a girl, no greater hoyden ever existed.

When they were all little folks together, she and the smaller Gayres were close friends ; and on wet days they were wont to play at battledore and shuttlecock in the wide hall of the Bedford Square house, and drive imaginary coaches and tandems up and down stairs, to the distraction of their elders.

Eliza Higgs was the youngest and worst of the trio. She had a hard, well-filled-out, good-natured, lively face; wonderful brown hair; as stout and straight a pair of legs as ever gladdened a parent's heart; activity which seemed simply inexhaustible; and a capacity for getting into mischief which could only be regarded as miraculous. She was in love with Nicholas Gayre, and used to kiss him in a manner the boy resented with many shoves and angry remonstrances; but, on the whole, he liked Eliza very much indeed, and preferred her companionship, when any deed of daring was in question, to that of his more timid sister.

When Nicholas Gayre returned home for good he found the bouncing Eliza, Mrs. Jubbins, and the mother of several tallow-faced and delicate children. Mr. Higgs' affairs had arrived at such a state of entanglement that he tried to hang himself. Being cut down just in time, Mr. Jubbins stepped forward to the rescue, and proved the splendid fellow everybody had always thought him. He took the Higgs helm, arranged with Higgs' creditors, found money for the Higgs establishment; and finally, one Sunday morning, when he was escorting Eliza back from St. Pancras church, asked her if she would marry him.

Had Miss Jubbins known she had kept her brother single till he was fifty years old, only in order that he might propose for her god-daughter, she must have risen from her grave; but she did not know or hear Miss Higgs' murmured "Yes."

The young lady had been warned by her mamma that a proposal was imminent, and told on no account to indulge in any little affectations or pretences.

"Our position is too serious, my dear, to be trifled with," said the astute lady; and accordingly Eliza—who could not forget the shock her papa had given them all, or the mere thread which stood between her and beggary, or, to do her justice, Mr. Jubbins' kindness—gave her lover to understand she would marry him with great pleasure.

When the happy man reached Bedford Square, he had one of those kisses Nicholas Gayre once received with such disfavour.

"God bless you, dear," he said; and went away because he wanted to be alone with his bliss.

That same afternoon, Mrs. Higgs, who was an eminently

practical person, with no tendency to let the grass grow under her feet, called on Mr. Gayre, and had a long chat with that gentleman.

"I left Liza crying," she said, with a cheerful countenance, after she had told her good news, "and you'd never guess why."

"Perhaps," suggested the banker—who thought the whole arrangement most sensible and proper, and "evincing a right feeling"—"because he is nearly thirty years older than herself."

"O dear, no," answered Mrs. Higgs; "she does not mind that at all."

"Had she any other lover?"

"Not that she cared for."

"Was she fond of any one who was not fond of her?"

"Good gracious! what are you thinking of? Certainly not, Mr. Gayre."

"Then, as I have exhausted all my guesses, *will* you tell me why your daughter was crying when you left her?"

"Because her name would be Jubbins. 'Higgs,' she said, 'was bad enough, but only to think of Jubbins!'"

"Ah, those novels, those novels!" exclaimed Mr. Gayre; and then with a glad heart, he offered Mrs. Higgs a glass of wine, for the banker was a very kindly man, and sincerely lamented the misfortunes of his friends, when they did not ask him for any money to tide them over their troubles; and he thought reverses in a certain rank of life were most lamentable, and that if any one member of a family could help the remainder to regain their former position, it was the duty of that individual to make even a great sacrifice in order to avert the social scandal of wealth being reduced to poverty.

In the matter of Eliza Higgs, as wife, mother, and widow, she behaved precisely with that admirable feeling and excellent sense Mr. Gayre expected. She could scarcely have been human, and failed to prove grateful to the man who thought her perfection, and deemed nothing in the world money could purchase, or love think of, too good for his young and handsome wife.

No happier couple could have been found in the whole of Bloomsbury, where Mrs. Jubbins was pointed out as an example to refractory misses, and a rebuke to skittish matrons.

She learnt to play whist almost as well as her husband, and Mr. Gayre often crossed the square in order to play a rubber, and spend a quiet evening in the Jubbins house, which was ordered on the same lines as found favour on the north side.

Mr. Jubbins, making money a vast deal more rapidly than
Mr. Gayre, spent but a small proportion of his income, and in-
vested the rest in good undertakings. He looked up to the
banker as his superior in age, rank, and wealth, and Mr. Gayre
liked to be so looked up to ; therefore the intercourse between
the two houses grew closer and closer.

Things were in this state when Nicholas Gayre commenced,
under his father's tutelage, to learn the knowledge and mystery
of banking; and though he never associated freely with, or
took kindly to, the Bloomsbury connection, it was impossible
for him to avoid seeing a great deal of it.

"Where could you find kinder or more excellent people?"
asked the old man, who saw, or fancied he saw, a sign of the
cloven foot—the West End mania—in his son.

"All your friends, sir," answered Mr. Gayre jun., "do,
indeed, appear to be most kind and excellent persons." ("At
the same time," he added mentally, "it is quite possible to see
too much of them.")

He made no mention, however, of this feeling to his father.
Long habits of military discipline, and sincere affection and
profound respect for a parent who had always acted kindly and
liberally towards him, tied the ex-officer's tongue concerning
questions far more vexed and important than the choice of
acquaintances or the selection of guests.

He did not abandon his own circle. but he concealed the
weary impatience he felt of the Bloomsbury dinner-parties and
social evenings. The Israelites never could have loathed the
wholesome manna and the too plentiful quails to the same
extent that Nicholas Gayre learned to hate whist and port-wine
and whitebait and lark-pudding and City talk ; but in a most
difficult position he behaved himself remarkably well, and
though his father's friends never, perhaps, felt themselves quite
at ease when he was of the company, they liked to speak
about young Gayre, who, in spite of his having "been at
Balaclava, you know, and all through the Mutiny, had given
up his profession and his brilliant prospects to please his father,
and was settling down in Lombard Street as if he had been
sitting behind a desk all his life. like one of our own sons, sir."

Years had come and years had gone, since the days when
Nicholas and his sister and Eliza Higgs romped through the
large house in Bedford Square; but the first thing Colonel
Gayre thought of, when he saw Mrs. Jubbins in the bosom of
her family, was concerning those sounding smacks she had

been in the habit of bestowing so lovingly and lavishly upon
him. He had forgotten all about them and her, till his father
piloted him across Brunswick Square, and took him up into
the great drawing-room, the windows of which almost faced
those of Mr. Gayre's own house, and said proudly, " I have
brought an old friend to see you, Mrs. Jubbins. I do not
suppose you remember my son Nicholas."

Did she not, poor soul? Had not a wandering thought
gone forth to him across the seas even on her wedding-day?
—though Heaven knows there was not a taint of disloyalty in
her thought to the best husband that ever lived.

" I am so glad you have come back to us, Colonel Gayre,"
was her greeting.

Then it all returned to him—the battledore and shuttlecock, the mad galloping up and down stairs, the surreptitious
descents to the kitchen, the visits to the housekeeper's room,
the kisses, the quarrels, the jam, the scoldings, the delights
snatched with a fearful joy and terror from under the very eyes
of Higgs *père*. The change was so complete and so absurd,
Colonel Gayre felt the corners of his mouth twitching under
the shelter of that friendly moustache, which had so often
protected his character for gravity; but he managed to say
what he ought to have said, and say it well. And then Mr.
Jubbins appeared, and the visit passed off pleasantly; and the
Jubbins children, who were supposed by a Bloomsbury fiction,
to inherit the beauty of their mother and the virtues of their
father, were introduced, and politics, as well as more material
fare, were discussed; and the head of the house hoped Colonel
Gayre would never feel a stranger in it.

Then once again the years went by, and during the course
of them Mr. Jubbins waxed richer and richer, and Mrs. Jubbins
comelier, and the Gayres got a little poorer; and everything
seemed going on in the same monotonous groove much as
usual, when one day in the spring of 1865, Mr. Jubbins, returning home from the City somewhat earlier than usual, complained of having caught a cold and not feeling very well.

Ever after he never felt very well, and it was during the
long and painful illness which supervened, and eventually
carried him where there is no more pain and no more sorrow
(and Mr. Nicholas Gayre hoped no more whist), that Mrs.
Jubbins won her golden spurs as a wife.

Nursing him she lost flesh and colour, but never cheerful-
ness. To the last she took a smile with her into the sick-room;

and when Mr. Jubbins died, it was with his poor wasted hand clasped tight in hers.

"The best woman in the world!" said old Mr. Gayre enthusiastically, an opinion his son did not feel inclined to controvert.

He considered Mrs. Jubbins' conduct towards her husband unexceptionable; and if she failed to interest her old play-fellow, it was rather because of some deficiency on his part than any shortcoming on hers.

After the death there ensued more than a nine days' wonder. With the exception of a very small sum secured to the children and a few legacies of no great amount, everything was left unconditionally to the widow.

"Literally everything," said Mr. Gayre senior, who was executor.

"She'll have the whole City of London asking her in marriage," thought Mr. Nicholas; but he did not say so.

He knew nothing vexed his father to such an extent as any reflections on the City; therefore, if the Lord Mayor and Aldermen and every member of the Corporation had come courting to Brunswick Square, he would have refrained his tongue from comment.

But, as a matter of fact, nobody did anything of the sort. Mrs. Jubbins afforded the many admirers she no doubt possessed small chance of declaring their sentiments.

For a year she lived in the strictest seclusion, having Mrs. Higgs, now also a widow, resident with her, seeing no one except a few old and intimate friends, and mourning most deeply and unaffectedly for the husband whose loss, as she told Mr. Gayre, she felt more deeply day by day.

This was all as it should be; yet at the end of a twelve-month, Mr. Gayre decided there is a limit even to mourning and propriety, and that it would be a serious loss to the world if such a woman took her grief to nurse for ever.

"It is time she began to wean it," thought the banker. This was after the great crash of 1866, and his attention had been directed even more than usual to the solid advantages conferred by a large income. "She's the very wife for Nicholas, if he can only be brought to think so. What is there against the match? Nothing. What is there in favour of it? Every-thing." And, indeed, so many golden reasons seemed to point to the Jubbins-Gayre alliance as a most desirable one for both parties that the banker decided some step ought to be taken, unless Nicholas meant to permit such a prize to slip through his careless fingers.

So entirely at length did this idea take possession of his mind that he determined to broach the subject to " my son Nicholas."

It was one Saturday morning, and senior and junior were alone in the private room at Gayres', when the old man, without any leading up to the question, asked,

"Do you never think of getting married, Nicholas?"

"Well, no. sir," answered Nicholas; "at least, for a long time past I have not. Once in a life, surely, is enough for a man to make a fool of himself;" which remark had reference to a wild romantic passion of the speaker's youth which had come to a disastrous conclusion.

"Ah, you must forget all that," said Gayre. "I am sure you would be a great deal happier married. All men should marry, more particularly men who, like yourself, have an old name to transmit, and an old business to bequeath. I know nothing which would give me such pleasure as to see you united to a good wife. You have been such a dutiful son, Nicholas, you deserve to meet with a woman who could give you more love even than your old father has done."

There was a touch of deep feeling in Mr. Gayre's voice as he spoke; and as Nicholas did not know very well what to answer, he only said,

"Thank you, sir."

"And there is a woman," proceeded the banker, "who, I am sure, would make you happy, and I think would take you if you asked her."

"Indeed!" exclaimed his son.

"Yes, Eliza Jubbins." The plunge was made, and Mr. Gayre felt he could go on. "A most suitable match in every respect, Nicholas. She is a few years younger than yourself. She is still a very handsome woman; you know how she acquitted herself as a wife. You remember what a daughter she was. She has—but there, I won't mix money matters up with the business. If she had not a penny a year, she would still be a treasure in herself. We know all about her since the day she was born. No after-clap can come in that quarter; and I believe—I do believe—she always felt a great regard for you."

It would be idle to state that so astute a man as Nicholas had not known for some time previously whither his father's desires were drifting. Nevertheless, this plain intimation of what Gayres expected from him in the way of a fresh sacrifice came with the force of a blow.

Marry Eliza Jubbins!—become stepfather to the young Jubbinses!—son-in-law to clever, manœuvring Mrs. Higgs! Settle down for the term of his natural life among the Bloomsbury connection—go voluntarily into the penal servitude of eating, drinking, sleeping, thinking, visiting, with a class he knew he could never really care for, seemed to this man too dreadful a doom to hear mentioned by another.

Nevertheless, he did not say "No." Long experience of his father had taught him the wisest policy in all family games was to play not trumps, but the most insignificant and inoffensive card he could find in his hand.

One of those he threw out now.

"It is early days to talk of anything of that sort," he objected. "She has not been a widow much more than a year, and her tears are not dry yet."

"Dry them yourself, my boy, then," recommended Mr. Gayre, with a chuckle of delight at finding Nicholas took his suggestion so coolly. "There is no time for winning a woman equal to that while her eyes are still wet. Besides, I feel sure she has a fondness for you. I am old, but I can see; bless you, I have not lived all these years with my eyes shut."

"That I am certain you have not, sir," replied Nicholas, in a tone in which respect and a pleasant flattery were dexterously blended. "Yet I must confess it seems to me premature to discuss such a matter."

"Not in the least—not in the least. Jubbins has been dead over a twelvemonth," said the banker, practically "going into figures."

"Still—to say nothing of my own objections—I do not think Mrs. Jubbins would feel grateful if she knew we were already disposing of her in marriage."

"There may be something in what you remark," agreed Mr. Gayre. "Spite of her excellent sense, Eliza was always a little given to sentimentality. We'll speak no more about the affair, then, for the present; only, Nicholas, you will promise me to think about it."

"Yes, I will do that, on the condition that no word is dropped to Mrs. Jubbins. I must feel myself quite free; for, to be quite plain, I do not believe I shall ever marry."

"That is simply nonsense, my son. You owe something to your family. You are almost the last of the Gayres. John has no sons; we have not even a distant relation of our own name. If you do not marry, and have children, who is to carry on the business?"

Mr. Nicholas made no reply to a question his father evidently considered crushing; but he thought two things— one, that the future might safely be left to look after its own affairs; and another, that if things went on in Lombard Street as they were going, at the end of another thirty years there would be no business called Gayres' to carry on.

CHAPTER VII.

WILL HE PROPOSE?

IT was to the house in Brunswick Square, which had for years been tenanted by the Jubbins', that Mr. Gayre repaired on the afternoon following his visit to Chislehurst. Opinion in Bloomsbury was divided as to whether the banker had proposed to the widow and been rejected, or was still making up his mind to put the momentous question.

Concerning the first alternative, Mrs. Jubbins could have enlightened her friends; but with regard to the second it was impossible for her to say, even mentally, aught save "I hope and I fear." There were days when she hoped, and there were days when she feared; yet as months and years glided away, she grew very sick with "hope deferred." She believed the man, the only man she had ever truly loved with the one love of a woman's heart, would some day ask her to be his wife; nevertheless, she did not quite understand him; surely that wound, which had changed the frank, brilliant, charming youth into a still more interesting, if less comprehensible, man, ought to have been healed long ago?

Mrs. Jubbins had some reason for believing he meant to marry her. Old Mr. Gayre, keeping to the letter of his promise, if not to the spirit, confided to Mrs. Higgs that "my son Nicholas was thinking seriously of her daughter, and he, Mr. Gayre, should feel glad if the young man proposed, and Mrs. Jubbins accepted him." To Mrs. Higgs, the idea of her daughter wedding into the Gayres seemed a thing almost too good to realise, and in her exultation at the suggestion she forgot to maintain that reserve Mr. Gayre had stipulated on. So Eliza was given to understand Nicholas had intimated he meant to "think of her:" and Nicholas, like his father, fulfilling the mere letter of his promise, did for a whole year think of his old playfellow with an ever-increasing dislike towards the connection. He did not want directly to cross his parent's wishes, but he felt to make Eliza Jubbins his wife would be to settle his own future in an utterly distasteful manner.

He liked the lady well enough—but liking is not love—and though he knew her money would be of use, both to himself and the bank, those thousands, made out of oil, repelled rather than attracted him. Then there were the juvenile Jubbins—commonplace in mind and features, spoiled, delicate, antagonistic, to his perhaps over-fastidious taste. Though the Bloomsbury world, or that other world quite away from Bloomsbury, with which he still kept up a friendly intercourse, did not suspect the fact, he had long outlived the old attachment Mrs. Higgs and her daughter often talked about with bated breath.

He was single, not from any actual objection to the married state, or fancy for one especial fair, but simply because no woman calculated greatly to delight so stern and cynical a judge of the sex had crossed his path. Possibly he was looking for perfection. If so, he had certainly as yet not found it. Upon the other hand, seeing that mediocrity and common-place virtues are often supposed to form a very good embodiment of a higher ideal, it seemed really hard he could not please his father and delight Mrs. Higgs, and return Mrs. Jubbins' attachment and reward her constancy; but all this appeared to Mr. Gayre impossible. The more he thought the matter over, the longer he contemplated himself hedged in by City notions, surrounded by a mere moneyed clique, tied to the apron-strings of Bloomsbury gentility—travelling life's road in company with the men he had to meet in business, and acting the part of a model stepfather to the Jubbins brood—the more truly he felt that, putting all question of romance, or love, or the glamour which does encircle some women, totally aside, such a marriage was, for him, out of the question.

At the end of a year from the time his father first broached the subject he was still " thinking the matter over ;" after which period all necessity for him to think about it ceased—his father died.

For six months after that event, Mr. Nicholas Gayre, a wanderer here and there, debated what he should do with his life ; then all in a hurry he made up his mind ; sold the lease of the Brunswick Square house, took another in Upper Wimpole Street, removed the furniture, books, plate, and china left to him under his father's will, and, with the help of three old servants, soon found himself much more at home than had ever been the case since he left the army and took to banking.

It was about this time Mrs. Jubbins' hopes revived. During the period when, according to his father's desire, he had been

F

thinking of the widow as his future wife, Mr. Nicholas Gayre's manners became quite unconsciously cold and distant to the constant Eliza. Now no longer bound by his father's old-world notions; free from the Bloomsbury servitude, wherein he had duly fulfilled his term; free to think and talk of other things besides money, and stocks, and investments, and commercial imprudence, and mercantile success; free, further, to marry whom he chose, or no one at all, Mr. Gayre grew quite amiable, and fell easily back into the familiar, though not close, intimacy which had marked his intercourse with the Jubbins family after his return from soldiering.

As a matter of course, the good-looking Eliza took it for granted he would step into his father's place as adviser-in-chief concerning the Jubbins property.

The title-deeds, the scrip of all sorts, the shares, the trade secrets, were under lock and key in Gayres' strong-room. At Gayres' Mrs. Jubbins continued the account her husband formerly kept there. Had he felt curious about the matter, Mr. Nicholas Gayre might have ascertained almost to a penny what she spent, and how she spent it. There was nothing which pleased the lady so much as getting into a muddle, and being compelled to ask Mr. Gayre to help her out of it.

She made mountains of mole-hills in order to write notes to him, and, herself a most excellent manager and capital woman of business, tried to pass for one of the most incompetent of her sex. Mrs. Higgs died, and then, of course, Mrs. Jubbins needed advice more than ever. Two of her young people, spite of money and doctors and care, and everything which could be thought of to restore them to health, drooped and died. All these events retarded Mr. Gayre's proposal, no doubt; still, there were times when Mrs. Jubbins doubted whether he ever meant to propose. Had she known as much of the world as Nicholas, she would have understood friendliness is the worst possible symptom where a man's heart is concerned. Mr. Gayre had as much intention of proposing for one of the princesses as for the widow. Preposterous as the idea seemed in his father's life-time, it seemed trebly preposterous now. He did not exactly know what she expected, though indeed he guessed; but he had long before made up his own mind that, so far as he was concerned, Mrs. Jubbins should remain Mrs. Jubbins till the end of the chapter.

A longer interval than usual had elapsed without his seeing her, when he turned his steps in the direction of Brunswick

Square. As he approached the familiar door Mr. Gayre surveyed Mrs. Jubbins' residence with an amount of interest and curiosity he had never before experienced, and he certainly felt a sensation of pleasure at the sight of windows clear as whiting and chamois and that other commodity, better than either, vulgarly called "elbow-grease," could make them, enamelled boxes filled with flowers on the sills, curtains white as the driven snow and of the best quality money could buy, spotless steps, polished knocker, and all those little etceteras which point to money, good servants, and a capable mistress.

"It is not Onslow Square, certainly," thought Mr. Gayre, "but we will see what we can do with it."

"Now, this is really kind of you!" exclaimed Mrs. Jubbins—a handsome and well-preserved woman on the right side of forty—stretching out a white plump hand in greeting. "You see, I am still unable to move," she added, with a laugh which showed an exceedingly good set of teeth, pointing as she spoke to a stool over which a *couvre-pieds* was thrown, in the modestest manner possible. "Why, it is quite an age since you have been here!"

"Yes, indeed," he answered, in his suave decisive manner—"almost three months. I fear you have been suffering much anxiety. Why did you not send for me sooner?"

"Well," she began to explain—"well—" Then, after a pause, "I know you must have so many engagements."

"None," he answered, "believe me, that could ever keep me absent if you said you needed my poor services."

Mrs. Jubbins had been a bold child, but she was not a forward woman. Quite the contrary. Supposing she could have won Mr. Gayre by saying, "Will you marry me?" he must have remained unwon for ever, and for this reason she did not take advantage of his pretty speech, but merely inclined her sleek head in acknowledgment, as she asked,

"*Have* you been able to go to Chislehurst?"

"Yes," he said. "And The Warren is a most lovely place."

"Which you would advise me to take?"

"If you really wish to go out of town for the summer, certainly."

"Tell me all about it, please;" and the Jubbins relict leaned back on the sofa, crossed her hands, and closed her eyes.

She was worth—heavens, ladies, how much was she not worth?—and could consequently, even in the concentrated presence of Gayre, Delone, Eyles, and Co., lean back, cross her hands, and close her eyes to any extent she liked.

Mr. Gayre looked at her not without approval—looked at her comely face, her broad capable forehead, her straight well-defined brows, her wealth of hair—not combed over frizettes, a fashion then still much in favour, but taken straight off her face to the back of a shapely, if somewhat large head, and there wound round and round in great plaits almost too thick and long even for the eye of faith.

Such hair—such splendid hair—as Mrs. Jubbins possessed, quite of her own and altogether without purchase, belongs to few women.

Mr. Gayre knew it to be perfectly natural. He had been well acquainted with it in his youth, and in his experienced middle age he could have detected a single false lock; but there was nothing false about Mrs. Jubbins. All she had was as genuine as her money, as the Spanish mahogany furniture which had belonged to her husband's grandfather.

"The Warren," proceeded Mr. Gayre, "is simply charming. A cottage in a wood; but such a cottage, and such a wood! Lord Flint, it seems, bought about twenty acres covered with trees, cleared a space on the top of the hill, and built a summer residence for his bride. Shortly afterwards he succeeded to the earldom; but still spent some portion of each year at the cottage, laying money out freely on the house and grounds. He died last summer; and as the widow does not now like the place—whether she liked it when her husband was living, I cannot say—she wants to let it; so there the house, fully furnished, stands empty for you to walk into, if you like."

At the mention of a lord, Mrs. Jubbins, who dearly loved nobility, old or new, opened her eyes and assumed an upright attitude.

"A place of that sort would be too grand and fine for me," she objected, in the tone of one who wished to be contradicted.

"It is not at all grand," answered Mr. Gayre, "and the furniture is not fine. I daresay it cost a considerable sum of money; but really everything looks as simple and homely as possible." And then he went on to talk of the gardens, and grounds, and terraces, and woods, finishing by remarking, "Though quite close to London, one might be a hundred miles away from town, the air is so pure and the silence so utter."

For a few moments Mrs. Jubbins made no reply. Then she said, with a delighted little laugh,

"Only fancy me living in the house of a real lord—not a lord mayor, but a peer!"

"It is a very nice house for any one to live in," observed Mr. Gayre, wondering, if she rented the residence, how often in the course of a month she would mention Lord Flint, and the Earl of Merioneth, and her ladyship the Countess.

"Who would believe it!" exclaimed Mrs. Jubbins. "And yet, do you know, I think I must have been dreaming of something of this sort. I have had the strangest thoughts lately. Whether it is this lovely weather following the long dreary winter, or being kept a prisoner by my ankle, or what, I am sure I cannot tell; but often of late I have found myself wondering whether I was doing right in staying so much at home, and spending so little money, and making no new acquaintances, and continuing the same round from year's end to year's end, as though Brunswick Square were the world, and no other place on the face of the earth existed except Bloomsbury."

Mr. Gayre smiled, and hazarded the remark that neither of them ought to speak against Bloomsbury.

"No, that is quite true," agreed the lady; "but yet, you see, you have gone west, and everybody else seems going west, or buying places out of town, except myself. The Browns have taken a house in Porchester Terrace, the Jones have gone to Bournemouth."

"And the Robinsons no doubt will follow suit," suggested Mr. Gayre, forgetful that Mrs. Jubbins' circle of friends did include a family of that name.

"Yes, Mr. Robinson is building himself quite a mansion down at Walton-on-Thames, and they expect to be able to move in August. I tell her she won't like it—that there is no place on the Thames to equal London; but they all seem eager to go; after a time there will be nobody left in Bloomsbury but me;" and Mrs. Jubbins sighed plaintively.

"You will not be left if you take The Warren," said Mr. Gayre.

"I can't stay at The Warren for ever," she answered; "I shall have to come back here some day, unless—"

"Unless what?" asked Mr. Gayre.

"Unless I sell the lease of this house and remove altogether. I really think I ought to make some change. The children are growing up, and ought to be in a neighbourhood where they could form pleasant acquaintances. Bloomsbury is all well enough for elderly persons; and the tradespeople are very good; I don't think you could get better meat anywhere than Grist supplies; and though Ida is not strong, I fancy that is only natural delicacy, and has nothing to do with the air. But still—"

"If I were you," interrupted Mr. Gayre, who always waxed impatient under details that had seemed both instructive and agreeable to his father, "I should take this Chislehurst place for a year; at the end of that time you could decide whether it would be best to return here or remain on there, or buy a house at the West End. What lovely flowers! How they transform this dear old room! It looks quite gay and bright—"

"They make a dreadful litter," remarked Mrs. Jubbins, who was a very Martha in household details, though to hear her talk at times any one might have supposed Mrs. Hemans took a healthy and lively view of life in comparison with the buxom Eliza—" but they certainly do light up a house. The day before I sprained my ankle I went over to Porchester Terrace, and, dear me, I thought what a difference between the West End and Bloomsbury! When I came back our square seemed quite dingy; so I told Hodkins to arrange with some nurseryman to keep me supplied with plants. At first it did seem a dreadful waste of money, and I could not help wondering what your poor father would have said to such extravagance; but there, the world goes on, and one can't stand still and be left all behind, can one?"

"Gracious heavens!" considered Mr. Gayre, "if I had married her I should have been compelled to listen to this sort of thing all the days of my life;" then he said aloud, "Talking of my father, I want you to grant me a favour; will you?"

"Certainly; need you ask? What is it?" And then Mrs. Jubbins paused abruptly, as the notion occurred to her that perhaps the long-deferred hour was at last on the point of striking.

But Mr. Gayre's next words dispelled the illusion.

"You remember Margaret?"

Hot and swift the tell-tale blood rushed up into Mrs. Jubbins' face, and as she said, "Yes, is she in London?" a duller, but not less painful, colour mantled Mr. Gayre's brow.

"I do not suppose Margaret will ever come to London," he answered; "but her daughter is here, and I should consider it a great kindness if you would pay the girl a little attention. You know—or possibly you do not know—what a miserable, hopeless, irreclaimable sinner the father is. His own relations have cut him adrift; mine will have nothing to do with him; consequently, through no fault of her own, my niece is, by both sides of the house, left out in the cold. I should like her to be intimate with a good sensible woman such as you are; but perhaps I am asking too much."

"Too much! I shall be enchanted to do anything in my power for Margaret's daughter. Is she like her mother, poor dear Margaret?"

"My sister was pretty," answered Mr. Gayre, with a feeling of deep gratitude swelling in his heart for the friendly warmth of Mrs. Jubbins' manner. "My niece is beautiful. Her face does not seem so sweet to me as Margaret's; but most persons would admire it far more. She is, in fact, so beautiful, so lovely, and placed in such a painful and exceptional position, that I shall not know a moment's peace till she is suitably married."

"Dear, dear!" exclaimed Mrs. Jubbins; "I would go to her this moment if it were not for this tiresome ankle. Could she not come to me, though, Mr. Gayre? I am such an old friend of your family, she might dispense with ceremony, and let us make acquaintance at once. If she spent a few days here, for instance, and then supposing I were to take Lady Merioneth's house, that would make a little change for her."

"You are the kindest person in the world," said Mr. Gayre, with conviction.

"No, indeed I am not; only think, you know, if it were one of my own daughters. I am sure I quite long to see the dear girl. What a thing for poor Margaret to be parted from her only child!"

"My niece believes her mother is dead, and there seems to me no necessity to enlighten her."

"Ah! that makes it all the worse. When I remember— when I look back, and recall her lovely face framed in those sunny curls—"

"Looking back is worse than useless," interrupted Mr. Gayre, speaking hoarsely. "We cannot undo the past; the best plan is to act as prudently as possible in the present. That is why I ask your help—why I want you to look a little after the child of my unhappy sister."

"And that I will," declared Mrs. Jubbins heartily. "It

will be like having a daughter given to me in the place of my
darling Clara ; a daughter to think and plan for and love. How
I long to see her ! When do you think she can come here ?
Will you bring her ?--or shall I send a fly and Hodkins ? You
know he really is a most superior and respectable person."

This time Mr. Gayre forgot to smile at Mrs. Jubbins'
singular way of putting things.

"I will arrange the visit with my niece," he said, "and
give you due notice when you may expect to see us. I am a
bad hand at returning thanks ; but I feel your kindness more
than I can express."

"It is nothing," she answered vehemently, "nothing at all ;
it is I who am obliged. All my life I have been receiving
favours from your family, and doing nothing in return. You
have made me so very happy. I wonder if you would mind
my consulting you concerning another little matter I could not
avoid thinking about while tied to this sofa ?"

"I am all attention," Mr. Gayre declared. "What is this
matter ? Are you thinking of setting up a carriage ?"

"Well, you must be a wizard !" exclaimed Mrs. Jubbins.
"Do you know, often lately I have been wondering whether
my poor husband and your dear father would think a single
brougham and a very plain livery too great an extravagance.
You see things have changed so much during the course of the
last few years. There was a time when all one's friends lived
close at hand ; but now one must have a fly to pay visits ; and
really a carriage and coachman of one's own would not cost so
very much more."

"My dear Mrs. Jubbins," said Mr. Gayre, "you talk as if
you had to economise upon five hundred a year instead of
being obliged to starve on fifteen thousand."

"Yes," she answered; "but there are the children, and I do
so want to be a faithful steward, Mr. Gayre, and justify the trust
reposed in me. Yet there are two sides to the question, I am
sure. Our fathers moved with their times, and, as a mother, I
ought to move with mine ; and that brings me to what I wished
to say--not about the carriage, it can wait ; but--"

"Yes?" said Mr. Gayre interrogatively.

"You must promise not to laugh at me."

"I am very sure I shall not laugh at what you say."

"Well, then, I have been thinking most seriously whether,
if I take a house out of town--and the doctor says I must--it
would not be a good opportunity for changing my name."

"*I beg your pardon!*"

No italics could indicate the astonishment expressed in Mr. Gayre's tone.

"Are you thinking of marrying again?" he went on—severely, as the widow imagined, but really in a mere maze of bewilderment.

"No—O no," she said hurriedly. "It is not likely I shall ever marry again—I am certain I never shall; but I cannot blind myself to the fact that the name of Jubbins is in many ways a bar socially. Put it to yourself, Mr. Gayre—Jubbins! Awful! All the years I have borne it have never reconciled me to the name. Higgs was not beautiful, but Jubbins is worse."

"'A rose by any other name would smell as sweet,'" quoted Mr. Gayre, resolutely refraining even from smiling.

"Not if it was called Jubbins," answered the lady almost tearfully.

"Yes, it would," persisted the banker; "but whether or no, there are for the present, at all events, good and sufficient reasons why your late husband's known and honest name should be preserved. As you are aware, the formulæ for making those wonderful oils lie at our bank. When your sons come of age they will want to make use of them. The name is associated with the product. It is of pecuniary value. The De Vere Oil, for example, would not command any market. I have always admired many traits in your character, but none more than your excellent feeling. Give that fair play now. Just think what the name you bear has done for you."

"I know—I know."

"And do consider that, although you have an undoubted right at any moment to change your own name by marriage, you really have no right to change the name of your children."

"O Mr. Gayre, how good and clever you are! How clear you make everything!"

"And speaking for myself," added the banker, warming to the subject, "I can only say that, though I liked Miss Higgs much, I like Mrs. Jubbins more."

"You *are* kind!" exclaimed the widow, while the colour once more fluttered in her face, and, spite of her declaration that she would never marry again, she began to consider such an event not quite impossible. "What, must you go? Well, you have given me a great deal of your valuable time, and I am very grateful to you."

She could not rise on account of that troublesome ankle,

and, as Mr. Gayre held her hand while he spoke some words of thanks, he was obliged to stoop a little, and—unconsciously perhaps—fell into an almost tender attitude.

Mrs. Jubbins' heart beat so fast and so loud, she felt afraid he would hear it. The long-expected declaration must surely be hovering on his lips !

That was a supreme moment. Never before had he retained her hand so long ; on the contrary, he had ever previously held it as short a time as possible. Never had he before regarded her with a look of such admiration ; never had his tone been so low, or his words so earnest, or—

Just then a tremendous double knock—prolonged, ear-splitting, infuriating—resounded through the house. Was ever knock before so unexpected and so loud ? Mrs. Jubbins gave a start, which almost threw her off the sofa. Mr. Gayre dropped her hand as if he had been shot.

And, after all, it was no one coming up ; only Mrs. Robinson's card, and kind inquiries after dear Mrs. Jubbins' ankle. Mr. Gayre saw that card lying on a salver as he passed out, excellently contented with his afternoon's work, but, upon the whole, not quite so well satisfied with himself.

CHAPTER VIII.

"Is your father at home, Margaret?"

It was Mr. Gayre who asked this question. He had gone straight from Brunswick Square to North Bank, debating that matter of his own conduct all the way.

When he left the City he fully intended to have "a few words" with his niece; but he did not feel his own hands quite clean enough at the minute to cast stones at her, and accordingly would have deferred the operation till a more convenient season but for the action taken by the young lady herself.

"Yes; papa has not gone out yet," she said, in answer to his inquiry. "I will tell him you are here;" and she left the room, but, changing her mind, returned almost immediately, and, closing the door, observed, with a confusion which for once was not feigned,

"I want to say something to you, uncle."

"Say on then, my niece," he returned.

But she hesitated, looking at him piteously for help, till at last he felt compelled to ask,

"Well, what is it?"

"Can't you guess?"

"Whether I can or not, I decline to do anything of the sort. Come, say what you have got to say, and let us be done with the matter."

"It is—about—Susan Drummond."

"Yes; what about her?"

For one moment Miss Chelston doubted whether he remembered, and lamented her own folly in not letting a sleeping dog lie; but the next she felt sure he could not have forgotten, and said,

"You must have thought it so odd that I did not tell papa I had seen her."

"Did I? No, I do not think I did. I wonder now why

you told him such an untruth ; but I presume you had some reason, good or bad, for not wishing him to know."

" I was wrong," she confessed, in a tone of the deepest humility ; " but indeed I acted from the very best motives."

" It would be interesting to know what those motives were ; but I suppose you won't tell me."

" O yes, indeed—indeed I will ; I have been longing to tell you. Susan and I are the oldest and dearest of friends— I may say she is the only friend I have in all the wide world. I understand her perfectly ; and the reason I did not want papa to suspect she was in London—"

" Out with it," advised Mr. Gayre.

" Well, you see, at the time I thought things would be different here. Papa told me we should have a great deal of company, and that I would be asked out to parties and—and — all that sort of thing ; and I knew, since her uncle's death, poor dear Susan could not afford to dress—as—as people have to dress if they go into society ; and I thought asking her to come to us would only vex and place her in a false position."

" Anything else ?" suggested Mr. Gayre.

" Yes ; but you must not be vexed with me. I do hate riding, and I was sure papa would be wanting me to go out with Susan ; and I dare not—O, I dare not ! That horse you so much admired almost frightened me to death."

" You are quite sure you have nothing more to tell me ?" said Mr. Gayre, as she came to a full stop.

" Quite sure—quite sure, indeed."

Mr. Gayre looked her over with an amused smile. She did not lift her eyes to his, but stood with them cast penitently downwards, waiting for any comments he might have to make.

" I think," he began at last, " there is some truth in what you have just been saying, but I fancy there is not much. Now let me give you a little advice. Don't try to hoodwink me. In the first place, it is a mere waste of time ; and in the second, you will find it to your advantage to work with, instead of against, me. All I desire is your good. You are placed in a most difficult and exceptional position, and you have not so many friends you can afford to quarrel with any of them, more especially a girl like Miss Drummond."

" Quarrel, uncle !—I wouldn't quarrel with Susan for all the world ; but how could I know living in London would turn out so different from what I expected—so miserable?" ended Miss Chelston, with a gasping sob.

"You expected, perhaps, to be presented at Court?" hinted Mr. Gayre, with bitter irony.

"I did not think it was at all impossible," she answered.

"And what do you think now?" he asked.

"That I have been very silly; and O, it's all such a dreadful disappointment!" and, covering her face with her hands, she left the room fairly in tears.

"It *is* hard on the girl," thought Mr. Gayre, "and why should I have expected straightforwardness from her? The father does not know the meaning of the word; the mother was a poor weak timid fool; and I—well, my friend, I don't consider you have much reason to be proud of yourself."

"So you have sent Peggy off crying," said the Baronet cheerfully, opening the door at this juncture; "I am very glad of it. Hope you gave her a good scolding. As I told her yesterday—for I had an appointment after I got back from Enfield the other day, and was not home till long after she had gone to bed—as I told her, there is nothing in the world I detest like a falsehood. Let a man or a woman only speak the truth, and I do not much care how bad he or she may be in other respects, though no one who does speak the truth can be very bad."

"I think we may let the affair rest now," remarked Mr. Gayre. "More particularly as Miss Drummond ought never to know Margaret's silence was other than a piece of carelessness. It will be a great matter for your daughter to have so nice a friend staying with her. Have you settled when she is to come?"

"Yes. Peg wrote her as pretty a note yesterday as you'd wish to read. O, she was humble enough, I can tell you. It's not often I do come the stern parent business, but I did speak out. I said, 'If you think because Susan has only got a poor couple of thousand pounds she is not as welcome to my house as though she had millions, you are very much mistaken, that's all. I'm sorely afraid, Peggy,' I went on, 'you're an arrant little snob; and you don't inherit that failing from me any more than your want of candour. No one can say I ever held myself aloof from any man because he was not rich or well-born. What's the use of being well-born if one can't shake hands with a beggar?' No, that girl of mine wants taking down. She does think so confoundedly much of herself."

"It seems to me she has been taken down a great deal," observed Mr. Gayre. "She evidently came to London expecting to carry all before her; and, spite of your agreeable manners and large circle of desirable acquaintances, she finds herself alone in a great city, without a soul to speak to. However," added Mr. Gayre hurriedly, to prevent his brother-in-law once again taking up his parable, "I have at last succeeded in getting her one invitation, which I hope will lead to more. As we can't induce rank to notice her, I determined to try money. Mrs. Jubbins, of Brunswick Square, a lady I have known all my life, will be delighted to do anything and everything she can for Margaret."

"Come, that's encouraging," exclaimed the Baronet, "though Jubbins does not exactly seem a name one would find in *Burke*, and Brunswick Square is a little—eh?"

"If you mean that it is not Belgravia, you are right; but as no duchess has rushed forward to chaperone your daughter, it may be prudent to try and make the best of rich respectability."

"Why, my dear fellow, how you talk! Any one, to hear the way you go on, might imagine I was particular! Thank God, I am no such thing! I do not worship rank or money. And so your friends are very rich. What is the husband?"

"I don't know what he may be at present; he is dead; he was a most excellent person when living."

"Widow! Bless me, why don't you make up to her, Gayre?"

"Well, there are several reasons. One, however, may seem sufficient. She says she is not going to marry again."

"Pooh!" commented Sir Geoffrey, with an airy incredulity.

"At all events, she has let seven years pass without making a second choice."

"The right man has not asked her," remarked the Baronet, with decision : and he shook his head with such emphasis that Mr. Gayre knew he was thinking, if his wife "gave him a chance," and the fortune proved sufficient, he himself would attempt Mrs. Jubbins' conversion, and with brilliant success.

"She is a truly admirable woman in every relation of life," said Mr. Gayre.

"I am thankful to hear it—most thankful," answered Sir Geoffrey solemnly. "What a fortunate fellow you are, Gayre, not to be saddled with the responsibility of a daughter! I declare the future of mine is getting to be a nightmare to me. What on earth would become of poor Peggy if I died?"

"It is extremely difficult to say," observed Mr. Gayre, too wise to be entrapped into any promise by his simple brother-in-law.

"And we must all die," pursued the Baronet tentatively.

"So it is said; but there is no rule without an exception; and you may prove that exception."

Sir Geoffrey digested this remark, and, deciding he would not make much out of Mr. Gayre on such a tack, said, in a frank sort of manner, as if the idea had only just occurred to him.

"I really don't know that I should object to a City man as a husband for my girl if he could insure her a proper establishment."

"It is extremely good and wise of you to say so."

"You see I can give her no fortune."

"And, as a rule, money expects money nowadays."

"Upon the other hand," proceeded Sir Geoffrey, "she is my daughter."

"So she is; that is a great advantage," said Mr. Gayre.

For a moment it occurred to the Baronet that his brother-in-law was openly gibing at him; but, looking sharply up, he could see no hint of laughter in the calm cold face.

"And a title must always carry a certain weight," he ventured.

"But your daughter has no title, and as for yours—knights and baronets have in the City become somewhat of drugs in the market. What can Margaret, without a penny of dowry, do for any man? You have no property left for him to talk about. Your daughter has no social standing; she possesses the manners of a gentlewoman, I admit, and is extremely good-looking. Nevertheless—"

"For Heaven's sake, Gayre, don't make me more wretched than I am! It was my misfortune, not my fault, I did not marry into my own rank of life, in which case my relations *must* have seen to the girl. But as matters stand—"

"I think, Sir Geoffrey, I will wish you 'good-afternoon,'" interposed Mr. Gayre, rising in his wrath and striding across the small room to the door, with the almost forgotten military gait.

But ere he reached it, Sir Geoffrey caught him.

"My dear, dear Gayre," he began; and then, as his dear

Gayre wrenched himself from his detaining grasp and reached the hall, the Baronet, once again seizing his sleeve, went on, "you have misunderstood me quite."

Mr. Gayre, however, was not so easily to be appeased. Standing in the middle of the gravelled path, sheltered from the vulgar gaze by that high wall already mentioned, he delivered his parable. He rehearsed the righteous doings of the Gayres, and the sins of Sir Geoffrey.

"Good God," he cried, and certainly, as a rule, Mr. Gayre was no profane swearer, "if my father had liked, he could have given you seven years' penal servitude over that matter of my sister's settlement. But he refrained; and yet now you talk as if you had made a *mésalliance* by entering a family able to trace a longer pedigree than your own."

Through a little pantry-window, almost screened from the sight of visitors by a goodly *arbor vitæ*, Lavender watched the progress of this wordy war, saw Mr. Gayre's impatient and angry movement and his master's deprecating gestures, and the humble and almost cringing servility of his manner.

"Sir Geoffrey's gone and done it now," he considered. "Ah! I knew it was too good to last. He'll be off in a minute more, and I suppose we'll never set eyes on him here again."

And indeed departure seemed imminent. Mr. Gayre had his hand on the lock of the gate, and, spite of Sir Geoffrey's efforts to detain him, was evidently bent on making his way into the road; but just as he had turned the handle, and was on the eve of leaving Mr. Moreby's borrowed villa for ever, Margaret, her eyes still a little red, but her dress, as usual, perfect—Margaret, with one rose in her hair and another in her girdle, looking fair and fresh and pathetically humble, came round the end of the house, and exclaiming, "O uncle! you won't go without a cup of tea," changed her own destiny as well as that of others.

"You can't refuse *her*," remarked Sir Geoffrey *sotto voce*. "Upon my soul and honour, you took quite a wrong meaning out of what I said; and, hang it, whatever I may be, she's your sister's child."

"Have you two been quarrelling?" asked Miss Chelston, in quick alarm. "Don't do that, don't—just, too, when I had made up my mind to be so good and nice and sweet to you both and everybody. Uncle, you mustn't mind papa. Really he was quite unpleasant to me yesterday. Papa, uncle is in a bad humour; he scolded me half an hour ago till I had to go up-stairs and have a good cry by myself. Now come in to tea, both of you," she finished, with a pretty, imperious, and yet caressing air which became her wonderfully, and caused Mr. Gayre to consider, "After all, something may be made of her."

"Come," she repeated, taking Mr. Gayre's arm and leading him towards the house; "and you may follow us, you bad man," she went on, addressing her father, who, for answer, put his fingers within the bit of black velvet she wore round her neck and gave it a twist.

Father and daughter did not exactly pull together, yet still, upon the whole, they understood each other pretty well.

Though the tea was lukewarm and extremely bad, Mr. Gayre swallowed one cup, exactly as he would have with some wild Indian smoked a pipe of peace. Sir Geoffrey refrained from partaking of the beverage offered for delectation, remarking his "liver wouldn't stand it," which, considering what he forced his liver to stand, seemed on the part of that organ an extraordinary act of rebellion; but he was good enough to go into the dining-room and prepare a brew for himself that did not err on the side of weakness. This he drank a good deal faster than Mr. Gayre did his tea, while he drank communicating the good news of Mrs. Jubbins' invitation to his daughter, telling that young person she could never sufficiently prove her gratitude to the best of uncles, and, during the course of the conversation which ensued, artlessly inducing his brother-in-law to state many facts in connection with the state of the Jubbins finances he had not thought of imparting previously.

"By Jove, what a chance!" considered the Baronet; and then he proceeded to think, "if her ladyship would only be kind enough to quit a world she never really adorned, I'd have a try for that quarter of a million—buried in the earth, as one may say—and I'd get it, or else know the reason why."

Which only proves that even baronets may be liable to error. Sir Geoffrey thoroughly understood the weakness of human nature, but most certainly he failed to estimate its strength.

CHAPTER IX.

SUSAN.

SEATED in his library—a room which, in a bachelor's establishment, ever seems the pleasantest and most comfortable in
the house—Mr. Gayre, on the evening of that same day when
he fought Sir Geoffrey on his own ground, and felt perhaps
ashamedly conscious of having led Mrs. Jubbins astray, or at
least allowed her to stray, permitted his own soul the luxury of
a day-dream. During the course of his life he had not indulged in many; and now and then a doubt would intrude as
to whether anything could come of this vision, or if it would
end like the others in grief and humiliation and disappointment. But in that quiet twilight hour doubt seemed exor-
cised. After all, why should happiness not be his? If in
some things he had failed, in others he had succeeded : in no
respect could he be accounted an unfortunate man. The
stars in their courses had not fought against him, as they did
against Sisera. "I ought to have no quarrel with Fate," he
thought, "for Fate has done a great deal for me; and, perhaps," he went on, contemplating his air-castle with an eye of
faith, "she has been keeping the great blessing of a good pure
wife for the last."

Dreams, fair dreams! Were they only, after all, to be
dreams? Was his day to end in darkness, unillumined by the
golden beams of a mutual love? Was life to hold nothing for
him of the beauty and the glamour which only a woman can
shed over it? "Ah, no!" he murmured, and through the
gloom it seemed to him that a figure, clad all in white, came
gliding to his side; that a delicate hand lay clasped in his;
that a pair of tender brown eyes looked wistfully in his face;
that a soft touch smoothed the coming wrinkles from his brow;
and that at last, tremblingly, he clasped to his heart the wife
he had waited through the long lonely years to meet.

Already he felt as if he must have known her always. They
were strangers no more. He heard her speak, and her voice

sounded familiar to him. She smiled, and the waters of his soul reflected back the pleasant sunshine.

Had they, in some former and happier state of existence, wandered side by side through flower-decked meads and winding leafy lanes, it could not have seemed more natural to him than it did to find himself pacing the never before trodden fields of Enfield Highway, in which the mowers were busy with their scythes, filling the air with the delicious perfume of recently-cut grass.

Her little tricks of manner and speech and look and movement struck him with no sense of novelty.

" I must have been acquainted with Susan Drummond the whole of my life," he decided ; "that is to say, for a good many years before she was born." Her very name sounded to him accustomed ; homelike seemed its simple melody. Susan— Susan—Susan—Susan Drummond, with her fair honest face ; with her hair, which was neither brown nor yellow nor red, but a marvellous mixture of all three ; with her exquisite complexion and sweet tender mouth—he recalled them all ; and yet each individual and to be particularised beauty faded into nothingness beside the intangible and indefinable charm which had its source no man could tell where.

Had she been smitten with smallpox, or lost a limb, or become suddenly old, Susan would have been Susan still. There are women who retain, whether in youth or age, some subtle and inexplicable essence of womanliness as far beyond analysis as the scent of a rose. Whatever the fashion of the earthly tabernacle her soul inhabits, nevertheless from the windows of even the poorest habitation some passer-by catches the glimpse of a countenance never for ever to be forgotten.

Mr. Gayre at all events felt he could not, while life lasted, forget riding along the Green Lanes and through Southgate, and thence, by many devious roads, into Enfield Highway.

" Are you quite sure where you're going, Gayre?" asked his interesting brother-in-law, Sir Geoffrey, whom he had seduced into setting off on a wild-goose chase after a fellow who owned a wonderful hunter on the London side of Waltham.

"No, indeed, I am not," answered Mr. Gayre despondently ; " but I mean to inquire about my man at each 'public' we pass."

Which performance, greatly to the Baronet's satisfaction, was gone through duly and truly with negative success, till the pair reached a certain hotel, noted in the old days, that still did a roaring trade by reason of excursionists to the Rye House and Broxbourne Gardens.

"Does I know a gemman as owns a 'ansome bay 'unter? Why, in course I does—Squire Temperley, of Temperley Manor. But, Lord love you, sir, it ain't of no manner of use riding on to see 'im! 'E's been away—let's see—a matter of three week with the gout, which do nip him up sore."

Mr. Gayre mused. It was not his fashion to rush into dialogue.

"What sort of looking man is your Squire?" he asked at length, while he slipped half-a-crown into his informant's hand.

"Well, sir, 'e's not unlike yourself in build and figure, only 'eavier and a trifle more advanced in years"—Mr. Gayre winced; "a very pleasant gemman, and most out-and-out rider; didn't mind taking in 'and any 'oss—got the most splendid 'unter to be seen in all these parts—a regular wild one; no person can, to say, really ride 'im but 'imself and young Mr. Arbery."

"Young Mr. Arbery? Who is he? Not Squire Temperley's son, of course?"

"No, sir; Mr. Arbery is the son of Mrs. Arbery, Granston 'Ouse, just above 'ere. 'E's just back from the Australies, and we 'aven't seen *yet* the 'orse could throw 'im."

Having with a commendable pride finished which statement, the ostler, whose manners happened to be of a more free-and-easy description than obtained in Lombard Street, was good enough to "throw his eye over Mr. Gayre's steed," and remark "she was a tidy sort of beast, who I dessay can go."

"Well," asked Sir Geoffrey, coming out of the bar, where he had been taking something, "just for the good of the house," "have you dropped on your friend's track yet?"

"Yes, I think so," answered Mr. Gayre; and having received some further information on the exact position of Granston House, the pair departed, only walking their horses up the Great North Road, but nevertheless eliciting an observation from the ostler that "he hoped he might be blanked if those gents didn't know something about riding."

On they went past the church and into the older part of the village, which even so late as 1874 was little more than a mere straggling street. They had got into the region of a few unpretentious shops, when Mr. Gayre started so suddenly that his mare sprang forward with a bound which elicited a profane inquiry from Sir Geoffrey as to "what the —— ailed the —— brute."

His brother-in-law did not answer. Apparently he was devoting his whole attention to "the —— brute," but in reality his eyes were following two persons who chanced to be sauntering slowly along the footpath; one was a lady wearing a white straw hat and piqué dress of the same colour, both trimmed with black ribbon; the other the young fellow he had seen in the Park.

He had found his quarry, and yet, though he passed the pair so close that he could almost have laid his hand on Mr. Arbery's shoulder, he did not pull up and accost him.

Shyness was a fault from which, as a rule, the banker might be considered perfectly free; but at that moment he felt it impossible even to turn his head in the direction of the very persons he had come to seek.

Not so Sir Geoffrey. That woman must indeed have been old at whom he would have failed (to use his own expression) to take a squint; and, following his usual practice, he proceeded to honour with a hard stare a girl whom he had already decided possessed "a deuced good pair of ankles;" then,

"Lord bless my soul!" he exclaimed, in a tone loud enough for all the village to hear, "if it isn't Susan Drummond!" and Mr. Gayre, at last looking back, beheld Sir Geoffrey standing in the middle of the road, with his horse's bridle slipped over his arm, shaking both Miss Drummond's hands, and expressing his delight and wonderment at meeting her in such an out-of-the-way place so volubly that he was well-nigh unintelligible.

"Gayre, Gayre," he cried, "stop a minute—this is Susan; Susan Drummond, you know. By Jove, who'd have thought of coming across her here? Susan, this is my brother-in-law; gad! I never was so surprised in all the days of my life! What in the world are you doing in Enfield Highway?"

Watching her, Mr. Gayre saw a shadow of disappointment creeping over her face, lit up the instant before with a delighted smile of pleasure.

"Did not Maggie tell you I was here?" she asked.

"How should she know?" demanded the Baronet.

"Why, I saw her one day in Hyde Park, about a month ago; didn't she tell you?" repeated the girl.

"Not a word; if she had you may be very sure I'd have been down here before now. I—" and Sir Geoffrey was about to plunge into the whole story of Peggy's statement that she did not know even the address of her old friend, when a look from Gayre arrested the words on his tongue.

"You know what a careless forgetful baggage it is," he said, with great presence of mind, "and how much fonder she always was of telling things to other people than her own father; however, now I've found you, I won't lose sight of you again; you must come over and see Peg, and have all out with her. Come and pay us a long visit."

But Susan made no answer except, "You are very kind; but you always were kind to me, Sir Geoffrey."

"Papa Geoff," amended the Baronet. "Where are you stopping? Who are you with? What are you doing? I am amazed. Who'd have thought of seeing you here?"

"There is nothing remarkable in seeing *me* here," she answered, "but it is astonishing to see you. I should just as soon have expected to see Chelston Church spire coming up Enfield Highway as you. What can have brought you to this part of the world?"

"My brother-in-law wanted to find some fellow about a hunter—" Sir Geoffrey was beginning, when Mr. Gayre interposed.

"This is the very gentleman I wanted to see, I think," he said, looking towards Mr. Arbery, who had stepped into the background. "As I did not know your name," he went on, speaking to Miss Drummond's companion, "we have had a great deal of trouble in finding out who you were and where you lived."

"Well, it's all right now, isn't it?" exclaimed Sir Geoffrey. "Susan, my dear, I am so glad we came; you can't think how pleased I am to see you again."

"This is my cousin, Mr. Arbery," she said, acknowledging the Baronet's hearty words with a smile which chased the shadows from her face; and then, with a pretty grace, she introduced him to Mr. Gayre, which ceremony duly performed, they all walked on together to Granston House, where the young man said his mother would be delighted to see them. It is more than doubtful whether Mrs. Arbery was anything of the kind; nevertheless, she received the unexpected visitors with a good grace, and asked them to stop and take early dinner.

"We always dine early," explained Will Arbery; "but you can call it luncheon;" and then, while Sir Geoffrey was making himself agreeable to Mrs. Arbery, whom he afterwards spoke of as "shaky—deucedly shaky," and Susan left the room, probably to add a few touches to the appointments of the dinner-table, Mr. Arbery and Mr. Gayre talked, not merely about Mr. Temperley's hunter, but other equine matters.

At the meal to which they all subsequently sat down the conversation was general. It turned a good deal on Australia, and Mr. Arbery, who found much to say, and said it well, interested Mr. Gayre considerably with his account of life on a great sheep-run. He had three brothers settled in Australia, and one sister—all married. "So when I get back," he added, "there will be five of us out there, old married folks. If we could only induce my mother to come too, we should be as happy as possible."

Mr. Gayre looked at Miss Drummond, who smiled amusedly in reply, while Mrs. Arbery said, " I shall never cross the sea," in a tone which told the banker this was a sore subject in the family.

"But 'pon my soul," exclaimed Sir Geoffrey, "it seems to me a splendid idea. Why can't we all go? What do you say, Susan—will you pack up and let us leave England together ?"

"No," she answered ; "like my aunt, I never mean to take so long a voyage."

" I have asked her already, and she refused me," declared her cousin.

"That is very true, Will," she said ; "but perhaps, if you had implored me to share the sheep run instead of helping to catch wild horses, my answer might have been different."

At which they all laughed—Mrs. Arbery a little sadly, Mr. Gayre with a sense of relief, Sir Geoffrey delighted to find his old favourite "as saucy as ever," and Will Arbery after the fashion of a person who felt himself fairly hit.

"No, Susie, it wouldn't," he said, looking at her with fond, but merely cousinly, affection. " You are far too much of a 'bloated aristocrat' for Australia ; you like purple and fine linen, and servants, and regular meals, and nice furniture, and—"

"I like civilisation, if that is what you mean," she summed up. " I think a sheep-run in Cumberland or Wales, or even Ireland, might be all very well ; but I confess I should not care for it a thousand miles from a post-office."

Hearing which declaration Mrs. Arbery sighed deeply, and Mr. Gayre drew his own conclusions. He understood there sat the wife Mrs. Arbery would have liked for her son, and he

could not exactly understand why "cousin William" had
elected to go further afield, till a few weeks afterwards, when
Susan was good enough to enlighten him.

"I don't fancy," she said slyly, one day, "men usually fall
in love with a woman because their mothers think the particular 'she' will make a good daughter-in-law."

After dinner they went out on the lawn, which was perched
high over the road, and where the whole "Way" might have
watched them promenading had it chosen; then they wound
round the house to a pretty trim flower-garden, laid out in the
Dutch style, and from thence Susan, and Mr. Gayre, and Sir
Geoffrey, and young Arbery strolled down the pleasant meadows, in which the grass was being cut and the hay being
made.

A stream bordered by pollards meandered at one side of
the fields; large Aylesbury ducks were disporting themselves
in the water; afar off, beyond the level marshes, rose the
rising ground, near Sewardstone and Chingford; there was a
great silence in the air, and it seemed to Mr. Gayre as if suddenly he had left some old life of unrest behind, and entered a
land where trouble could not enter.

Even Sir Geoffrey assumed quite a different aspect sauntering through those Elysian Fields with his hat off, discoursing
learnedly with young Arbery about country affairs, or turning
to speak to Susan as she and Mr. Gayre lagged behind.

"You wouldn't like to jump that stream now, would you,
Susie?" he asked, as they came to a standstill at one particular
bend of the river.

"No," she laughed. "I do not feel so young as I did
once, and besides, this is wider than the Chel even at the
Pleasaunce."

"I am not so sure of that," said the Baronet, surveying the
sluggish water dubiously. "Well, perhaps you are right.
Lord, Lord! shall I ever forget that day when I was out in the
Long Meadow looking at Lady Mary—do you remember that
chestnut filly, Sue?—the prettiest thing, the very prettiest!—
seeing you come tearing down the green walk, with Lal Hilderton behind you, racing like two mad things! I shouted out to
you to mind the river; but you just gathered your skirts about
you and took it like a deer. Gad, I never saw a patch upon
it before or since! And, afterwards, you stood mocking Lal,
he on one side and you on t'other."

"He did not follow, then?" suggested Mr. Gayre.

"If he had, he'd have pitched right in the middle of the water. Lal was no jumper."

"Ah, but couldn't he paint, Sir Geoffrey?" said Susan, with just the faintest mockery of an Irish accent as she uttered a completely Irish sentence.

"Yes, certainly he was clever with his pencil," agreed Sir Geoffrey.

"And who was this Mr. Hilderton?" asked Mr. Gayre, feeling really he could contain himself no longer.

"O, an old neighbour," answered Susan carelessly. "He was intended for the Church, but preferred art and went to Rome to study. For the credit of Chelston, we hope he will be a great man yet. About three years ago he was good enough to come down to see us aborigines, and caused quite a sensation in a velvet suit and a red tie."

"And all the ladies fell in love with him, I suppose?" said Mr. Gayre bitterly.

"I think a great many did," agreed Miss Drummond. "He really is very handsome."

What a strange girl!—one who spoke of men and life and wooing and marrying as if she were seventy years of age ; who addressed the representative of Gayre, Delone, Eyles, and Co. as though she had frisked and frolicked about Chelston Pleasaunce with him ! How frightfully easy were her manners !— well, perhaps not so easy as indifferent ; and yet—and yet who was the only woman that since that crazy fancy of his youth, had ever seemed winsome to him.

Already he loved her distractedly ; already he felt, on the slightest provocation, madly jealous. The first six words she spoke had not disenchanted him—quite the contrary. She was different from the girl he expected—stronger—a woman better worth loving and winning—a woman such as, in all his previous experience, he had never before met, and—

"I think, Gayre, we must be seeing now about getting back to town," said Sir Geoffrey, who, fond though he might be and was of Susan, felt the pastoral business, unenlivened by champagne and the hope of a dupe, wonderfully slow.

To this proposal Mr. Gayre at once assented. He felt that whatever his own wishes might be, he and the Baronet could not stay at Granston House for ever ; and accordingly, declining young Arbery's hospitable suggestion that they should stop and have tea, and ride home in the cool of the evening, it was finally settled their horses were to be saddled and taken to the back gate, where Susan undertook to pilot the visitors in ten minutes.

"The back gate is really the carriage-gate here," she explained; "only we have no carriage, and nothing in the stable, except a cow and a donkey."

Killing that ten minutes—a process which Sir Geoffrey thought occupied about ten hours—they paused beside a Marshal Niel which ran over the drawing-room window.

"Give me a rose, Susie," said the Baronet; and then, as she complied, added, "Give Gayre one, too. Now," he went on, "you must fasten it in my coat, in memory of old times. What jolly little buttonholes you used to make up for me at Chelston! Only look at Gayre—see what a mess he is making of the performance. Better let Susie take your rose in hand."

Now the fact was that Mr. Gayre had never in all his life worn a flower in his coat. Affecting a severe simplicity, he eschewed jewelry, perfumes, buttonholes, and every vanity of latter-day male life; but not knowing what on earth to do with the rose Susan had given him, feeling he could not go about dangling it in his hand, he was, when Sir Geoffrey spoke, vainly attempting to coax it to stay in his left-hand lapel.

"Will you really take pity upon me?" he asked; and the blood came up into his face as he put this question.

"O, certainly!" said Susan; and while fastening the stem, she looked up at him, blushing too, but with a merry light in her brown eyes.

"Gad," exclaimed Sir Geoffrey, complacently surveying his decoration, "they'll think along the road we've been to Broxbourne Gardens!" a remark which induced such an expression of disgust on Mr. Gayre's countenance that Susan laughed outright, and explained the correct form of bouquet generally borne home in triumph from that place of gay resort.

"What people will imagine, Sir Geoffrey, is that you must be a great rose fancier, and are returning from Paul's at Waltham," she said; which suggestion of his brother-in-law being mistaken for a florist so tickled Mr. Gayre's fancy that, his good-humour quite restored, he joined in Miss Drummond's merriment.

"You are a bad, bad girl!" declared the Baronet, pinching her cheek. "Come now, before we leave, you must tell me what day I am to drive over for you."

Then instantly Susan's manner changed. She didn't know; she was afraid she could not go; perhaps Margaret might be able to arrange to run down by train and spend a day with her ; excuses Sir Geoffrey cut short by saying decidedly,

"Now look here, my girl, no use our beating about the bush ; you're huffed, that's what you are, but you needn't be. Peggy will be only too glad if you'll come and stop with us— not for a night or two, remember, but on a long visit. She's just as lonely a girl as you will find in London, and she has not a friend on earth she likes as she does you. Of course, you know, we are down in the world a bit, but you cannot be the Susan I know if that makes any difference."

"I was sure the poverty touch would fetch her," he remarked afterwards to Mr. Gayre ; and it did "fetch" Miss Drummond so far as to induce her to say " she would try to go and see Maggie," if that young lady would write and name an hour when she should be likely to find her at home.

"I think I did that pretty well," remarked the Baronet, as he and his brother-in-law rode straight down the wide Highway to Edmonton, cheered by Mr. Arbery's parting assurance that whichever road they took back they would fancy the longest. " I think I did that pretty well, considering we had nothing but water at dinner. How people can drink water, as if they were beasts of the field, beats me altogether."

"If you were on the march and couldn't get any, you might change your opinion."

"I might," said Sir Geoffrey, in a tone which implied he did not think such a change very likely.

"However," he went on, "I am going to stop here for a minute to 'bait ;'" and, suiting the action to the word, he rode up to the door of the inn where he had previously partaken of spirituous refreshment, leaving Mr. Gayre to walk slowly on and admire the prospect of flat country which alone met his eye, look where he would.

"I feel another man now," declared the Baronet, when he overtook his brother-in-law. "Well, you haven't told me yet what you think of Susan."

"She seems a very nice girl," answered Mr. Gayre coldly, as it seemed to Susan's enthusiastic admirer.

"Nice ! I believe you. There's not a dark corner about her. I've known her—how long haven't I known her ?—the dearest little woman ! I used to think it was a pity I could not harness her and Peggy when they were children ; such a pair they'd have made—Susie in blue shoes, and my young one in red, blue and red sashes, blue and red necklaces to match; and later on, while Peg was posturing before a look-ing-glass—if you believe me, from six years of age she was always putting flowers in her hair and smiling at her own reflec-tion—Susie would be out in the paddocks with me, or sitting in the dining-room while I told her stories."

"Stories!" repeated Mr. Gayre in amazement, wondering what sort of fairy tales the Baronet's repertory contained.

"Yes, stories," said Sir Geoffrey defiantly. "I don't mean, of course, nursery tales or foolish stuff such as most children are crammed with; but good sensible stories about duels and races, and shooting, and spins across country—things likely to improve her mind. Lord, how she used to drink them in! holding her breath almost till we got to the end of a run, and clutching the arms of her chair with both hands, and well-nigh gasping as I told her about flying over hedges and taking bull-finches, and all the rest of it. She'd never have been what she is if it hadn't been for me. One evening I made a great mistake. I don't know how I happened to get upon Dick Darrell, who was the hardest rider and the wildest devil I ever did come across. He was going to be married and settle down, and the young woman was stopping at Darrell Court with the father. Dick thought he'd have a burst with the hounds; and if you believe me, when I came to where at the last fence he went clean over his horse's head and broke his neck, Susan fell to crying to such an extent, my housekeeper wouldn't let her go back to the Hall that night. Ay, it seemed a hard thing to take Darrell home stiff; such screaming and weeping and wailing I never heard—the old man childless and the bride a widow, as one may say."

"What became of the bride, as you call her?" asked Mr. Gayre, with some interest.

"O, she stayed to comfort the Squire; and comforted him to such purpose that they made up a match between them."

"I thought as much," remarked his brother-in-law sardoni-cally. "Where's your rose, Chelston?"

"Faith, I don't know," answered the Baronet, glancing at his coat, and for the first time noticing the flower had disap-peared. "I must have knocked the head off as I was mount-ing this fidgety beast."

Mr. Gayre smiled, but said nothing. On the whole he was not perhaps displeased that Sir Geoffrey had lost his Marshal Niel, as he had already lost the whole of his other possessions.

Seated in the twilight, then, it was of Susan Drummond

and Enfield Highway and fields of emerald green, and a blue sky just flecked here and there with snow-white clouds, and the air filled with the fragrance of new-mown hay, that Mr. Gayre thought, as he dreamed his day-dream, and built fancy castles with towering pinnacles that glittered in the sun. Why should he not win and wear her? Why should he not marry and be happy? Why should she not come stealing to him through the gloom, and fill his empty heart, and change his lonely life into one of utter content?

She was young, very young, no doubt; and he was old—yet not so old, after all. She was poor, and he was rich enough to give her all he fancied she could desire. Women had figuratively torn caps about him; why should he despair of awakening an interest in Susan Drummond? She had no lover—he felt sure of that; quite sure the depths of her nature had never yet been stirred.

The twilight deepened; it grew so dark he could not see the objects surrounding him; and yet he dreamt on, till suddenly the door opened, and an old servant, who had been with him " through the wars," said,

" Mr. Sudlow, Colonel, wishes to know if he can see you."

" Yes," answered the " Colonel," coming back to earth and its realities. " Ask him to walk in; and bring lights and coffee."

CHAPTER X.

LIGHTS and Mr. Sudlow appeared together—the former in tall silver candlesticks. massive, and of an antique pattern; the latter in all the splendour of evening dress. As they shook hands Mr. Gayre surveyed his visitor.

"Going to some scene of gay festivity?" he inquired.

Mr. Sudlow coloured a little.

"No, nowhere very particular," he answered. "I just looked in on—on my way. I thought you would not mind. I have called so often lately and always found you out."

"Yes, it has been unfortunate," remarked the banker; but he did not proceed to indulge in expressions of regret, or tender any explanation of or apology for his absence. He only asked Mr. Sudlow if he would take some coffee, and while he sipped his own stood leaning against the mantelpiece, looking thoughtfully down on the flowers that filled the wide hearth.

For a few moments the younger man did not speak; then he said, as if in a sort of desperation,

"Mr. Gayre, *when* are you going to introduce me to your brother-in-law?"

Mr. Gayre, thus directly appealed to, laughed, took another lump of sugar and stirred his coffee, before he answered,

"I am sure I cannot tell; fact is, the more I see of the worthy Baronet the less I consider his acquaintance a blessing to be desired."

"But you promised me," expostulated Mr. Sudlow; "you did—you know you did!"

"Did I? Well, perhaps so; only circumstances alter cases, and with the fresh understanding I have recently gained of Sir Geoffrey's character, I should certainly advise any one able to keep him at arm's length to do so."

"But it is not Sir Geoffrey I want to know—it is his daughter."

"My dear fellow, don't excite yourself; of course I understand it is the daughter. But you can't make her acquaintance without at the same time making that of the father; and, as a friend, I say have nothing whatever to do with Sir Geoffrey Chelston. You think you can take care of yourself, I know," went on Mr. Gayre; "that the owner of Meridian Square will be more than a match for the Baronet, without an acre of land or a house of his own. On your own head, then, be it. You shall become acquainted with a gentleman who, to quote those words of Mr. Pickwick which so deceived the widow Bardell, will teach you more tricks in a week than you would ever learn in a year."

"And when?" asked Mr. Sudlow suggestively.

"Only to consider the impatience of youth!" exclaimed Mr. Gayre. "Perhaps you imagined I would take you to call this minute," he added, with cruel irony; "but I won't hurry you along the road to destruction. One of these afternoons we will search out Sir Geoffrey, about the time he arises from slumber, and before he goes forth to seek whom he may devour. But one word of caution, Sudlow," went on Mr. Gayre, with a short bitter laugh: "don't let him choose you a horse."

"You may be very sure I won't," returned Mr. Sudlow with energy.

"I am aware you think you play billiards pretty well; still, were I in your place, I would not pit my skill against the Baronet's. Further, do not lend him any money; do not let him persuade you to put your name to paper; be very wary of all games both of chance and skill; refrain from laying or taking odds—"

"Anything else?" asked Mr. Sudlow, a little sulkily.

"Well, no, except that you would do well to have nothing whatever to do with Sir Geoffrey Chelston."

"You must permit me to be the best judge of that."

"All right, so you shall; only I should be very sorry to see Meridian Square, and all the other elegant and convenient, if less profitable, properties you possess, converted into ducks and drakes; and that is a conjuring trick the Baronet will perform with incredible rapidity unless you are very careful."

"I believe he has bit *you*," said Mr. Sudlow, with a certain triumph.

"You are mistaken in that belief," answered Mr. Gayre, the coldness which had characterised his manner during the interview deepening into displeasure. "In which direction are you going, Sudlow? I will walk part of the way with you. I want a stroll and a cigar."

In some places and with some people Mr. Sudlow was often bold, not to say arrogant; but the banker exercised a deterrent influence over him, which he felt perhaps rather than understood.

With almost any other man he might have prolonged the conversation, and indulged in further argument; but since his youth he had looked up to and feared Mr. Gayre. Habit accordingly proved stronger than indiscretion, and muttering something about the Strand, and looking in at one of the theatres, he took the hint so plainly given, and rose to go.

They passed together into the quiet street, and under the peaceful stars sauntered slowly along, speaking no word for some little time, each busy with his own thoughts, whatever those thoughts might be.

It was Mr. Sudlow who broke the silence, and his first remark proved he had been considering how to give Mr. Gayre a rap over the knuckles.

"I was surprised to meet Miss Chelston the other day."

"In the Park?"

"No, I have not seen her *there* for a long time. At Baker Street Station."

"Romantic," commented Mr. Gayre, who, had he spoken frankly, would have said he felt a great deal more surprised than Mr. Sudlow.

"A railway-station is as good a place to meet a lady as any other in these days," retorted the younger man.

"It may be, you ought to know."

"She was going to Kew."

"You mean my niece, I suppose?"

"Yes; and we travelled down in the same compartment."

"Indeed!"

"She went to one of the old houses on the Green."

"Once more referring to Miss Chelston?"

"Of course; I did not know it was necessary to go on

repeating a woman's name in conversation, like 'my lord' in an official letter."

"O!" and Mr. Gayre walked on, smoking steadily, and refused utterly to ask a single question, though Mr. Sudlow waited and longed for him to do so.

"True love will excuse many things," began the banker at last; "still, as neither Sir Geoffrey nor his daughter is aware you fell in love with my niece the first day you saw her riding remarkably badly in the Park, I really do not think I should ever mention that you followed Miss Chelston in the manner you seem to have done. The Baronet might think you had been—spying."

"How do you know I was not going to the Green too, on my own business?"

"I do not know, of course; I only suppose. And under any circumstances I should not advise you to mention the matter—I really should not."

"I only mentioned it now to show you—"

"To show me what?" asked Mr. Gayre, as the other paused and hesitated; "to show you could form my niece's acquaintance without my help. Make no mistake on that point, my friend—you might get to know a milliner's apprentice by travelling in the same compartment with her to Kew on Whit-Monday, but not that of a girl in a higher rank of life."

"You are always so hard upon me," complained Mr. Sudlow. "You generally take a wrong construction out of what I say."

"Then learn to express yourself in such a way that misconstruction is impossible," returned Mr. Gayre sternly. "At all events, understand clearly that though Sir Geoffrey Chelston is an unprincipled *roué*, his daughter has never caught even a glimpse of Bohemia, and I mean to take very good care she never shall. Fortunately she has not the slightest inclination in that direction; I believe a girl never lived more capable of understanding and resenting the impertinence of modern puppyhood than my niece."

"Do you suppose I was going to offer her any impertinence?"

"How can I tell? All I know is you had better not."

"Mr. Gayre, on my honour—"

"Your honour! Well, well, let that pass; proceed."

"I wish you would not so constantly catch me up—you make me forget what I intended to say."

II

"That is a pity, for you were, if I mistake not, about to remark you admired the calm dignity of Miss Chelston's manners, when answering the observations made to her by a gentleman 'who travelled in the same compartment all the way to Kew,' as much as her beauty. Come, Sudlow, confess my niece snubbed you effectually."

"She did not do anything of the sort."

"Do you expect me to believe she *talked* to you?"

"No, no! O, no! She did not talk, but she was quite polite. Said 'no,' and 'yes,' and 'thank you,' and that."

"Evidently regarding you as an outer barbarian all the time," suggested Mr. Gayre, with relish. "Yes, I know her style. Frankly," he added, "for your sake I am very sorry this has happened; why can't or won't you remember all girls are not barmaids, and that the fascinating manner and brilliant conversation which prove so effective across a marble-topped counter are really worse than useless with young ladies who have been discreetly brought up?"

"You are always preaching to me," observed Mr. Sudlow.

"And with so little result I think I shall leave off preaching altogether."

"You are offended, and I declare nothing in the world was further from my intention than to annoy you.".

"We had better let the subject drop."

"But you will introduce me to your niece?"

"I shall have to reconsider that matter. Second thoughts are often best."

"But, Mr. Gayre, indeed, I meant no harm. Pray do not speak to me in that tone. You know I would not voluntarily vex you for the world."

Mr. Gayre burst out laughing. It was the best thing possible for him to do under the circumstances.

"Three quarrels in one day!" he exclaimed. "It would be wise, I think, to get me home and send for a doctor. Nevertheless, Sudlow, it was truth that I told just now. You must mind your p's and q's when I introduce you to Sir Geoffrey Chelston."

"I'll take good heed to every letter in the alphabet, if that is all," exclaimed Mr. Sudlow, relieved. Yet as he walked away, after parting from Mr. Gayre, who seemed disposed to carry out the programme he had indicated, so far as hieing him back to Wimpole Street was concerned, he muttered under

his breath, "O, if I only once could get the chance of giving
you change in your own coin, I'd make your ears tingle! I
wonder what has come to you lately! You always were given
to gibing, but since the Baronet appeared on the scene you
have grown unbearable."

Once rid of his companion, Mr. Gayre only retraced the
way for a short distance towards Wimpole Street. Instead he
turned in the direction of Manchester Square, and walking
evidently for the sake of walking, and not because he desired
to reach any definite goal, occupied himself in reflections upon
the occurrences of the afternoon, devoting a considerable
amount of attention to that statement of Mr. Sudlow's concerning Miss Margaret's visit to Kew.

"I wonder who it is she knows at Kew?" he thought.
"Shall I try to get her married? or, following the Canon's
sensible advice, settle a small annuity on her and wash my
hands of the whole business? Heavens! what dirty water I
always seem to be dabbling in now! There was a time when
I would not have soiled the tip of my finger with it. Alas! and
alas! Nicholas Gayre, Love has, I fear, played you a scurvy
trick once more. You had better don cap and bells at once,
for you are a far greater fool than Sudlow, and all for the sake
of a woman concerning whom you know next to nothing. I
wonder if she will be able to sweeten this Marah—extract any
healing out of such a Bethesda?"

For, indeed, when Mr. Gayre exhausted the subject (and
his mind was so constituted he could not help exhausting any
subject which concerned himself, whether agreeable or the
reverse) he found he had since that memorable day in May,
when the horse Mr. Arbery was riding shied at a steam-roller,
been travelling across a wilderness, in which the few springs
were very bitter and the pools brackish, and playing an extremely risky game. What he said was quite true. There had
been a time when he would not have meddled in Sir Geoffrey's
concerns for any consideration. You cannot touch pitch and
not be defiled was a truth the Gayres never cared to forget,
and Nicholas Gayre could not disguise from himself the fact
that his brother-in-law could in no moral sense be regarded as
clean. The more he saw of him the more hopelessly disreputable did the man appear. Washing an Ethiop white would
have been a possible task in comparison with taking even a
part of the stain out of the Baronet's nature.

In the days gone by, when Sir Geoffrey kept his account in Lombard Street, on the first occasion of his drawing below the large amount which Gayres expected to be kept as a balance, a letter was despatched to Chelston Pleasaunce, directing his attention to the fact, and begging that the mistake might be rectified; but, finding the same "mistake" repeated, Mr. Gayre, Senior, requested that the account might be closed.

This was the beginning of a coolness which lasted up to the time when Mr. Nicholas Gayre sought out his relative in North Bank—a coolness which Sir Geoffrey's own conduct intensified into total estrangement. The banker thought of all this as he walked along the London streets under the quiet stars, and a feeling not unlike shame oppressed him as he considered how utterly at variance his own conduct had of late been with the traditions of his house.

"And all because of a woman's face," he decided. "Well, I can't draw back now. I went into the Chelston pest-housef with my eyes open, and whatever happens I have only myself to thank. Sir Geoffrey is not any better than I expected to find him; and my niece is not much worse than I expected to find her. She is false; but she is not fast, thank Heaven. I wonder who it is she knows at Kew? She ought not to be running about London by herself; but I do not see that I can interfere in the matter." And having, just as he reached his own door, arrived at this sensible conclusion, Mr. Gayre put his key in the lock, and passed into the library, where he saw a letter lying on the table.

"It is from Sir Geoffrey, Colonel," said his servant; "a messenger brought it up from the club. He did not know whether any answer was required; so I told him you were out, and that I had no idea when you would be back, but if a reply was expected I could take it myself."

Mr. Gayre made no comment. He only lifted the note with the usual dread and repugnance with which he always approached the Baronet's communications, and, tearing open the envelope, read:

"Dear Gayre,—Peggy is certainly turning over a new leaf. What do you think she proposed this evening? Why, that we should both run down to Enfield early to-morrow and look up Susan. I can't tell you how pleased I am. I have promised to be a good boy and get home betimes to-night, so as to be in condition for the journey.   Yours, G. C."

"Now what is the English of this move?" marvelled Mr. Gayre. But he need not have exercised his mind over this question. For once Miss Chelston was playing a perfectly straightforward game. "Circumstances alter cases," and she felt as anxious for Miss Drummond's company as she had once been desirous of avoiding it.

CHAPTER XI

"SHOULD AULD ACQUAINTANCE BE FORGOT?"

PEACE reigned in Mr. Moreby's villa. The summer glory lay golden without, sunshine dwelt within. Susan had come, and the house seemed transformed. The rooms were the same, the furniture was the same, and yet everything looked different; the place had that charm of home it never possessed before. Susan was there, with her bright cheerful face, her pleasant laugh, her useful hands, her constant thoughtfulness, her unselfish heart, her tireless consideration for others. Mistaken! No, Mr. Gayre understood here at last was a woman sound to the core; a woman a man would be safe in loving, and who herself could love till the last hour of her life. Already he felt as if he had known her for years—as if there had never been a time when he and Susan Drummond were total strangers.

They sat at tea in the charming room overlooking the lawn; sun-blinds excluded the light and heat, the windows were filled with flowers. Sir Geoffrey lay almost at full length in an easy-chair; his daughter was looking her best, and trying to seem demurely unconscious of Mr. Sudlow's admiring glances.

Miss Drummond presided over the tea equipage, and Mr. Gayre was taking her part against the apparently good-natured accusation of extravagance which Miss Chelston was bringing against her.

But Susan needed no champion; she was perfectly well able to defend herself.

"If one is to have tea at all one may as well have it good, and I am very sure the extra cost cannot be a shilling a week. I excessively dislike tea that has been 'brewed.'"

"So do I, Susan," exclaimed Sir Geoffrey, who had been coaxed into accepting a cup of the refreshing beverage, and was considering how to escape drinking it. "I'd just as soon take a dose of senna."

"Your tea is certainly extremely nice," capped Mr. Gayre.

"We are all teetotallers at Enfield, you see," went on Susan, in calm explanation—"my cousin from choice, my aunt on principle, and I and the servants from necessity."

"O Susan, how can you say such things!" expostulated Miss Chelston, shocked.

"Have I said something very dreadful?" asked Miss Drummond of the company generally.

"No, faith," cried Sir Geoffrey; "after the wine your uncle used to have at the Hall you must find water an awful cross to bear."

"Happily the water is very good at Enfield. But what I meant to say was, that as we have no other extravagance we surely are justified in making good tea."

"You shall make it as you like here, Susan. That lazy little minx always leaves it to the servants, and nice stuff they turn out;" and the Baronet set down his cup and took a little stroll to the window, and peeped under the sun-blind and remarked he thought a breath of air was stirring, and then asked Susan when they were to have a long ride together. "I'll find you a mount," he added.

"I think there is one of my horses Miss Drummond would like," remarked Mr. Gayre.

"O, you don't want to ride; do you, dear?" suggested Miss Chelston softly.

"Yes, I do, very much indeed. But I must first get a habit; I won't bring eternal disgrace upon you, Maggie, by wearing that old thing I had on when we met in the Park."

"It was a horror," said Miss Chelston.

"Ah, well, it won't offend your eyes again. I mean to have one of the latest fashion, short and narrow, so that if I am thrown I sha'n't have a chance of helping myself."

"Order it from my tailor, Susan," advised Sir Geoffrey; "he never expects to be paid under six years."

"You had better have it from mine, Miss Drummond," said Mr. Sudlow; "he is a very good man, and allows fifteen per cent for cash with order."

"What a pull you rich fellows have over us poor devils!" groaned Sir Geoffrey; "we are forced to pay through the nose for everything."

"Thank you, Mr. Sudlow, for your suggestion," answered Susan; "but I am having the habit 'built,' as my cousin phrases it, by the 'local practitioner.'"

"Good gracious, Susan, you might just as well put your money in the fire!" said Miss Chelston.

"Wait till you see this great work of art," advised Susan. "I ventured to pay the old man a compliment about the fit, which he received with lofty indifference, merely saying, 'Yes, I think we are pretty good sculptors!'"

Mr. Gayre laughed, Miss Chelston looked disgusted, and Sir Geoffrey declared, "By Jove, that wasn't bad!"

"What is the colour of the thing?" asked Miss Chelston.

"The colour of the uniform of the Irish Constabulary," said Miss Drummond, "invisible green. I am not going to enter into competition with you, though I do think that precise shade of blue in your habit divine."

"And so becoming," added Mr. Sudlow, as a general sort of statement, which he made particular by a look at Miss Chelston.

"And so becoming, as you truly remark," observed Miss Drummond, laughing, "*to some persons.*"

At this juncture Sir Geoffrey bethought him that the room was unbearably hot, and that he would take a turn round the garden to "stretch his legs a bit."

It was some time before he appeared sauntering over the lawn, for it had been necessary for him to pause in the dining-room and refresh exhausted nature from a convenient decanter.

Shortly Mr. Gayre joined him among the flowers, and then learned his brother-in-law was deucedly sorry, but he had an appointment he could not possibly miss.

"Don't let me drive you away, Gayre, though," he said. "Make yourself as much at home as you can; and look here, you bring your friend up some evening to dinner. The girls make luncheon, dinner when I am out; but name your day, and I daresay we can manage something fit to eat. Susan and Mrs. Lavender shall go into committee."

"Are you going to instal Miss Drummond as housekeeper?" asked Mr. Gayre.

"Bless you, she has installed herself. Peggy will do nothing but dress. There never was such a girl for finery. She'll have to marry somebody rich, for she'd very soon bring a poor man to the workhouse. Has it struck you that Sudlow's mightily taken with her?"

"He seems to admire her very much."

"Well, then, clearly understand, if he means business I won't stand in the way. Anybody with half an eye can see there's not a bit of breed about him, but you say he's well off; nobody without money need think of Peggy. It would be a great relief to me to have her well settled; so now you know my views, and, as far as I am concerned, your friend can propose as soon as he likes."

"But, good Heavens, he was only introduced to her the other day!"

"I know that; but 'happy's the wooing that's not long of doing;' and between you and me, the sooner we can get her off our hands the better. A great deal of running could be done in a short time; and the days slip away when you are living in a borrowed house and have to trust to your wits for money. I thought I would just give you a hint of what is in my mind."

"Most kind of you, I'm sure."

"Well, my idea is a man can't be too straightforward, and I may tell you the sooner Peggy is married the better I shall be pleased."

"Surely you don't want, though, to throw her at the head of the first person who seems to admire her? Don't be in such a hurry; give the girl a chance. She may meet plenty of men more desirable in every way than Mr. Sudlow."

"She may," agreed Sir Geoffrey, "and also she may not; besides, Gayre, a 'bird in the hand,' you remember; and don't you make any mistake about sentiment, and all that sort of thing, as regards Peggy. She is as cold as a stone. She cares for nothing on earth but herself. If she had been different she might have done well for both of us."

"Then you *had* some plan in your head when you brought her to London," thought Mr. Gayre, "which she has baulked."

"And she's not a bit clever," pursued Sir Geoffrey, anxious, apparently, thoroughly to convince Mr. Gayre of the desirability of closing with the first eligible offer. "All that can be said in her favour is she's pretty, and she knows how to dress herself."

"Two very good points about a woman," commented Mr. Gayre.

"Well, well, I only tell you for your guidance."

"But, Sir Geoffrey, she is not *my* daughter; if you want to get her married you had better set to work for yourself, had you not?"

"I! What can I do, a poor fellow out at elbows with Fortune, who has had the devil's own luck in life? Besides, it is not from my side of the house she gets her selfishness and want of brains. If I had thought more of myself and less of other people I should not have been placed as I am. I have been too considerate, too honest, Gayre—that is about the state of the case. Ah, if I had to begin life over again, I would act very differently!"

"I wouldn't vex myself about your own imperfections, were I you."

"No; it's of no use crying over spilt milk. But, to come back to what we were saying, you keep that matter in mind, and remember if your friend likes to propose I shall make no objection. Some men would want to know a lot about family and all the rest of it, but, thank Heaven, I have no prejudices. Everybody must have a beginning, and all I shall require to be satisfied about is, can he pay her milliner's bills and keep her as a girl with such a face ought to be kept? Ah, talk of the —here she comes! Well, Peggy, how are you going to amuse your uncle? for I must be off. I am so sorry, Mr. Sudlow— confoundedly sorry; but Gayre has promised to bring you up to dinner some day very soon. You'll come, quite in a friendly way, won't you? We are very plain people, but sincere. I never ask any man to the house I don't want to see."

In which statement there was so much truth Mr. Gayre felt that even mentally he could not controvert it, while Mr. Sudlow, almost trembling with pleasure, said he would be only too delighted to accept the invitation.

"That's all right, then," said the Baronet heartily. "Now I really can't stop another minute. You'll excuse me, I'm sure, Mr. Sudlow. Till our next merry meeting, Gayre. Fare- well, Peggy. You'll see the last of me, I know, Susan;" and he turned back a pleased face to his brother-in-law as Miss Drummond slipped her hand through his arm and went with him into the house.

Something in that action seemed to touch Mr. Gayre to the heart. He had heard ere then of guardian angels, but never previously did it fall to his lot to see a pure and lovely woman taking charge of such a sinner as Sir Geoffrey Chelston.

"We must also be thinking about going," he said; but Miss Chelston pleaded so prettily for a longer visit that the gentlemen consented to remain till nearer dinner-time, and finally it was arranged they should all go out for a turn in Regent's Park.

"O, delightful!" exclaimed Susan, when the question was referred to her. "I do think this part of the park so exquisite."

Half-an-hour later they were all strolling along together—Susan in a black silk dress, Margaret in a brown, which became her as well as the blue cloth habit had done. Regent's Park was looking its very best; the ornamental water shimmered and glittered under the beams of the evening sun. The leaves of the trees were fresh and cool, and free from dust; the birds were singing in the mimic plantations; there was a great peace in the hour and the scene, which seemed to lay a soothing hand on the hearts of two, at all events, who looked wistfully at the landscape.

"It is very, very pretty," said Susan to Mr. Gayre; and, looking in her face, he agreed with her; *it* was, indeed, very, very pretty.

"Are Kew Gardens well worth seeing?" asked Susan, after a minute's pause.

"Yes; I like the wild part best, however, where one gets away from the excursionists."

"Maggie and I are going down to Kew to-morrow; perhaps we might be able to see the gardens."

"They are open every day," said Mr. Gayre.

"It was not that I meant; we intended to visit two dear old ladies that we used to know at Chelston. They are the sisters-in-law of the former Rector. They used to live with and keep house for him. Such charming ladies! You can't think how lovely they were; the pink in their cheeks was so delicate, and their eyes so clear and blue, and they dressed so plainly, yet so spotlessly, if you know what I mean; and the poor loved them so much, and with reason. Well, the Rector died. But I am afraid I tire you, Mr. Gayre."

"Tire! Your story enchants me."

"The Rector died, and then it seemed such a terrible thing for them to go into lodgings and live on their poor little income. I am sure I lay awake at nights crying about them, for they were such darlings. And then, in a minute, like something in a fairy-tale, a distant relation died, and left them a house on Kew Green for their lives. They took their lovely china and Indian curiosities up there. I helped them pack. And a niece, a widow, lives with them; and they put their incomes together; and it really is a delightful ending to what might have been a sad tale. They have a nephew, an artist. I think you heard Sir Geoffrey mention him."

"Is he the son of the widow?" asked Mr. Gayre.

"No; his mother died long and long ago."

" And is he still in Rome, or has he returned to England?"

" I have not heard anything about him for a long time.   I
shall know all to-morrow."

" At last," thought Mr. Gayre, " I have met a woman in
whom is no 'shadow of turning.' She is as transparent as
glass. She is frankness and truth itself." And he felt mightily
relieved; for, after all, there seemed no wrong in his niece's
trip to Kew.

" Save that she ought not to have gone alone.   But then,
if she never went out except with a chaperon, she might stop
at home for the term of her natural life."

Altogether it was an anomalous position.   Mr. Gayre, when
he considered the matter dispassionately, found it extremely
difficult to define the rank to which his niece belonged.

" How fond, Miss Drummond," he said, " you seem to be
of every thing and person connected with Chelston !"

" If you only could imagine," she answered, " how happy I
was there, you would not wonder at my loving even the vaga-
bond curs running about the roads."

Chelston, she went on to tell him, was the loveliest place
in all the wide world.   Had he ever been there?   Yes, once.
Did he remember this, that, and the other about the Pleasaunce,
the yew hedges, the fish-ponds, the cherry orchard, the great
mulberry-trees, the vineries, the billiard-room, the library ?

" At one time I used almost to live at the Pleasaunce," she
explained.   " Sir Geoffrey *was* good to me ;" and then in a few
words she told how, when but two years of age, her father died
out in India, and her mother drooped and pined, and was
buried in Chelston churchyard six months afterwards.

" I never knew what it was, though, really to miss my
parents," she said.   " Everybody was so kind.   I do not think
any child could have been more petted and spoiled than I.
My dear uncle would not even let me go to school to be
taught, as poor old nurse used to lament, to be like other
young ladies ; and I am very sure Maggie is right in saying I
did not learn much from the governesses, who were supposed
to teach useful knowledge.   Dreadful, was it not ?"

And Miss Drummond, remembering many pleasant speeches
Miss Chelston had made to her in Mr. Gayre's presence, turned
a mischievous laughing face to that gentleman, who, though he
only smiled in answer, thought if his companion were to be
regarded as an example of total ignorance, education might be
dispensed with.

"I used to hear so much about you," Susan went on, "I feel as if I had known you all my life. And then—papa was an officer too."

"I wish I were an officer now," answered Mr. Gayre heartily, "only that in such case I might not have had the pleasure of making your acquaintance. Should you like to go back to Chelston, Miss Drummond?"

"I think not," she said, with a sad dreamy look in her wonderful eyes. "You see we cannot take up the past again just as it was. It is like reading a book a second time, or hearing a song, or seeing a sunset. It is never the same twice. My past was very beautiful, but it is ended. You can't put last year's leaves on the trees, and we—we can't stay children and girls for ever. Pretty nearly all the people I loved are dead or gone. No, I should not care for Chelston without my kind old uncle, and Sir Geoffrey, and all the other friends I was so fond of." And for a moment Susan turned aside, while Mr. Gayre, who had his memories of loss, if not of love, walked on in silence too.

Just then, while Mr. Sudlow and his companion were gravely discoursing concerning the latest *on dit*—the Queen and Royal Family, the picture of the year, and the play which was considered most amusing, or the book attracting the greatest attention—Mr. Gayre saw a gentleman striding along the path, who, with eyes bent on the ground and hat pulled over his brow, passed beautiful Miss Chelston without a look, and would have served Miss Drummond in like manner had that young lady not arrested his attention with a cry.

"Lal!" she said, "Lal!" and then they grasped hands, both hands.

"O, I am *so* glad!" she went on, "I am *so* glad!"

"Where in all the wide world, Susan, did you spring from?" he asked, his face radiant with pleasure. "It is like the good old long ago, meeting you again."

"I am stopping with the Chelstons," she answered. "O Mr. Gayre, would you mind telling Margaret this is Mr. Hilderton?"

Sweetly and decorously, without any undue haste or excitement, came back the fair Marguerite. *She* did not call the young gentleman "Lal." *She* did not greet him with effusion; she only said, "How very odd! We intended to go to Kew to-morrow."

Susan's friendship, however, was of quite another kind. No

cause to complain of the warmth of her greeting. She insisted on knowing "Where he was," "What he was doing," "How he was doing." While Miss Chelston seemed to be considering how she could most gracefully efface herself, Miss Drummond asked fifty questions.

"I have a studio in Camden Town, Susan," said the young man, "and your face is in a picture there. Come and see it— do."

"Certainly I will," she answered. "Not to-morrow, but the day after. *Is* it not wonderful to have met you?"

"I don't know," he answered; "I live not very far away." And then, raising his hat to the rest of the party, and shaking hands with Susan, he was gone.

"How could you," asked Miss Chelston chidingly—"how could you think, dear, of saying we would go to Mr. Hilderton's studio? The thing is utterly impossible."

Sir Geoffrey's daughter tarried behind Mr. Sudlow to make this remark, and her friend retorted,

"I never said *you* would go; but *I* shall."

"Now, Susan darling!"

"Now, Marguerite!"

And the two women stood tall and lovely and defiant in the evening light.

"If you would accept of my escort, Miss Drummond," said Mr. Gayre softly.

"O, how very, very good you are!" exclaimed Susan, turning towards him with that charming smile which seemed her greatest possession; "I should be so glad if you would go with me. Not because I mind what Margaret says in the least. She knows, nobody better, that Lal and I have been good brother and sister always, and shall be the same, I hope, till the end of our days. But if you went with me, you might see some picture you admired, and then you could talk of it to your friends, and, perhaps, somebody might buy it. Lal is very, very clever; but—"

"Is that the Lal who did *not* jump the river at Chelston?" asked Mr. Gayre.

Miss Chelston had, apparently in stately disgust of her friend's frivolity and impropriety, resumed her walk with Mr. Sudlow.

"Yes, poor Lal! I am afraid he will never jump any river anywhere," said Miss Drummond sadly. "Don't you know that sort of man? But, of course, you must be acquainted with all sorts of men. There are people who can write books, and paint pictures, and compose music; and yet not sell a book or a picture or a song. I am afraid Lal won't do much good, as far as making money is concerned, and yet he has such genius. He did a crayon likeness of uncle, which was indeed his living self. Poor, poor Lal! Isn't he handsome?"

With a light heart Mr. Gayre agreed the young man was uncommonly handsome.

"I do not think it is well for men to be so very good-looking," observed Miss Drummond. "I know his beauty has been Lal Hilderton's ruin. His aunts denied him nothing, and the women about Chelston, young and old, thought he was a nonsuch. Poor Lal! I have often felt sorry for him. You will look at his pictures, won't you, Mr. Gayre?"

If she only could have realised the fact she had but to speak a little longer in similar terms to insure the purchase of Mr. Hilderton's whole collection!

CHAPTER XII

HIGH FESTIVAL.

Days swept by. Since Mr. Gayre left the army, days had never sped along so quickly. All his scruples were gone, his painful self-examinations ended. He almost lived at North Bank; he walked and drove and rode with his niece and her friend. Save for an uneasiness he could not explain, an occasional doubt which would intrude, he was perfectly, utterly happy and content.

For some reasons best known to himself—most probably because he wished at once to begin operations upon the widow's heart—Sir Geoffrey decided to accompany " his girls " to Brunswick Square when the luncheon " came off."

" I think it would be only a fitting mark of respect to your kind friend," he observed to Mr. Gayre, who merely said " Very well," and having duly apprised Mrs. Jubbins of the pleasure in store for her, announced that he would defer his own visit till some future occasion.

According to the Baronet's account everything went off delightfully. He knew he had made himself most agreeable. Mrs. Jubbins' acquaintance with that class of "nobleman" (brought prominently before the public by the Tichborne trial) was of the slightest. Indeed, she had never before known but one "Sir" intimately, and he was only a red-faced, snub-nosed, loud-talking gentleman in the tallow trade, who had been knighted upon the occasion of some royal expedition to the City. In comparison with him Sir Geoffrey's manners, when on good behaviour, must have seemed princely. Truly, as the widow told Mr. Gayre afterwards, his brother-in-law was " most affable," " and I am quite taken with your dear niece," went on Mrs. Jubbins. " She is a most lovely girl, and so sweet and winning; but I can't say I care for her friend. What do you suppose she asked my maid?"

" I really cannot conjecture. Was it something very dreadful?"

"Very impertinent, at any rate," declared Mrs. Jubbins; "she asked her *if my hair was all my own.*"

"Miss Drummond," said Mr. Gayre, when he next went to North Bank, "may I inquire what induced you to put such a singular question to Mrs. Jubbins' maid as you did about that lady's hair?"

"It was not Susan, it was I," interposed Miss Chelston. "I did not mean any rudeness, though it seems Mrs. Jubbins is very angry with me. So she has been complaining to you, has she?"

"Yes, but she said it was your friend. Miss Drummond, what *are* you laughing at?"

"I can tell you," said Miss Chelston, as Susan murmured "Nothing." "She is wondering if Mrs. Jubbins let down her back hair to prove to you it was 'all real, every bit of it;' for that is what she did the other day, when expressing her righteous indignation to Susan."

"My acquaintance with that back hair is of too long a date for practical assurance to be necessary," answered Mr. Gayre, joining in Susan's mirth, which was now uncontrollable.

"Her hair is as coarse as a horse's mane," put in Miss Chelston spitefully.

"O no, Maggie. It is not as fine as yours; but it is magnificent hair, for all that," said Susan.

"I do wish you would call me Marguerite!" exclaimed that young lady. "I have told you over and over again I detest hearing Maggie, Maggie, Maggie, from morning to night!"

"I'll call you Griselda, if you like," said her friend slyly.

"What I cannot conceive," remarked Mr. Gayre, "is how Mrs. Jubbins came to imagine you were Miss Drummond, and Miss Drummond you."

"It was all papa's fault," answered Miss Chelston. "You know the ridiculous way he talks about Susan being his own girl and his favourite child, and his two daughters, and all that sort of thing; and poor Mrs. Jubbins, whom I really do not consider the cleverest or most brilliant person I ever met, got utterly bewildered. Besides, Susan set herself to be so very agreeable that I know I must have seemed a most reserved and unpleasant young person by comparison; and, of course, Mrs. Jubbins imagined *Mr. Gayre's niece* could not be other than delightful. She still believes Susan to be me. For some reason, when Susan called the other day to inquire concerning the health of Mrs. Jubbins' ankle, she did not think it necessary to explain the mistake."

I

"I thought it would be wiser to give her time to forget that little matter of the hair," observed Miss Drummond.

"You had better try to make your peace, my dear Marguerite," suggested Mr. Gayre, a little ironically. "I know no kinder or better woman than Mrs. Jubbins; and it will grieve me very much if she and you do not get on well together."

"If I can make her credit I am really your niece she will forgive me readily," said Miss Chelston, in a tone which told Mr. Gayre she understood the widow's feelings towards her uncle, and did not approve of them.

Indeed, the whole question had been very freely commented upon by Sir Geoffrey and before Miss Drummond.

"I shouldn't wonder," declared the Baronet, "if they make a match of it yet. I think she'll bag her bird, after all. He's a strange fellow, but I daresay he'll settle down in the traces one of these days. I am sure he might have her for the asking, and I don't think it would be a bad thing for him, eh, Susan?"

"It does not strike me as very suitable," answered Susan.

"She's not exactly his sort, but she'd make him comfortable, I'll be bound. With such a lot of money *any* woman must be considered suitable; besides, Mrs. Jubbins is not bad-looking, and she's a good soul, I feel satisfied."

"Is not Mr. Gayre rich enough?" asked Susan. "I should have thought it was not necessary for him to marry Money."

"Bless you, my girl, nobody is rich enough. Gayre must have plenty; but I daresay he could do with more, and it would be an actual sin to let such a fortune slip out of the family."

Susan did not say anything further, but she thought a great deal; and she often afterwards looked earnestly at Mrs. Jubbins, wondering whether Mr. Gayre would ever marry that lady, and supposing he did how his notions and those of his wife could be made to work harmoniously together. She liked Mr. Gayre immensely; but somehow she felt she did not like him quite so well since the Baronet broached that idea of marrying the widow for the sake of her money.

And yet he was so kind and considerate. It was he who made her visit utterly delightful. Margaret and she had their little tiffs and misunderstandings. Sir Geoffrey—well, Sir Geoffrey did not seem to her quite the Sir Geoffrey of old. "We go on," as she observed so truly to Mr. Gayre; and oftentimes we find old friends do not suit us if they have not gone on our way.

Much as faces change—age, sadden, alter—they do not change half so much as souls. This is what makes it so hard to take up a friendship again after a long separation. We may get accustomed to gray hair that had kept its sunny brown in our loving memory—to wrinkles—to dim eyes—to the bowed head and the faltering step; but what we never grow reconciled to are the moral changes wrought by time, the faults which have become intensified, the latent weakness we never suspected, the falsehood where we would have pledged our lives there existed only truth, the frivolity and the selfishness where we never dreamed to find other than high aims and noble aspirations.

To the young the process of disillusion seems terrible, and Susan found that to be forced to see her friends' faults was very bitter indeed.

Nevertheless, spite of Sir Geoffrey's eternal Jeremiads on the subject of money, and his daughter's jealousy, irritability, and lack of ordinary straightforwardness, Susan did enjoy stopping at North Bank. It was such a delightful change from the deathly quietness and dull monotony of Enfield Highway, from her aunt's lamentations, and the conventionality, not to say stupidity, of her cousin's intended wife.

Constant variety was the rule at Sir Geoffrey's: except when Margaret and she were alone together, Miss Drummond never felt dull.

"I daresay I should tire of the life after a time," thought Susan; "but a little of it is delightful."

Flower-shows, concerts, exhibitions—Mr. Gayre took the girls to everything that was going on. Sometimes Mr. Sudlow was of the party, but the banker never seemed particularly desirous of his company. He was waiting to see whether some better chance might not open for his niece. The closer he came in contact with that gentleman the less he liked him, "and yet he is good enough for her," was his deliberate conclusion.

Happiness, in those bright sunshiny days, made Mr. Gayre almost amiable. Dimly it occurred to him that if he married Susan he could then give Margaret the opportunity of meeting men of a different class and stamp altogether. He had quite made up his mind to ask Susan to be his wife; but he did not want to be precipitate. He wished to woo her almost imperceptibly, to make himself necessary to her before he spoke of love, and win her heart, if slowly, surely, and run no risk of even a temporary rejection. He could not do without her. She was the woman he had been waiting for through the years —sweet, tender, spirited, truthful. Life seemed very beautiful to him then—well worth living, indeed.

Properly speaking, Miss Drummond's sojourn at North Bank was rather a succession of short visits than one continuous stay. Every alternate week she returned to Enfield, remaining there from Friday till Monday—sometimes for a longer period; besides this, she and Miss Chelston went to stop a little time with their old friends at Kew; and when Mrs. Jubbins took up her abode at Chislehurst she often had both girls staying there.

The widow was in a state of the highest excitement concerning a great party she meant to give. The Jones had celebrated the change to their new house with a ball; the Browns had got up a picnic really on a scale of unprecedented magnificence; whilst it was known the Robinsons intended to ask all the world and his wife to a tremendous entertainment, when their new " mansion " at Walton was ready for occupation.

" So I really must do something," declared Mrs. Jubbins to Mr. Gayre ; " it would be a sin and a shame to have such a house as this and not ask one's friends to it."

" Better give a garden-party," suggested the banker ; " and then the young people can have a dance in the evening."

So said, so done ; the invitations were written and posted. Every one Mrs. Jubbins had ever known was asked, and a great number she never had known.

Sir Geoffrey begged her to give him some blank cards, and promised to secure the presence " of a few young fellows well connected, and so forth."

The Jones, Browns, and Robinsons, and many other rich families—all of the same walk in life—had each two or three intimate friends who wanted, of all things, to make dear Mrs. Jubbins' acquaintance.

Mrs. Jubbins even asked Canon and Mrs. Gayre and the Misses Gayre, and received by return of post an emphatic refusal. The widow was unwise enough to mention that she expected Sir Geoffrey Chelston and his beautiful daughter to be of the company.

" What a set your brother has got amongst !" said Mrs. Gayre to her husband. " I should not be at all surprised to hear any day he had married that Jubbins woman."

" Neither should I," groaned the Canon. "There is one comfort, however, she is enormously *rich*."

" O, I don't believe in those City fortunes," retorted Mrs. Gayre : " look at your father !"

" My dear !" exclaimed the clergyman, less in a tone of endearment than of mild remonstrance.

The garden-party, to which Mrs. Jubbins had bidden a crowd of people, and with which she intended to inaugurate a new epoch, wherein " she should enjoy her money, and have some good of her life,' promised indeed to be a unique affair. Where expense is no object it is comparatively easy to compass success ; and on this occasion, if never on another, the widow announced her intention of not troubling her head about six-pences—a resolution which met with unqualified approval from Sir Geoffrey.

" In for a penny, in for a pound," he said. in his off-hand, agreeable way ; and then he asked Mrs Jubbins how she " stood " for wine, and offered to take all trouble concerning her cellar off her hands, by having anything she wanted sent down by his own wine-merchant, " who supplies an excellent article," finished the Baronet " and is a deuced nice sort of fellow."

" Affable," however, though the Baronet might be, friendly as well. and indeed on occasions homely in his discourse, Mrs. Jubbins was not to be enticed into taking her custom away from the houses that had won the favour of Mr. Jubbins deceased, and Mr. Jubbins' father before him. She would as soon have changed her church ; sooner, indeed, because in her heart of hearts she inclined to a moderate ritual, while the Jubbins had always pinned their simple faith to black gowns, bad music, high pews. and the plainest of plain services.

At every turn Sir Geoffrey's proffered suggestions met with a thankful but decided rejection.

For the commissariat department, concerning which the lady's ideas were of the most liberal description, Mrs. Jubbins felt that she and her butler and her cook, and the City pur-veyors, would prove equal to the occasion.

" I am not afraid of being unable to feed my friends," she said to Sir Geoffrey ; " only, how am I to amuse them ?"

" Let them amuse themselves," answered Sir Geoffrey. " Gad, if they can't do that they had better stop away."

He had laid out his own scheme of entertainment, and also given a private hint to Miss Chelston it would be wise for her to make " some running with that Sudlow fellow." " Remember the crooked stick, my girl," he advised, "and while we are in comparatively smooth water try to get a bit ahead. You mind what I say to you. If you don't, the time won't be long coming you'll repent having neglected my advice."

Plants by the van-load, muslin by the acre, relays of musicians, luncheon and supper from a firm of confectioners well known to City folks, waiters whose dignity would not have disgraced a Mansion House dinner: The Warren looking charming in its setting of green trees, guests alighting as fast as the carriages could set down, a hum of voices, dresses of every possible fashion and colour, ladies young and old, winsome and *passée*, girls and matrons, gentlemen in every variety of male costume, people who had respected Mr. Jubbins, and people who respected Mr. Higgs' daughter ; the combined odours of all the flowers on earth, as it seemed, mingling with the sound of rattling china and jingling glass ; everywhere a Babel of tongues : guests sauntering solitary over the gardens, wondering how they were to get through the next few hours ; groups chattering on the lawns ; sunshine streaming on the grass through a tracery of leaves and branches ; rabbits scudding away into the plantations ; windows open to the ground ; light curtains swaying gently in the summer air ; white pigeons with pink feet and wondering eyes looking down on the company from the roof ; millionaires exchanging words of wisdom about "stocks," and "Turks," and "Brazils," on the terrace which once "his lordship" had no doubt often paced ; Mrs. Jubbins nervous, triumphant, handsome ; her children in a seventh heaven of delight ; Sir Geoffrey Chelston in a perfectly new white hat and pale-blue necktie, talking to everybody his discerning glance told him might be made worth the trouble ; Margaret radiantly beautiful, in a dress which suited her hopes and expectations ; Susan more simply attired in accordance with her certainties ; Mr. Arbery escorting a young lady whose ultimate destination was Australia ; Mr. Lal Hilderton looking handsome, forlorn, and discontented ; a sprinkling of clergymen ; a few unmistakable West Enders ; this was what Mr. Gayre saw when he walked up from Chislehurst Station to The Warren on that glorious afternoon in August.

The number of persons who declared it was "a perfect day" could only have been equalled by those who talked about Lord Flint and the Earl of Merioneth and the widowed dowager. Though all dead or absent, the "noble family" seemed to pervade the whole place.

The rooms were inspected, their appointments criticised, the style of architecture examined in detail. Opinions differed as to the convenience of the residence as a family mansion; but every one agreed it was just the place for a party. Such a number of rooms, and all on the ground-floor!

"It is like wandering through the courts in the Crystal Palace," said one young lady.

"As fine a billiard-room as I'd ever wish to see!" exclaimed Sir Geoffrey.

"Never could have believed any man out of Bedlam would build such a place; it is offering a premium to burglars," grumbled an old alderman.

"Dear me, I should not care to sit in these great drawing-rooms by myself!" cried a portly dowager, who, next minute, confided to all whom it might concern, "I am such a poor timid creature, though—a mere bundle of nerves."

"Just fancy lying awake at night and listening to the wind howling through the trees! I would as soon live in the middle of an American forest," ventured a lackadaisical miss to her neighbour, with a shudder.

"I like it," answered the neighbour, who happened to be Susan Drummond.

"You don't mean to say you *live* here?" in a tone of mingled awe and horror.

"No, but I stay here sometimes."

"And where do you sleep? Surely not in one of those dreadful rooms with only a pane of glass between you and robbers!"

"I am not afraid. For twenty years I resided in a much more lonely house than this."

"Really! I wonder how any one can do it; I could not! I should *die!*"

"Come into the garden, do," entreated a voice at Susan's elbow; and, turning, she saw Lionel Hilderton.

Crossing the spacious hall, they walked together to the gardens, which were curiously planned on sloping terraces, rustic steps, formed of logs laid lengthwise, leading from level to level.

"What a rambling sort of place this is!" remarked the young man irritably, as he regarded the evidences of wealth which met his eye at every turn; "and these huge gatherings are a complete mistake. I don't know a soul here."

"You know *me*," said Susan mildly.

"Yes, you of course; but then everybody wants you; and what a set of people they are!"

"Some of them seem very nice, I think," dissented his companion.

"O, you find good in every one; but they are a lot of dreadful snobs, you may depend. Of course I have not a word to say against your friend Mrs. Jubbins, though she has about as much appreciation of art as that cow;" and Mr. Hilderton pointed down to the plantations, where a milky mother was seeking food under difficulties calculated to try her patience. "She—Mrs. Jubbins I mean, not the cow—asked me the other day what I would charge to paint her a picture exactly a yard long. I found out she wanted it to put in a frame she had by her not worth twopence. Of course I said I could not paint to measure. If these sort of people do not know better they ought to be taught."

"I think I should have taken the order," said Susan.

"I would not, then. If I have no respect for myself I have for my art. To please you I consented to paint her prosaic self and hideous children, but I feel I can't stand any more of that sort of thing."

"You know I did all for the best."

"Of course I understand that; and I am most grateful to you; but you cannot think how trying it is. You remember that picture of 'Esther' for which your friend Mr. Gayre said he would try to find a purchaser? Well, he sent a dealer—actually a dealer, a man with dirty hands and diamond ring, and heavy gold chain and thick nose, a Jew of the worst type—who had the impudence to criticise my work. He was good enough to say 'Esther' herself was not so bad, and he was willing to buy that painting, though the perspective was defective and the minor figures unfinished. I told him he must take 'Mordecai' as well—that I could not part the pair. He declared he would rather be without 'Mordecai' if I gave him the picture; but at last, finding me firm, offered eighteen shillings extra!"

"Poor Lal! What did you do?"

"Do! I ordered him to leave the studio, and next day had a note, saying I could send a line 'to his place' if I thought better of the matter."

"So you failed to sell 'Esther' after all?"

"I was forced to take his terms. I had not a sovereign left."

They went a little further without speaking a word; then Mr. Hilderton took up his parable again.

"And to see all these people absolutely wallowing in wealth! It is utterly heart-breaking! Don't you think so, Susan?—now, honestly, don't you?"

"Well, no," she answered. "If they can derive happiness from money and you from art, surely it is better they should have their money and your art."

"But I can't be happy without money. I want ever so much. I'd like to be as rich as Rothschild, if I could."

"In that case would it not be wise to accept as many commissions as you can get, even if the people who give them are not particularly interesting? Were I you I should try to paint Mrs. Jubbins and her children as well as possible, and then she might get you more orders. To be quite plain, Lal, as you are in such want of bread-and-butter, you ought not to quarrel with it."

What answer the artist might have made to this extremely wise speech will never now be known, for at that moment their *tête à-tête* was interrupted.

"O, here are the truants!" exclaimed Miss Chelston gaily : she and Mr. Sudlow, coming from an opposite direction, met Susan and Mr. Hilderton somewhat unexpectedly. "We could not think where you had gone; Mrs. Jubbins has been sending in all directions after you. Aren't you tired of walking about? You missed some exquisite singing; dancing will commence presently—you had better come in and get cool."

"I am not at all too warm," answered Miss Drummond; "but I won't miss the dancing as well as the singing."

"And remember I am to have the first waltz," said Mr. Hilderton.

"You shall have it, though you did not ask me before," she laughed.

And then they all bent their steps in the direction of the house, Mr. Hilderton drawing his companion a little back in order to ask,

"Who on earth is that man Sudlow?"

"Haven't an idea," replied Miss Drummond, in the same low tone; "some one Mr. Gayre knows."

"He is rich, too, I suppose?"

"I fancy so; but I don't know."

"He has eyes for nobody but your friend Miss Chelston."

" Your friend, too, or at least she used to be."

" Ah, she is like every one else in this vile place. She cares for nothing but money."

" I am sure you wrong her," said Susan.

" It does not much matter whether I do or not. I am only a struggling artist. You see she scarcely speaks to me."

" It is her quiet manner ; she does not mean to be unkind."

As they stood near one of the windows watching the quar-tette slowly ascending from terrace to terrace, Mrs. Jubbins was saying at that very moment to Mr. Gayre, " Judge for yourself ; I feel positive my idea is correct."

" I should not have thought it ; but ladies no doubt under-stand all these matters better than we do," answered the banker courteously.

" And it seems such a pity, for she is so good and charm-ing, and he is so poor and so impracticable."

" We must try if we can't do something for him."

" Yes, you are always thinking how you can serve others." This was quite a stock phrase of Mrs. Jubbins, and one which Mr. Gayre had long ceased to deprecate. " But I really can't see how he is to be helped ;" and then the widow went on to relate the " painting by measure " episode, and also another painful experience she had undergone in her efforts to " bring the young man forward."

" Dear old Deputy Pettell came down to call on me the other day, and you know what a judge *he* is of pictures ; he has bought thousands of pounds' worth one time and another. Well, I had got Mr. Hilderton to take my darling Ida as a shepherdess with a crook and sheep—such a pretty idea—and there was the portrait in the smaller drawing-room, and Mrs. Robinson and her nephew Captain Flurry and Mr. Hilderton in the other. Of course the painting instantly arrested Mr. Deputy. ' What have we here?' he asked ; and he put on his spectacles, and I was just going to remark I hoped to intro-duce the artist, who fortunately was at The Warren, when he said, ' My dear Mrs. Jubbins, where did you get this awful daub from? It is one of your girls, isn't it? I suppose that long stick she is balancing over her shoulder is meant for a crook ; but those things can't be sheep—they have not even the remotest resemblance to that animal.' "

" What happened then?" asked Mr. Gayre, as the widow paused in her impetuous narrative.

" From the next room," answered Mrs. Jubbins, " there

came this, quite loud and distinct: 'The man only knows a
sheep *by its head and trotters!*' I declare, Mr. Gayre, I thought
I should have dropped; and I felt so angry with Mrs. Robinson for laughing outright—you are aware the Robinsons never
liked the Pettells. But don't mention the matter before Miss
Drummond," added Mrs. Jubbins hurriedly, as that young
lady, leaving her friends, turned to enter by the window. " I
wouldn't have her vexed for the world!'

Time—relentless time—flew by. The afternoon had gone,
the evening was going, the time for the last train coming.
Everywhere, as it seemed, there was dancing—in the dining-
room, the larger drawing-room, the library, so miscalled from
the fact of a few volumes of forgotten magazines being there
imprisoned within glass cases, locked and bolted as though
each book were valuable as some old Elzevir.

The musicians were placed in the wide corridor which
divided the private part of the house into two portions; and in
the various rooms set apart for their use light feet twinkled in
the mazes of the dance, and light hearts grew lighter and bright
eyes brighter as the old, old story, which will never stale till
the heavens are rolled up as a scroll, was told in words or
implied in glances more eloquent than any form of mortal
speech.

" There never was such a party." At last every one seemed
agreed on that point—the many who approved of the affair, and
the few who did not. As a "social gathering" it proved a
supreme success. No stand-aloofism; no proud looks and
uplifted noses; no " How the deuce did you come here, sir?"
sort of expression. The City did not seem antagonistic to the
West, or the West supercilious to the City; while the latest
fashion in suburbs did not disdain to ask a few kindly questions concerning " dear old Bloomsbury."

There a High Church clergyman was exchanging confidences with a wealthy Dissenter, who had given Heaven only
knows how much to the destitute and heathen. Young Graceless was dancing with Miss Reubens, who was reported to have
a fortune of a hundred and fifty thousand. Beamish, the author
of *Fashion and Fancy*, brought to Chislehurst by Mr. Hilderton,
was showing some tricks in the card-room, to the great mental
disturbance of a few old stagers, who looked upon levity in the
midst of a game of whist as a sort of act of bankruptcy; while
Sir Geoffrey Chelston having button-holed Mr. Jabez Fallis,
the great match manufacturer, who was then running a tre-

mendous opposition to Bryant & May, had just concluded a deal with him for a pair of carriage-horses, subject to inspection and a vet.'s approval.

"The price may seem stiff," remarked the Baronet (at the same time confidentially recommending Mr. Fallis to try some sparkling hock; "the very best I ever tasted; and I thought I knew every vintage worth talking about"); "but there is not such another pair or match in London—three parts thoroughbred; action perfect, temper ditto; except that the mare has a star on her forehead and the horse hasn't, might be twin brother and sister. Now I tell you," and the Baronet dropped his voice confidentially, "how they come to be in the market. Bless you, I know all the ins and outs of these things;" and as he made this perfectly true assertion, Sir Geoffrey poured his new friend out a fresh beaker of Mrs. Jubbins' wonderful hock. "Graceless—that young fellow coming along now to get an ice for the pretty girl he has been waltzing with—who is she, did you say?—had, owing to a little misadventure— young fellows will be young fellows, but you can't make old dowagers understand that—got into the black books of his great aunt the Dowager Countess of Properton. Well, he knew her ladyship's one weakness was horseflesh; so as a sort of propitiatory offering, he got over from Ireland two of the sweetest things ever put into harness. They were just a bit wild at first, as all Irish horses are; they need coaxing and humouring, like the Irish women, and then they'll go through fire and water and to death for you, if need be. He and I trained them: took them here and there, first wide of London, then nearer and nearer, and into the Park, till they were at last well-nigh perfect; then what d'ye think happened?"

"I can't imagine; perhaps one on 'em fell lame," said the match-maker, lapsing into a once-accustomed vernacular.

"Lord, no," said Sir Geoffrey; "but the Dowager died. When Graceless went down to the funeral, he found his name not in the will. That was last week. There are the horses eating their heads off; and to come to what I said, Mr. Fallis, if they don't do their twelve miles, half country and half over the stones, in less than forty minutes, why, I'll eat them, and that's all about it."

The hall was set about with great banks of flowers. Sitting, half hidden by ferns, palms, begonias, and a hundred sweet-scented flowers, that certainly were that night not on deserts wasting their perfumes, Mr. Gayre at length espied Miss Drummond, whom he had for some time past been seeking. She was nestling behind a great oleander, with a scarlet shawl wrapped around her shoulders, her hands idly crossed in her lap, and her head resting against the wall. Her whole attitude was one of listless weariness; and it seemed so strange to see Susan Drummond, of all people in the world, sitting apart idle and silent, that Mr. Gayre was about to approach and ask if she felt ill, when Mr. Hilderton, hastily brushing past, exclaimed,

"Come, Susan, this is our dance."

"I think not," she said; "but, in any case, I mean to dance no more to-night."

"The translation of which is, you don't mean to dance with me."

"I intended you to understand my words literally."

"If I were Mr. Sudlow your answer might be different."

"As you are not Mr. Sudlow, and as he will certainly not ask me, there is no use speculating about my possible answer."

"If you will not dance, then, come and have an ice."

"No, thank you. Like a dear good Lal, do leave me in peace. I want to be quiet for a few minutes. I really am very tired."

"The next time I ask you to do anything for me—" began the young man.

"I'll do it if I can possibly; but not to-night."

"That is all very fine. I am going, Susan."

"It delights me to hear it."

"Perhaps some day you will feel sorry for this."

"I do not imagine I shall; but you had better leave me now to try to get up strength to bear the regret you prophesy is in store."

"Susan, I never thought I should almost hate you."

"Neither do you hate me seriously, Lal; you will regret your words to-morrow."

"Is Miss Drummond not well?" asked Mr. Gayre at this juncture, calmly and innocently, as though he had just come on the scene.

"I am only tired, Mr. Gayre," Susan answered for herself; while, without deigning an answer of any sort, Mr. Hilderton, an ugly scowl disfiguring his handsome face, turned away abruptly, and strode out of the hall.

"I fear greatly you are ill," persisted the banker anxiously.

"No, indeed; but I do feel very, very tired. I have been

standing, talking, or dancing all day, and am beginning to think with Mr. Hilderton, these continuous parties are mistakes. One has too much for one's money," she added, with a laugh.

"You are about the only person here who thinks so, I imagine," said Mr. Gayre. "Let me get you a little wine. Sir Geoffrey has been chanting the praises of some hock, as though he had a cellar-full to dispose of. Will you try its virtues?"

"Not even on Sir Geoffrey's recommendation," she answered. "I think I will try instead the efficacy of night air. Anything to be quiet for a short time; anywhere to get away from the sound of those eternal waltzes and mad galops."

"May I—will you allow me to accompany you?" and the banker's courteous manner formed a marked contrast to the rude familiarity which had characterised Mr. Hilderton's speech.

"I should be very glad; but I do not like taking you away from your friends."

"I have not many friends here," he answered; "and if I had—" But he stopped in time, and drawing her hand within his arm in the paternal manner he affected, led her out on to the drive.

"The terrace is crowded," he explained; "which way shall we go?"

"Down towards the Hollow, please," said Susan; and accordingly, winding round the end of the house, they struck into a narrow tortuous path which led to the plantations.

"How pretty it is!" remarked Susan, looking up at the lighted windows, from which the music floated out into the peaceful night, and sank tenderly down into the heart, softened as music and bells always should be by distance.

"Yes, not a bad sort of 'Love in a cottage' place."

"Too large for that," she answered.

"What a bad character to give Love! Do you think he could not fill all those great rooms?"

"He might; but still The Warren does not fulfil one's ideal —at least my ideal—of Love in a cottage : three small sitting-rooms, if Love were inclined to be extravagant, a tiny tile-paved kitchen with latticed casement, a thatched roof, in the eaves of which martins and swallows make their nests—it is said martins will never build where man and wife disagree—a trellis-work porch covered all over with honeysuckle and jasmine—roses, crimson, white and pink, peeping in at the windows. No, The Warren is too stately a cottage for ordinary lovers. The very place, of course, for folk of high degree, but not for common mortals. Do you know, I have often wondered how a lord makes love."

"Very much like anybody else, I should think," answered Mr. Gayre.

But Susan shook her head in dissent.

"I should say not, though of course I am no judge; for I never knew but one lord, and he was a dreadful old man. People said he beat his wife, and certainly she looked miserable; and I knew—for I saw it—that he kept a book in which every household item was entered. You would hardly believe that the diary ran something in this fashion:

"'At luncheon to-day: Mr. Gayre, Mrs. Jubbins, Sir Geoffrey Chelston, Miss Chelston, Miss Drummond. Game-pie, cutlets. blancmange, stewed fruit: *nothing sent down.*'"

"You cannot mean that!" exclaimed Mr. Gayre in amazement.

"Indeed I do. The book had been handed to the house-keeper to convict her of some sin regarding three sponge-cakes, I think, and she showed it to me. I looked at a page or two, and saw my own name with this comment: '*Miss Drummond was helped twice to cold beef.*' O! and I remember also: 'Mem.—Never to ask young Hilderton again; *he drank three glasses of old madeira.*' And poor Lal really did not know what he was drinking."

"By the bye, I wanted to speak to you about Mr. Hilderton," began Mr. Gayre. "I could not avoid hearing what he said to you in the hall just now."

"Yes!" said Susan, surprised; and she waited for the next words her companion should utter.

CHAPTER XIII.

APPARENTLY Mr. Gayre found his subject less easy than it seemed at first mention, for, instead of proceeding to say what he had to say, he repeated his former statement in a different form.

"Believe me, I played eavesdropper quite unintentionally. It was impossible for me to help hearing your conversation."

"No," answered Susan, varying her monosyllable, but not its sense. "It does not matter in the least," she went on, imagining Mr. Gayre intended to convey some sort of apology. "Lal spoke loud enough for all the world to hear."

The banker laughed. "That is quite true," he said. "Of course, Miss Drummond, it would be both impertinent and intrusive were I to make any remark on Mr. Hilderton's words. All I want to say is—"

"Don't say anything hard about poor Lal," she interrupted. "He is trying at times ; but so few people understand him."

"I think I do."

"No, indeed, you cannot. Even to-night, for instance—" and then Lal's champion paused suddenly.

"Even to-night, for instance?" repeated Mr. Gayre, with quiet suggestiveness.

"I dislike half sentences, and yet I cannot finish mine," said Susan. "I may tell you this much, however," she added, "that the day's festivities have tried his not particularly equable temper a good deal. After all, if you think over the position, it cannot be pleasant for a poor man who does possess genius to mix amongst people incapable of recognising genius till it is successful !"

"You bring me to the very point I wanted to reach," replied the banker. "I wish to help Mr. Hilderton to make the genius he undoubtedly possesses profitable ; but I scarcely know how to set about the matter. He is a little ' difficult.'"

"Not a little—very," amended Susan. "So difficult, that

I really sometimes fail to see how even his best friends are to put him in the straight road for fortune."

"I am quite willing to try, if you assist me with a few hints. Knowing the interest—the *great* interest—you take in Mr. Hilderton's future, it would give me the sincerest pleasure to aid him by any means in my power."

"I certainly like Lal," answered Susan slowly, struck by something in her companion's tone—something implied which she instinctively felt she ought to show him she understood—"very much indeed ; both for his own sake, and on account of old times ; but—"

"I suppose one cannot expect a young lady to say more," Mr. Gayre observed, almost as if by way of inquiry.

"I hope, Mr. Gayre, you do not imagine for a moment—"

"What, Miss Drummond ?"

"That I care for Mr. Hilderton excepting as a friend ? A dear friend, of course ; but one who could never by any possibility be more to me." Susan was a little angry, and spoke with a plain decision no man could really have misinterpreted.

Mr. Gayre did not, at all events, though it suited his purpose to ask,

"And why should I not imagine he might some day be more to you ?"

"Because," she answered, "I thought you knew me better."

Just for a moment there came a wild temptation over him to say he did, to cast his arms around her and strain her to his heart, and then and there, under the silent stars, with lights gleaming through the open windows above, and music floating down to where they stood, tell the tale of how love in middle age had come to him, and made life all beautiful and good and sweet, since a certain May day, when for the first time he saw, in Hyde Park, Susan Drummond's fair dear face calmly watching the antics of Squire Temperley's hunter.

But he was prudent ; he did know her so well that he felt sure, if the faintest consciousness of liking him over-much had entered her mind, those charming lips would never have spoken the words which filled his heart with such delight. He would wait ; he would not frighten, even by a gesture, this innocent, fearless, winsome bird, which seemed inclined to flutter towards him and settle on his hand.

"To be quite candid," he answered, and in his voice there was no trace of the strong constraint he put on his speech, "I thought I *did* know you better. It was an idea which would never have entered my own mind; but Mrs. Jubbins felt so sure, so satisfied—"

"Dear, kind Mrs. Jubbins," murmured Susan. "She has indeed been good to Lal."

"Then there is really nothing in the affair?"

"Nothing whatever; nothing on either side," she said eagerly, yet with pretty confusion. "Still, none the less, Mr. Gayre, you will help him, won't you?"

None the less! If she could only have read his soul she would have understood all the more—a thousand times the more.

"I will do my best, my very best for him," answered the banker earnestly; "but you must help me, Miss Drummond. You will teach me how to give him hints and avoid offence."

"Not a very easy task," she declared; "but I will try to teach you the geography of that very strange country, Lionel Hilderton's mind; that is to say, so far as I may," she added, with an unintentional significance. "And now you must not say I am like a child who does not know what it wants if I ask you to take me in again. I feel as much too cold as I did too warm ten minutes ago. The night air out here is chilly."

"Wrap your shawl closer around you," said Mr. Gayre anxiously. "I am afraid you are not well. You have been over-exciting yourself."

"Perhaps I have a little," she agreed; "but that is nothing, and I feel so much happier, so very much happier, since we talked about Lal. I do not know how to thank you enough; I do not indeed."

Mr. Gayre could have told her; but once again he refrained. Who would willingly, even for reality, break the soft spell of such a dream as the man then revelled in?

"And so," to change the subject, he said, looking up at The Warren, "you think Love would not be a suitable tenant for Lady Merioneth's cottage?"

"Well, you see," explained Susan, leaning a little on his arm as they ascended the slope, her head bent somewhat back, her eyes scanning the long terrace and the brilliantly-lighted windows, "the poets. so far as I can remember, have never yet represented Love as a millionaire."

"What do you think of Mr. Sudlow as combining both characters?"

"I may be wrong," she answered, "but I fancy he feels his

position as a rich man too much to act the part of Cupid very naturally."

"And yet he is deeply smitten with my niece."

"So I see," Susan agreed; and they proceeded a dozen steps or more in silence.

They were slowly ascending towards the house. Mingling with the tones of the music they could hear the voices of those guests who were pacing to and fro, or standing upon the terrace. Now there came to them the curious, muffled, yet continuous noise produced by a hundred light feet skimming over polished floors—a moment more, and they were able to catch glimpses of the dancers themselves. Soon it would be all over, that brief time spent in paradise, which Mr. Gayre knew he should never, while life lasted, forget. Involuntarily almost he slackened his already tardy steps, and said.

"Do not walk so fast, Miss Drummond. You are tired."

"Fast!" she repeated; "slow, rather, even for a snail;" at the same time, however, following his example, while she turned a thoughtful dreamy face towards the gleaming lights and the laughing groups, and the flitting figures as they appeared and disappeared within the rooms.

"If you could choose your lot in life," asked the banker, breaking in upon her reverie, "what would it be?"

"You ask a very strange question," said Susan, turning towards him a glance eloquent in its wistful astonishment.

"Do I? And yet one I should imagine easily answered. We all have, or have had. I suppose, our dreams of what we should like life to prove. If some enchanter put it into your power to-night to select your path, where would you have it lie? Across the hill-top or winding among lowly valleys? Should you select to be rich and great, or humble and out of the battle? Perhaps, like Agur, of whom we are told so very little you would pray for a happy mean?"

"I don't think I should," she replied.

"What would you ask for, then?' he persisted. "Wealth power, love, genius?"

She shook her head.

"Is it that you will not tell me, or that, never having thought the question out previously, you are unable to decide?"

"I never have thought about the matter before." she said. "Still, I fancy I know what I should most wish to be able to do."

"And that is—?"

"You must not laugh, Mr. Gayre, if I tell you—I could not bear you to laugh."

"On my honour. I won't laugh, no matter how extraordinary your desire may seem."

"I should wish, then—"

"Yes, Miss Drummond?" for she stopped and hesitated.

"To be able to make the best of whatever lot was appointed for me. If I were wise I know I should not ask for riches, or competence, or happiness, or talent, or renown; but simply that I might have strength and wisdom given me to be, not merely content in the state of life assigned, but to make a 'good thing of it,' as Sir Geoffrey would say." And for a moment, in the starlight, Mr. Gayre could see a smile wreathe Susan's lips and chase away the grave shadows that had seemed to change the whole expression of her tender lovely face.

For a moment the banker was startled—actually startled. He had long felt the girl's daily life and practice to be a lay sermon; but he was scarcely prepared for such a confession of faith as that involved in the words she uttered. Just at first he did not understand, even dimly, what she meant, and days and weeks and months, and even years, were destined to pass before the man thoroughly comprehended youth in its ignorance may conceive a simple and sublime ideal that shall yet, with tears and struggles, with sorrow and pain, eventually impress something like the image of Divinity upon broken and contrite hearts, or souls worn, weary, and buffeted by the billows of temptation, by the agony of remorse !

Had he only known it, he was standing then under the starlight side by side with his better angel. Yet the world and the things of the world left him without other answer to her words than the question.

"Are you a fatalist, Miss Drummond? Do you believe we cannot even rough-hew the marble of our lives?"

"I believe," she answered, "that as we cannot forecast the events of the next twenty-four hours, as we are unable to tell in the morning what may occur before night, 'free will' resolves itself into whether we shall be good or bad children in our school and playtime. Fact is, Mr. Gayre," added Susan, with a gaiety which had a touch of underlying sadness, "I have been enjoying life too much lately, and so I want to prepare myself to bear the dark days bravely when they come—as come they must."

"You add the Spirit of Prophecy to the Voice of the Preacher, Miss Drummond."

"Thank you for listening to the words of both so gravely," answered Susan; and as she spoke she would have taken her hand from his arm, and turned to enter the house by a glass door opening on a corridor which split the cottage in twain, and gave egress to all the reception and some of the principal bed rooms, had not Mr. Gayre detained her.

"Indeed, indeed." he said, "I meant no sarcasm. I feel there is truth underlying your words, though I confess I do not exactly comprehend them. Why should you, in your sunny youth, talk so wisely concerning dark days? Why should you, from whom all true men would keep even the knowledge of sin and trouble, imagine it could ever prove necessary for you to 'make the best of your lot in life'?"

"Because I have known sorrow, and am certain I shall know more; besides. Mr. Gayre, even if such a thing were possible, I should not *like* to live a perfectly prosperous and easy life. One ought to see both sides."

"True daughter of Eve, you want to pluck of the tree of the knowledge of good and evil! I really cannot recollect ever having heard you take so despondent a view of life before. Is it Mr. Hilderton's poverty, or Mr. Sudlow's plenty, or this gay and festive scene, which causes you to regard existence as so utterly gloomy an affair?"

She did not answer for a moment. Somehow, as he paused and listened, he felt rather than heard she was catching a sobbing breath; then just as it seemed he could contain himself no longer, as if he must pour forth the full torrent he had so long restrained, she said, with a little touch of her usual vivacity,

"There are some people, you know, Mr. Gayre, in whom the spectacle of a crowd induces a far greater melancholy than the sight of a single corpse; especially if the corpse has had anything to bequeath. Well, in a different way that is my case to-night. I suppose it is only because I am so tired that I project myself (that is a good word) to a time when not merely in those now brilliantly lighted rooms there won't be a single guest, but when I myself, Susan Drummond, shall feel

> 'Like one who treads alone
> Some banquet-hall deserted.'

Forgive me, Mr. Gayre; ah, I did not mean to make you

gloomy too. I am going to Mrs. Jubbins; I want to ask her a favour." And with a smile she left him at the porch, and, crossing the wide hall, made her way to the inner drawing-room, from which a few days previously had proceeded the speech that struck Deputy Pettell dumb. Following close upon her, Mr. Gayre saw the girl glide behind the easy-chairs and lounges, where dowagers sat fanning themselves, and exchanging weighty confidences concerning household matters, and the perfections of their children, till she reached Mrs. Jubbins, standing near one of the windows talking to Mr. Brown, who felt even his great mansion at Walton-on-Thames shrink into insignificance beside Lady Merioneth's "little box," into which, by a mere freak of Fortune, the widow had walked as "coolly and unconcernedly as if she were as intimately acquainted with noblemen's houses as with the old place in Brunswick Square." For a minute Susan stood quietly waiting, her face white as her dress, and a far-off yearning expression in those soft tender brown eyes the banker had never seen before. Then suddenly Mrs. Jubbins turning became aware of her presence. Whatever Susan's request, it was evidently granted with pleasure. The hostess touched the fair cheek with her fan, lingeringly, lovingly. Mr. Gayre could have blessed the buxom Eliza for that graceful caress. Then as Miss Drummond, threading her way back as dexterously as she had come, passed through the archway into the long drawing-room, where dancing was in progress, Mrs. Jubbins made some remark to the Walton-on-Thames Crœsus the banker knew had kindly reference to his niece's friend.

Still standing by the door, he saw Susan's white dress flitting down the corridor. It went on and on, past the hall, past the dining and morning and billiard rooms, past the library and the state bed-chambers; finally disappearing down a passage at right angles with the main gallery. Through the music, through the tip-tapping of the dancers' feet, through the buzz of conversation, and the clatter of plates, and popping of corks in the supper-room, he heard the closing of a distant door, and Susan Drummond did not again that night bless his sight.

What could have gone wrong? What was the matter with her? He waited and waited for her re-appearance, but waited in vain. All the guests who wished to catch the last train had gone. Weary chaperons were casting stern and reproachful glances at girls who persisted in just one dance more, one more still; even Mrs. Jubbins' prosperous face began to show signs of wear and tear. Amongst the musicians a man fell out occasionally to rest. The hours had told on the waiters, some of whom looked limp as to their cravats, and dishevelled about the head. Still the young people went on dancing fresh and gay, as though the party were just beginning; but Susan came not, and Mr. Gayre's anxiety and curiosity concerning what had become of her grew all the more intense, because he did not wish to ask any questions concerning the missing guest.

With discontented and cynical eyes he was looking at his niece as she floated to the melody of a ravishing waltz round one of the ballrooms. pioneered by that captivating sinner Graceless, when one of the old Bloomsbury set, a contemporary of Mr. Jubbins, who had scores of times religiously played out rubber after rubber of whist in Brunswick Square, accosted him.

"Not dancing, Gayre?" began this individual, who was the human embodiment of snow in harvest; "leaving it for the juniors? You're right—no fool like an old one, you know! Well, and what do you think of all this? Things were different in my day, and in yours too, for that matter. It is enough to make Jubbins turn in his grave. If your wise father had been alive we'd have seen nothing of this sort. He'd have read madam a lecture. There are people here whose names would not be thought much of across a bill-stamp, eh? You've come to look after your niece, I suppose! Handsome girl! doesn't take after your side of the house, at any rate. It is astonishing, though, how hard it is to get men to marry beauties. They fight shy of them when it comes to that, and I am sure I don't wonder at it.

"Have you had any supper? I give you my solemn word I could not get a mouthful fit for any Christian man to eat till a quarter of an hour ago, when I seized the butler and made him bring me a cut of cold beef out of the larder, and a pint of draught ale. I know their draught ale of old. Jubbins always dealt with Flowers, and she keeps up the charter.

"I shall be glad to be at home and in my bed, and I daresay you will, too. It is hard upon you, just when you must be beginning to feel you want rest and quiet, having that girl on your hands. However, Mrs. Jubbins will, perhaps, help you to get her off. She played her own cards so remarkably well, I daresay she can put your niece up to a thing or two.

"And so it was you looked out this fine place for the widow, eh? You know the sex! Give women their way about finery, and fashion, and folly, and you may lead them where you like by the nose. You're a sly dog, Gayre! Not a bad sort of peg this to hang up your hat on for life, though the money that pays the rent was made out of dirty oil. You're a sly dog!"

Having emphasised which pleasant utterance with an evil chuckle and a dig in the ribs, the old friend of the family took himself off, leaving Mr. Gayre speechless with indignation.

"You look as if you had lost a shilling, and not found even sixpence," said Sir Geoffrey, at this juncture taking up a position beside his brother-in-law. The Baronet was just beginning really to enjoy the evening. He had drunk himself sober, if such an apparent paradox is intelligible. It was a way Sir Geoffrey had, or rather, as he frequently explained, a way his constitution had. At the first start, when he began his libations —if that, indeed, could be said ever to begin, which was only suspended by sleep—strong liquors did apparently produce an effect faintly simulating intoxication; but as time went on these evidences of a weak brain disappeared totally.

"Fact is," said Sir Geoffrey, "drink steadies me." He spoke of it as a seafaring person might of ballast. He did not roll when he had his due complement aboard, and he was extremely ingenious in accounting for the extraordinary phenomenon, that the more champagne, or brandy, or "whatever was going" he swallowed, the soberer he became.

"It is like this, you know," he declared: "every family, I take it, must, in the course of a few generations, drink a certain amount; I daresay statistics could get at the amount. Well, then, don't you see, if three or four of the lot fail to take their fair share, there must at last come some poor devil of a scapegoat like myself, who has to drink for the lot. I call it hard, deuced hard! I am sure, even on the score of expense, I'd like to live on tea and lemonade; but Lord! when you've a constitution like mine to deal with, what are you to do?" A question so abstruse and so impossible to answer, that nobody tried to grapple with the difficulty presented by the singular nature of Sir Geoffrey's internal arrangements.

In a state then of steadiness and comprehension a teetotaller might have envied, Sir Geoffrey, seeing Mr. Gayre part company with the Bloomsbury friend, sauntered across and made that remark anent the banker's shilling and sixpence expression of face.

Desirous, no doubt, of emulating the little busy bee, Sir Geoffrey lounged about the rooms, affably entering into conversation with utter strangers, and, indeed, helping to do the honours for Mrs. Jubbins, as he might had Lady Chelston gone to a better world, and the widow and himself been engaged. Now and then, in this chance ride across country, he met with a crushing retort or a nasty fall; and, from experience, he knew pretty well what "the crusty, white-haired, and red-nosed old party had been saying to Gayre."

" Deuced mixed lot this," he observed, with a solemn shake of his knowing head. "I thought I'd seen a thing or two during the course of a life which has not been wholly spent in the quiet country; but hang me if I ever could have imagined such a set out as this!"

"It must, indeed, seem a change to you to find yourself among so many solvent and respectable people," retorted Mr. Gayre, who was glad to vent his irritation on any one.

"That's right, pass the blow round, my lad! It does not hurt me," said the Baronet. "Solvent?" he went on, looking about him, "no doubt of that; but respectable? h'm—m—m! I notice some folks here who, unless I am greatly out in my reckoning, have sailed uncommonly close to the wind. But then *their* haul was ten thousands, or hundreds of thousands, which makes all the difference, Gayre, all the difference."

"The whole thing is a confounded bore," remarked his brother-in-law, who did not feel inclined at that moment to take up the cudgels for trade morality.

" Peggy's having the fun of the fair," observed that young lady's parent. "I don't think she has sat out one dance, and I have seen her send away would-be partners by the dozen. Lord, what a sly jade it is! How does she do it? Just a modest downcast look, and an uplifted appealing look, or the slightest turn of the shoulders, or an indolent movement of her fan, and she has all the men about her. I have been watching her, and wondering. It is extraordinary. That sort of thing would not attract me; but it seems to suit other people. It is not my style."

"No, I don't think it is," agreed Mr. Gayre, who knew too well the type of frisky and frolicsome young lady the Baronet delighted in.

"But she's a splendid girl," proceeded Sir Geoffrey; "just look at her now. Faith, in that dress—I wonder how much the bill for it will tot up too?—she resembles nothing except some rare tropical bird. Gad! what a splendid colour she has to-night, just like the inner leaves of a damask rose! And her feet—there is not a woman in the room has such a foot and ankle; all the Chelstons had good feet. Poor Margaret had pretty feet too, though a trifle low in the instep. Seriously now, Gayre, don't you think it's a thousand pities Peggy should be thrown away on mere wealth? She'd make a capital countess, and even as a duchess she would only be the right thing in the right place."

" Well, if you know any stray earl or duke in want of a wife, you might mention the matter to him," suggested Mr. Gayre.

" I declare the more I see of Peggy the less I feel I can bear the notion of her being wasted on such a fellow as Sudlow. Why, he's a perfect cad, and a stick in addition. He can't skate, and he can't ride, and he can't dance, and he can't shoot; what the deuce can he do?"

" Take care of his money," answered the banker; "and all I hope is he may give her a chance of helping him to take care of it also."

"Well, I suppose we must make the best of a bad business," said Sir Geoffrey, with religious resignation; "I am sure I try to do so. I gave her a hint or two before we came here; I told her she must not neglect her opportunities. The worst of her is she's such a flirt, always was, always will be; I don't mean in any dangerous way—bless you, no! She'll take good care to get into no harm; I could trust Peg anywhere, trust her as I could myself;" which, indeed, was saying so little for the charming Peggy's discretion, that Mr. Gayre had to turn away his face and hide a smile. " I wish she'd some female relations up in all that sort of thing," proceeded Sir Geoffrey, with an easy wave of his hand, indicating that he meant the art of securing eligible husbands, "just to give her a chance; she wants training. Heavens! well schooled, she might marry whom she pleased. It's no use thinking of what's past; but if her poor mother—"

At which juncture the Baronet stopped and sighed, and shook his head and sighed again.

"Out of the fulness of your own abundant experience," suggested Mr. Gayre, "don't you think you might advise your daughter for her good—tell her how to set about the great sport of hunting men?"

"No, my dear fellow," answered the Baronet, who, if he imagined his brother-in-law was sneering at him, took care not to seem cognisant of the fact. "In the first place, to be truly successful, it should be pursued as a business, not a sport; and in the next, only a woman can really teach a woman how to deal with the other sex. If a man, now—yourself, for instance—stood in want of a few tips, couldn't I give them? and wouldn't I, with pleasure? But, bless my soul, your running is all straight enough. Here are you, and there's the widow; you've only to say 'Come,' and she'll come fast enough, and why the deuce you don't say it baffles me."

"I must request, Sir Geoffrey—"

"O yes, I know all about that; but requests don't alter cases, and though you may insist on people shutting their mouths, you can't compel them to close their eyes. Well, she's as pleasant and hospitable a woman as I'd ever desire to meet, and I will say she, or somebody for her, has a judgment in the matter of wine I wish were universal. You'll weed out a lot of these people, no doubt," and he nodded towards the room where what he called the "old fogies" were "playing at company." "Poor soul, she knows no better; but you'll teach her, Gayre—you'll teach her; and—she'll make an apt pupil;" having delivered which last opinion, the Baronet was turning away, probably to quite assure his mind as to whether Mrs. Jubbins' brandy was as good as her hock, when, inspired by a fresh idea, he paused to ask,

"By the bye, where's Susan? I haven't seen the little baggage for ages. She looked a bit bleached, I thought, a while ago; wonder where she's got to? There's Lal Hilderton. face, as usual, black as a thunder-cloud. No doubt he knows. Hilderton—Lal—come here, can't you! Where's Susan?"

"Haven't seen her for an hour or more."

"Where the deuce can she be?" remarked Sir Geoffrey. "How are you going to get back to your 'diggins' to-night, Lal?"

"Irish tandem," was the curt reply.

"Come and have something, then, to give your horses spirit for the journey," said the Baronet, taking the young man's reluctant arm, and leading him tenderly towards the supper-room.

Where was Susan? where could she be? Miss Chelston did not know; for, pausing with Mr. Graceless close to where Mr. Gayre stood, she propounded the very question to her uncle he was longing to hear answered by some one.

"She is not going back to town to-night," said Mrs.

Jubbins, appearing at the moment Margaret was prettily expressing her wonder and astonishment. "She is tired; she
has been doing too much, and I've sent her to bed."

For a second Miss Chelston looked at the speaker with
incredulous surprise; then, seeing the hostess was not jesting,
she pressed her fan against her chin, puckered her forehead,
raised her eyebrows, murmured, "I am *so* sorry," and next
moment the maize dress, with its splashes of colour, was
whirling amongst the dancers, a dream of beauty and delight.

CHAPTER XIV

ON THE WAY HOME.

" Poor Susan! poor. dear, kind, tiresome Susan!" lamented Miss Chelston. "These are the sort of things she always would do. Almost kill herself to please people who scarcely considered it worth their while to say thank you; always ready to wear herself out for anybody."

"I call the whole proceeding extremely silly, to say the least of it," observed Mr. Sudlow.

" Do you ?" said Mr. Gayre.

"Yes, I do," retorted Mr. Sudlow. in a tone intended to convince young Graceless he was out of the banker's leading-strings at last.

" And what," said Mr. Gayre, " should you call the proceeding, if you said the most of it ?"

"That's a question I decline to answer," answered the gentleman tersely styled " the cad " by Sir Geoffrey; hearing which valiant reply. Mr. Graceless burst out laughing.

They were all driving back to London together—Miss Chelston. Messieurs Sudlow. Graceless. and Gayre—with Sir Geoffrey on the box; three of the party in extremely bad temper. and one not too well pleased at finding himself booked as inside passenger for a fourteen miles' journey. unable to smoke. and thrown on the companionship of two men and a girl. with none of whom he had an idea in common.

As for Miss Chelston. she felt most truly it was the day after the fair. Such triumph as she had compassed was over. and her triumph could not. in such an assemblage. be considered great. Amid better surroundings. her beauty. her figure, her grace. her manner, her voice, must have placed her on a high rung of the social ladder; but upon the City magnates she was thrown away. The old men regarded her merely as a good-looking girl without a fortune, who, no doubt. knew more about spending money than saving it; while their sons felt somewhat shy of a Baronet's daughter whose ways and looks and tones seemed different from the ways, looks, and tones of belles renowned in civic circles. She was the right thing among the wrong set of people. She had striven her best to please; she had smiled on the sons of prospective Lord Mayors; she had, in her quiet, undemonstrative way, flirted with wealthy young stockbrokers and rising junior partners in great City houses; she had borne herself meekly towards large and portly mammas, and refrained from looking amazed at the doings of Cockney heiresses; and yet, when the sum of the day and evening was told, she felt her talents had not returned her even fair interest. If Mrs. Jubbins' party represented the best her uncle could do for her socially, bad indeed was the best. She had only really felt herself in a proper element while dancing with one or other of the " fellows " Sir Geoffrey offered as his graceful contribution to the Chislehurst festivities; and as she knew too well what they were, and what they had, and that each of them was looking out for a flat, or an heiress, or both, on his own account, it goes without saying that even in the delicious curves of that final waltz with Mr. Graceless she was perfectly well aware nothing could ever come of such an acquaintance, save, perhaps, if hereafter she got into a safe and unexceptionable clique, a little regret at ever having known so polished and presentable a blackleg.

With the result of the day's proceedings Mr. Gayre felt, if possible, more dissatisfied than his niece. He had arrived at the conclusion that he did not understand Susan in the least; that she would require more careful management than he anticipated; that below her sweet amiability and charming frankness there lay a depth of character and a power of will, both of which it might be necessary to gauge and to conciliate. Time was when he thought he knew her thoroughly; day by day it was dawning upon him he really knew her less. The old qualities which had so captivated him on first acquaintance remained unchanged, but fresh and unexpected qualities were, in addition, constantly appearing. She was like a garden which a man first values for the sake of a few simple and homely flowers almost gone out of fashion, and behold, as the days go by, other plants thrust their tender leaves above ground, and he is kept in a constant state of uncertainty as to the manner of blossom which shall next appear.

As an acquaintance, even as a friend, perhaps she had drawn nearer to him; but as a lover, no. Mr. Gayre was too sensible a man, far too well learned in the lore of a world which contains both men and women, to blind himself to facts. Before he knew Susan Drummond he would have laid it down as a general proposition that all women were enigmas. Since he had known Susan he would have done battle on the point that he was acquainted with one woman who wore her heart on her sleeve ; but now—now—now Mr. Gayre could not exactly tell what to think. Leaning back in his corner, he felt sorely tempted to speedily put his fortune to the test, and "maybe," he considered, "lose it all."

O sweet Susan, sleeping that night among the Chislehurst woods, dreaming your maiden dreams in the house where noble lovers had kissed and been blessed, had wept and been parted till eternity, how was it possible for you to imagine a middle-aged man's heart was being rent because he failed to read aright your simple sincerity?

He felt wild to know his hands held no prize the girl seemed to account of value. Wealth, rank, jewels, pleasure, idleness—the five curses and snares of womanhood—she held, apparently, of no worth whatever. What did her youth long for, his middle age could give? Now he was beginning to understand her better, he saw Susan was prepared to sit down to the feast of life with a purpose of abstinence for which he could find no possible reason. She loved riding, dancing, society, travelling. Even to the simplest excursion she brought a zest and a sunshine he had never seen equalled. Yet he fully understood she expected at some not remote day to resign all chance of such pleasures, and live quietly at Enfield with her aunt.

"I mean to grapple with the mysteries of farming next year," she said to Mr. Gayre one day. "I don't think I could serve my country better than in trying to solve the problem of how to make land pay. Aunt cannot. I see where she goes wrong ; but that is quite another matter from seeing how I am to go right."

"I will come over and help you," offered Sir Geoffrey. "I know all about farming. If my tenants would only have followed my advice I need never have left Chelston. Now they have got another landlord they wish, I'll be bound, they had considered me a little more. Do you remember, Susan, the talks your uncle and I used to have about cropping, and how he broke up the ten-acre lot, and sowed flax entirely on my advice?"

"Very well indeed," answered Susan demurely. She had

good reason for remembering the circumstance, since, owing to dry soil and the utter impossibility of irrigation, the result proved a dead failure.

"I'll only make one stipulation," proceeded the irrepressible Baronet—"that you lay in a cask of beer. I ask nothing more expensive. Hang it, there never was a man with simpler tastes! But water! and New River water, too! Fugh!" and Sir Geoffrey drew down the corners of his mouth—he could not turn up his nose, because it was aquiline—and pulled a grimace expressive of the most intense disgust.

"I must talk to my aunt about the ale," said Susan.

"Come, you don't mean to say, my girl, you are going to turn yourself out to grass like Nebuchadnezzar, and drink nothing stronger than water, as if you were a cow or a dog? Why, even a horse knows better. Gad! I wouldn't keep a brute that refused honest liquor."

Susan and Mr. Gayre simultaneously broke into a peal of laughter.

"I am growing rather in love with teetotalism," said the former. "It is cheap and healthful."

"The cheapness I admit, but the health I deny," retorted the Baronet. "I only know one fellow who denies his blood natural nourishment, and he's covered with as many boils and blains as Job; only Job got cured, and he never will. Serve him right, too."

Once, when opportunity offered, Mr. Gayre hazarded an inquiry to Sir Geoffrey concerning the why and the wherefore of Miss Drummond's conviction that she would have to content herself with a humdrum existence and very modest surroundings, and though the answer he received seemed to him scarcely satisfactory, it was at least plausible.

"Susan's a confoundedly sensible sort of a girl," said the Baronet. "Always was. Bless you, I used to call her little old woman when she wasn't more than eight hands high. She ought to have been a big heiress, a fine haul for some lucky young fellow, but the house in which her father left his money went smash, and she never got a penny out of the wreck but a beggarly two thousand pounds. Her uncle Drummond was a man who could not save a farthing—most extravagant old dog; so when he died, and the son came into the estate, there was poor Susan adrift with about sixty pounds a year, and no near relation except the ancient party at Enfield. Many a girl would have broken her heart; but that's not Susan's way.

She'll make the best of a bad business, and when that young
Arbery's gone back to the Antipodes, take sole management."

"Yes, I understand all that," replied the banker; "but
why should she speak as if she was going totally out of society?
Now, she comes here, for instance; why should she imply she
will not be able to continue to do so?"

"Well, for two reasons, I suppose : one, I don't fancy the
aunt will care to be left alone; another, Susan knows Peggy
must marry; and she's not so blind as to imagine my good
daughter would care for her as a constant or even occasional
inmate. Peg's jealous of her, that's the truth. Besides, Susan's
not grand enough, or rich enough, or dressy enough, or stuck
up enough to please her ladyship. Yes, you may stare, but
though Peggy's my own child, I can see her faults. I don't
know where she gets them, upon my soul, I don't—not from
me; and as for her poor mother, if your sister hadn't much
wit, at any rate she was a loving clinging creature. You mayn't
believe it, Gayre, but I've often felt very sorry for Margaret.
Most men would only think of themselves, but, thank Heaven,
that's not my way;" and Sir Geoffrey paused, either because
he was stricken dumb with the contemplation of his own
merits, or because he wished to give his brother-in-law time
to recover from the astonishment he believed such unparalleled
magnanimity might well excite.

Whatever his emotions, Mr. Gayre controlled them admirably.

"Still, I fail to comprehend Miss Drummond," he persisted. "Most girls look forward to marriage as an end to all
difficulty, the beginning of a brilliant and delightful existence.
Why should she not feel certain that a husband as rich and
handsome as Cinderella's prince will one day cross her path?"

"Because, as I told you before, Susan is as wise as Solomon. She knows well enough it is not so easy to pick up a
rich husband; if it were, clever though she is, she is not the
sort of girl to hook a big fish. Besides, her own sense must
tell her that if Peggy, a Baronet's daughter and so forth, hangs
fire, she has not much chance of going off to any good purpose. Fact is," went on Sir Geoffrey, shaking his remarkable
head till his hat actually quivered, "men can't afford to marry
nowadays, unless the lady brings something in her hand,
and something considerable too. There's no end to the
expenses of a married man. They begin with the engagement ring, and they don't end when he is screwed down in his
coffin. It's no joking matter, I can tell you. Men don't care

a straw, at this date of the world, what a girl is; what they
want to be told is what she has. For himself, a man is always
worth his own value in the matrimonial market, but a woman
isn't; there's such a deuce of a lot of them."

Mr. Gayre was thinking of these utterances, and many
more, as they drove steadily on through the chill twilight of
that summer's night, when suddenly the carriage stopped, and
Sir Geoffrey shouted to some one they had just passed, "Jump
up, man; we'll make room for you on the box; you've done
enough for glory; come along!"

"Thank you, I'd rather walk," answered a sulky voice,
which belonged to Lionel Hilderton, and none other.

> "With my left leg for leader,
> And right leg for wheeler,
> I'll distance all racers, says Pat.
>   Hoo-roo!
> I'll distance all racers, says Pat,"

chanted the Baronet. "Don't be a fool, Lal," he added, in
sober prose. "It's thirteen miles from here to Camden Town,
if it's a step. If you have no mercy on yourself, have some on
your boots!"

Even Susan Drummond could scarce have found an apology
for the reply to Sir Geoffrey's genial speech, which though
muttered, was distinctly audible to every person in the carriage.

"Have your own bad way, then, my friend," retorted the
Baronet; "I'll not baulk you. Walk and be —— !"

"Poor Mr. Hilderton!" exclaimed Miss Chelston as they
drove on.

"Lovely woman!" commented Mr. Sudlow.

"Yes, it's what we are all bound to go through," said Mr.
Gayre, who, having now a perfect knowledge of the name of
that lovely woman, derived the keenest enjoyment from Mr.
Sudlow's remark.

"And the most delightful part of the business is, that by
this time next year he will be thinking what a special Providence it was that she refused to smile on him," capped young
Graceless.

"I hope you like *that*, my lady," thought Mr. Gayre, striving in vain to catch a glimpse of his niece's face.

Almost in silence the dreary journey was got through somehow. If there ever had been a time when Mr. Graceless
enjoyed the society of a respectable woman it was long past;
and after the utterance of a few commonplace phrases, he began

to think what a nuisance it was he could not smoke, to wonder whether the old City "duffer" would stand to the bargain made with Sir Geoffrey, how much the Baronet would expect for his share of the spoil; and finally, exhausted by these mental labours, he fell asleep, for doing which he afterwards apologised by explaining he had "made a long day," viz. thirty-four hours, not having gone to bed at all on the night preceding to Mrs. Jubbins' party.

As for Mr. Sudlow, he was in a white heat of rage at the presence of this interloper. He felt jealous, envious, disappointed. Although Miss Chelston had, during the early part of the day, shown him a good deal of favour, when once dancing commenced he found himself put somehow out of court. Graceless, without a sovereign in his pocket, was, in a ballroom, a greater man than Mr. Sudlow; and not merely Graceless, but all the guests introduced by Sir Geoffrey.

"They dance like *seraphs!*" said one gushing young lady to the disgusted Dives, who did not dance like anything on earth or in heaven except like himself, who walked through a quadrille with the solemn grace of a poker, and extracted, apparently, a vast deal less pleasure out of a wild galop than he would have done from a religious procession.

"He likes no concert where he can't play first fiddle," said the Baronet, afterwards summing him up; and as he certainly did not do that at The Warren, it goes without saying Mr. Sudlow's enjoyment of the evening's proceedings was not of an ecstatic character.

On and still on, weary mile after weary mile; the gray dawn came raw and miserable; objects by the wayside began to be visible, and it was with a jaded feeling of relief the revellers found themselves at last jolting over the London stones. How hard and cold the river looked in the first beams of the morning sun! What a blessed sight the Houses of Parliament seemed, holding as it did an assurance Middlesex was reached once more! On and still on. What an endless distance they appeared to have driven! How cramped and stiff they felt! How exasperatingly maddening Sir Geoffrey's cheery and wide-awake tones sounded, as he hailed his brother-in-law to ask,

"Shall we go round by Wimpole Street, Gayre? Drop you at your door with pleasure."

"Certainly not," answered Mr. Gayre; "we will get out here;" and, suiting his action to his word, he opened the carriage-door and stepped out, leaving Mr. Sudlow to follow his good example.

"I'll take your place now," said the Baronet, jumping down from the box. "It's getting a bit chilly. No, Graceless, keep where you are ; we'll find you a sofa, never fear. Hope you'll be none the worse, Mr. Sudlow ; by-by, Gayre !" and Sir Geoffrey put up the window, and remarked to all whom the intelligence might concern that it was deucedly cold.

"What does he mean by it?" was the astounding question Mr. Sudlow put to his companion as the carriage rolled away.

"What does who mean by what?" asked Mr. Gayre, in amazement.

"Your brother-in-law ! What does he mean by taking that fellow Graceless to his house and talking about finding him a sofa ?"

"Are you mad, Mr. Sudlow?" said the banker. "Do you suppose Sir Geoffrey Chelston cannot ask any one he likes to his house without your permission ?"

"He has no business to allow his daughter to associate with such a man."

"May I inquire by what right you presume to dictate with whom his daughter shall associate ? What is Miss Chelston to you, that you should even express an opinion on the subject ? You are tired and a little irritable, Mr. Sudlow ; so I will only say, that it seems to me you have of late, more than once, strangely forgotten yourself !"

CHAPTER XV.

SIR GEOFFREY'S TACTICS.

"LEAVE me to deal with the fellow, Gayre," said Sir Geoffrey cheerfully. "You are not fit for the task. In your own way you are confoundedly clever—no doubt of that; but aptitude for business is one thing—gad, I wish I wasn't such a fool about figures and money!—and a knowledge of human nature another. You made a mistake with your friend—one you would not have caught your simple brother-in-law committing. He never ought to have gone with us to Mrs. Jubbins—never. He thinks now Peggy and myself are no better than her lot, and that *he is as good as we are.* He thought great guns of you once; now he knows your 'native heath' is much the same as his own—" and as the Baronet left his sentence thus unfinished, in order to light a fresh cigar, Mr. Gayre felt the pause which ensued more explicit and humiliating than any words could have proved.

It was three days after the party at The Warren. Mrs. Jubbins had been discussed, re-discussed, praised, criticised, disparaged, blamed; and now there was nothing left for the majority of her guests to do save call and see whether "the Earl of Merioneth's house" seemed as grand a place when viewed in cold blood as it had done while filled with visitors who walked through the rooms to the strains of music and the popping of champagne corks. Things during that three days had not been going pleasantly with Mr. Gayre; on the contrary, when he went to Chislehurst, ostensibly to inquire how Mrs. Jubbins felt after her exertions, he found Miss Drummond was walking through the woods, accompanied by Mr. Hilderton. The widow told him this fact with a look of mournful significance, and he really felt too much dispirited to inform the lady he was satisfied his niece, and not her friend, had won the poor prize of a struggling and sulky artist's heart. No, many a man was caught on the rebound, and he did not know, he could not be sure. After all, the girl might scarcely understand her own mind ; possibly she mistook the actual state of her feelings. This sisterly sort of intimacy, this familiar intercourse, was dangerous—very.

Supposing Susan were Mrs. Gayre, would he allow, would he tolerate it? Certainly, Mr. Gayre decided, he would do nothing of the kind. It was all very well to talk, but Lal was not her brother; worse still, he was disgustingly handsome—and young. Yes, just the lover a girl might fancy ; and Susan was only a girl, and the common-sense view of the matter must be considered the right sense. The whole thing was unusual and incorrect. He thought he would drop a word of warning ; but, somehow, when the culprits appeared, he found it would be very hard to make Miss Drummond understand the full enormity of which she had been guilty, and decided that to lecture her on the subject of "propriety" would be like discoursing to a child concerning those sins which it is the endeavour of older persons, who have eaten of the tree of the knowledge of good and evil, to keep hidden from its innocence.

At dinner, to which meal Mr. Gayre stopped, for Mrs. Jubbins would take no denial, Susan was charming; less gay than formerly, perhaps a little sad, certainly most sweet. She had been teaching Ida to ride, and caused some laughter by an account of that young lady's mishaps.

"I don't know what in the world we are to do without her, Mr. Gayre," said Mrs. Jubbins, referring to Susan, not her daughter ; "we shall feel lost."

"When is the parting to take place?" asked the banker, who felt delighted to hear Miss Drummond's sojourn at Chislehurst was soon to be ended.

"I am going to Enfield to-morrow," said Susan

"*To Enfield!*" repeated Mr. Gayre ; "not to North Bank?"

"I have written to tell Maggie I cannot return there just at present."

"So we shall *all* have to go into mourning," said the banker ; at which remark Lal Hilderton scowled. He thought this rich man was sneering at his old friend.

The next check Mr. Gayre met was received from the artist. In the most courteous manner possible he asked Mr. Hilderton to paint Miss Chelston's portrait, and was met with a flat refusal.

"I don't intend to paint any more portraits," declared Lal, with rude directness.

Susan looked at him reproachfully and sighed. Mr. Gayre saw the look and heard the sigh.

"It breaks my heart to think of her being tied to such a bear," said Mrs. Jubbins afterwards.

"Why did you ask him here?" inquired the banker.

"I did not ask him. He came, and I could not well tell him to go. Of course he will not come when she is gone;" which was very poor comfort for the middle-aged lover.

Calling the following afternoon at North Bank, in hopes of hearing why Susan had decided on returning to Enfield, and when she might be again expected in Mr. Moreby's villa, he found Mr. Sudlow partaking of afternoon tea, and was unpleasantly struck by a change in his manner, rather to be felt than defined. They had not met since the morning when Mr. Gayre administered what he meant for a crushing rebuke, and the banker was certainly not prepared to find this former disciple had cut his leading-strings, and was walking quite independently about the world, "showing his d——d cloven foot," said Sir Geoffrey.

Few things could have discomposed Mr. Gayre to an equal extent. Hitherto Mr. Sudlow had looked up to him, adopted his views, being guided by his advice, received his admonitions modestly and in a good spirit, as if he knew they proceeded from one having authority; but now all that was changed. He ventured to disagree with the banker, not once or twice, but many times; he spoke more familiarly to Sir Geoffrey than young Graceless would have done; and only the beautiful coldness and propriety of Miss Chelston's demeanour prevented his addressing that young lady "as though she was some girl standing behind a counter, by Heaven!' declared the Baronet, talking "the cad" over after his departure.

Much exercised about the change which seemed to him to have been wrought so suddenly, Mr. Gayre told Sir Geoffrey that remark concerning young Graceless, and delicately hinted it was not impossible some of those rumours the best of men are not always able to escape, had reached Mr. Sudlow's ears.

"It is not that," answered the Baronet. "I don't pretend to be better than my neighbours. No one can say I have ever set myself up as a paragon of virtue. I admit I have faults; who is without them? Even you, Gayre, are not immaculate, I'll be bound. As for myself, I am too easy, too frank, too trustful, too willing to forgive, too ready to be duped. But it's nothing he has heard about *me* that has caused this transformation. Your friend Sudlow needs taking down a peg; his comb wants cutting, and I'll cut it. Leave me to deal with the fellow."

And then the credulous Baronet, who wore his heart on his sleeve for all the daws he came in contact with to peck at, delivered himself of that pleasant sentence which annoyed Mr. Gayre more than he would have cared to acknowledge.

Sir Geoffrey had an absolute genius for "finding out the raw," and knew there was nothing under heaven that hurt Nicholas Gayre's vanity more keenly than associating him with the old Brunswick Square "set."

Resolutely the banker had for years held himself aloof from his father's connections. In the City he was considered proud, exclusive, and a genuine "West-ender." At the West End, among acquaintances made during those blessed days when he served the Queen and never thought of Lombard Street save as a sort of gold mine, he was known as an officer who had won distinction and a banker who was "rolling in money;" while both in the City and at the West End people held him to be exceptionally respectable. And now, merely for the sake of a girl's brown eyes, he had voluntarily let himself drift into close companionship with one of the most disreputable men in England—gone to a party at which, a year before, he would not have been seen for any consideration; where dreadful people, who were "merely rich," felt themselves at liberty to call him "Gayre," and address him in a "hail-fellow-well-met" manner inexpressibly galling; and, as if this was not sufficiently mortifying, on the top of all came Sir Geoffrey's statement, which *he knew to be true*, that Mr. Sudlow now believed socially his former Mentor stood very little higher than himself.

"It is always best to look matters straight in the face," proceeded Sir Geoffrey, when he had got his cigar well alight. "There's Peggy to be married, and Sudlow's the only man who has turned up we can marry her to. I hate the fellow, but what am I to do? Of course, I must not let my own likes or dislikes interfere when the girl's happiness is at stake. It's a pity I can't find a husband for her in a decent rank of life; but it is no use fretting about that now. Well, the next thing to be done is—get the man up to the point. I don't intend to have him dangling about here, wasting all our time and trying my temper You wouldn't believe what a confounded nuisance he is. Why, I have often to stop in, and lose perhaps the chance of some good thing, because he does not know when to go. It's all very well for him, but we're no further forward than we were last June. I can't bear such dawdling. Gad! the fellow ought to snap at the chance of marrying a Baronet's daughter."

"Apparently he is in no hurry to 'snap,'" said Mr. Gayre, with ill-natured frankness.

"He will be in a hurry before he is much older, or I'll know the reason why," remarked Sir Geoffrey, "which brings me back to the point I started from. It is quite evident, Gayre, that under your management the matter makes no progress. Now I am going to take the conduct of affairs. I don't ask your help because I would rather play my game alone. Fact is," finished the Baronet, "the beggar must be brought to book, for I can't hold on in this way much longer. If I had not been pretty lucky the ball must have stopped rolling weeks ago; and I feel it deucedly provoking for so much of my hard-earned money (no man knows how hard I work) to go in keeping up this house. Were I alone, any attic at a few shillings a week would serve my turn. Besides, I have heard a word drop that young Moreby's mamma has found a wife for him; and if such is the case, you'll see this place will be sold, and then what's to become of poor Peggy? Mark my words —this place will be in the market ere long; you know how right all my intuitions are;" and Sir Geoffrey shook his head with the air of a man who believed there was not a cranny or crack in it unfilled by wisdom.

He had good reason, at any rate, for his belief concerning Mr. Moreby's villa, since the "word dropped" assumed the shape of a letter from Mrs. Moreby's lawyer containing a plain intimation that the sooner he could find another residence the better his client would be pleased.

Except in that trifling matter of paying ready money, or indeed any money at all, no one could complain of undue delay on the part of Sir Geoffrey. Were a horse to be bought or sold, a bet to be laid, a flat to be fleeced, or any other little business of pleasure or profit in hand, the Baronet was "up to time;" and most certainly now he had decided "some steps must be taken about poor Peggy," he did not mean to let grass grow under his feet.

Accordingly next time Mr. Sudlow called, as of late he had got into the habit of doing, unaccompanied by his former friend and Mentor, he found the drawing-room unoccupied, and not the slightest sign of afternoon tea. On the contrary, the gipsy table, which might be regarded as the basis of operations, was put tidily away in one corner of the apartment; the chairs stood also in orthodox positions, and the stands and vases were destitute of flowers.

Mr. Sudlow stared about him bewildered. He had never before imagined the prettiest room in young Mr. Moreby's villa could look so cold and formal. The afternoon also was dull and depressing. No sunshine streamed across the tiny garden, and no fragrant logs burnt in the grate. "Logs are deuced useful sort of things," Sir Geoffrey was in the habit of sententiously remarking.

On that especial day, however, at five o'clock P.M., affairs were chilling in the extreme; and as he stood by the window Mr. Sudlow shivered.

"Bah! what a place this must be in the winter," he considered, "with all that water flowing at the rate of about an inch an hour down below there!"

"How de-do?" said the Baronet, appearing at this point in Mr. Sudlow's meditations, and greeting his daughter's admirer with friendly familiarity and two extended fingers. "Bit raw, ain't it? Come into the next room—fire there; like a fire myself all the year round;" with which statement Sir Geoffrey conducted Mr. Sudlow into the adjoining apartment, where that gentleman found blazing logs and a strong smell of stimulants.

"I suppose we must consider the best of the weather's over now," remarked the host as he threw on another billet.

Mr. Sudlow ventured to hope a fine day or two might still be expected, but Sir Geoffrey would not listen to the suggestion. "We're in September now," he said, "and, faith! winter will be upon us before we can turn round."

After that there ensued a pause. Sir Geoffrey was able, as a rule, to maintain a good even stream of talk, but neither man could be described as a brilliant conversationalist.

"What will you take, Sudlow?" asked the Baronet, inspired by a happy idea, sauntering towards the sideboard as he spoke.

Mr. Sudlow thanked Sir Geoffrey, but declined to take anything.

"It's a beast of a day," said Sir Geoffrey, "'pon my soul it is; worse than if it was raining. Have something, man; I am sure you need picking up; I know I do."

Firmly Mr. Sudlow, or, as the Baronet sometimes loved to describe him, that good young sneak, resisted the temptations and declined the blandishments of his ladye-love's papa. "I never touch wine between meals," he said, repeating a statement Sir Geoffrey had heard before at least fifty times.

"Gad, I envy you; I only wish I could do without it," answered the Baronet; and to prove how imperatively necessary he found it to "pick himself up," he forthwith poured out and swallowed a tumbler of champagne, laced with what he called a mere touch of brandy.

Mr. Sudlow looked on during this performance, but spoke never a word; indeed, what word could he have spoken?

"I feel a new man," said Sir Geoffrey, in that capacity strolling back to the hearth and critically scanning the last log he had thrown on. "Do—take even a glass of sherry, Sudlow."

But Sudlow only shook his head.

"Deuced chilly, I call it," went on the Baronet, settling himself in the depths of an armchair and stretching out his long legs towards the fire. "Well, and what mischief have you been up to since I saw you last?"

"Not much," answered the lively suitor, who detested Sir Geoffrey's jokes, and yet did not well know how to take offence at them. "How is Miss Chelston?"

"O, she's all right," was the reply—"packing."

"Packing!" repeated Mr. Sudlow.

"Yes; of late days she's had unfortunately to manage without a maid, poor girl; so she's doing the best she can, with the help of Mrs. Lavender. They've been at it all day; but I'm afraid to inquire progress."

"Is Miss Chelston, then—"

"She's going out of town," finished the Baronet, with kindly consideration; "and, faith, I'm very glad she is, though I don't exactly know what I am to do here all by myself—you'll take pity upon me, and look in often, won't you?—for the girl has been too long cooped up, losing all her colour, and so forth."

"Is she likely to remain away for any length of time?" asked Mr. Sudlow.

"Can't tell, I'm sure, what she'll do when she gets among her friends—go the round of them, I suppose. I'll not bid her come back to North Bank, you may be sure, while she keeps well and is enjoying herself elsewhere. In the length and breadth of England I suppose there is not so unselfish a father as myself."

Sudlow murmured some remark under his breath, which Sir Geoffrey chose to accept as complimentary; for, after repeating his statement in different and more comprehensive terms—viz. that when another person's interests were to be considered, he never thought of " Geoffrey Chelston "—he remained for a short time looking at the fire with a pensive and satisfied expression of countenance.

With more courage than might have been expected under the circumstances, Mr. Sudlow essayed a few commonplace observations; to all of which Sir Geoffrey replied heartily, yet in a manner which suggested to the visitor that his mind was wandering elsewhere.

" Is there any chance of my having the pleasure of seeing Miss Chelston this afternoon?" ventured the lover at last.

The Baronet laughed.

" My good fellow," he said, " it would be 'as much as my place is worth ' to ask such a thing. My daughter can't endure to be seen unless she's in parade dress, every bow and brooch and hairpin in its proper place. Funny girl! Now she's in her dressing-gown I wouldn't like to beg for a two minutes' interview myself."

" I did not mean to intrude, of course; I only wished— but perhaps you will kindly tell Miss Chelston I trust she may have an ' extremely pleasant journey.' "

" I don't know much about the journey," answered Sir Geoffrey; " but she's certain to have a good time when she gets to the end of it. Much obliged to you, I'm sure. I'll say all that's proper and civil. What, must you go? Can't you spare me even a few minutes more? No? Well, I'll walk with you to the gate. By the bye, I saw you the other day, though you did not see me."

" Indeed! May I ask where?"

" In Meridian Square. You were pottering about! Had I seen any one to mind my horse I'd have got down to ask what the deuce was possessing you to hold a house-to-house visitation in a neighbourhood like that. The whole population must have been at one-o'clock dinner, I think. At any rate there were mingled odours of fish, onions, bacon, and cabbage, and not one of the aborigines visible. You *are* in a hurry! Good-day. Look in as often as you can. *Good*-afternoon!" And the Baronet, as he shut the gate after Mr. Sudlow, slowly closed one eye with a waggish expression of such infinite, if silent amusement, that it really seemed a pity there was no one at hand with whom he could share the excellent joke evidently in progress.

"Sulk away, my friend," soliloquised the Baronet. "The more you sulk the better I shall be pleased. You've had two or three nasty falls this afternoon, or I'm much mistaken. Perhaps for the future Jack will think twice before he again feels quite so certain he is as good as his master."

"So your niece is not at home," suggested Mr. Sudlow to the banker the first time he was fortunate enough to meet that gentleman.

"Where is she, then?" asked Mr. Gayre.

"Gone out of town."

"O! Gone for how long?"

"I don't know—not till she has finished the round of all her friends, as I understand."

Secretly Mr. Gayre reflected that Miss Peggy's absence would not prove of long duration if it depended on that contingency; but he only said,

"Well, you see, Sudlow, you and I are the only people left in town. Soon I shall be the last rose—for you doubtless mean to take your departure shortly."

"Yes, I think I shall get away for a while," agreed Mr. Sudlow. "I never remember so slow a season."

"Take comfort; it is over, at any rate."

"Which way are you going, Mr. Gayre?"

"If you had asked me two minutes ago I should have said to North Bank; but as my niece is not there the journey would be useless. Sir Geoffrey is sure to be out."

"*He* has not left town," said Mr. Sudlow, in an aggrieved tone.

"Now his daughter is gone you may be very sure he won't stop long behind. I understood him to say some time ago he was only staying on her account."

"I suppose," remarked Mr. Sudlow ruefully, "he has plenty of friends always ready to invite him."

"Possibly, probably; but I really have no information on the subject."

"I daresay now he'll be going to some great place in the country to shoot."

"He may; I do not know."

"If I could speak French well I'd go abroad," said Mr. Sudlow, a little inconsequently; "but it is such a nuisance to be in a foreign country, and experience a difficulty about even asking for a glass of water."

"If Sir Geoffrey were here he would advise you to get over

that difficulty by never asking for a glass of water;" with which easy observation Mr. Gayre managed to end the dialogue and betake himself to Wimpole Street, whence he despatched a note to his brother-in-law, asking, "What have you done with Margaret?"

During the course of the following day back came Sir Geoffrey's reply:

"Dear Gayre,—Don't you trouble your head about Peggy. She is out of town, staying with friends—that is what Peggy is doing; and she is going to remain out of town for the present. As for myself, now I have that anxiety off my mind, I intend running down to Snatchwell's place in Staffordshire to have a turn among the long-tails. You had better come too. Lots of game; pleasant house to stop at; colourless wife, with no harm or good about her; excellent cellar; host who likes his guests to enjoy themselves. Snatchwell would have been just the husband for Peggy—son of an ironmaster, or something of that sort, who left him a large fortune. But then, you see, there's Mrs. S.; and even for Peggy I don't feel disposed to bring myself to the gallows. If you like to look up any evening you name, shall be glad to see you; but the place is all, after a manner, done up in holland and brown paper, and there are no servants except Sweet Lavender.—Yours,   G. C.

"Think about Staffordshire."

"Then she is really out of town," decided Mr. Gayre. "I scarcely believed it. Who *can* he have found to take charge of her?"

SEPTEMBER had come and gone. Spite of Sir Geoffrey's gloomy prophecies concerning an early winter, that year summer, as if loth to part company with everything fair and beautiful, lingered in England till even in late November such a blue and sunshiny sky looked down on mead and stream and copse as often fails to gladden the eye in rose-laden and leafy June. It was October—a dry glorious October, with foliage turning red and yellow and brown and russet on the trees, when the cones hung low on the pines, and late pears and apples and plums shone mellow on the espaliers; and there was just enough of chilliness in the autumn air to make a fire pleasant, and the country looked its very best, and the stubble gleamed golden in the bright sunshine, and sportsmen winding through woods only just beginning to get somewhat bare and thin of foliage gave animation to almost every sylvan landscape.

The Warren was looking enchanting. Down in the plantations there was an autumnal rustle and scent; but immediately around the cottage it might still have been July, so firm was the turf, so fair the lawns, so bright the gardens, so gay the verandah, with flower and leaf and berry; whilst as for Mrs. Jubbins, the gladness of Nature seemed reflected in her face.

So happy and good a season the widow had never known. The glory of an Indian summer was streaming across her life just as the sunshine lay golden upon the Kentish fields. Three, often four, days a week Mr. Gayre now spent at her house.

Ostensibly he came to shoot; but then he might have found far more pheasants, far finer sport, elsewhere. Were not great houses open to him? Had not grand and notable persons asked for the pleasure of his company at their country seats? It was optional with him, she knew, whether he chose to chase "the wild deer and follow the roe" in Scotland, or kill a stray rabbit on his lordship's twenty-acre lot. For him the rivers of Ireland danced and glittered in vain, the York-shire moors held no charm, the stately hospitality of great men's houses presented no temptation.

At last, thought the widow, after the years, the long patient years, of waiting, he had become quite one of the family; and by Christmas perhaps—who could tell?—the day might be settled when, the last drop of bitterness extracted from her cup, she should exchange the name of Jubbins for that of Gayre. As regarded the banker himself, she felt he had grown too delightful; while still superior to all created beings, he was yet more human, more accessible, less cynical. He took the keenest interest in Ida's equestrian exercises; he talked to the boys about their future—he was very earnest that one at least of them should pursue the path Mr. Jubbins had trod before.

When he spoke about "oil" it seemed to the widow that product became nectar. Attar of roses never smelt sweeter than rank sperm or olive when purified by Mr. Gayre's clever tongue.

At last he was identifying his interests with hers—"taking notice" of her children, advising her—not coldly, but as one who took a pleasure in the subject—as to their future; and all this had come to pass since she left Brunswick Square and migrated to Chislehurst.

Blessed Chislehurst! blessed Warren! thrice blessed Lady Merioneth! As she paced the rooms once trodden by that noble personage, as her feet pressed the carpets formerly honoured by the footsteps of nobility, and looked out of the windows on the woods for which her money paid, but in which Mr. Gayre shot, the widow forgot to remember she had been Higgs and was Jubbins—forgot everything in heaven and on earth save that she believed at length her long fealty was to be rewarded, and that ere long she would be solemnly asked whether she Eliza would take this man Nicholas for better and for worse.

Poor Mrs. Jubbins! Men were deceitful ever; and Mr. Gayre only made the few pheasants and rabbits he ever "potted" at The Warren an excuse for hearing tidings of Susan Drummond.

Since the great party they had met thrice—twice at Chisle-hurst, once at Enfield, whither Mr. Gayre repaired with a mes-sage (which might just as well have been sent on a post-card) from Sir Geoffrey.

It struck him Mrs. Arbery was not particularly delighted

with his visit, and that Susan seemed a little anxious and *distraite*; but when next she walked with him round and about The Warren he could see no difference in her, save that she had grown more sweet and beautiful than of yore. When would Sir Geoffrey and his daughter return to London? That was the only question Mr. Gayre now accounted to be of any real importance. Politics were to him as vanity, and the state of the money market a matter of supreme indifference. He could not propose to Susan at The Warren, where his most telling sentence might be spoiled by a shout from one of Mrs. Jubbins' untrained and ill-mannered cubs. It was equally impossible to say what he wanted to say out at Enfield, under the eye of Mrs. Arbery. No; he had decided the when and the where his declaration should take place, if Heaven only so ordained matters that his brother-in-law and niece returned to North Bank before all sunshine departed. He knew the very spot in the Regent's Park where he meant to lay all he had of value on earth at her dear feet. He would entice her there, and before those wonderful brown eyes lay his heart bare.

He had thought the whole affair out; there was nothing to conceal, nothing of which he need be ashamed. It was for her sake only he had sought out his relations, for whom he was now prepared to do a great deal. Her will should be his law. Aught a man may do he was ready to essay, if only she would lay her hand in his and say, "We will walk through life together."

Occasionally perhaps he felt a twinge or two concerning Mrs. Jubbins; but if a woman likes to deceive herself, is a man to blame?

Mr. Gayre felt Miss Drummond was not likely to censure him greatly for not asking the widow in marriage. Susan moved among the City people; but she was not of them. She had scarcely a thought in common with the bulk of the persons Mrs. Jubbins knew. She was good to Ida, tolerant towards the boys; but O! and O! what a gulf, wide and long and deep, worn by centuries of culture and thought and breeding, lay between her and the rich dowagers who "condescended" to exchange a few words with Mrs. Jubbins' young friend, as she flitted about the place, getting a book for one, a few flowers for another, a cushion for a third—"making yourself cheap," so Miss Chelston once truly and indignantly remarked —a thing, by the way, Miss Chelston was never likely to do.

As for Mr. Sudlow, he was wandering to and fro upon the

earth, like a perturbed spirit. He had gone to every usual and unusual seaside resort within a reasonable distance of London, and nowhere found Miss Chelston, either in the flesh or in the visitors' list. She had vanished, and nobody apparently, except her father, knew whither; Mr. Gayre did not, or Lavender, or Mrs. Lavender, or the housemaid, or Mrs. Jubbins, or Miss Drummond. Mr. Sudlow had tried them all, openly and craftily; but it is impossible to tell what one does not know, and the suitor could only, by dint of trouble and time and scheming, extract at the last the answer he had received at the first.

"Miss Chelston was out of town with some friends." Nobody could tell when she would return, nobody seemed to know whether she would ever return; nobody was able to throw the smallest light on Sir Geoffrey's plans for the future, save that there seemed some idea of giving up Mr. Moreby's box at Christmas.

"And I did hear a word let drop, sir," said Mrs. Lavender, smoothing down her apron, "that very likely Miss Chelston might winter abroad with a relation of Sir Geoffrey's," which revelation was in acknowledgment of a sovereign pressed into the worthy woman's hand. Had she vouchsafed this information at first instead of at last, she would never have received that twenty shillings sterling coin of the realm.

"Dem!" said Mr. Sudlow, as he flung himself away, leaving poor Mrs. Lavender utterly amazed. "Dem!"

Clearly if Sir Geoffrey failed to understand many good things, he had a perfect comprehension of such a nature as that possessed by the son-in-law he hoped to secure.

"Dem!" said that worthy, which monosyllabic curse meant he felt he must now take action.

"And he went out of that there gate," said Mrs. Lavender to her spouse, "and tore down the road as if he were a dog with a tin kettle tied to his tail!"

A week later, Mr. Gayre had but just finished dinner, and was in the act of filling himself a glass of claret, when the door opened, and, unexpected and unannounced, Sir Geoffrey Chelston made his appearance.

"I know you don't care to see me in your house," began the Baronet, directly the first greetings were over; "I must be a confounded deal less sharp than I am if I failed to know that. But under the circumstances I thought you would not mind. *Sudlow has proposed.*"

"No!" exclaimed Mr. Gayre.

"Fact, my dear boy, and a deuce of a time he has been about it, in my opinion. If I had not packed Peggy bag and baggage out of town, we should never have got him up to the point. Yes, five days ago I was staying with a young fellow in Norfolk, who has just come into fifteen thousand a year and some splendid shooting—gracious Heavens, only to think of the luck every one seems to have but myself!—when a letter arrived, forwarded on from my club. It was from our friend, asking my permission, wanting to pay his addresses, and all the rest of the business ; a very proper sort of epistle altogether, except that, apparently, he had forgotten all about money matters ; at any rate, he said nothing on the subject. So I wrote back from Antler Castle a diplomatic little letter, thanking him for the honour he did my daughter and myself ; but in imating it was not exactly the alliance I desired. I didn't say what I wanted, but I made him feel he was scarcely in the rank—you understand."

Mr. Gayre did. The charming Baronet had pursued precisely the same tactics in his own case he was now practising on behalf of his daughter ; but it was not necessary to go into that question, so the banker only said,

"Did he write again?"

"No, *he came.* By the greatest piece of good fortune, Dashdale—that's my friend, you know—happened to be at the station with tandem, dog-cart, livery servants, and everything likely to impress an out-and-out cad like Sudlow, when he heard that individual inquiring how he could get to Antler Castle. 'Who is it you want there?' asks Dashdale (a deuced ready off-hand sort of fellow Dashdale). 'Sir Geoffrey Chelston,' says Sudlow. 'You're not a dun, I hope!' cries Dashdale between fun and earnest. Sudlow, I believe, got very red, and said, 'No, he wasn't a dun.' 'Jump up, then,' says Dashdale ; 'give him his head ; stand clear, there.' And before Sudlow was well settled in his seat, as sweet a pair of bays as ever you clapped eyes on were spanking along the road at a pace which took away our friend's breath.

"'If you believe me,' says Dashdale, 'the cockney held on—held on, by—— !'"

"Well?" asked Mr. Gayre.

"Dashdale—most deuced hospitable man—made him stop for dinner, stop the night, stop for breakfast, stop for luncheon, and then ordered round the brougham and sent him over to the station. 'Any friend of my friend Chelston,' said Dashdale, 'is welcome to anything I can do for him.' If I had coached him up, Dashdale could not have played into my hands better. Of course, in a house like that, Sudlow got a glimpse of the usages of decent society. Thank God, I am no snob. I would just as soon eat a crust of bread-and-cheese at a way-side pub as dine off silver; still, I confess I was glad that, for once, Sudlow should see the sort of thing I had been accustomed to. There was not much bounce left in him when he asked me for half an hour's conversation in the library."

"And the end of it all?" inquired Sir Geoffrey's patient auditor.

"I'm coming to that. He wanted my daughter; what was my objection to him? I said, 'General rather than particular. I looked for something beyond mere wealth in a husband;' and I fooled him into believing Dashdale might suit me for a son-in-law, as, indeed, he would, only he's engaged to his cousin, a girl with the wickedest pair of eyes, and the sauciest smile, and the best seat across country you'd desire to see."

"Yes," said Mr. Gayre.

No revelation the Baronet could make would have surprised his relative!

"That arrow stuck. 'You see,' I said, 'you are *only* rich.' 'Surely it is something to *be* rich!' he urged. Of course I agreed to that. 'But then a great deal more is needed. In our rank we look for other things besides money. I am a great advocate,' I went on, 'for people marrying in their own set. My daughter would be miserable if asked to associate with persons beneath her.'

"'I should not ask her to do anything of the sort,' he declared.

"'I do not know,' I said. 'I have noticed a tendency in you to think people great and grand merely because they have so many thousands a year. In your estimation, if I may say so without offence, a lord mayor is an individual to be cultivated. Personally—though I am not in the least pre-judiced—I would rather not associate with lord mayors, and I certainly don't intend to let my daughter associate with them. You have forced me to speak plainly,' I finished; 'and now no offence being, I hope, given, take my advice, and look out for some City heiress.' And with that I rose to end the conversation."

"It would have ended with me at a much earlier period,"

said Mr. Gayre. "How you can be so intolerably rude,
Chelston, passes my understanding."

"Rude! I was particularly polite. I didn't 'Confound
his impudence!' or bluster about my family. I was obliged
to show him where he had gone wrong, but I tried to spare
his feelings as much as possible. However, he would not
let me go. He was willing to do everything in his power.
A golden key would unlock the door into almost any society
nowadays; and, with his money and my daughter's beauty,
birth, and breeding, he thought—he felt sure, indeed—
there would be no difficulty in getting into the very first
circles.

"'Make no mistake about that,' I said. 'Society is not
a theatre, where you have only to pay your money and walk
into the stalls. Besides, what earthly reason have you to suppose my daughter would marry you? Has she shown the
slightest partiality for you?'

"'Well, he could not say she had. Still, he thought he
might have a chance if I would only give him opportunity;'
and I let him talk on and on, and at last over-persuade me
into giving a sort of reluctant and conditional consent to his
writing to Peggy. He wanted to see her, but I would not
allow that. 'I can't have the girl harassed as you have harassed me,' I told him. 'She is a timid sort of creature, and
it hurts her, I know, to give pain so much; she would be just
as likely as not to say 'Yes' when she wanted to say 'No.'

"Then he entreated me not to prejudice her against him.
'Honour bright,' I promised; 'if I say nothing in your favour,
I'll say nothing in your disfavour;' and he was going to end
with that, when I remarked, 'O, by the bye, before we go any
further we had better understand each other about one thing
—*settlements.*'"

Mr. Gayre smiled cynically, but Sir Geoffrey did not choose
to see that smile.

"Would you believe," he said, "the beggar did not want
to make any settlements; so we had a very stiff ten minutes
before I could make the least impression on him. 'He did
not approve of settlements.' 'Very well, then,' I said, 'you
don't propose to my daughter.' 'Whatever the amount of
her fortune might be, he would settle a similar sum.' 'Then,
I said, 'you don't propose to my daughter.' 'He would settle
three hundred a year.' 'O no,' I said, 'you don't propose to
my daughter. Hang it, sir!' I went on, 'have you come here

to insult me? You've nothing *but* money to throw into the scale; and, by Heaven, if you don't throw in a good lot of that, wife of yours daughter of mine shall never be! Do you think I am going to have my only child left to the tender mercies of any husband? No, no, Mr. Sudlow, you have deceived yourself. I am not as simple as I look. I have not lived fifty years in this wicked world for nothing. And if my daughter marries, she shall marry as befits her station. Settlements liberal and all in order—good establishment—plenty of servants—carriage—everything in the best style—money no object whatever. Now you know my views, and there is an end of the matter.'"

"And Mr. Sudlow—?"

"Your friend accepted the inevitable. 'Pon my soul, there are people who like you the better for thrashing them. When I found out my gentleman's game I did not spare him, and now he is as tractable as you please. He has my permission to write to Peggy through me, and I have told her she is not to take him at first, but that she must take him at last. I wish they could have been married immediately, but that's impossible. He has to find a house *she* likes, buy furniture *she* selects, purchase the carriage *she* prefers (if he behaves himself I'll give them a pair of horses such as you don't often see), make settlements to be approved by *my* solicitors. Gad, when you think of it, Gayre, marriage is an awful thing for a man! Then, on the other hand, Peggy must provide a *trousseau*—not a mere makeshift sort of business, but the best money can buy; and afterwards comes the worst difficulty of all—what are we to do with the girl in the period between the time she is engaged and married? There is only one person I can think of fit to matronise her. I must see Susan Drummond on the subject. She can help me in that quarter, I know."

"Do you think of going over to Enfield, then?" asked Mr. Gayre.

"To Enfield! Not I, faith! I am not so fond of cold water, old women, and sour looks as all that comes to. I'll just drop Susan a line, and ask her to run over and see me as soon as ever she can. We must take time by the forelock now, or else time may reverse the operation."

"But you don't suppose Miss Drummond will run over, as you call it, to see you?"

"Won't she? Ah, you don't bet; if you did, I'd lay long odds Susan will come at any inconvenience to herself. You don't know Susan—that's flat, my lad. And now I must go, and you will be very glad to see my back. It's a queer world, too. Only to think of the Chelstons and the Gayres, and the Chelstons and the Sudlows!" Having delivered himself of which suggested parable, Sir Geoffrey, after stigmatising claret as cold unhealthy stuff, which thinned the blood and destroyed the digestion, poured himself out a tumbler of Mr. Gayre's rare vintage, and swallowing it with a wry face, as though it were medicine, walked out of the house with a gravity of demeanour and steadiness of gait which deceived Mr. Gayre's servant into believing the Baronet was soberer than any judge.

For one rash moment Mr. Gayre had felt tempted to declare Miss Drummond should not be at his brother-in-law's beck and call, that it was monstrous to ask the girl to come to North Bank even for ten minutes during his niece's absence; but the next, caution won the day; only he resolved that upon the very first opportunity which offered he would try to gain a right to stop all that sort of thing.

But then, good Heavens! if Susan married him she would be almost Sir Geoffrey's sister-in-law; and this seemed so utterly monstrous an idea that Mr. Gayre had, spite of his own will, to sit down and consider the complication of relationship which would ensue.

Aunt to Marguerite and Mr. Sudlow and the Minor Canon-esses, sister-in-law to the Canoness and Canon Gayre! The banker felt quite disheartened.

"There ought to be some law passed to relieve people of these liabilities." he considered; and then he decided to haunt North Bank till he heard when Susan might be expected to pay that extraordinary visit suggested quite as a matter of course by Sir Geoffrey, if indeed she ever paid it at all.

"I ASKED you to come over in a way our worthy friend here evidently considers extremely free and easy, that I might get ten minutes' uninterrupted chat with you. We've known each other too long to stand on ceremony, eh, Susan?"

"I should think so indeed," answered Miss Drummond, but the colour rushed into her face as she spoke.

"What on earth," wondered Mr. Gayre, "can make the girl blush so painfully at times, while on other occasions she does not seem to have a drop of tell-tale blood in her body?"

"Can you tell me where Miss Matthews is to be found?"

"She is living at Shepherd's Bush," answered Susan.

"There, I felt sure you could help me out of the wood. How is she off?"

"Not very well, I fear," was the reply.

"All the better for my purpose," said the Baronet gaily. "Sorry, of course, on her account, and all that," he went on; "but if she is not overburdened with this world's goods, she may be the more inclined to let bygones be bygones."

Susan shook her head gravely. "What is it you want her to do?" she asked.

"Come here for three months, and I'll make it worth her while."

"I am afraid," said Miss Drummond, pursing up her pretty mouth till it was like nothing so much as a sweet pink rosebud; then meeting Sir Geoffrey's eye, her lips opened, and she broke into a sudden and irresistible peal of laughter, in which the Baronet himself joined heartily.

"Faith, it seemed no joking matter at the time, Sue," he said, as soon as he could speak; "and there's Gayre wondering what the deuce we are laughing at."

"I can guess," remarked Mr. Gayre, with a poor resemblance of merriment.

The three were at luncheon together. Mrs. Lavender had

what she called "tossed up" a very pretty repast, over which Sir Geoffrey Chelston, clothed, shaved, and as sober as his previous night's doings would permit, presided. That luncheon was indeed his breakfast, and with the aid of several highly-seasoned and savoury dishes, assisted by strong cordials, he was trying to get that troublesome stomach of his into good temper.

" Have a glass of sherry, Susan, do," entreated the Baronet. " Capital sherry this. Now I want you to coax Miss Matthews to come and take charge of the house for three months. I am sure she would do anything for you."

" I do not think she would do that," answered Susan, with an attempt at gravity creditable under the circumstances.

" Not if I promised to be a good boy and behave myself? She need not fear any recurrence of the indiscretion. Deuce take the girl ! what's she laughing at now?"

" O Mr. Gayre," panted out Susan, " if you could only see Miss Matthews !"

" He need not wish to see her, I'm sure. Touch of the tar-brush about her complexion, and figure indescribable. But fact is, Gayre, I did offend Miss Matthews—as conscientious a woman as ever entered the house. An excellent person, but most confoundedly ugly—perhaps that was the reason she was good. There is no merit in ugly people being virtuous. I can't think what the deuce possessed me ; or rather—I know, it was some of the worst whisky that ever came out of a cheating inn-keeper's cellar. She needn't have made such a fuss about the matter, though. If she looked in her glass she must have been perfectly sure what I did was committed in a moment of mental aberration. Never previously," finished the Baronet, " in the course of a long and, I may add, comparatively sinless life, did I so far forget myself."

" She would not have minded it so much, I am sure," inter-posed Susan, " if Dottrell had not chanced unfortunately to come into the room."

" Where, if you believe me, Gayre, on my sacred word of honour, I was making that worthy lady tread a measure like Young Lochinvar. I must have been confoundedly drunk ; not with the quantity, only with the quality, of what I had taken. And when I got home, and found the old girl in the drawing-room, I believe I chucked her under the chin, and insisted she should dance a minuet with me. She declared I kissed her, too ; and I daresay I did, for I was quite off my head. As a matter of choice, I wouldn't have done such a thing in my sober senses for a thousand pounds; and then, in the middle of the performance, Dottrell, our then butler, appeared on the scene.

"She appealed to him for protection, and straightway opened out on me. I sat down, for the simple reason that I could not stand, and she did hold forth. Father Mathew and Mrs. Grundy together could not have hatched up such a discourse. She would have gone on till now, only Dottrell calmly remarking. 'You had better come away, ma'am ; Sir Geoffrey does not understand a word you're saying,' with firm decision took hold of her arm and marched her out of the room."

"And the next morning?" questioned Mr. Gayre, who now began to understand more thoroughly than ever the reason why Sir Geoffrey found his domestic affairs somewhat difficult to manage.

"The next morning Dottrell woke me out of a sound sleep in order to deliver a letter from Miss Matthews.

"'Put it down,' I growled, for I had such a headache I could scarcely open my eyes.

"'Beg pardon, Sir Geoffrey, but Miss Matthews wants to catch the 11.25 train, and—'

"'Let her catch her train, and be blanked to her !' I said, settling down again, for I had clean forgotten all about that last night's minuet. But it was of no use. Dottrell proved too much for me, and I had to sit up and face the matter.

"'Won't she take an apology?' I asked.

"No, she wouldn't ; all she meant to take was her salary and departure. But now, look here, Susan. You tell her I'm a reformed character ; and that I'm never at home till morning ; and that you'll go bail for my good conduct ; and that Peggy, who is now quite grown up, and a dragon of propriety, keeps me on my best manners ; and that she shall have fifty pounds for the three months, paid in advance. She'll come then, bless you ! she'll come. If she should want any further guarantee, refer her to Gayre. He'll tell her the man never lived who had a greater respect for elderly women than myself. Why, rather than offend one of them, I'd keep out of their way for ever."

It was too much. Even Mr. Gayre had to laugh, as if he saw some fun in the Baronet's utterances, while Susan faithfully promised she would say all she could in Sir Geoffrey Chelston's favour.

"And you'll say it this afternoon, won't you?" he entreated, "because time happens to mean money to me just now."

—To this arrangement Susan at first demurred a little. The afternoon would be far advanced before she could get to Shepherd's Bush. Miss Matthews might not be at home. Mrs. Arbery would certainly feel uneasy. But each of these points Sir Geoffrey combated, and she yielded; the while Mr. Gayre sat inwardly fuming at the way his brother-in-law made use of the girl, and the manner she allowed herself to be so treated. Mr. Gayre failed to see the beauty of making oneself cheap. He could not understand that the moment Susan began to think she was of too much importance to answer to the beck and call of those she cared for, she would cease to be Susan Drummond, and become a totally different person.

"If you are going by the Metropolitan," said the Baronet, by way of conclusion, "we can walk together as far as Baker Street. Will you come with us, Gayre?"

Almost gnashing his teeth, Mr. Gayre said he would. Where was now his chance of speaking to Susan? He felt at his wits' end. He did not know what to do. Should he write? Should he go down to Enfield, or wait his opportunity, or—

"This is your hat, Gayre," cried Sir Geoffrey, interrupting his meditations, "and here is Susan. I always did say I never saw a girl who could put on her bonnet as fast as you. However, as you know, a 'bonny bride is soon buskit;' which reminds me that I am to be father, and give you away some day. You remember our compact?"

"Very well indeed; and I will hold you to your promise," answered Susan.

And then, as Mr. Gayre held the door open for her to pass out, he wondered to himself what on earth his ladye-love could see in such a reprobate as Sir Geoffrey to laugh and make merry with him and smile on his battered wicked face, as though it were pure as that of an angel.

Nevertheless, they were a pleasant trio as they walked to Baker Street; and Mr. Gayre, after he had got Susan's ticket and seen her into the train, he and Sir Geoffrey accompanying the lady on to the platform per favour—lamented his own want of daring in failing to take a ticket also to Shepherd's Bush.

But if there is a "divinity which doth hedge a king," there is a higher divinity which hedges a modest innocent woman. Not for all the world would Mr. Gayre then have so timed his proposal as to hurt the girl's self-respect, and daunt her fearless self-reliance.

"She has no business to be running about London in this way by herself," he thought; but he felt he dared not be the man to teach Susan Drummond she was doing wrong.

Next morning's post brought a note to North Bank, saying Miss Matthews utterly declined to accept Sir Geoffrey's offer; but she—Susan, the writer—had met, at the house of Margaret's ex-governess, a lady willing to enter upon the duties he required at once.

"I am sure she is just the person you would like," finished the fair scribe; "*not young*" ("Good Lord!" groaned Sir Geoffrey), "a widow" ("'Ware hawks, but she can't catch me," considered the juvenile Baronet); "rather nice-looking and pleasant-mannered" ("That's a bit of comfort"); "has a grandson she wants to keep at school" ("Then she must be out of her teens, at any rate"); "and seems to be in all respects the sort of person you require. I enclose her address."

To which Sir Geoffrey replied:

"You settle with her, my dear Susan. Anything you say I'll stick to. If she can come into residence before the week is out, so much the better."

Upon which authority, it may be assumed, Miss Drummond acted forthwith, since Mr. Gayre was duly and truly informed "an elderly party was coming to keep things straight at North Bank."

"She'll be a deuce of a nuisance, I know," finished the Baronet; "but we must have something of the sort. Those few days I had to stay at home and play propriety after the Chislehurst spread nearly killed me. Besides, my time is my money; and it wouldn't pay me to play the part of Mrs. Propriety. Once Peggy has given a sort of modified consent, she shall come home; and I've asked Susan to tear herself away from the delights of Enfield, and stay with us for a while to brighten up the house."

It was not long ere Mr. Sudlow won a reluctant and dignified acceptance from Miss Chelston.

"She feels she scarcely knows enough of me yet," explained Mr. Sudlow to Mr. Gayre; "but even that looks well, does it not?" asked the happy lover, invading the sanctity of Upper Wimpole Street one morning before Mr. Gayre had finished his breakfast. "She would not have said so much if she had not intended taking me some time, would she?"

Declining to commit himself to any positive statement, Mr. Gayre nevertheless admitted he thought his niece must, at all events, be entertaining the idea of Mr. Sudlow as a husband.

"I am afraid Sir Geoffrey will be very hard to deal with on the subject of settlements," ventured Mr. Sudlow.

"Time enough for you to consider that question when you have arranged matters with my niece."

"You know I object to settlements—"

"So I remember you said before; and we need not go over that old ground again. Keep your objections for Sir Geoffrey. It is his daughter, not mine, you hope to marry."

What Mr. Sudlow wanted to know was whether Mr. Gayre meant to behave handsomely on the occasion. Five thousand pounds, he hinted to Sir Geoffrey, would not empty the Lombard Street coffers, while it might prove of material assistance in the housekeeping battle; but the Baronet warned him off this treacherous ground.

"Gayre is a deuced odd sort of fellow," he said; "and if he is going to give anything, he'll give it without being asked, perhaps slip a *dot* into his niece's hand when she is going away to change her dress. But a certain person, who shall be nameless, couldn't get sixpence out of him unless he took the notion. Our best plan is to let him alone."

Which was all very well for the Baronet, considered Mr. Sudlow; but not so well for the person undertaking to board, lodge, and dress the beautiful Marguerite for the remainder of her days.

"You see it is not as if Miss Chelston had a fortune in her own right," ventured Mr. Sudlow at last.

Mr. Gayre looked at him and smiled.

"I suspect," said the banker, "if Miss Chelston had possessed a fortune in her own right, or in right of anybody else, Sir Geoffrey would not have bestowed it on you. Take my advice—if you get youth and beauty, and birth and breeding, don't break your heart because there is not money too. You could not have got one of the four in the person of my niece but for the folly of Sir Geoffrey Chelston, formerly of Chelston Pleasaunce."

"You seem to consider my wealth nothing."

"On the contrary, it is your wealth which has given you the chance of marrying my niece; and when you are married to her I hope you will live in a manner befitting her rank and her means. And for Heaven's sake, Sudlow," added Mr. Gayre, with sudden energy, "give up collecting your own rents. Dunning weekly tenants is scarcely an employment suitable for a man whose wife may one day hope to be presented at Court."

Mr. Sudlow turned pink and scarlet, and blue and crimson, in about as many seconds; and his moustache quivered as he asked,

"Who told you I did anything of the kind?"

"Sir Geoffrey. He says he saw you doing it. And now do take a word of advice. Your social future is before you to make or to mar, and, what is of a great deal more importance to me, my niece's future can be made or marred by you. If you mean to continue to do these sort of things say so, and the matter shall be broken off at once. It is quite competent for you to lower yourself; but my niece shall not be pulled down to your level. Why, in Heaven's name, don't you sell all that wretched property, and try to put your many talents out to interest in some way befitting a gentleman?"

"Whenever you can prove your ability to introduce me to really good society," retorted Mr. Sudlow, "I will follow your advice. Meantime permit me to say I do not consider the persons I find you know most intimately are in any respect superior to myself."

"You had better repeat that statement to Sir Geoffrey Chelston," said Mr. Gayre, "and ascertain his opinions on the subject. I was wrong to interfere in the matter. It does not much signify to me whom his daughter marries, or whether she ever marries at all."

With which explicit statement Mr. Gayre rose, and would have ended the conference, but that Mr. Sudlow, with profuse apologies, begged him to overlook his little ebullition of temper.

"You *are* hard on a fellow, you know," he finished. "You delight in catching me up and twitting me for taking care of my money; though you would be the first to find fault if I squandered what my father left me."

"But for my grandfather your father would not have had much to leave," answered Mr. Gayre.

And then the talk drifted away from the dangerous question of rank to the surer ground of money, and peace seemed restored by the time Mr. Gayre announced his intention of starting for the City; and Mr. Sudlow asked him to come round by Bond Street, as he wished to buy a ring, and desired the benefit of his experience.

"I do not profess to be any judge of jewelry," answered Mr. Gayre; "but I will accompany you with pleasure, though I consider your purchase somewhat premature. However, if the ring is never possessed by my niece, it will do for some other young lady; only there is the loss of interest to consider, Sudlow."

"I don't care a straw about that," declared Mr. Sudlow valiantly. "Once your niece says 'yes,' and if only those confounded settlements can be arranged, I shall be the happiest man in England."

"That's what they all say before marriage," commented Mr. Gayre, searching about for his umbrella.

They were just turning into Vere Street as a cab pulled up opposite Marshall & Snelgrove's. Before the driver could get down, a small gloved hand turned the handle, and in a second the owner of that hand was on the pavement, and helping another lady to descend more slowly.

"Why, it is Miss Drummond!" exclaimed Mr. Sudlow; then he stopped; for the flash of glad surprise in Mr. Gayre's face, and the eager step made involuntarily forward, were revelations more extraordinary than welcome. A man could scarcely have clapped hands during the fraction of time it required to make the banker's secret plain reading to Mr. Sudlow; and then both gentlemen were raising their hats and greeting Susan, and remarking how extremely strange it was they should have met.

The cabman duly paid and discharged, Miss Drummond introduced the banker and his companion to Miss Matthews, during the progress of which ceremony it tried even Mr. Gayre's gravity to look upon the highly respectable lady with whom, in the great drawing-room at Chelston Pleasaunce, his brother-in-law had essayed to trip a measure. Nearly six feet tall, gaunt, short-petticoated, with slim ankles and lean legs, and long, thin, flat feet, with a face like a horse, kindly dark eyes, black hair turning gray, a good Roman nose, prominent teeth, more than a suspicion of a moustache: a less likely woman to appreciate the delicate attention of being chucked under her chin never existed.

As for Susan, she felt she dared not look at Mr. Gayre; there was a suspicious twitching about her mouth and a tremor in her voice Mr. Sudlow could not comprehend, though both phenomena were perfectly intelligible to his companion.

"Going shopping, Miss Drummond?" asked Mr. Sudlow, who, in his new character of an almost engaged man, had already commenced to take an interest in so purely feminine a weakness.

"Yes, really," answered Susan, with a little nod and a happy smile, and that sudden and vivid blush which was beginning sorely to perplex Mr. Gayre. What on earth could make her colour up at such a simple question?

"I always envy ladies their ability to sew and their liking for turning over silks and satins," observed the banker.

"My purchases," said Susan, "must be of a much more modest description;" while Miss Matthews didactically observed she did not know what ladies would do without the resource of needlework.

As there probably never existed any one less able to suggest even a vague solution to such a conundrum than Sir Geoffrey's brother-in-law, wide though the field of speculation opened up by Miss Matthews' sententious remark might be considered, the banker wisely declined to enter on it. Instead he inquired when Miss Drummond meant to go to North Bank, and finding "Very shortly—next week, perhaps," took his leave, and, accompanied by Mr. Sudlow walked off, followed by warm encomiums from Miss Matthews, who professed great astonishment that her former employer could be possessed of so desirable a relative.

"And what is the younger gentleman's name, Susan? I failed to catch it."

"Mr. Sudlow—a captive of Margaret's spear and bow."

"Will it come to anything?"

"I don't know. I hope not. He is only rich."

"If he is rich, then you ought to wish it may come to a great deal. Margaret would be wretched married to a poor man; and she must be far happier and safer in the house of a husband than residing under the roof of her reckless and dissolute father."

"Poor Sir Geoffrey!" remonstrated Susan. "You are far too hard upon him."

"No, indeed, my dear, I am not; and the only fault I have to find with you is that you wilfully shut your eyes to the real character of that dreadful man. I am so sorry you are going there; it is really not respectable for a young girl to associate with a person who bears so bad a character as Sir Geoffrey Chelston."

" He has never been bad to me," retorted Miss Drummond sharply—"always good and kind and thoughtful. One can only speak of people as one finds them."

" Ah, Susan—"

" Now it is of no use, Miss Matthews," interrupted the girl, with that decision which often astonished Mr. Gayre : " I shall always like Sir Geoffrey. I should like him even if he picked pockets."

" So he does," said the Roman Conqueror, as the Baronet had been wont to call his daughter's governess ; " so he does, if all accounts be true."

" I don't care whether they are true or false. What is the use of being fond of a friend only when he does right ? I should want my friends to be fond of me if I did wrong—as you would be, you know you would ; so never ask me again to turn my back on Sir Geoffrey."

As days went by, the object of all this charming loyalty might have been regarded almost as a reformed character. The Baronet was devoting himself to getting his daughter well settled with the same earnestness he brought to bear on betting, card-playing, and horse-dealing.

"Sudlow finds those settlements a rasping fence." he said to Mr. Gayre; "but he shall take it, by ——— ! or give up all hope of Peggy;" and because he was steadfastly purposed to frustrate the slightest attempt to balk the jump. he rose betimes, and stayed about the house, and watched over Miss Chelston, who was now at home, like a hen with one chicken. The engagement at length became a fact accomplished, and Sir Geoffrey was pleased to signify that he would put no obstacle in the way of a speedy marriage.

" You satisfy my lawyers," was his terse way of putting the case in a nutshell to Mr. Sudlow, "and you'll satisfy me. To save all trouble and argument, I have given them their instructions, by *which they will abide;*" and if any disinterested person had been by to see the shake of the head with which the Baronet emphasised this utterance, he could not have imagined that Miss Chelston's worthy papa was destitute of worldly wisdom.

For, indeed, there had come a certain change over Mr. Sudlow which puzzled and annoyed Sir Geoffrey. It was not that he cared for his lady-love less ; but he certainly seemed in no hurry to endow her with the amount of his worldly goods upon which the Baronet insisted. That meeting with Susan

N

Drummond told him how small the fair Marguerite's chance of inheriting her uncle's wealth might be considered, and hitherto he had always calculated that she would, sooner or later, come in for a good slice out of Lombard Street.

He longed to tell Sir Geoffrey and his daughter what he had discovered, he was waiting his opportunity to do so; but he did not wish to show his new card before Mrs. Morris, who sat constantly on guard doing lace-work, which she sold to various patronesses for the benefit of her grandson, whose school-bills were made the excuse for that sort of genteel begging greatly in favour with ladies so situated that they are obliged to wrest a living from society by hook or by crook.

He earnestly desired to get the matter off his mind before Miss Drummond again appeared at North Bank, and at length his chance came one evening, when Mrs. Morris had been obliged to go to bed with a severe headache, and Sir Geoffrey was fidgeting about the room, trying all the easy-chairs in succession, and thinking what an awful nuisance a daughter was, and wondering why Lady Chelston could not, excepting for contrariness, have presented him with a son instead, and marvelling when Mr. Sudlow would take his departure, and feeling sure there had never existed on the earth before so exemplary a father as himself.

Something was said about Mr. Gayre not coming so often as formerly to North Bank.

"I suppose," added the Baronet, "the fact is he has other fish to fry at Chislehurst. I confess I feel rather surprised at his choice myself. I hoped he might have gone in for something different; but money attracts money, there can be no question about that."

"And Mrs. Jubbins is so immensely rich," put in Miss Chelston softly.

"Are you quite sure it is Mrs. Jubbins?" asked Mr. Sudlow.

"Why, of course, man," answered Sir Geoffrey; "who else is there? Who else should there be?"

"I daresay you know best," said Mr. Sudlow; "still, I have a notion that when Mr. Gayre marries it will not be the wealthy widow."

"You speak as if you had some one in your eye," exclaimed the Baronet, roused into attention.

"So I have."

"And who is she? O, pray tell us!" entreated Miss Marguerite. "What I would give to see her!"

"You can compass your desire without any great expenditure of either time or money," said Mr. Sudlow triumphantly, for he felt the moment for making a *coup* had come. "Unless I am greatly mistaken, Miss Drummond will be metamorphosed into Mrs. Gayre before we are any of us much older."

"Susan Drummond!" repeated the Baronet, sitting bolt upright in his chair, and holding the arms with both hands, while Margaret, literally, for the moment, bereft of speech, remained dumb. "I think you are wrong there, my friend," added Sir Geoffrey, after a pause, which seemed to last for years.

"Am I?"

"How in the world could such a notion have got into your head?"

"I can't imagine how it failed to get into yours," answered Mr. Sudlow, with a fine scorn.

"Poor dear Susan, what a preposterous idea!" said Miss Chelston gently.

"You will find it a true one, I imagine," persisted the new prophet.

"Fancy Susan my aunt!" suggested the beauteous Marguerite, in the sweetest accents, the time her heart was full of rage and malice and all uncharitableness.

"You might get a worse, Peggy, but never a better," said the Baronet, who, having now grasped the position, decided there was something in it. "If the land lies as you think, Sudlow, I for one shall be delighted. On the face of God's earth there walks no grander woman than Susan Drummond; and while I should have made the Jubbins welcome, I'd go out of my senses with delight if matters turned out as you think."

"You are very disinterested, Sir Geoffrey."

"Not I, faith; I know Susan would never take from my girl for herself. She'd be the making of Gayre—and—and—us all. I wonder how it was I never thought of such a thing? Gad, if it had rested with me they should have been man and wife long enough ago."

Mr. Sudlow opened his mouth to reply, but an imploring look from Miss Chelston caused him to shut it again. "After all," she said, "my uncle may not have an idea of the kind."

"I hope and trust he has," cried Sir Geoffrey. "You have brought me the best piece of news to-night, Sudlow, I have heard for this many a day! Susan married to Gayre! why it

sounds too good to be true. I'll go straight away down to
him, and ask if there's anything in it. We can walk part of
the way together;" and the Baronet rose from his chair with
all the more alacrity that he thought he now saw his way to
getting out of the house and rid of his future son-in-law at the
same moment.

"For heaven's sake, Sir Geoffrey, do no such thing!" entreated Mr. Sudlow. "Your brother-in-law would never forgive me if he thought I had been meddling in his concerns.
Whatever you do, pray keep my name out of the affair; or,
rather, refrain from mentioning the matter at all. I—I may
be mistaken; but I considered it only right to give you a hint.
I did not know the match was one you would like. I fancied
there might be objections, both on the score of age and
fortune."

"Did you?" said Sir Geoffrey grimly. "Understand, if
you please, I consider Susan Drummond a fortune in herself.
Why, with her family and Gayre's money, they might do just
what they pleased: and as for that trifle of disparity, Gayre is
a good fellow, and deserves a good wife: and, faith, if he gets
Susan, he'll have something to be proud of."

"I never admired Miss Drummond particularly myself,"
remarked Mr. Sudlow—for which diplomatic speech he was
rewarded by an appreciative glance from his ladye-love—"but
from the first hour he saw her I know Mr. Gayre did."

"Showed his taste," commented the Baronet. "However,
I'll take no notice of what you have told us. Never spoil
sport has always been my maxim. Upon my soul, I feel as
much pleased as if anybody had given me a thousand pounds."

Which creditable feeling was certainly not shared by his
charming daughter. She knew exactly what Mr. Sudlow was
thinking, and her own opinion chanced to be identical with
his. If Mr. Gayre married Susan he would not feel disposed
to endow his niece with all he possessed. Miss Chelston had
long fastened her gaze on the Lombard Street coffers, and it
could not be said she regarded with pleasure the idea of Susan
getting any share of the spoil.

"Don't say anything more about this before papa," she
hinted, during a brief absence of Sir Geoffrey for the purpose
of draining a bumper to the health of the future Mrs. Gayre.
"Do you think my uncle is really thinking of marrying dear
Susan?"

"I am quite sure he would like to marry her," answered

Mr. Sudlow; and then he explained how the knowledge had come upon him like a flash of lightning. "'Pon my honour, a child might have knocked me down," he finished.

"It was wonderfully clever of you," said Miss Chelston, with a pleasant flattery of voice, and word, and look; "but then you are so clever. Don't you think the disparity is dreadful, however?"

"Yes; but if Miss Drummond does not mind that, I am sure Mr. Gayre need not."

"O, don't; I can't bear to think of it," murmured Miss Chelston, shuddering; and then Sir Geoffrey, refreshed and invigorated, sauntered back into the room, where he began to yawn with such good effect that Mr. Sudlow felt reluctantly compelled to say good-night.

"Now, look here, my girl," said Sir Geoffrey to his daughter, as he took his hat, preparatory to getting the "cobwebs blown off him," "take my advice, and neither mell nor meddle in this business. You'd love dearly, I know, to stop the match, but it will be a deuced fine thing for you should it ever come off. As for Susan, if she can fancy your uncle—and he is not an old man for his age; he hasn't had to bear the anxiety I have —I'm sure she'll never repent taking him. When she comes here keep a quiet tongue about the matter. We'll want your uncle's help yet, I'm afraid, in that matter of the Sudlow fish; so for the Lord's sake don't let any of your woman's whimsies put his back up."

Only to a certain extent did Miss Chelston comply with Sir Geoffrey's wishes. Miss Drummond spent a few hours at North Bank one day, and promised to return shortly and stop a fortnight. It was then she and her friend had a serious talk about the Sudlow engagement.

"O Margaret! don't marry him; don't, like a darling," entreated Susan, at the close of a long and confidential interview. "You do not care for him, and you do care for Lal Hilderton."

Miss Chelston laughed scornfully.

"Should you recommend me to marry Lal and make as good a match as you seem disposed to do?"

"Perhaps not," said Susan, "for there is that reason, you know, which might cause any one to feel afraid of marrying Lal; but you have led him on and on, and—"

"Now, remember, I cannot bear being lectured, more particularly by you," interposed Miss Chelston.

"Well, then, tell Mr. Sudlow you can't marry him, and I won't say another word. Recollect, so long as I have a home you need never want one. And I am sure—"

"Make yourself very sure, dear, I mean to marry Mr. Sudlow. I shall not so far insult my own taste as to say he is the man I would have chosen. But beggars, you know—"

"O Maggie, Maggie!"

"O Susan! At the end of twelve months I wonder which of us will be the best off?"

"Good-bye, then, you poor mistaken child, and remember what I said."

"I certainly shall not forget a word you have said, dear;" and with a sweet smile, Miss Chelston kissed her friend and saw Susan depart, and then sat down biding her time, which arrived that evening before dinner.

Mr. Sudlow was in evidence; Sir Geoffrey in high spirits, because his brother-in-law had walked up to North Bank; Mrs. Morris was putting the finishing touches to her toilette; Mr. Gayre was looking at the evening paper, when, in quite an artless and gushing manner, Miss Chelston opened her first parallel.

"I have such a piece of news for you, papa," she said gaily.

"Good news, Peg?"

"Very good; it concerns Susan Drummond."

"Let's hear it, then," cried the Baronet.

"She is going to be married"—involuntarily Sir Geoffrey turned towards Mr. Gayre, but that gentleman never moved nor stirred, neither did the crisp sheet he held rustle—"to Oliver Dane. You remember Oliver, don't you? Old Mr. Dane's grandson," went on the fair Margaret, almost without a pause, and maintaining an admirable composure. "He is at present in some house in the City—Colvend and Surlees—but he is going to start on his own account, whatever that means, and the wedding is to take place before Christmas."

"I don't think it will," said Mr. Gayre from behind his newspaper; and as he spoke a dead silence fell on those present—they were waiting to hear more.

"*Mr. Oliver Dane*," proceeded the banker, deliberately folding up the *Globe*, "*was this day charged at the Mansion House by his employers, Colvend and Surlees, with forgery and embezzlement, and remanded, bail being refused.*"

CHAPTER XVIII

EARLY next morning Mr. Gayre was making his way into the
Camden Road. Overnight, pacing the silent desolate streets,
he had decided what to do. He would break the news to
Susan. Unless Fortune meant to turn utterly against him, he
felt that he should be the first to carry the tidings out to
Enfield, and so score one trick in a game that would require
the most careful playing. While his niece was firing her shot
about Oliver Dane, it had seemed to him that he fell from
heaven to earth. The whole time occupied by her narrative
could have been reckoned by seconds, yet years ere then had
appeared to him a shorter period.

How he had held his paper so that it did not even rustle,
how he compelled his voice to utter the words he spoke without a tremor, were mysteries he could not have explained
himself. Save for a certain ring of triumph in his tone he was
unable to repress, Oliver Dane and Susan Drummond might
have been total strangers to the banker.

This was the hidden rock he had always instinctively
known stood in his way to port. Now he fully understood
the reason of Susan's unaccountable blushes. At last he comprehended why she was at once so friendly and so indifferent.
Everything which had puzzled him about the girl was clear at
last; far, far too clear. But she could not marry this man.
All was not lost. On the contrary, in this awful trouble he
would be of such comfort, he would so watch over her. so
sympathise with her every mood, that for very gratitude's sake
she must at length give him love. And then he strove to
think he would rather not change matters even if he could. It
was far, far better she should have had a lover and found him
worthless. At his age it was scarcely to be expected a young
girl could give him the first, romantic, unreal dream-love of a
woman's life; but the love that lasts would be his—the love
founded on a rock—on respect, esteem, reason, and affection.
No more wild, unpractical, dangerous friendships with hand-

some young fellows like Lal Hilderton; no running about at
the beck and call of that sinful reprobate Sir Geoffrey; no
more gallops with her easy familiar cousin the centaur. The
brightness of her morning was gone, and she would now settle
down and make a more charming wife, with the traces of
tears on her cheeks, than she ever could have done in the
sunshine of a ridiculous and impossible engagement.

It is always wise to make the best of a bad bargain; and
as Mr. Gayre rode leisurely along, he became so exceeding
wise that he finally felt thankful such a person as Oliver Dane
was in existence.

"I will make myself necessary now," he decided; "and,
when her sorrow is a little spent, she will not be able to do
without me."

A pleasant vision, truly. Poor dear Susan, with those
wonderful brown eyes, coming to him, not as a ministering
angel, but as a sorely wounded dove, weeping out her grief on
his bosom, sobbing her tears in his arms, feeling him a tower
of refuge in her time of trouble, and giving this disinterested
suitor the last, best, strongest love of a strong unselfish nature!

Men of Mr. Gayre's type are all too apt to imagine Providence delights to play into their hands.

Certainly on that autumn morning, between six and seven
o'clock, Mr. Gayre felt God was on his side.

The longer he thought about the matter the more satisfied he
became that things were working round to promote his own
happiness and Susan's welfare.

Out of evil good would come. When she had got over the
fret of losing her lover, she would bring him, Nicholas, the whole
of her great, loyal heart. Had the man died, had untoward
circumstances separated her from Oliver Dane, she might never
have recovered the blow. But forgery, embezzlement, the dock,
and a felon's doom, must, he argued, hurt a woman's pride, and
crush her love, and clear the course for a suitor like himself,
unexceptionable in all respects save that unlucky item of age.
Not for one moment did it ever occur to Mr. Gayre that Oliver
Dane might be innocent. He knew Colvend and Surlees well.
Mr. Colvend, indeed, kept his private account at Gayres', and
he had often heard that gentleman speak in almost affectionate
terms of young Dane, "remanded on the previous afternoon,
bail being refused."

He was aware that at one time Mr. Colvend had thought of
taking his clerk into partnership. Such a termination of the

business connection was spoken about both by Mr. Colvend and Mr. Surlees. Of late Mr. Surlees, however, had seemed dissatisfied with their *employé*. The question possessed so little interest for Mr. Gayre, that when both principals wrangled a little about Dane, he only considered that person a bore; but now he remembered all their utterances, and came to the conclusion the young man must have been engaged in a course of fraud for years. He knew Mr. Dane's appearance perfectly well—his voice, accent, and manner had always struck the banker as quite unsuitable to his actual station.

"A gentleman to the backbone, sir," old Mr. Colvend remarked; and now that "gentleman" was as good as convicted.

"Surlees is not a person to show mercy," considered Mr. Gayre. "It will be penal servitude. Well, not so long ago he would have been hanged!" Cheered by which consolatory reflection the banker proceeded on his way.

It was a lovely morning. The Seven Sisters' Road looked its best as Mr. Gayre rode along. Tottenham Valley, which lies just behind the Manor House Tavern, seemed literally steeped in sunshine; the morning air blew fresh and pleasant; the ground was hard, and echoed cheerily the sound of the horses' hoofs. Yes, though the blow had been severe, Mr. Gayre felt he was recovering from it. Things were not so bad that they might not have been a great deal worse. This trouble, properly utilised, must draw Susan nearer to him— nearer and nearer still. Now he knew his ground, and he had never known it before. Putting up his horse at a tavern in Enfield Highway, he walked on to Mrs. Arbery's house. As he pushed open the small gate he caught the flutter of a woman's dress in the garden; and, next moment, Susan turned and saw him.

"Why, Mr. Gayre," she cried, "what has brought you here so early? How is Maggie? There is nothing wrong with Sir Geoffrey, is there?"

She did not know, she had not a notion of the trouble impending; and for a moment Mr. Gayre's heart smote him when he thought of the sorrow he was bringing to the dear fair girl, who had never looked sweeter or lovelier than at that instant.

"My niece is well, thank you," he answered, "and Sir Geoffrey was well also when I saw him last night. I have come to see you, Miss Drummond. I want to tell you something I think you would rather hear from me than—strangers."

" Something bad ?"

" I feel you will—I know you must—think so."

" Whom does it concern ?"

" Mr. Dane."

" My God !"—her lips rather shaped the words than said them—" is he ill, *or dead ?*"

" Neither. But let us go into the house. This garden is so exposed, and—"

Without a word she led him into the pleasant drawing-room, which commanded a view of Sewardstone and the Essex hills ; shut the door close ; and then, turning to the banker, said,

" Now, what is it ?"

" I bring very bad news." He hesitated.

" I know you do ; what is it, Mr. Gayre ? Don't keep me in suspense. What is it you have come to tell me ?"

" Have you read this morning's paper ?"

" No, I have not looked at it. O Mr. Gayre, what is wrong—what has happened ?"

For answer he produced a copy of the *Times*, which he had bought on the road, and gave it into her hands, indicating a particular paragraph.

" I thought," he repeated, " you would rather hear of this from me than another."

She did not answer. She was reading the brief passage in yesterday's police report, which told her her ship had gone to pieces on the breakers. She finished it to the end ; then lifted her eyes to Mr. Gayre's with a look of dumb entreaty which haunts him even now.

" My love ! my love !" she murmured, and sat down transformed.

The Susan of old would never walk among the flowers in Mr. Arbery's garden again. That Susan was dead and buried ; and Mr. Gayre stood marvelling to see the change. Coming events cast their shadows before ; and the banker now understood that yearning look in those sweet brown eyes. The minor chord that gave such a strange sadness every now and then to the music of her young life meant trouble was on its way to meet her—the crushing trouble she now saw face to face.

Minutes passed, but she never spoke. After that one cry of agonised despair she sat silent and motionless, while Mr. Gayre, unable to suggest one word of comfort, stood looking at her, with a great pity and a wild jealousy and a mad joy all contending together in his breast.

Through the window which looked out on the Essex hills, bright sunshine fell in golden bars across her hair, her white soft throat, her hands lying loosely clasped together in her lap. The girl's whole attitude was that of utter abandonment. For the moment she seemed stricken down. She and hope and youth and gaiety had shaken hands and parted. To have seen her then, any one might have imagined Susan Drummond would never laugh or smile or jest again. The iron had entered into her soul. *Forgery, embezzlement!* The words were branded on her heart. The man she knew so well, the man she loved, accused of such awful crimes! It appeared impossible; and yet there before her eyes lay the story in black and white. His accusers said he had forged their signature; the proceeds of his imputed crime were found at his lodgings. The notes paid over the counter of the Union Bank were discovered in his portmanteau, which was packed as if for a journey. What did it all mean? Tossing in a sea of distressed conjecture, Susan still held fast to one saving rope—*he was innocent.* If the whole world declared him guilty she would not believe the verdict. In some moment of mental aberration she might have committed a great sin (Susan felt she would do wickedness for the sake of those she loved); but Oliver Dane? No! While the sun rose and the sun set she could never believe that. He might have faults, and he had—Susan knew them—but he was perfectly incapable of such an act as this. He would want her. Vaguely this blessed thought began to shoot up—two fair green leaves of promise to beautify the arid desolation of the barren land to which she had been so suddenly transported. He could not do without her help. He had no relation, she knew, who would come forward at such a crisis. To all useful intents and purposes, he and she stood utterly alone in the world. Adam and Eve were perhaps less solitary in the Garden of Eden than her lover and herself in what some persons consider this over-populated world.

Directly that idea of help crossed her mind, she looked at her watch, and said,

"There is an up-train in about twenty minutes. I shall just be able to catch it, Mr. Gayre, if you will excuse me."

"Catch it! Where are you thinking of going?"

"To Oliver. I must go to him at once, you know—"

"No; by Heaven, that you sha'n't!" broke out Mr. Gayre fiercely; then recollecting himself, he added, "Can't you trust me, Miss Drummond? Only say what you want done, and I will try to do it. If time, or money, or influence can help you in this strait, command all so far as they are within the compass of my power."

"Thank you," she answered earnestly, "thank you;" and almost involuntarily she stretched out her hand, which he took and held in both of his while she went on. "We are so lonely, Mr. Gayre ; we are so far more lonely than any human being could imagine."

He bent his head and kissed her hand—that white hand which she made no attempt to withdraw, which lay in his as a frightened bird nestles in the palm of some one who has rescued it from fear and death.

"If you can trust me—" he was beginning, when the door opened and Mrs. Arbery's voice was heard exclaiming a little sharply :

"What are you doing? Breakfast is ready, Susan." Then, catching sight of Mr. Gayre, who was standing very close to her niece—indeed, quite bending over that young person in a manner which seemed to indicate private communications of importance were passing between them—she added, in a tone of severe and astonished dignity, "I *beg* your pardon, I am sure."

"Come in, aunt," said Susan, "we are not talking about any matter which can be kept secret. Will you tell her, Mr. Gayre?" and the girl turned her face, from which all the delicate rosebud pink had flown, towards the window, and looked with unseeing eyes at the distant hills, while the story of Oliver Dane's downfall was recited for Mrs. Arbery's benefit. It was a long story, which did not take long in the telling. The bare facts contained enough of sorrow and disgrace without any necessity for further detail. Mr. Gayre said as little as he well could, but that little proved more than sufficient. If Susan's lover had been tried, convicted, and sent to penal servitude, Mrs. Arbery could not have felt more fully convinced of his guilt.

She listened to the narrative in utter silence, and when it was finished said calmly,

"I am not at all surprised."

"No?" questioned Mr. Gayre, for Susan did not speak.

"He is a young man I never liked," Mrs. Arbery explained. "It was an engagement I never approved."

"You cannot mean, aunt, that you believe him guilty?"

"I certainly do not mean that I believe him innocent. Everything is against him."

"Yes," said Susan bitterly. "Everything is against him, everything has been against him; but that is no reason why you should think him a thief. Do you suppose if I heard you or Will had committed any sin I should believe the story? O aunt, though you dislike Oliver, do not be hard on him. I can't bear to hear you speak against the man I am going to marry—I can't, I can't!" and her voice trailed away into low sobbing.

Mr. Gayre looked at Mrs. Arbery, who, laying her hand on Susan's shoulder, said,

"My dear, I do not wish to be hard on him. If he has done wrong he is suffering for it; but as for your ever marrying him now, of course—"

"Are we not to have any breakfast to-day?" cried Will Arbery at this point in his mother's diatribe. "Why, what has happened? What is the matter?" he went on, looking in astonishment at the group collected at the upper end of that long pleasant drawing-room. "What is wrong, Susan?"

"Don't tell him," pleaded the girl; "let him read it;" and as Mr. Gayre handed the *Times* to the young man in silence she rose, and, twining her arm about her cousin's neck, looked over his shoulder while he glanced at the brief report.

'O Susan, I *am* sorry for you!" he exclaimed. "What ought we to do? Mr. Gayre, you know, I suppose, how we can be best of use."

"You believe him innocent, Will?"

"Innocent! Of course I do. It is some awful mistake; it can be nothing but a mistake," he added, turning to the banker.

From the manner in which he uttered the words they might have been intended either as an interrogation or a statement of opinion. Mr. Gayre chose to accept them in the former sense, and gravely answered that he hoped so.

"Mr. Dane may be able to explain the circumstances. As yet, you must remember we have only heard one side—that of his employers. When his statement is made the whole complexion of the affair will probably be altered."

"I do not need to wait for his statement," said Susan, with streaming eyes. "I know."

Mr. Arbery took a few turns up and down the room.

"Don't you think," he asked, appealing once again to Mr.

Gayre, "the thing for me to do would be to see Mr. Colvend at once?"

"Better let me do so. I know both the partners."

"It—wasn't at your bank, was it?" hesitated Mr. Arbery.

"No; the Union. Mr. Colvend only kept his private account with us."

"What sort of a man is he?"

"Extremely kind. At one time he took the liveliest interest in Mr. Dane's future."

"Do you know Oliver, then?" asked Susan, drawing a quick gasping breath.

"I have seen and spoken to Mr. Dane. Had I been aware you were interested in him, Miss Drummond, I should have made a point of cultivating his acquaintance."

"Standing here talking," remarked Mr. Arbery, in a general sort of way, "won't mend matters. Mother, if you will give me a cup of tea, the sooner I get off the better. Cheer up, Susan; I'll bring you back good news, never fear."

"I am going with you," she said.

"No, Susan," said Mrs. Arbery. "Understand that I distinctly forbid your doing anything of the kind. I will not have you compromise yourself. You know what I have been impressing upon you for a very long time past. You thought me prejudiced, and now you see something far worse than ever I imagined has come to pass."

"It is quite true," answered Susan—"something much worse than any one could ever have imagined has come to pass;" and she sat down again with something more nearly approaching a sullen expression clouding her face than Mr. Gayre had ever seen disfigure its fair beauty before.

"Shall I send *you* a cup of tea, dear?" asked her aunt, apparently quite unconscious of having given any offence; "it will do you good." But Susan only shook her head.

"Come into the other room, or Mr. Gayre won't touch a morsel; and he has ridden a long way to do you a kindness," whispered Will Arbery. Whereupon Susan rose, and, taking her cousin's arm, walked silently across the hall.

Mr. Gayre watched her at the morning meal, which was the great meal of the day in Mrs. Arbery's house.

She allowed herself to be helped to ham. She accepted a proffered egg. She took a piece of toast. She did not again decline that cup of tea, suggested as though a cup of tea were a panacea for all the ills of life. She made pretence of cutting up and toying with her food ; but she touched none of it. She never looked at nor spoke to any one. She asked no question. She made no remark. Will Arbery argued out the Dane complication exhaustively, and Mr. Gayre exhibited considerable ingenuity in suggesting plausible reasons why it seemed the most natural thing in the world for three hundred pounds, paid over the counter at the Union Bank, on the strength of Messrs. Colvend and Surlees' forged signature, to be found in the lodgings of one of their clerks, a trusted *employé*, a gentleman they had once thought of taking into partnership—but Susan made no sign.

Mr. Gayre then shifted his ground. He spoke of the high opinion he had always entertained of Mr. Dane, of the conviction he felt from the beginning he was far too clever to be hampered with two such partners as Colvend and Surlees.

" Excellent men," proceeded the banker, warming to his subject, " but fifty years at least behind the times. Colvend's notions are those of the last century."

Just for the moment a faint flush, or quiver of the eyelids, or pitiful tremor of the mouth rewarded these utterances ; but it was uphill work, and Mr. Gayre felt he was growing almost as anxious for the moment of departure as Mr. Arbery professed himself to be, when suddenly Miss Drummond's eyes, which she had lifted for a moment, became larger and brighter ; her whole manner changed ; her colour came and went, and, exclaiming almost incredulously, " It's Sir Geoffrey ! it really is Sir Geoffrey !" she ran out of the room and opened the hall-door, and met him in the middle of the straight prim gravelled walk.

" Why, Susan, my girl !"

" O Sir Geoffrey !" and then the Baronet found himself, for the first, and, it may be added, the last time in his life, holding in his arms a perfectly respectable young woman utterly beside herself with grief and anxiety, and what she considered a lack of intelligent sympathy.

" There, then," said Sir Geoffrey, stroking and soothing her down exactly as he might have done had she been a horse, " take it quietly, my beauty. There's nothing really to be frightened about. Dane—Dane's all right, you know. Gayre and I will stand bail for him. Tut-tut ! what's all this trouble ? Bless the creature, how she clings to me ! There's nothing wrong ; there is nothing to trouble you ! You are safe now your old papa Geoff has come to the rescue. Bless you, he'll

go and rout up the magistrates, and make them send your lover
back to you at once. It is an outrageous proceeding. Never
heard of such a thing—never in all my life. Now, now, now,
don't cry any more. If you do, you'll not be able to see him
when he comes back. What's that you are saying? I don't
think him guilty, do I? You silly little mortal! Why, I'd
just as soon believe myself capable of doing such a thing;"
which comparison struck Susan even in her then state of mind
as scarcely conveying the amount of comfort Sir Geoffrey
amiably intended.

"Dry your eyes, Susie, and come into the house and tell
me all you know about the matter, and we'll see what's best to
be done."

With which and suchlike fatherly words of rebuke and
encouragement Sir Geoffrey led Susan into the drawing-room,
where, as he stated, to his immense astonishment, he found
Gayre.

"God bless me!" he exclaimed, "to think of meeting you,
of all men in the world, here! Why, I'd ten minds to call for
you on my way—I passed the end of your street. I've never
been home all night—but I made sure you were snugly tucked
up, dreaming of Consols and Lord knows what besides! Now,
I call this really friendly of you. I was just saying, Mrs.
Arbery," he went on, as that lady, frigidly decorous and deeply
exercised in her mind, made her appearance on the scene,
"that among us we'll put things right for our little girl."

"You mean very kindly, I am sure," answered Mrs. Arbery,
"but there are some things which never can be put right. If
you could only persuade my poor Susan of this, you would be
performing an act of the truest friendship."

"We'll see about all that after a while," answered the
Baronet cheerfully; "time enough to discuss all those sorts of
questions when Dane is able to put his oar in. Now, Susie,
wake up, and say what you want me to do. As I told you, I
haven't been to bed at all; but that makes no difference—I
am ready to go anywhere and see any one."

"I want you to take me to see Oliver," murmured Susan,
in so low a tone her words failed to reach Mrs. Arbery's ear.

The girl was still holding Sir Geoffrey's arm, and almost
whispered her request. Just for a moment the Baronet looked
grave, then he said briskly,

"So I will—so I will. Run and put your bonnet on, and
we can talk as we go up."

"Sir Geoffrey," broke in Mrs. Arbery, "I really cannot allow my niece to go to London with you."

"Very sorry indeed to hear it."

"Her engagement has been a source of disappointment, trouble, and anxiety to me ever since I first knew of it."

"I can well understand that. Engagements very seldom do meet the approval of any save the pair engaged, and their satisfaction seldom lasts beyond a week after marriage. I myself think the whole thing a mistake; but, bless your soul, you might as well try to prevent the sap rising as hinder two young people falling in love."

"Young people should fall in love suitably."

"So they ought," agreed the Baronet; "but then, you see, as a rule, they don't, and in this world we have to deal with things not as they should be, but as they are."

"That is very true, Sir Geoffrey," answered Mrs. Arbery, who in her own family and amongst her own friends conducted herself after the fashion of a Mede and Persian; "and it is precisely because I object to things as they are that I feel bound to forbid my niece to hold any further communication whatsoever with Oliver Dane."

While Mrs. Arbery was speaking, Sir Geoffrey felt Susan's hand slip from his arm, and saw her gliding out of the room through the nearest door. He listened gravely to all the "elderly party" had to advance, then took up his parable.

"In my best days," he began, "I never was what is called a ladies' man" (Mr. Gayre smiled grimly); "but I believe I understand the sex; or, to be more exact, I feel the sex is made up of a number of women differing mightily from each other, which is a fact your ladies' man never can grasp. I don't attempt to generalise men. Why should I attempt to generalise women? And so, to return to what I had to say, don't you curb up Susan too tight. If you do she'll give you a lot of trouble. Take the right way with her, and, bless your soul, I'd undertake to drive her with silken thread; take the wrong way, and—"

"So far as I understand your mode of speech," said Mrs. Arbery, white almost with passion, "you mean to encourage my unfortunate niece in pursuing a line of conduct opposed at once to propriety and common sense?"

"I always lament having to disagree with a lady," said Sir Geoffrey, with a low bow—the one gentlemanlike talent the Baronet possessed was his bow, afoot or on horseback—"but

as you drive me into a corner, I feel bound to tell you plainly
I consider propriety and common sense were never opposed to
anything Susan Drummond liked to do. If you can show me
that they were, I will abandon common sense, and 'go in' for
another and better sense called Susan Drummond."

"Bravo, Chelston!" cried Mr. Gayre, almost involuntarily.
In acknowledgment of which the Baronet said:

"All right, Gayre; thank ye."

"And despite of what I say, and Mr. Gayre said when he
first came this morning, you actually mean to take Susan to see
a felon?" went on Mrs. Arbery.

"Softly, softly," entreated Sir Geoffrey. "Wait at least till
the man is proved guilty before you call him hard names.
And even supposing the worst comes to the worst—"

"Which it must," interrupted Mrs. Arbery, with great decision.

"Well, even in that case, I don't think it would be well to
use such a word when speaking of Oliver Dane. We are none
of us infallible. We don't know what we might do if we were
tempted. A man may make a mistake, but—"

"These fine distinctions are quite thrown away on me,"
retorted Mrs. Arbery. "Right is right, and wrong is wrong."

"Oliver has done no wrong, aunt," said Susan, reëntering
the room at this juncture. "Give me some good wish before
I go—some good wish for both of us;" and she held up her
sweet face to be kissed.

But Mrs. Arbery would not kiss her. Once again she
expressed her disapproval of the whole expedition, and was
especially irate against her son, who, declaring Susan should go
where she liked, and that he would go with her, drew his
cousin's hand within his arm, and angrily left the house, leaving
Sir Geoffrey and Mr. Gayre to follow at their leisure.

CHAPTER XIX

IT was a fortnight later. Oliver Dane had once again been brought before the magistrate, and committed for trial. The evidence against him was conclusive; not a creature except Susan believed in his innocence. Even Sir Geoffrey, who said he was "deuced sorry for the fellow, deuced sorry indeed," shook his head mournfully, and lamented over the weakness of poor human nature which, he implied, was alone responsible for ruining the whole future of "as promising a young man as you would wish to see."

"Heaven only knows," he exclaimed, "what demon could have possessed him. I am sure any of his friends would have found the money. I would, if I'd had it, and there were lots, I'll be bound, in the same mind. That woman getting the cheque cashed was a bad sign—a widow too—and handsome, ah!" and Sir Geoffrey shook his head. "There must have been some screw awfully loose. Wherever a woman leads, trouble follows. Wonder who she is? Awkward mess altogether. Dane is the last man in the world I should have thought likely to go wrong in that way; but, dear me, what a dance any petticoat may lead the best of us! You and I can't be too thankful, Gayre, can we?"

"Some persons are more lucky than wise," agreed the banker, thinking Sir Geoffrey was a case in point.

"That is very true. It is not always the best rider clears the ditch. But, as I was saying, it is altogether a most confoundedly awkward business. Though I am sorry for Dane, I don't think he is doing right, and I told him so. 'You ought to plead guilty, and settle Susan's mind,' I said. 'If the case were mine I could not keep a girl on the tenter-hooks. This sort of thing might be all very well in dealing with a man, but it isn't fair to a woman.'"

"And what did he say?" asked Mr. Gayre.

"Just the usual thing—that he could not tell an untruth

even to settle Susan's mind; that he had not forged the signature; that the money was forwarded to his lodgings by some one unknown; that he had his suspicions; that unless he could change them into certainties it would be worse than useless to speak; that he quite understood it was impossible for Susan now to marry him; that the engagement must be considered at an end; that his life was wrecked; that she, the noblest of women, must not sacrifice her life through any mistaken idea of loyalty to him; that her devotion was the bitterest drop in a bitter cup; that he had not the slightest hope of an acquittal; but that he could not plead guilty, or tell Susan he was dishonoured in deed as well as in the eyes of the world. Then I said, 'Your boasted affection is a very poor sort of affection; I would not treat any girl after such a fashion. I am disappointed in you. I knew your father to be a fool, and your grandfather a screw, but I did *not* think you were a scoundrel.'"

"Rather rough on the fellow," commented Mr. Gayre.

"Rough! not a bit too rough! 'Look at what the consequences will be!' I said. 'Susan is just the girl to exalt you into a sort of martyr. She will go on believing in and fretting about you. She will lose her youth and her good looks. She will not marry, and, if she do not die, she will live a sad sweet old maid, nursing other folks' babies instead of her own.'"

"You drew quite a touching picture," said Mr. Gayre.

"And *then* he wouldn't," declared the Baronet, with a great oath. "No, —— me if he would! I don't know when I went through such an interview, and without a drop of anything either to give me a fillip. Give you my word, Gayre, I felt quite exhausted when I came out. Had to go into the nearest pub, and ask leave to sit down. It's heartless, you know; that's what it is. Hang it! I'm not particular, you are aware. If a man commits a crime I wouldn't turn my back on him; but to keep on with this sort of infernal humbug to a girl like Susan Drummond, why—why, it's the very deuce!" finished the Baronet, who was delivering these sentiments in his own house and at his own table.

"I suppose it is not on the cards that the man may be, by possibility, innocent?"

"Innocent! for Heaven's sake, Gayre, don't you get sentimental! It's all very well to humour Susan's notion for a while, and let the girl down gently; but we, who have been

out in the world, and know a thing or two, must not talk like
children. Run your eye over the whole matter. Here's a
young fellow brought up by a grandfather, who won't allow him
sixpence of pocket-money, and puts him into an attorney's
office. Young fellow won't be an attorney, goes and enlists;
old Drummond buys him off, and has him stopping at the
Hall for a while. Then he fails in love with Miss Susie;
grandfather, delighted, thinks she will be an heiress; grandfather finds out she won't be an heiress, and insists on the
engagement being broken off; young man comes up to London
in a huff, and, through favour, gets into Colvend's house.
Everybody believes it's all over between him and Susan.
Eventually the grandfather makes some conditional sort of
promise to find money enough to buy a small share in the
business. After a while, Surlees begins to find fault with the
young man, the idea of the partnership is abandoned, and
Dane announces his intention of going into business on his
own account. Grandfather discovers he and Susan mean to
get married, and declares he will cut young man off with a
shilling. Young man has got a little into debt, and wants
money besides for capital. Surlees gets a hint that all is not
square, and begins to look into matters, which present some
serious complications. Holds his tongue to make quite sure
—means to speak to Dane when he has all the proofs complete. At that juncture a three-hundred-pound cheque, signed
Colvend and Surlees, is presented across the Union counter
and paid. Notes are found in Dane's rooms, in a portmanteau ready packed. Make what you can of the case, my
friend—it looks confoundedly black against Mr. Oliver."

"Yes," agreed Mr. Gayre—"yes."

"But there is no good in talking to Susan yet. I told you
exactly what would happen if Mrs. Arbery persisted in taking
up the curb another link. Most foolish, self-opinionated old
woman. Thinks because she won't drink half a pint of ale,
the Almighty has given her dominion over every living thing
that moveth upon the earth. If she had only let Susan go her
own way at her own pace for a while she would not have sent
the girl mad, as she has done. When she told me about Susan
having left Enfield, and taken up her abode with Miss Matthews,
I said, 'It's your own fault, ma'am; she'd never have got the
bit between her teeth if you'd driven her easily.' But, bless
my soul and body, there are other persons in the world who
have a will beside Mrs. Arbery. No—excuse me—I can't get

the girl back ; and if I could, I wouldn't try. The end of it will be she'll marry Oliver Dane."

"But you don't really think that likely?" exclaimed Mr. Gayre.

"I'll tell you what I think—that Dane won't marry her. How could he? The dear grandfather will give him nothing; Susan has but two thousand pounds. Say he only gets a couple of years, what will he be fit for when he comes out? No, the thing is not to be thought of. But our plan at present is to take no notice—to her, at any rate. After the trial we'll see what we had better do."

"Miss Drummond appears to have no doubt of his innocence."

Sir Geoffrey shrugged his shoulders. "All the fault of the old party out at Enfield Highway. She would tighten that curb. It's just the same with a woman as a horse ; and you know, Gayre, the result of fretting a young high-spirited creature by holding it in when there's no need to do anything of the sort. Bless you, I always try to give them their head for a bit ; and if Mrs. Arbery had taken no notice, and let Susie have her own way about this confounded business, the girl would have begun to entertain doubts concerning her lover, and wanted to know who the woman was, and why Surlees could not get on with friend Oliver, and so finally come gradually round to a sensible view of the matter ; whereas—" and the Baronet, finding words inadequate to express the pass to which Mrs. Arbery's management had brought affairs, poured himself a good measure of champagne into a large tumbler, "throwing on the top," as he expressed the matter, "just a flavour of brandy."

If Sir Geoffrey had not been a baronet the mode in which he tossed off this bumper and smacked his lips approvingly after it might have been considered vulgar ; but circumstances alter cases, and circumstances altered most cases with Mr. Gayre's brother-in-law.

"Ah," said Sir Geoffrey, leaning back in his chair, stretching out his feet to the fire, and looking with an air of childlike contentment at the leaping flame, "you may talk as you like about your clarets— !"

"I am not aware that I have spoken about clarets at all," mildly responded the banker.

"Deeds speak as loud as words, and you always drink that poor, thin, sour stuff—for poor and thin and sour it is, though you do pay a price which makes my hair stand on end; but then a rich banker is one quantity and a poor baronet another. However, as I was remarking, you may depend upon it a man's face takes the cast of the tipple he affects. Now claret produces lines, wrinkles, and gives a sneering sort of expression to the countenance. I'd drop it if I were you, and go in for something more generous and exhilarating. Why should you look older than your age? You are a mere boy in comparison to the battered craft you are good enough to call brother-in-law. Let me see, you are younger than poor Margaret—"

The banker shook his head.

"Well, the difference either way, I know, is very trifling, and we know what a baby thing she was when I married her. Why don't you turn your attention to matrimony, Gayre? I you can't make up your mind to the widow—and I suppose you can't or you'd have been stepfather to the Jubbins fry long ere this—there are plenty of girls who, I am sure, would be only too glad if you could be induced to say a civil word to them."

"I fancy you are right about the widow," went on Sir Geoffrey, finding his brother-in-law did not speak. "Of course she has money; but then you have plenty of your own, and money is not everything, though it is a great deal, as nobody knows better than I do. Why shouldn't you marry, and have a nice wife and pleasant home? You're just the sort of fellow girls would take to, and make up romances concerning; I know them; bless your soul, they'd turn you into a hero, and fall down and worship at once. Think of it, Gayre. 'Pon my honour, I don't like to see you drinking claret and living in a big house all alone, with only servants about you. Providence never intended such a thing. It is you that have made the mistake; but you may remedy it yet."

"If I take to champagne and brandy and making love to young ladies?" questioned the banker.

"I don't suppose you would care to make love to old ladies, which, by the bye, reminds me of something I wanted to say to you. I sha'n't be able to induce Mrs. Morris to stop on; and I declare solemnly I have not chucked her under the chin or insisted on her dancing a *fandango*."

"Why does she wish to go, then?"

"The usual thing; all women are alike; they have a craze for what they call respectability, and a knowledge of what constitutes impropriety, which knowledge I myself regard as sinful. Mrs. Morris has arrived at the conclusion this house is not an abode in which she ought to continue to reside. She has her doubts about it and me. She fails to understand why visitors do not call; why my daughter is not asked out; why we never give parties; why you have not Peg staying in Wimpole Street; why I can't be induced to return to six o'clock tea, nine o'clock prayers, and eleven o'clock bed; why we have not more servants; why we do not keep a carriage; why I run household bills; why I do not pay every fellow who has a 'heavy account to make up.' She feels, in fact, the air of North Bank may be injurious to her social health. It seems she has got a presentation to Christ's Hospital for the boy. So now, as she can do without me, she means to leave. Nice and grateful, is it not?"

" How extremely awkward!" said Mr. Gayre.

"I wanted her to stop till Peggy was married, but no she won't. 'My dear Mrs. Morris,' I urged, 'you have surely reached a time of life when you might be able to defy Mrs. Grundy and all her works.'

"'No woman is ever so old as to be able to disregard appearances, Sir Geoffrey,' she replied; 'and for myself, though I *have* a grandson—'

"'Yes, yes, yes,' I interrupted, 'I know you were married at sixteen and your daughter at fifteen—the usual thing—so you can't be much over thirty; but still—'

"'Pardon me,' she returned, 'I am over forty (upon my soul, Gayre, she must be close on seventy), but I feel it is as imperative for me to regard my character now as I did when I was in my teens.'

"'Most creditable, I am sure,' I replied; 'but forgive me if I ask what is the good of shouting "Wolf!" when there is not an animal of the sort outside the Zoological Gardens? Let us walk across and see the wolves, Mrs. Morris, and say you will stop a little while longer.'

"But she wouldn't, Gayre; she was as stiff as you please. She set her lips tight and she drew down her nose (have you ever remarked the stiff-neckedness of Mrs. M.'s nose?), and looking straight at me, and fixing me with those steel-blue eyes of hers, said, 'You must excuse me, Sir Geoffrey, but my mind is quite made up. Miss Matthews told me from the first your place would not suit me, and she was right. The place does not suit me; and if I may venture to say so, your place would not suit any gentlewoman who respected herself.'"

"What are we to do about Maggie, then?"

"That is just what I wanted to talk over with you. I have been trying to get one of Lal Hilderton's old aunts—people I had Peg with when they were in Wales—to come up from Richmond and take charge, but it was no use. They say she has treated Lal iniquitously, and that in consequence their dear nephew has taken to smoking, drinking, and going to the deuce generally, which of course is pleasant for a father to hear."

"My fair niece can't help flirting, and I do not think Mr. Lionel Hilderton required any goading along the road to ruin."

"Precisely my own idea; thank you, Gayre. Now I am going to propose something I know will astonish you, but don't make any rash comment till you have considered the matter in all its bearings. *The right person to take charge of Peg is her mother;* and if you'll help me a bit with the pecuniary part of the matter, I am willing to let bygones be bygones, and for the sake of my girl make it up with your sister."

"You cannot be serious, Chelston."

"I never was more serious in my life. I have a right to take back my wife if I like. The story is an old one now. At the time many persons thought Margaret was dead, many imagined we separated by mutual consent, many that I was the sinner; only a very few knew the rights of the case. Well, we make it up, we take a small house somewhere, and there's your natural protector for Peg at once. Bless you, I've thought it all out, and feel sure this is the course we ought to pursue. Don't say anything yet. Mrs. Morris does not remove the light of her countenance for a month. Think it over: a mother for Peg, a home for Susan, who can't live always with that gruesome old maid at Shepherd's Bush, all trouble and anxiety ended, a very small additional allowance from you, and the thing is complete. I never was a man who thought of myself, and I assure you I have forgiven Margaret from the bottom of my heart over and over again. She was a very sweet girl, that sister of yours, Gayre, and I can see her now as I saw her that day we first met at Brighton;" and the Baronet stooped, as though to hide a tear, while his brother-in-law rose and paced the limits of Mr. Moreby's dining-room.

At last he said,

"You *have* indeed taken me by surprise, Chelston."

"Yes, I thought you would be astonished," said Sir

Geoffrey, in the tone of a modest man who felt serenely conscious he had performed a good action.

"You say you do not expect me to give you an immediate answer."

"Take your time—take your own time," observed the Baronet tolerantly. "I am the most considerate man on earth. No person can say with truth I ever made capital out of my matrimonial troubles. Now did I?"

"I am very sure you never did," agreed Mr. Gayre, thinking as he spoke that he knew the reason why.

WHATEVER small amount of comfort it may be possible to extract from being the principal figure in a *cause célèbre* was denied to Oliver Dane. Nothing could have been more prosaic and commonplace than his trial. As usual, the Old Bailey was crowded ; as usual, the benches were filled by that curious class of persons who are to be found in all parts of London—lounging on the seats of the Thames Embankment and Leicester Square, in the waiting-rooms of railway stations, and the Law Courts, and the few other places of free resort— engaged in the herculean task of killing time. Before a comparatively unappreciative audience the great scene of his life's story was played out. Fashionable ladies were conspicuous by their absence. Stock Exchange gentlemen, with their hats well on the backs of their heads, and their hands deep in their trousers pockets, utterly failed to put in an appearance. The thousand shades of business to be met within the confines of the City likewise felt the case was one which presented no attraction. A defaulting clerk, a common case of forgery and embezzlement : " Pooh ! not worth crossing the road to hear."

A good murder or a big swindle would have attracted an appreciative audience ; but the crime of which Oliver Dane stood accused being common as picking pockets, it was before a comparatively speaking empty house, Messrs. Colvend and Surlees' *ci-devant* clerk made his bow.

Through the windows of what is called the Old Court the gray lights of a winter's day streamed coldly upon audience, judge, aldermen, barristers, jury, and prisoner, who was young, rather over middle height, slight, well-formed, dark-haired, dark-eyed, standing looking calmly at the judge, and quitting himself, as even Mr. Gayre could not but acknowledge, like a man. Confinement and anxiety had worn but not otherwise changed him. He was still the Oliver of those happy blissful days which now seemed farther away than childhood. And Susan,

who, with a little bunch of forget-me-nots fastened prominently
in her dress, had come to sit out the trial, when she saw the
dear face of old in such a place, felt the hot tears coursing
slowly down her cheeks and dropping heavily behind her veil.
On entering the dock, for one moment he glanced around,
and in that moment she made the slightest gesture with her
hand and touched the knot of blue flowers nestling in her
breast. That was all; but he knew. And then, turning his
gaze resolutely away, he never again let his eyes stray towards
her—never once till the trial was over and the torture ended.
Mr. Gayre sat one side of the girl and Miss Matthews on the
other. Will Arbery had left England, and all other friends
were either witnesses for the defence or too angry or indifferent to support her lover at such a crisis. But for Susan,
Oliver Dane might well just then have felt himself forgotten
by God and forsaken by man. Innocent or guilty, it seemed
as though his fellows had deserted him. In his cell he had
not felt half so lonely as he did in the crowded court. Mr.
Gayre he had seen and Miss Matthews likewise. Mr. Surlees
stood near the dock leaning against a partition. Familiar as
he was with the City, as a matter of course the names and
appearances of many men present were known to the prisoner.
He recognised his solicitor talking to a man he concluded
must be the counsel engaged for his defence; a burly coarse-
looking individual, famous for his skill in brow-beating witnesses, he was aware had been retained for the prosecution.
He saw the place of honour under the canopy filled by an ex-
Lord Mayor, gorgeously attired, with the "sword of justice"
hung over his head on the wall behind his seat; then his
glance wandered to the judge, and after that his thoughts began to stray.

It seemed as though all the sin and misery of the centuries
rose out of their forgotten graves, and came trooping, ghostly
phantoms, into the place which had witnessed one terrible
scene of their earthly tragedy. The prison taint was around
him, the prison smell in his nostrils. He could see the dock
filled with wretched men and despairing women; widows'
sons and gray-haired sires; fingers, soon to be cold and still
in death, playing nervously with the herbs placed to preserve
those who were free from prison fever—fever kept for the
benefit of the captives.

Old stories, long forgotten, recurred to memory; all the
legends of that shameful place where, in the name of "Jus-

tice," so many innocent men were condemned in the good old days to infamy, torture, and death, came jostling his elbow, laid their skeleton hands on his throat, thrust their pallid faces between him and the judge, and glided—a ghastly awful procession—down the stairs, from step to step of which they carried, in dumb agonised silence, the burden of their woe.

All at once a voice brought him back from dreamland to the fact that he was the latest member of that terrible crowd. On the boards where such tragedies had been enacted it was his turn to play a minor part.

"Guilty or Not Guilty?"

"Not Guilty, my lord."

And then Mr. Gayre knew Sir Geoffrey's pleadings had been, after all, in vain.

"It will be of no use urging extenuating circumstances after that," thought the banker, looking hard at the accused, while a feeling of pity, inconsistent in a merchant and a rival, stirred his heart.

At once the court settled to work. The prosecutor's case was fully stated. No detail which could hurt the prisoner and his friends was spared; his birth, education, antecedents, means, failings, were shouted in the ear of the public.

He was shown to have been always somewhat wild—a boy hard to control, impossible to train; a lad determined to take his own course to perdition; a youth destitute of gratitude, who turned and stung his best benefactor, an old and infirm gentleman of large fortune and the possessor of extensive estates.

"Our learned friend is a master of his craft," thought Mr. Gayre, himself not wholly indifferent to the suggested iniquity.

Sledge-hammer work the learned counsel evidently considered quite good enough for the Old Bailey and Oliver Dane; and accordingly down he came, mercilessly crushing all flowers of grace and beauty the young man's life might have been supposed to hold. Everything charming, in word, deed, or manner, was either a sin or a snare—often indeed both. He had bowed his grandfather's gray hairs low with sorrow; he had been seen on racecourses drinking champagne and betting freely; he had utterly deceived his excellent and simple employer, Mr. Colvend; he had been insolent to Mr. Surlees; he had declined the chaste pleasures, the intellectual converse, of Mr. Colvend's house, and descended to the lowest social stratum to be found even in London. He had consorted with thieves and vagabonds; he had gone into their haunts, and treated them with gin. One of the fraternity who called at his lodgings, had been invited to partake of mild refreshment, which assumed the character of brandy in its integrity. He (the learned counsel) was aware an endeavour would be made to explain these and other awkward facts; but the overpowering evidence on the part of the firm must render all such efforts worse than useless. To see a man of parts—a gentleman by birth, education, association—one who, favoured by Nature and caressed by Fortune, might have hoped to climb to the highest rung of the world's ladder—standing, like the common felons with whom he had consorted, in the dock, wrung his (the learned counsel's) heart—at which point the learned counsel thumped that organ. But he had a duty to perform, and he meant to perform it, without fear and without favour, just as he knew the intelligent jury he had the privilege to address would perform theirs, regardless of ridicule, undaunted by calumny, undeterred by the false, though amiable, representations of the prisoner's too partial friends.

Stripped of its verbiage, the whole speech, which did not occupy above fifteen minutes in its delivery, was absurd in the extreme—so absurd that Mr. Gayre could see even the prisoner's lip quiver under his close moustache ("Hang him!" thought the banker; "this poor dog whose day is ended has a sense of humour"); but it told. Old Bailey juries and the learned counsel were old and fast friends. If jurors never exactly understood the barrister, the barrister understood jurors.

"They don't want much," he explained, in the easy confidence of private life, "but they do like it uncommonly strong. Pitch into a man, give it him right and left, and you get a verdict. Mistakes! Bless your innocence" (only the learned counsel employed a stronger phrase), "a judge of the realm can't make a mistake. If a man is not ripe for hanging to-day you may feel very sure he will be over-ripe next year; and it is better to garner the criminal crop early rather than late; that is all." And, strongly convinced the Oliver Dane crop was ready for the sickle, the learned counsel hitched up his robe, settled his wig firmly on his head as though a thunderstorm were impending, and "went for" that ungrateful young gentleman with a fury and acrimony which would have delighted those writers for the press who denounced the Cato Street conspirators. He, the learned counsel, meant to show twelve honest men what an unmitigated and irredeemable scoundrel the prisoner at the bar really was. And then he proceeded to examine Mr. Surlees, who was the first witness called on behalf of the prosecution; while Susan Drummond spoke no word, and turned no look towards her companions, though Mr. Gayre could see she dug the fingers of one hand into the palm of the other till it bled; then she began as of deliberate intent and tore her handkerchief into strips. The banker beckoned his servant, who stood not far off, and handed the man a leaf from his pocket-book. During the course of that trial Susan all un-wittingly tore five handkerchiefs and a fan to tatters, festooned her watch-chain into loops till she broke it, slit her gloves be-yond the possibility of further use, and picked the whole of the fringe off one side of her mantle.

A sadly untrained young woman! If Sir Geoffrey had been going to the scaffold Miss Chelston would have adjusted every frill and tucker, fastened her brooch, smoothed her hair, and rubbed her eyes into a state of touching redness, ere descend-ing to receive the condolences of her friends.

After all, it must be a great trial to people who believe these and such-like items compass temporal salvation to meet with persons who do not.

Mr. Surlees, judging from his evidence, seemed to be a man who was at one in his opinions with Miss Chelston. He had never thought Dane a business sort of young man; he con-sidered he was too fond of new-fashioned ways. Mr. Colvend being infatuated about their clerk, he deemed it only his duty to warn his partner he did not believe Dane could ever become a fitting person to take into the house. He had received more than one warning about the prisoner—half a dozen, perhaps, in all. They assumed the shape of anonymous letters. He could form no idea from whom they emanated. In consequence, he examined the books. He found some discrepancies in them; he was intending to ask Dane to explain, when his attention was called to the fact of a cheque being missing. His sus-picions at once fell on the prisoner. He spoke to his partner. who wanted to speak to Dane. Instead of speaking to Dane. however. a detective was sent for. The detective proceeded to the clerk's lodgings. where the notes, with which the cheque was cashed at the Union, were found in his portmanteau, packed as if ready for a journey.

Being cross-examined by Mr. Tirling, the prisoner's counsel. Mr. Surlees was entreated to describe his idea of a business young man. Mr. Tirling convulsed the court, always ready to laugh at nothing, but did no good to his client. The airy and humorous way in which this learned counsel delighted in putting things, in slyly chaffing his learned friend, poking fun at the judge, and driving Mr. Surlees to the verge of distraction, amused but did not convince twelve "conscientious, impartial, and intelligent men."

Mr. Tirling wanted to know more than Mr. Clennam ever thought of, when he went to the Circumlocution Office. The learned counsel commenced operations with requiring a definition of a business sort of young man—not too fond of new-fashioned ways. Finding Mr. Surlees incapable of putting his notions into the concrete, he asked all sorts of questions concerning the model or dream young man. Mr. Surlees turning sulky at a very early stage of these proceedings, and the judge interposing with a remark that he did not really think the learned counsel's questions had the smallest bearing on the point at issue, Mr. Tirling argued the matter out with his lordship, and, being practically granted permission to ask such questions as he liked, proceeded to inquire whether Mr. Surlees took Charles Lamb's good clerk as his model.

"I think all C. Lamb's clerks very excellent; I only wish we had a few like them," was the unexpected reply. Whereupon, said the newspaper reports, the court was convulsed, the fact being the laughter was confined entirely to the bench and the bar.

"Mr. Surlees' acquaintance with Elia does not appear to have been intimate," suggested his lordship, wiping his wise old eyes. Whereupon there ensued a smart little dialogue between the bench and the learned counsel concerning Lamb and Leadenhall Street, Talfourd and the Inner Temple, which might have seemed more agreeable to the prisoner had he been unaware the discussion could not possibly influence his fate for good or for evil, that, forgetting all this pleasant fooling, the judge would eventually sum up dead against Oliver Dane!

Mr. Tirling inquired whether Mr. Dane wrote a "fair and swift hand," whether he was clean and neat in his person, whether he kept his books fair and unblemished, whether, in the mornings, he was first at the desk, whether he was temperate, whether he avoided profane oaths and jesting, whether the colour of his clothes was generally black in preference to brown, and brown rather than blue and green. And finding Mr. Surlees unable to answer any of these queries in the negative, the learned counsel suddenly dropped his friendly and conversa-

tional manner, and demanded with great sternness what further
or higher qualities he could wish in a clerk.

Driven to bay Mr. Surlees answered,

" Honesty, for instance."

" That won't do," retorted the learned counsel. " You
conceived a prejudice against my unfortunate client long before
any doubt concerning his honesty crossed your mind. Remember you are on your oath, sir. Now, what was your particular
objection to Mr. Dane ?"

It was like applying the thumbscrew torture, and Mr. Surlees stammered out that he thought their clerk talked too much,
and was a fop.

Instantly Mr. Tirling smote the witness hip and thigh.

" Did Mr. Surlees know the meaning attached to fop?"

" Yes, Mr. Surlees thought he did."

" Would he be kind enough to explain ?"

Mr. Surlees declined this challenge. " There were," he said,
" words the meaning of which could not be explained by the
help of other words."

" There are, are there ?" retorted Mr. Tirling; and straightway begged his lordship to take a note of this reply.

Instead of doing anything of the sort, his lordship said he
thought the learned gentleman was travelling very wide of the
subject indeed ; to which remark the learned gentleman replied
his lordship would, ere long, comprehend the reason for the
course he was taking, and with all due submission begged to
state he felt if he were to do justice to the prisoner—than
whom no more cruelly maligned individual ever deserved the
sympathy of his fellow-creatures—he must be allowed to continue the cross-examination in his own way. The judge gave
consent by silence. The opposing counsel looked up at the
ceiling, and smiled as one who should say, " Let him have his
fling. It is all of no use ; but he must do something for his
money." The prisoner knew if his chances had been bad ten
minutes previously they were worse now. With all the veins of
his heart he wished he had employed no solicitor, secured no
counsel, but just let things drift.

What was the loneliness of his prison cell in comparison
with this idiotic splitting of hairs, and attempt to make a man
out a liar who, to the best of his knowledge, stood there trying
to tell the simple truth ?

" Now attend to me, sir, if you please ;" it was Mr. Tirling
who spoke this sentence. " On your oath, do you consider

P

Oliver Dane to be a person of weak understanding and much ostentation? O, you don't? You are quite sure of that? Very well. Do you believe it was his ambition to attract attention by showy dress and pertness? Certainly not. Thank you, Mr. Surlees; I thought we should get at something after a time. Did he strike you as a gay trifling man? Once again, no. I trust these answers will be remembered. Was he, then, a coxcomb or a popinjay? Again No. Now really this is very singular. You described Mr. Dane as a fop, yet when one comes to exhaust the matter it actually seems he has not a single fop-like quality. Perhaps the other cause of dislike was founded on equally unsubstantial grounds. You say, sir, Mr. Dane talked too much; why, even Charles Lamb's model clerk was permitted the occasional use of his tongue. What did Mr. Dane say, when did he say it, and how? O, you decline to answer! Well, let that pass. Now I want to know who called your attention to the fact that a cheque had been torn out of the book?"

With this question Mr. Surlees tried in vain to fence; Mr. Tirling was determined he would—as he unpleasantly expressed the matter—"have an answer out of him," and at length elicited that Mr. Surlees was the Columbus of this great discovery; that he had "called his own attention" to it.

Then, indeed, the learned counsel felt delighted. In the playful exuberance of his spirits he figuratively danced round and round the merchant, dealing him verbal blows, catching him with a jest and gibe under the fifth rib; getting him into a corner, and making him contradict himself half a dozen times in as many seconds; closing with him as if for a mighty tussle; and then at quite an unexpected moment intimating in a scornful manner he had done with him.

This might have been all very well had his ingenuity proved able to tell the jury how notes paid across the counter of the Union on one day came, on the next evening, to be found in Mr. Dane's possession. It was a circumstance which of course might be capable of explanation; but then neither Mr. Dane nor Mr. Dane's counsel managed to do anything of the sort. The notes had been sent to him, so said the prisoner; the parcel containing them was dropped into the letter-box of his lodgings, the only information which accompanied it being that they "came from a friend." Certainly such a story did not seem feasible. It was just within the bounds of possibility that it might be true; but then it was so much more probable that it might not. Incredulity was writ large on the faces of those twelve men with whom the result lay. There are things that cannot be got over save by faith, a quality for which the British juryman is not usually remarkable; and if he had ever possessed it in the case of Oliver Dane, it may safely be said every step of the trial, every fact extracted in cross-examination and from the witnesses produced for the defence, must have tended to weaken the conviction of Oliver Dane's innocence.

There never seemed a clearer case of heartless ingratitude and flagrant fraud.

On the part of Mr. Colvend, at all events, there could be no suspicion of prejudice or dislike. Every answer he gave clearly proved his affection for the prisoner—his grief and surprise when he heard of the accusation against him; yet his evidence, reluctantly given, could only be summed up as against Oliver Dane. Had the matter rested with him, the young man would not have been given into custody; but that he believed in his guilt was evident. He knew he was going into business on his own account, and had offered to assist him; would gladly have lent him three hundred pounds or more had he been aware such a sum was important. Not a word was said or sentence spoken during the whole course of the trial which did not make the case blacker against the criminal.

"He ought to have pleaded guilty," thought Mr. Gayre. "Chelston was quite right; every fresh scrap of evidence is an additional nail in his coffin. Even *she* must be convinced now;" and he looked down at Susan, who, raising her anxious eyes, whispered, as if in answer to his unspoken words,

"Remember all this does not change my opinion in the least. He is innocent. I do not expect you to think so, but I know it."

The end was nearly at hand. Sir Geoffrey Chelston, who had been intimate with all the Danes—Oliver included—came forward to state he believed Dane to be a most honourable fellow, one he had never seen but once on any racecourse. Pressed as to whether the prisoner was not fond of horses, he answered, "Of course; all gentlemen are;" which last assertion might as well have been omitted, if he wished to impress the jury with any of the advantages to be derived from his own acquaintance. There was only one witness whose testimony could have proved useful on behalf of the prisoner; but both Mr. Gayre and Oliver Dane had so managed that her name was not even known to Mr. Tirling.

"Wouldn't do, you know, Gayre." remarked Sir Geoffrey, talking the matter over with his brother-in-law. "Susan must not be mixed up publicly with that poor fellow's troubles. Besides, nothing can materially change the aspect of matters for him ; it is a mere question of so many months, more or less ; and what can a few months more or less signify to him ? while it would be perfect damnation—excuse the word—for the girl to be bracketed with a fellow residing, even temporarily, in one of her Majesty's gaols."

"And, at the most, all she could say is he might have had her money without ever asking for it," answered Mr. Gayre. "We must keep her out of the matter. It is a redeeming point in Dane that he seems more anxious by far about her than himself."

"So he ought to be. Hang the fellow ! what business had he to induce such a girl to engage herself to a pauper ? Now the only amends he can make is to leave her free to marry somebody else."

"She won't do that, I think," said Mr. Gayre, a little hypocritically.

"Won't she ! Leave her to Time for a while. Old Time is the only fellow that thoroughly understands women. He heals love-wounds, and turfs over graves, and dries up tears in a way you would scarcely credit. 'Pon my soul, I've known him work miracles, and so you'll find it with Sue ; only whatever you do, don't cross her fancies," finished the Baronet, who already looked on Susan as Mrs. Gayre, and the Lombard Street strong-room as unlocked for his benefit.

It was, therefore, more with an interested eye to the future than from any sympathy with the unfortunate lovers that Sir Geoffrey worked for Oliver Dane "as though he were my own son."

Nevertheless, spite of the fact that he was a baronet, his testimony told, in the minds of the jury, against Mr. Colvend's clerk ; and not even the circumstance, that in cross-examination, to the great satisfaction of every one, the judge included, he threw the learned counsel for the prosecution, could make things better for a man accused of robbing his employers. Sir Geoffrey was quite sure of two things—one, that Oliver Dane did not bet ; another, that he did not habitually attend races.

"I'd know a betting-man," declared the Baronet, " if he were a bishop, or came on the course in wig and gown. I never saw Dane on any race-ground but once, and that was at the Derby, with a lot of other young fellows like himself. More by token," he added, nodding his head, and looking with a malicious twinkle at the learned counsel, "that was the very same year you laid against Bluegown, and lost a pot of money. I shall never forget your face when the roar came, ' Bluegown, Bluegown !' "

There was such a laugh over this agreeable reminiscence that the judge's admonitions to Sir Geoffrey were quite unheard; and the Baronet, dismissed by his opponent, who desired no continuation of so unpleasant a tale, lounged easily out of the witness-box, before it dawned on any one his lordship was remonstrating with him concerning the impropriety of his conduct.

After Sir Geoffrey came Lionel Hilderton, who was called to prove he and Oliver Dane had gone together into the low haunts of London in order to study faces and find models likely to prove useful in connection with his own work. They had found their way into very questionable neighbourhoods, and treated persons who were very like blackguards and thieves ; but if they had, what then ? " No doubt you "—this pointedly, and in his most offensive manner, to the genial gentleman who was badgering him—" have, in the way of your trade, consorted, ere now, with bad characters. You would be very much offended, I daresay, if any one called you a pickpocket because you may have defended one."

"Such license of language really cannot be permitted," observed the judge.

"Then why," asked Lal, his dark eyes flashing with anger, "does your lordship allow that person such license of language in addressing me? It is hard to get a blow and not to have a chance of striking out in return;" following on which remark there ensued a very pretty little quarrel between bench and witness. Lal defied the judge, and the judge threatened to commit him. Lal said he did not care, and that, on the whole, he would rather be committed; and it was at length only through the interposition of the learned counsel engaged on both sides his lordship was pacified, and the young man induced to hold his tongue, and the cross-examination proceeded.

" Were you ever engaged in a fight with the police?" asked his persecutor.

" Yes, and I'd fight them again if they were insolent. What right had they to interfere with a man who was doing them no harm?"

"Do you not think it was wrong to go to such places as the police warned you were not fit for any decently-dressed person to enter?"

"No, not a bit more wrong than going to church," retorted Lal.

"Perhaps you don't go to church, Mr. Hilderton?"

"Yes, I do, to study the British Pharisee."

"Dear—dear—dear!" murmured Susan, in an agony, wringing her hands; "what madness could have induced them to call Lal?"

"He has done all that lay in his power to convict his friend," decided Mr. Gayre, but he did not utter this idea aloud. "Won't you come away now, Miss Drummond?" he entreated, for he knew the beginning of the end was at hand.

"No; O, no!" she murmured.

"I wish you would not stop, dear," said Miss Matthews.

"I must stay to hear—the worst," Susan almost whispered.

Still the dreary proceedings dragged their slow length along; but at last came the judge's summing-up. It was dead against the prisoner, who stood listening, with crossed arms and an unmoved front, to the words of wisdom and reprobation which flowed in smooth passionless accents from the bench. The question of the prisoner's guilt or innocence was left, of course, to the jury; but the jury were told how to decide. The crime of which the young man before them was accused struck at the foundations of society. It was for the jury to disembarrass their minds of the extraneous matters which had been obtruded on their notice, and deliver a verdict on the merits of the case. His lordship felt he need not remind the gentlemen of the jury that the fact of the prisoner being well born, well educated, well connected, could not palliate his sin, if they believed he had first stolen a cheque, then forged his employers' signature, and subsequently appropriated the proceeds. It was for the jury to say whether they considered this serious charge proved.

Apparently, the jury had arrived at their decision before they even left the box; for they were not ten minutes absent before they trooped back again solemnly. They had arrived at a verdict.

"How say you, gentlemen?"

And then Susan Drummond, though she knew what was coming, held her breath.

" *Guilty !*"

It seemed as if a thousand voices took up the word, and shouted it in her ears. For a moment she felt like one drowning ; the waters had indeed covered her soul.

"Let me take you out," said Mr. Gayre, touching her arm ; but she seemed not to hear him. Every sense was concentrated on the judge, who, in measured accents, proceeded to say he would not add to the distress the prisoner must feel at the position to which a long course of folly and extravagance had brought him. When he looked back over his wasted life —a life which he could so easily have made honourable and prosperous—it might well seem as if in the loss of the esteem of all honest men, in the wreck and ruin of his own career, in the reproaches of his own conscience, were the elements of a sufficient and terrible punishment ; but the crime of which a jury of his own countrymen had found him guilty, was one so dangerous to the community, so necessary to check in a vast city—the capital of the greatest mercantile nation in the world, or that the world had ever known—his lordship felt it necessary to pass the severe sentence of seven years' penal servitude.

"My God !" exclaimed the prisoner, like one stunned ; and at that moment Susan would have risen, but that Mr. Gayre prevented her from doing so.

"Don't make a scene," he entreated, "don't ;" while from the dock came a cry of "*I am innocent !*" ere the warders hurried the living man into the seven years' grave that yawned before him.

CHAPTER XXI

" EVENTS ARRANGE THEMSELVES."

"SEVEN years, by Jove!" said Sir Geoffrey, pacing the length and breadth of Mr. Gayre's dining-room, his head sunk on his breast, his hands clasped behind his back. "Seven years! Good God Almighty!" and the Baronet, in a vague sort of way, fell to considering what he, Geoffrey Chelston, could have made of seven long years spent in penal servitude, had the Gayres dealt with him "according to law."

"Seven years without drink or dice or pretty barmaids—without flats or cheats, or horses or racecourses—with no society save the dumb company of those who had been 'found out'—with the shape of his head and ears too painfully defined—clad in a suit for which no tailor could ever dun him—forced to go to bed with that silly creature the lamb, and compelled to rise with that greater nuisance and greater fool still the lark—obliged to go to church, and knuckle down to the chaplain, and eat, begad, any beastly stuff a rascally Radical Government elected to thrust down the throat of gentlemen in trouble—a damned lot!"

Thus the tenth Baronet, who had put his name and ancestry and title and money out to such extraordinary interest, stung into mental activity by the fact of so severe a sentence being passed upon a man who had not shaved the wind one whit closer than himself, regarded the "might have been" of his own case, while ostensibly considering the sore plight of that "unlucky devil," Oliver Dane.

"It all comes of keeping a fellow too tight," went on the Baronet, talking to Mr. Gayre as though the banker were an utter tyro in the ways of this wicked but pleasant old world. "A man must have his fling some time, and if he hasn't it early he'll take it late. 'Pon my soul, I'm as sorry for Dane as if he were my own brother! It's a deuced hard case. I am sure I said all I could for him. Had he been my father I couldn't have sworn harder, and yet I feel as though I were in some sort to blame—as if I might have said more, you know. I declare, Gayre, to my dying day I shall never forget his cry, ' I am innocent !' "

"But he was not innocent," objected Mr. Gayre.

"I am not so sure of that: standing almost in the presence of his Maker, as one may say ; for seven years' penal servitude in this world appears to me far more like eternity, and a very bad eternity, than walking over the border into a land the parsons seem to think will be made pleasant for most of us who are not hardened and desperate ruffians—a well-connected and respectable young fellow like Dane—Heavens ! I remember him quite a little lad running about in knickerbockers—would be scarcely likely to tell a lie."

"No one could have felt more sure of his guilt than yourself," said the banker angrily ; "what is the use of talking in this strain now ?"

"None—not a bit ; and that's just what makes me take the whole thing so much to heart. Innocent or guilty, such a sentence is enough to make a man, if he had not the very strongest faith—which, thank God ! I have—turn atheist. Seven years cut clean out of a fellow's life ! Better have hung him at once. Could that old fool of a judge understand what seven years of penal servitude means to a gentleman well born, well bred, well connected ? I feel as if I'd like to go and assault somebody—I might get the case ventilated then. And then there's poor dear Susan breaking her soft tender heart ; and, as I told her this morning, I am only able to stand like a brute and do nothing ; and then what d'ye think she did ?"

"Thanked you for your sympathy, I have no doubt."

"She never said a word. She just came up to me, and put her arms round my neck and kissed me, and laid her pretty head on my shoulder and cried like a child. I am a rough and tumble sort of chap, and nobody ever suggested there was any gammon or sentiment about Geoffrey Chelston ; but, upon my soul, Gayre,"—and the unsentimental Baronet, instead of finishing his sentence, fetched a deep breath. "A woman like Susan Drummond can make what she will of a man," he went on, "hand in hand with her, a fellow need never wish to wander out of that path to heaven which we are told is so confoundedly narrow and straight."

"I never heard the path was straight," remarked Mr. Gayre, "though I fancy many persons find it so."

"Hang it all, you need not take me up so short ! Besides,

I gave the spirit of the text, and surely that's enough. And as for Susan, narrow or straight, or both, she'd lead the worst sinner that ever lived to the happy land school-children sing about. Faith, it was very pretty to hear them at Chelston, Gayre; poor Margaret used—"

"Miss Drummond does not seem to have been able to lead her particular sinner to a very happy land, in this world, at all events," said Mr. Gayre, ruthlessly cutting across his brother-in-law's pastoral reminiscences.

"Now don't be ironical," entreated Sir Geoffrey.

"Ironical! Good gracious!"

"Well, ironical, or sarcastic, or what you choose, you were sneering at Dane, you know you were, and it's not kind to sneer at a fellow who has got into hot water and been badly scalded."

"I don't know what you mean," returned Mr. Gayre. "I suppose we have all a right to express an opinion, and when a man embezzles and forges—"

"Well, you need not be hard on him; and you are much harder than I like to see—you are, Gayre, upon my conscience."

"And upon *my* conscience," retorted the banker, "I utterly fail to understand the drift of all your profound remarks. It is impossible, in the face of the evidence you heard yesterday, for you or any man to believe Dane innocent, and, being guilty, he deserves punishment. Seven years is a heavy sentence, no doubt, but employers *must* be protected. Supposing you left your purse on that table, and a housemaid stole it, would you give her a sovereign and entreat her to remain in your service? You know you would not; you would send for the nearest policeman and give her in charge—"

"I'd do nothing of the sort," interrupted the Baronet. "She should never have a chance of robbing me again, but—"

"You would give her a chance to rob somebody else," suggested Mr. Gayre.

"I'd rather do that than lock her up," said Sir Geoffrey, standing to his guns. "I do not believe in all this law and lawyer business, and punishing and deterring and the rest of it. If a fellow goes wrong, give him a chance of doing right. How can any one get right working like a navvy at Portland? Supposing these two City Solons had left Dane free, and let him repay their money, it would have been better for everybody, themselves included."

"In that case, he might have married Miss Drummond, and lived happily ever after," sneered Mr. Gayre.

"I shouldn't have gone so far as that," answered the Baronet. "And, indeed, I doubt if Susan would have wished to marry him; now she does; that's the first effect of his lordship's sentence. The girl considers her lover a martyr, which brings me to what I particularly wanted to say. For Heaven's sake, Gayre, don't hurt her feelings by speaking as if you thought him guilty! If you do, she'll hate you for ever. There is no manner of use in reasoning with a woman—women can't reason any more than they can grill a steak. Let Susan have her way. If she likes to believe Dane innocent, it won't do you or me any harm. Soothing is the way to treat such a wound. If any likely young fellow were about, now would be his chance; no time for winning a girl's heart so good as when it has just been broken, and while her eyes are still wet with crying! Gad! I mayn't know much about the business world and money and so forth, but I do understand women! Though I am not as young as I used to be, if I were single I'd engage to have Susan Drummond for wife in three months."

"Upon the whole it is fortunate for her that you are not single," remarked Mr. Gayre.

"O, I don't mean to say that I should wish to marry Susan," returned Sir Geoffrey; "only that I know I could. We should not suit each other in the least. I'd drive her mad; and she —well, fact is, Susan would be a bit too good for me. She ought to run in harness with some steady fellow, who does not drink or gamble, who has not been driven half mad with trouble, and compelled to pick up a wretched living as I am. I'd like to see her married to some excellent man she could be proud of—rich, respectable, that sort of thing; what I never can be now, Gayre. It would be an awful business if she made a mistake a second time. Just fancy her tied for life to a sulky beggar like Lal Hilderton, or to such an infernal cad as your friend Sudlow!" Having planted which sting in his brother-in-law's soul, Sir Geoffrey walked to the sideboard, and refreshed himself with about half a tumbler of Chartreuse that had been produced for his especial benefit, as he said he felt deucedly queer, and could think of nothing so likely to pull him together a bit.

"I don't know what I am to do with Sudlow," he began, after partaking of this moderate draught. "He's as shy of those settlements as if they were a ten-foot wall. I bring him up to them again and again, but he always refuses the leap. Now it's this, now it's the other; something has been left out, or something has been put in. He goes to my lawyers; for I can't have him bothering me, and he won't, he declares, incur the expense of letting his own solicitor arrange the matter— I am sure he is afraid the attorney would sell him—goes to my lawyers, and argues each point with them. Heaven only knows who is to pay the piper. I know I sha'n't be able."

"And I really don't think Sudlow will," said Mr. Gayre.

"Things are getting deucedly awkward. I must give up Moreby's crib ere long. His mother's legal adviser says I may rent the place on, if I choose to pay in advance, but that he cannot advise his client to permit the present unsatisfactory arrangements to continue, and be blanked to him. Then I am all at sea as to what I am to do about Maggie. Clearly Sudlow mustn't be hanging round the house while the girl is alone in it; and I can't be mewed up in North Bank for ever. If I am to stop at home all day, the pot would soon cease boiling. You must see yourself it is of no earthly use trying to get 'companions;' they won't stop; money won't make them— love might. I believe old mother Morris expected I would propose for her. It's deucedly awkward, confoundedly awkward. I've looked at the position from, I think, every possible and impossible point of view, and the more I think the more satisfied I feel there is but one course open, and that is making things up with Margaret."

"Well, of course, you know your own business best," said Mr. Gayre, who understood whither all this was tending.

"There are few men who would propose such a plan," said Sir Geoffrey, helping himself to a little more Chartreuse; "but I do not profess to be led by popular opinion. My notions are not worldly, but I hope they are Christian. Dear, dear, when I look back to the old times, and think of Margaret and the Pleasaunce! Ah! she was a lovely young creature, Gayre, and nobody can deny the Pleasaunce was as sweet a spot as ever a set of rascally Jews got hold of! Lord! when I shut my eyes I can see her standing beside one of the windows in the great drawing-room at Chelston, framed in a tracery of leaves and roses, the red in her cheeks pink as the roses, and her forehead white as her dress. The fairest picture: the quaint old furniture and the sweet young bride. Ah, the house is dismantled, and Margaret gone! Many a man has hung himself for less, Gayre."

"It is not a particularly agreeable theme for Margaret's brother," observed the banker.

"Rough on you," agreed Sir Geoffrey, "deucedly rough. Hard for me—harder for you. Impossible to wash such a stain clean out of any family; and to think that the cowardly fellow escaped without having to pay even a farthing damages!"

"It would not have benefited Margaret much if he had," said Mr. Gayre, who knew into whose pocket the damages would have found their way.

"The more I think over the matter, the more satisfied I feel Peggy and her mother ought to be together," declared Sir Geoffrey, ignoring his brother-in-law's remark.

Mr. Gayre also was aware when it was prudent to maintain silence, and discreetly held his peace.

"Have you thought over what I said to you a little while since?" asked the Baronet, finding this astute fish declined to "rise."

"What did you say? Put your idea into plain words."

"You might help a man a little, more especially when he is making such an offer as I am making now. Hang it! if Margaret were *my* sister, and *you*, her wronged husband, were proposing to let bygones be bygones, and have her back, you could not take things more coolly than you are doing."

"I do not feel elated, if that is what you mean," said Mr. Gayre.

"Well, of all the cold, bloodless fellows I ever met," Sir Geoffrey was beginning, when a look in the banker's face warned him to desist. "We can't be *all* alike, however," he added in a tone of bland apology for the fact.

"We can't all be Geoffrey Chelstons, if that is what you mean," agreed the banker.

"We can't be all Gayres either. Gad, in many ways I wish we could. But now to revert to Margaret. You would like the past to be forgotten, eh?"

"It cannot be undone."

"That's true; but where's the use of harping upon that? It would gratify you to know your sister had resumed her old position and rank, and so forth, eh?"

"I don't know that it would. There is an old proverb about letting sleeping dogs lie. Were Margaret to return to England, many sleeping dogs in the country would wake up and begin snarling at her."

"O no, they wouldn't. Scarce a soul ever knew the rights

of that affair. I am sure, Gayre, even you must say no man could have kept stricter silence than I."

"Whatever your reason may have been for holding your tongue, I never found fault with you for doing so," returned Mr. Gayre dryly.

"That's City all over. I wonder if you would have made such a speech while you were in the thick of the dashing fellows who saved India for us? But never mind, I know you better than you know yourself, and feel quite sure business has not really spoiled one I can remember as generous and trustful and enthusiastic a young man as ever wore her Majesty's uniform."

Mr. Gayre did not answer this bitter-sweet encomium. Once again Sir Geoffrey had touched the raw, as that worthy understood.

"Well, well," he said, "we can't be hard-hearted men of the world, and keep the soft tender hearts of boyhood in our breasts, too. Still, thank Heaven, all I have gone through has not made me cast iron. I can't forget, though you do. I wish we could have been more like brothers, Gayre. I'm an unfortunate devil, I know; but I always was fond of you, and misfortune is not crime. I did think you would be pleased at my notion about Margaret—poor misguided soul! However, of course, I can't expect you to see with my eyes; so Peggy and I must do the best we can for ourselves, and that best will be bad enough. Good-bye. Heaven only knows when I shall see you again. I hope you may always be prosperous, and never know what it is to hunger for a kind word or look, and get neither;" with which Christian aspiration, that sounded uncommonly like a curse, Sir Geoffrey was turning towards the door, when Mr. Gayre stopped him.

"Wait a moment, Chelston," he said. "Don't go yet."

The banker was standing before the fire, looking into its glowing depths, and did not see the smile which overspread Sir Geoffrey's face as he paused to ask,

"Well, what is it now?"

"That is what I wish to know," answered Mr. Gayre. "Why can't you tell me in so many plain words exactly what you want? If you know anything about me, you ought to understand the sort of talk in which you have been indulging is completely wasted. I despise flattery as much as I distrust sentimentality. You never liked one of us; you thought we might serve your turn. As for Margaret, a pert serving-wench would have found more favour in your eyes than my sister. I declare," added the banker, in a burst of fury, "when I think of all Margaret suffered at your hands, I hate myself for ever having crossed your threshold again, or eaten your bread, or let my hand touch yours in amity."

"You know I can't hit back, Gayre; and it really was deucedly good of you to forget old grievances—utterly imaginary, upon my soul—for the sake of Peggy."

A dull red line, like a band, came slowly across Mr. Gayre's forehead. Perhaps he was conscious of that tell-tale mark, for he never turned towards Geoffrey as he answered,

"I would have done a good deal for my sister's daughter, but I find that daughter almost as impracticable and selfish as yourself. I don't know what can be done for her."

"Don't you? If you chose to give Peggy a fortune, no man would find her waste it in making presents, for example."

"But I *don't* choose to give her a fortune."

"I know you don't; you are far too like her to do anything of the sort. I was only remarking, if you tried the experiment of giving Peggy any of this world's goods, you'd find she'd take deucedly good care of number one. She can make a pound go further than I could five. Faith! spite of her beauty and the long line of ancestry she is able to claim on my side, I often think it would be a pity to spoil two houses with her and Sudlow. There is a regular trade smack about the girl at times which positively amazes me. It just shows that what's bred in the bone, you know—"

"Where is all this tending?" interrupted Mr. Gayre.

"I don't know that it is tending anywhere except to lodgings at fifteen shillings a week and good-bye to Sudlow," answered Sir Geoffrey. "I had better be going, Gayre. I am confoundedly sorry I came."

"What is the amount of annual income over and above the sum I allow my sister you require to set up house with Lady Chelston at the head of affairs? Remember, I promise nothing. I do not even know that Margaret would return to you; if she did, I fail to understand what is to be said to her daughter concerning a mother she believes died long and long ago. Still, I should like to know your price; you came to tell me that price; out with it, man."

"Well, as you force me to say, I think ten thousand pounds down, and five hundred a year for Margaret's and my life, at

our death to go then to Peggy, would be just to me and not
unfair to you."

"Just to *you!*" repeated Mr. Gayre.

"I don't expect you to think much about the justice to
me," replied Sir Geoffrey equably. "Why should you? Why
should a rich man consider a poor one? Why should you,
who have always been first favourite with Fortune, think for a
moment about an out-at-elbows fellow like myself? The ball
is at your foot, not at mine; play it, knock me over! Only
deal kindly with Margaret and the girl, and I am content to
hang on to life by my eyelids as I am doing now, till a pauper's
grave receives all that is mortal of the tenth Baronet of
Chelston."

"As for ten thousand pounds down, I won't give you a
thousand pence."

"Then I needn't detain you longer. I am sorry I mentioned the matter at all, only I thought, and still think, Margaret is the proper person to take charge of her child. No
one but a mother can see to a girl, and I'd have made things
as pleasant as possible. I'd have stopped out of her way
except when it was necessary for me to enter an appearance.
I'd have left Margaret and Peggy to manage matters just as
they liked, and only put in a word if asked to do so. You
and your sister could have selected a residence to suit her;
bless you! though I make no fuss or pretence, I'm full of consideration. I'd have left her as free as air. If she ever wanted
to ask a few friends, she could have sent out the invitations as
if from Sir Geoffrey and Lady Chelston; and I'd have come
up to time. Of course I understood, after the way she had
treated me, she might feel more comfortable if I were not constantly at hand to remind her of the past. Poor dear soul!
She couldn't help being a simpleton, I daresay, but still—"

"Sir Geoffrey, will you have the kindness to leave my
house?"

Mr. Gayre was almost beside himself with rage.

"Certainly, certainly," answered Sir Geoffrey, with the
greatest equanimity. "If you don't mind, I'll just have
another sip of that Chartreuse, and then I'll be off."

"Finish the bottle if you like," said Mr. Gayre, who knew
the Baronet was certain to do so without his permission.

"Thankee, I will; there's not much left;" and Sir Geoffrey,
having exactly filled his tumbler with the precious liquor, and,
in an easy affable way, drained its contents to the last drop,

nodded to Mr. Gayre and walked out of the room. Next moment, however, he reappeared.

"I say, Gayre," he began, putting his remarkable head inside the door, "you've treated me deucedly badly to-day, I consider; but still, hang it, if blood is thicker than water, a brother-in-law is a brother-in-law; so I thought I'd just come back and give you a bit of a hint. It's not very likely you'll ever see Peggy again—for I'm sure your friend the cad, upon whom we've wasted such a lot of valuable time, will never be got over that rasping settlement fence, and I'll have to start the girl out as nursery-governess or lady-help, or something of that sort—still if you ever should, don't tell her that you think Dane guilty. Though she is my daughter, she's as nasty and venomous a little toad as ever held the making of a truly respectable and conventional woman. She'd tell Susan instantly. Poor Susan! Now, there is breed. The Drummonds never married beneath them—never."

"Not even into the Mrs. Arbery clique," suggested Mr. Gayre.

Sir Geoffrey was out on the doorstep ere the banker had got half through this sentence, and before it ended had crossed the street and was sauntering along the kerb, shaking his head with repressed delight, and smiling to such an extent, the few persons he met turned to look back after his retreating figure.

"That sprat will catch that herring," he decided. "I'll screw fifteen hundred perhaps out of him, and he'll make Margaret's allowance a thousand a year. It will be a wonderful relief to me. I sha'n't then care a snap of my fingers whether Sudlow marries Peggy or not; I should never be a penny the better if she did."

Sir Geoffrey's spirit of prophecy proved in many respects correct. Mr. Gayre's first determination was, indeed, to sever the whole connection; but eventually calmer thought prevailed. He could not blind himself to the truth that it would be making the best of a bad business to adopt his brother-in-law's suggestion, and place "Peg" under her mother's care. He had no intention of paying a large sum in order to effect the needful reconciliation, but he would be willing to pay something. It was easy enough to resume outwardly friendly relations with Sir Geoffrey, who never took offence unless he meant to make a profit by doing so. A hint was given to Lady Chelston of the happiness which might be in store; and had her husband been the best man living, she could scarcely have expressed greater thankfulness for his generosity or more fervent hope that nothing might occur to prevent the proposed arrangement being carried out. Sir Geoffrey walked jauntily about London with so jubilant a manner people imagined he must have had a fortune left to him. Even Mr. Sudlow began to feel satisfied some extraordinary piece of luck had fallen in the Baronet's way, and yielded a point in the settlements, over which there had been ceaseless wrangling. Mrs. Moreby's lawyer and several rather pressing creditors were quieted and satisfied without that awkward business the exchange of money, and things seemed to be going almost—to quote Sir Geoffrey's own words —" too smooth," when one evening, while he was sitting over his wine with a few choice spirits he had invited to a " quiet dinner and rubber to follow," Lavender appeared, carrying a telegram on one of Mr. Moreby's salvers.

Unwitting of evil, the Baronet cut open the envelope, and with a bland " Excuse me," read :

" *Margaret died this afternoon, very suddenly. I start for France by night mail.*"

"'Talk about Job !" thought Sir Geoffrey ; but, with suppressed and creditable emotion, he said aloud, " This," and he touched the telegram, " announces the death of one very near and dear to me. Gentlemen, will you excuse me, and make yourselves at home ? I shall just have time to catch the express to Dover. Lavender, a hansom, quick, with a horse that can go. O, I have no gold ! Can anybody lend me five pounds ? Thank you, very much."

And the Baronet was gone to bid good-bye to Peggy.

CHAPTER XXII.

THE WIDOWER.

At his wife's funeral Sir Geoffrey developed quite a new accomplishment. HE WEPT! Circumstances had kept him compulsorily sober; and sobriety did what brandy never could have done—made him maudlin. Mr. Gayre did not believe in his brother-in-law's tears, yet he felt touched by them. They fell like rain; they were to be seen of all men. The undertaker, who knew his money to be safe, was quite affected, and afterwards spoke of Sir Geoffrey's emotion as "most creditable to all parties." In gloomy silence the Baronet, thinking of what might have been, and of what, indeed, was so near being, stood and looked at the changed calm face of his once beautiful wife. He could not have shed a tear then—he explained that he felt turned into stone—had the whole of the money in Gayres' bank been offered to him as the price of that precious crystal; but in the watches of the night, which, contrary to custom, he was forced to spend in bed, "tossing and turning and burnt up with a consuming thirst, begad!" he evolved a brilliant idea, which he confided to his brother-in-law next morning.

"Look here, Gayre," he began. "I wonder why we can't have sensible breakfasts like this in England, instead of that eternal tea or coffee which plays the very deuce with a man's nerves and digestion. That is not what I was going to say to you, though. I didn't get a wink of sleep last night—couldn't sleep, you know. All the past rushed back upon me like a wave—well, well, it's no use talking about last year's snow—and it came into my head that you'd like to have Margaret laid at Chelston. Of course everything is gone; but I fancy I could manage that matter. As for me, one place will be as good as another—where the tree falls, you know (a most inapt simile, because as a rule the tree is never allowed to lie long anywhere). But I do think if the poor girl could speak, she would say, 'Lay me at Chelston!' Lord, when I think of her trotting about at Christmastide, with a present for this one and something for the other, I feel as if my heart would break; I do, upon my soul, Gayre!" And the Baronet walked out of the room, ostensibly to hide his emotion, but really to consider at leisure the extent to which Mr. Gayre would "fork out" for the glory and privilege of having his sister buried among "decent people."

There is an intuition, which seems to be the exclusive birthright of dogs, children, women, fools, and scoundrels, that serves its purpose better than any exhaustive line of argument. This intuition Sir Geoffrey possessed to its fullest extent, and through it he understood his brother-in-law would at length rise to the bait offered. In good earnest Sir Geoffrey could have made no proposition more grateful to the banker's feelings. If Lady Chelston were once laid to rest amongst her husband's kindred, the world might say its worst, and still be checkmated. If Sir Geoffrey made the arrangements for her funeral; if his friends attended it; if he, for once, donning a black hat instead of a white one, appeared as chief mourner, Mr. Gayre felt he could for ever after snap his fingers in the face of Mrs. Grundy. The best he had ever hoped was to lay his poor, erring, and doubly-sinned-against sister in some quiet grave in a strange country and amongst a strange people; but now the prospect opened fairly amazed him. Of course he knew he would have to pay in meal or in malt for that niche in the Chelston vault; but he was willing to pay for it. Sir Geoffrey had touched everything that was weakest and most vulnerable in his nature.

"Poor Margaret!—poor dear child! If she could know, she would like it," he thought; and the long years of trial and shame and sorrow and seclusion faded away from memory, and in fancy he once again saw his little sister running races with him up and down the stairs, and along the halls and passages of his father's house and the house occupied by Mr. Higgs. He could hear the swish of the stiffly-starched white dress, and the pitter-patter of the tiny feet; behold once again the flutter of a light-blue sash, and feel the long curls touch his cheek, as, with a laugh and a bound, she rushed out upon him from some unsuspected ambuscade.

And there, still and cold, in an upper chamber, lay all that remained of the little sister grown to womanhood, who had made what they all once thought so great a match; who had suffered horribly and sinned grievously, and repented in the sackcloth of loneliness and the ashes of isolation, and to whom he had not perhaps been so kind as he might, and visited less frequently than he cared to remember. And life was over for her; and he could have made it happier. And yes, certainly, if it were possible to bring her to Chelston, she should lie there, though all the stately matrons and discreet widows and tender virgins mouldering to dust turned in their coffins with righteous indignation when this poor frail sinner was carried into the last earthly home the portals of which might ever open for her.

"You will want money," said Mr. Gayre to the Baronet, whose chronic state it was to stand in need of that necessary article.

But Sir Geoffrey knew when to hold his hand as truly as he knew when to reap, and at first refused to take the cheque Mr. Gayre had already drawn.

"Leave it, leave it, my boy," he said, with a spasm intended to act the manly part of indicating the emotion he was strong enough to repress; "time enough to spare for all that when we know for certain if our darling can rest where I want to lay her. If I am able to do that for her, I sha'n't feel so utterly miserable. It's all I can try to do, Gayre. And now I ought to be off at once. By the way, d'ye happen to have any loose gold about you? Lord, how money does sift away, at a time like this! No, no, no; I don't want a twenty-pound note. Can't you give me anything less?"

If Mr. Gayre could, he would not.

"Keep it," he said; "you don't know what you may need."

"Faith, no!" exclaimed Sir Geoffrey, struck by a sudden thought. "I had to borrow a fiver last night, or I couldn't have come. Well, good-bye, Gayre; and I'll wire you directly I have seen Wookes—that's the name of the fellow who has Chelston now."

"One moment. Don't you think—shouldn't you like—" suggested the dead woman's brother almost timidly.

"My dear fellow, a thousand thanks! I had forgotten—I had, upon my soul—what might—what, indeed, must—happen before it would be possible for me to return. Poor, poor Margaret! poor sweet dear!" And the Baronet, who had earnestly hoped he might be spared another look at that face he never saw in life cold and statuesque, took off his hat, and laying it on the table, lest he might, from sheer force of habit, cover his head again even in the death chamber ("which would play the very devil," he considered), ran his fingers through his hair, put on the most solemn expression at his command—and the Baronet's expression could not, as a rule, be described as jocund—and intimated to Mr. Gayre he was ready.

"Perhaps," said the banker, "you would prefer to go up-stairs alone."

"No, no, not at all. Why should not we—the only two who seem to have cared for her—stand beside her together? And you know, Gayre, I *must* leave her to your care."

As if, under any possible combination of circumstances, Sir Geoffrey would have been induced to remain sole, or indeed any, guardian at all of the "poor pale" thing laid helpless on its last bed up-stairs!

In that sacred chamber the Baronet did all, and indeed more than all, man could expect from man. He kissed the mask of life there stretched so stiff and stark; he touched the clay-cold hands; he severed with the aid of a convenient pair of scissors—which, indeed, suggested the idea to him—a lock of hair once golden, but now plentifully sprinkled with gray.

"Lord, Lord!" said Sir Geoffrey, in severe expostulation with the Deity, "that we should come to this! On such an occasion what *can* any trumpery laches on the part of a man or woman matter?" After which magnanimous query the widower left the room, made his way down-stairs, secured his hat, and, grasping Mr. Gayre by the hand, departed in the most cheerful spirits, producing a great effect on all the persons he met by his lugubrious countenance and the persistent manner in which he shook his head, as though he had tried a wrestle with grief and been sorely worsted in the struggle.

No man was perhaps ever more astonished than Mr. Sudlow when he read in the *Times* the death of "Margaret, wife of Sir Geoffrey Chelston, Bart., deeply lamented by her sorrowing and affectionate husband." He was so much astounded, indeed, that he found it necessary to call at North Bank, where there was no one to receive him except Lavender, from whom he failed to extract any save the most ordinary answers.

"He had known Lady Chelston—yes, well; he remembered her home-coming and the great doings at the Pleasaunce. She was a beautiful lady—more beautiful, according to Mr. Lavender's ideas, if he might say so without offence, even than Miss Chelston. Her married life, he thought he might go so far as to confess, could not have been a happy one. You know Sir Geoffrey, sir," Lavender proceeded to remark, "and it is not all ladies who could make allowance for his ways. Any-

how, they didn't agree, and they lived apart. It was better for
married folk to live apart if they didn't live happily together.
The Baronet was gone down to Chelston to arrange about
the funeral. None but intimate friends were to be present
(and something in the man's manner informed Mr. Sudlow he
was not going to be asked, and that Lavender knew it). Miss
Chelston (who at that moment of speaking happened to be
up-stairs closeted with her dressmaker) was out of town. Her
grief was terrible ; though she had not seen her ladyship for
years, still, in Lavender's opinion, a mother was a mother, and,
as Mr. Sudlow put the question so straight, he did not think
Sir Geoffrey ought to have kept his daughter all to himself as
he had done. Latterly there had been a talk of Miss Chelston
living for part of the year with her mamma. Lavender had
always heard Lady Chelston was a great heiress ; most likely
her fortune would come to her daughter, but even Lavender's
wisdom could not tell exactly how that might be ;" and then
Mr. Lavender, with a grave face and sad subdued manner,
shut the gate after Mr. Sudlow, and went back into the house,
and had a laugh with his wife over the suitor's discomfiture.

" I can't abear him," said Mrs. Lavender.

" Nor me," agreed Lavender ; " but he's better than nobody,
I suppose, and I do hear he's rolling in riches."

Meantime Mr. Gayre had returned to England, and in the
large dining-room of his house in Wimpole Street his sister's
body lay ready for burial. For several reasons Mr. Moreby's
villa seemed ineligible for so rare a purpose, and it scarcely
needed Sir Geoffrey's hint that any day the bailiffs might
enter into possession, which " would be confoundedly awkward,
you know," to decide the banker as to the course he should
pursue.

" Sorrowing and affectionate," considered Mr. Gayre, reading the announcement in the *Times.* " I daresay ! And now
Sir Geoffrey Chelston, Baronet, who so deeply laments his
dead wife, is eligible once again, what will he do with this
chance, I wonder ?"

Sir Geoffrey could have told him that the first thing he
meant to do was to offer himself and title to Mrs. Jubbins ;
but his *rôle* was to keep up the semblance of distracted grief
for poor Margaret, and no man understood the beauty and
wisdom of silence better than the bereaved husband. So far
grief had returned him excellent interest. Mr. Wookes instantly
placed, not merely the family vault, but also Chelston Plea-

saunce, at his service. Mrs. Wookes, and the young person
Sir Geoffrey with a deep sigh styled her "lovely daughter,"
were introduced to the worthy Baronet. Mr. Wookes spoke of
him as "my afflicted friend," and he was earnestly requested
to stop and partake of "some refreshment," which, under an
immense delusion, he certainly would have done, had he not
been compelled to hurry off to catch the afternoon express.

"There are so many things to see to at such a time," he
said; and Mrs. Wookes sighed, "Ah, yes, there are!" and
Miss Wookes stared at him hard with wide-open colourless
eyes; and Mr. Wookes insisted he and Mr. Gayre should
come down the evening before the funeral and stay the night;
and "whenever you feel disposed to stop with us, I can assure
you, Sir Geoffrey, both Mrs. Wookes and myself will give you
a hearty welcome," added Mr. Wookes, who, though truly
pious, would have welcomed Lucifer himself had he come with
a handle to his name.

"I really do not know how to thank you sufficiently," answered Sir Geoffrey, in his best manner, which Mrs. Wookes
often subsequently defined as "courtly," though she might
have employed a different word had the Baronet been a tutor.
"My daughter will be delighted when she hears I met with
such a reception at her old home."

"How is Miss Chelston?" instantly inquired Mr. Wookes.

"She is dreadfully cut up, poor thing, of course," explained Sir Geoffrey. "Still, she tries not to let me see all
she feels."

Then Mr. Wookes, in a grand pompous voice, immediately
said, "My dear;" and Mrs. Wookes understanding observed,
"Yes, I was just about to remark that if dear Miss Chelston
thought a change to so quiet a place would do her good, we
should feel honoured by a visit;" after which amenities, Sir
Geoffrey took a hurried leave, and entered the conveyance
waiting for him; first, *sotto voce*, desiring the coachman to
"drive to Chelston Station like the ——."

There is no time probably which passes so slowly as that
intervening between a death and a funeral; but at length the
interval was well-nigh bridged over by a succession of weary
hours; and the evening arrived when Mr. Wookes was to be
gratified with the presence of his "distinguished" guest, and
that guest's less distinguished brother-in law.

"I hope they've some decent wine," said Sir Geoffrey, as
the gates swung wide to welcome the visitors. "He looks

like an old boy who knows what's what, and the cellars here
are first-rate."

"It might have been prudent to bring some cognac with
you," suggested Mr. Gayre, with a fine sneer.

"O, I'll square the butler!" answered Sir Geoffrey amiably;
and then he looked out of the carriage-window and shook his
head, and remarked his heart was well-nigh broken, by ——, it
was! to think poor Margaret was not to be carried from the
house which properly belonged to her. "It may be partly my
own fault. I was always too easy and generous, and never
thought enough of myself; but, gad, that makes it no plea-
santer to see a place like this owned by a fellow who made his
money out of tallow, and to have to ask leave to bury my wife
in my own vault, cap in hand, like a railway porter;" which
recital of misfortunes was ended by their arrival at the house,
where Mr. Wookes in person appeared at the door to greet
them, and to tell Mr. Gayre how delighted he felt to welcome
any relation of his "esteemed friend Sir Geoffrey Chelston."

"You'd like a cup of tea, perhaps, before you go up to
dress," he said, with genial hospitality. "I always find a cup
of tea so refreshing after a railway journey. There was a
time when I would have proposed a glass of wine; but we've
changed all that—we are strict abstainers."

"And so not merely virtuous yourselves, but the cause of
virtue in others," observed Mr. Gayre, scarcely able to repress
a smile at the sight of his brother-in-law's discomfiture. For a
moment, indeed, Sir Geoffrey was too deeply indignant to
speak; but he regained his presence of mind during the course
of some didactic remarks from Mr. Wookes concerning the
prevalence of drunkenness, and the importance of the upper
classes setting an example of temperance to the masses.

"You are quite right, Mr. Wookes," agreed the Baronet,
who had already set his wits to work to consider how he could
get some brandy "or—or anything, by Jove," from Chelston.
"People do drink far too much—and eat too," added Sir
Geoffrey as a happy after-thought, feeling he was clear of the
vice of gluttony, at any rate.

Mr. Wookes reddened. He liked to see a good table,
and to partake plentifully of what he called "God's mercies"
spread upon it.

"As for eating," he observed, "though we cannot deny
that it is a sin to indulge any appetite to excess, still I consider that a moderate pleasure in and use of the bounties so

lavishly provided for our benefit are not crimes. You see, my dear sir," and he laid a fat pudgy hand affectionately on Sir Geoffrey's arm, " the difference is this—fish, flesh, and fowl, vegetables of all sorts, and sweets at discretion, do not cause quarrelling and murders; whereas spirits—and under the general head of spirits I include all sorts of wine—*Won't* you have a cup of tea?" he broke off to ask, feeling, perhaps, his arguments might seem a little lengthy to hungry and thirsty men.

"Thank you; I should like one greatly," answered Mr. Gayre.

" And I'd like a glass of *water*," declared the Baronet desperately, " to lay the dust. My throat is as dry as a London street in summer."

"Ah! that's because you are in such trouble," sympathetically said Mr. Wookes, who knew as well as possible Sir Geoffrey was one of the hardest drinkers in England, and who would have liked to offer him champagne had his new principles not been dearer to him even than a title.

They were, indeed, as new as his possession of the Pleasaunce, and he had been frightened into them by the sudden decease of a brother, who died, as one City wag expressed the matter to another, " of forgetting to put any water in his grog."

There is no bigot like a convert (pervert Sir Geoffrey would have said), and Mr. and Mrs. Wookes were already anxious to begin the holy labour of washing this Ethiop white. They belonged to the straitest sect : not a pint of beer was allowed about the premises; dinners were cooked, and horses driven, and tables set, and fruit forced, and gardens kept in order on the strictest teetotal lines. The lodge-keepers drank nothing stronger than milk ("like babes and sucklings," said the Baronet afterwards, in accents of the deepest disgust); no labourers were employed who refused to give up malt liquor. Indeed, Mr. Wookes had drawn such a cordon of sobriety round his domain that when Sir Geoffrey, during the course of the evening, made an excuse for stealing out, he found the very beerhouse in the little village hard by had been closed, and the premises converted into a coffee-tavern.

" Well, I'm blanked !" he thought; and, making the best of a bad bargain, decided he would go back and render himself agreeable to " old mother" Wookes, and get something definite settled about Peggy's visit to the Pleasaunce.

This was how he chanced to be "fasting from everything

but sin," when he attended his wife's funeral, and shed those tears that excited the surprise and won the admiration of all beholders.

"Tell you what, Gayre," he said, as they returned together to London, "another day in that house would have killed me. It was inhuman too, under the circumstances—downright inhuman, and confoundedly impertinent into the bargain. A man has a right perhaps to play tricks with his own constitution, but he has no right to try to leave another man with no stomach to speak of. *I* shouldn't force a fellow who came to my house to drink against his will. Why should I be compelled to swallow gallons of cold water?—bad as a drench, begad! Why, you see yourself the effect it had upon me. Whatever I might feel—and, as a rule, people haven't thought I felt much—they were mistaken, though—I could control myself; but I give you my word, Gayre, I am still as shaky as possible. I could cry like a woman now. It was an awful ordeal! But the poor dear, could she have seen, would, I think, have understood I bore no malice, and that I loved her to the last—I did, upon my soul!" And the Baronet once again took to weeping so profusely his brother-in-law began anxiously to examine the time-table, to see how soon they might hope to reach a "civilised station," to quote Sir Geoffrey, "where stimulants could be procured."

"I'm a fool," said the widower, wiping his red eyes, "an utter idiot; but the whole thing has been too much for me. I do think all the people behaved splendidly. Fancy, even old Dane coming—though, perhaps, that was as much to prove he didn't care about his grandson being in gaol as to show respect to Margaret's memory."

"He looks a dreadful old man," observed Mr. Gayre, wisely passing over his brother-in-law's final suggestion.

"He looks what he is. Only to think of that poor young fellow having to break stones, or carry stones, or whatever it may be, for seven long years at Portland, and this old wretch gloating over the guineas he can't take out of the world with him, and that might have saved the lad! Why such things should be allowed baffles me! And that dear poor Susan coming down here to ask him to help get up a petition, or a memorial, or something of the sort, and the wretch as good as shutting the door in her face! Drummond told me about it at the station just now. Give you my word, I scarcely knew how to contain myself."

"What can you mean?" asked Mr. Gayre; "what is Miss Drummond doing?"

"As I understand, the solicitor who acted for young Dane told her if she got a whole lot of influential people to sign a paper, and forwarded it to one or other of the big wigs, she might get the sentence commuted. I don't believe a word of it myself; but still the notion may serve to comfort her a bit till the worst of the trouble had worn off. One thing, however, I am sure of—the girl oughtn't to be going about herself asking for signatures. I wish I had time and money to take such a labour off her hands;" and the Baronet looked hard at Mr. Gayre, who, after a few moments' silence, said,

"I think I am the person to help Miss Drummond now."

"You're the best fellow living, Gayre!" exclaimed Sir Geoffrey, giving his brother-in-law such a slap on the shoulder that the banker winced. "I always said it, and I always thought it, spite of some few angularities—and which of us is perfect?—you are the kindest, and the most generous, and the truest man in England." Having finished which peroration, as the train stopped, the Baronet jumped out of the compartment at the civilised station, and returned refreshed.

CHAPTER XXIII.

A DOG IN THE MANGER.

INSTEAD of formally offering the "assistance of his experience" by letter, Mr. Gayre decided to call upon Miss Drummond, and actually got within twenty yards of the house at Shepherd's Bush, when he suddenly hesitated, turned, and commenced retracing his steps.

"What can it be?" he thought. "From the moment I first saw this girl a power stronger than myself seemed drawing me towards her; and yet at the very same moment some spirit of prescience said, 'if you allow your inclination to lead you now, you will in the future repent having done so.' It is odd, very odd, at each turn of the affair, a check or warning has met me; and now, here again, almost with my foot on the doorstep, I feel I cannot meet her this morning—feel almost as though I could wish we had never met. Her influence upon me too is not for good; strange, because she is all good! If there be any lasting virtue to be extracted out of my scheming brother-in-law (which I doubt), she could extract it. Though Sudlow hates her, he thinks it necessary to be on his best behaviour when she is present. The fair Peggy also is an atom more human, less affected, less straitlaced, altogether less unendurable when Susan makes one of the party. But, so far as I am concerned, it is really only since I knew her I feel capable of treason, stratagem, or spoil. If I could be sure of not being found out I would rob my neighbour, cheat my friend, commit a murder, and see an innocent man hanged for my deed, supposing any one of those acts would bring me closer to Susan. Then, when I married her, I should, I have no doubt, find she had all unconsciously brought the avenging sword to church with her. I wonder whether all this is temptation? I am half inclined to think so! For generations we have been such a lot of respectable Pharisees, that no doubt it needed an angel to teach us we are only common clay, subject to like temptations, &c. But hold! What about poor

Margaret? Is Sir Geoffrey an angel—was Sir Geoffrey ever an angel? Here is a difficult conundrum—Why do I feel myself a worse man since I have known Susan Drummond? Is it because she is a good woman? Pooh! what will the end of all this be, I wonder? Will time solve the riddle? I have a strong belief in the ability of time to solve most riddles, and— Ah, how d'ye do, Sudlow? who would have expected to meet you here?"

"I am often in this neighbourhood; but you—"

"Set out to call on Miss Drummond, and then changed my mind."

"Indeed! You would not have found her at home, however, if you had called."

"O !"

"She is staying at The Warren."

"Is my niece there too?"

Mr. Sudlow shook his head.

"Sir Geoffrey means to lunch with Mrs. Jubbins to-day."

"Does he know Miss Drummond is at Chislehurst ?"

"Of course; it was he told me."

Having successfully planted which thorn in the banker's bosom, Mr. Sudlow proceeded on his way, pleased to have scored even so poor a trick.

"He's jealous of his own shadow," considered the careful young man. "If it wasn't that my lady would snub me so dreadfully, I'd have a turn at making love to her myself, in order to vex the Baronet and drive Gayre mad. Marry him ! The money is not in Lombard Street would buy her *yet:* and when the time comes that it might, our dear friend will have found out practically roses wither and lilies fade."

"Sir Geoffrey will tell her she may depend on my help, and so spoil the whole effect," thought Mr. Gayre, with a feeling of savage disappointment. "Well, things must take their chance now. I can only wait results."

He had not long to wait. It was about a quarter to four on the same afternoon—the busiest part of a banker's day, only Mr. Gayre was not busy—when a clerk took a card into that gentleman's private office, intimating at the same time the lady whose name it bore "would like to speak to him."

Mr. Gayre's first impulse was to rise and rush out to greet this unexpected visitor; but prudence prevailed, and in his coldest business tone he desired that Miss Drummond might be asked to walk in.

Then he waited—waited till he heard the rustle of Susan's dress, as she drew nearer and nearer; waited till the door opened, and he heard the clerk's warning to beware of that step, which so often caused a customer or possible client to enter the sacred apartment with an undignified stumble. Then he rose ; he could refrain no longer.

"Pray be careful, Miss Drummond," he said ; " that step is so very awkward. I must really have it altered." And then it flashed through his mind, if Susan would only promise to marry him, he might, even at so late a period of his life, alter many things, beginning with himself, for example.

That was, indeed, a moment to be marked with a white stone in the banker's memory. The woman he loved stood there looking with her soft brown eyes, from which the remembered sunshine had departed, up into his face, with a sort of timid appeal that wrung a heart not over susceptible to the troubles of others. She had come to him voluntarily for help. It was the beginning of the end. It was for this he had turned back almost from the threshold of her home. That which he so foolishly construed into a warning proved to be an omen for good—an omen already fulfilled.

"I fear," she began—and there was a hesitation in her manner he had never previously seen in it—"I fear I am intruding, Mr. Gayre. I walked twice up and down Lombard Street before I could summon sufficient courage to ask for you."

He did not answer this remark for a moment. The contrast between the girl, strong in her fearless innocence, he had sauntered with on that memorable night beneath the stars at Chislehurst and this stricken Susan, who had since faced the then intangible evil she vaguely felt was advancing to meet her, seemed to him so cruel he could not find words in which to clothe his pity.

When he did speak it was lightly.

"Strange to say, I went almost to Miss Matthews' door this morning, intending to call upon you ; but then I turned back, fearing to intrude—"

"I am not with Miss Matthews now."

" No, so I understand ; but I was unaware you had gone to Chislehurst till I heard from Mr. Sudlow you were staying at The Warren."

" I shall only be there till to-morrow. I have taken lodgings at Islington."

"At Islington! Why? Forgive me ; of course, I have no right to ask."

"Certainly, you have every right. You want to know why I left Miss Matthews. We disagreed—about Oliver. I could not bear it—I could not. Everybody is sorry for me ; but nobody is sorry for him. Now I don't want people to be sorry for me."

"No one could help being sorry for you," said the banker gently.

She looked at him for an instant questioningly ; then tears welled up into her eyes, and she turned her head aside as she said, "I have come to ask you to help me, Mr. Gayre. It is very bold of me, perhaps, but—"

"I went to Shepherd's Bush this morning to know if you would not let me try to help you."

"How could you know I wanted help ?"

"Sir Geoffrey told me. He said you were endeavouring to get some petition signed. That is so, is it not?"

"Yes. And O, Mr. Gayre, if you will only put me in the way of getting the right people to sign it, I shall be unutterably grateful."

"Anything I can do for you, be sure I will do."

"Thank you !—I feel certain of that. And you won't advise me ; I am so tired of being advised—so weary of hearing I ought to sit down and fold my hands and do nothing, while he—is—and we were all the world to one another !"

"I shall not advise you," said Mr. Gayre, who felt no inclination to mingle his tears with the girl over the woes of Oliver Dane. "Only tell me what you are doing—what you want done—and I will assist you to the best of my ability."

"How kind you are !" she cried—"how good ! I will try to explain how it all came about. But I fear I am taking up your time. You are busy, are you not ? I had better write to you—may I ?"

"Might I not call upon you, Miss Drummond ? I shall be most happy to do so, if you name an hour convenient to yourself."

"*Any* hour," answered Susan—"any hour which suits you. I do feel grateful, though I cannot express my gratitude. How can I ever be thankful enough to God for raising up such a friend for me in my extremity?" Which being a question Mr. Gayre, under the most favourable circumstances, could scarcely have been expected to answer, he prudently affected not to hear.

"I may be fortunate enough to see you at Chislehurst this

evening," he said, instead of solving that difficult problem as to whether Miss Drummond, if she could read his heart, might regard his friendship in the light of an unmixed blessing. " I was thinking of calling at The Warren. Then, perhaps you will kindly give me your address, and let me know when I should be most certain to find you at home."

" But please do not mention the matter before Mrs. Jubbins," entreated Susan. " She does not say anything, but I know she is like every one else."

" Surely not *every one!* There are exceptions."

" Yes, I forgot. Sir Geoffrey, of course—kind good Sir Geoffrey."

" Won't you bracket us together, Miss Drummond?"

She looked at him searchingly for a moment before she asked, " Do you believe Oliver to be innocent, then?"

The question was put with such direct suddenness that Mr. Gayre found it difficult to parry.

" It is not easy to believe him innocent," he answered; " but—pray do not misunderstand me, Miss Drummond—I do not say he is guilty. Appearances are often against a man; and this is a case in which I, for one, should not care to express a positive opinion. Of one thing, however, I am certain —that, whether the verdict were righteous or unrighteous, the sentence was utterly beyond the offence; and, without going into the question of guilt or innocence, I will do all I can to help you and him. You must not be angry with me," added the banker apologetically, " because I have not the same faith in Mr. Dane you possess. Remember, I never was intimate with him in the slightest degree—"

" That is true," she murmured; " had you known you could not have doubted him."

" Besides," said Mr. Gayre, finishing his interrupted sentence, " I have seen something of the world, and understand how temptation assails, and often overcomes, even the very best amongst us."

" It did not overcome him," declared Susan.

" Then on your word I am to believe Mr. Dane sinned against, not sinning: is that so?"

" If you can."

" I will do precisely what you tell me. I consider myself a soldier under orders, and shall hold no personal opinions whatever. I think I had better let you out by this private door. You would of course rather avoid passing through the

bank. Good-bye for the present, Miss Drummond—no, please
don't thank me. If we meet at The Warren perhaps it might
be more prudent to say nothing about your having been here.
Once more, good-bye; depend I will do all in my power for
your friend."

And in another second Susan was once again in Lombard
Street, with the old dull pain tugging at her heart, spite of the
faith she had in Mr. Gayre's power to help young Dane, and
the certainty she felt he would try to do so.

"But O, he cannot be of the use he might if he only
believed in my darling !" she considered.

When, some two hours later, Mr. Gayre arrived at Chislehurst it was scarcely agreeable to find Sir Geoffrey acting as
Mentor to the youth of the family, who were listening to his
improving stories with enthusiasm, and encoring reminiscences
of flood and field in a manner which should have been gratify-
ing to the Baronet.

"She can't bear these old tales now," said Sir Geoffrey,
sotto voce, to his brother-in-law, indicating Susan, who was
seated apart in the larger drawing-room ; "but she'll mend of
that, poor soul. It has been worse than a death to her. You
must give her time, Gayre—give her time."

"Good Heavens! have I ever interfered with her in any
way?" asked the banker.

"No, no; I didn't mean that. Only *verbum sap.*, a nod's
as good as a wink, you know, and I really do love Susan like
my own child."

"And what was done to the mare that broke her leg, when
old Carey would take him over the bullfinch, Sir Geoffrey?"
inquired one of the younger Jubbins.

"Shot, Joshua—dead as a doornail. A rough sort of
fellow—Poaching Bill he was called—happened to come up
at the minute, and we sent him for a pistol to put the poor
brute out of his misery. Give you my word, there was not a
dry eye in the field, except old Carey's. 'I said I'd teach
her who was master,' declared the gray-haired ruffian, 'and
I did it.'

"'If you had broken your own neck it wouldn't have mat-
tered,' I remarked ; 'but by ——, sir, you've killed the finest
mare in the county, and if the other gentlemen present are of
my mind, you may hunt the county by yourself for the future.
Fair riding is one thing, and fair punishment is one thing ; but
brutality's another, and Geoffrey Chelston will never eat bread

nor shake hands with a man who has done a gallant animal to death, as you've tortured one this day.' "

" And did he hunt the county by himself?" asked the pertinacious Joshua.

"No, my lad; he went to another county, where they would have none of him either. The story followed him—I took precious good care it should—and so, at last, the talk and disgrace broke his own heart. His dying words, I understand, were, 'Curse Chelston!' but I didn't care for that. I always say, if you do right, no man's bad opinion need trouble you. And now, you see, Carey's in his grave, and I'm telling the story of his wicked cruelty to a set of boys who ought to know how to go across country as well as I do. If you'll persuade your mother to let you come down and see me at Chelston— But there, what am I talking about? Well, well, though I haven't the Pleasaunce any longer, you ought to know how to take your fences. There's Gayre, now; d'ye suppose he's a bit worse banker because he's as straight a rider as you'd wish to see? Gad, Nicholas, shall I ever forget seeing that wild Irish devil—that chestnut mare, Leda, I mean—take you first over the ha-ha, with only one foot in your stirrups, and then across the Chel, before you were fairly settled in your saddle? By Jove, it was as fine a bit of horsemanship as ever came in my way! She took the notion in her head and went for it; and there was Margaret screaming, and the grooms running, and I expecting you'd be brought back dead; and then you just turned the creature's pretty head—Lord, what a thing memory is! I seem to have that star on her forehead before my eyes this minute—and brought her back the way she had gone, gentle as a lamb."

With which, and suchlike pleasing and instructive anecdotes, the Baronet held the youthful Jubbins entranced during the compulsory absence of their mamma, who, in honour of Sir Geoffrey's presence, had proceeded to her room, in order to don a more elaborate dinner-dress.

The feeling Mrs. Jubbins entertained towards the brothers-in-law was, to a certain extent, contradictory. Whilst Mr. Gayre remained the love of her heart, she felt a pride concerning the easy and familiar terms on which Sir Geoffrey honoured The Warren with his presence she did not even try to disguise. The names of great persons grew to be as common on her lips as in the columns of the *Court Journal*. She repeated anecdotes of the nobility to her friends on the authority of the

Baronet, which were not really more untruthful than such anecdotes usually are. The private history and daily life of no
peer of the realm remained a sealed book to her. Thanks to
good Sir Geoffrey, she was *au fait* with everything which
occurred at Windsor and Balmoral. She felt that a visit even
from the Prince of Wales would not quite have overwhelmed
her. She had heard how his Royal Highness was in the habit
of greeting her friend at Ascot with " Geoffrey, my boy," and
" Chelston, old fellow," and asking his advice concerning
which horse the Princess should back for a dozen of gloves.
As for the younger Jubbins, they were simply rapturous on the
subject of Sir Geoffrey.

In his charming way he had pinched the girls' cheeks, and
declared they were " deyv'lish good-looking," " pretty little
things," " that when they went to Court they would put some
persons' noses out, begad !" with a good deal more to the same
edifying effect.

He got a pony on which Miss Ida could canter as easily as
if she was sitting in an armchair in her mother's drawing-room,
and himself accompanied that young lady while she ambled
along the Kentish lanes. He sent Lavender frequently to The
Warren, so that the smaller fry might under his aupices learn
to fall easy on the velvet turf once pressed by the august feet
of Lady Merioneth. He told the lads stories of his own
exploits and the exploits of other worthies like himself, and
promised that when he " pulled his affairs together a bit " he
" would make men of them." He proposed furnishing a sort
of armoury at Lord Flint's former abode, which excellent idea
had, however, to be abandoned in consequence of Mrs.
Jubbins' nervous terror of firearms.

" Why, my dear soul," he said to that lady, " if you'd only
let me take you in hand, I'd engage you should in a month
hit at a hundred yards."

" I never said what she'd hit," he confided to his brother-
in-law ; " but it did not matter, because she thinks everything
with a muzzle can bite, and is deadly afraid even of a toy
pistol. Those big women always are cowards—ever notice
that ? Courage decreases as fat is laid on—fact, I assure
you."

In a sentence, then, the Baronet had secured the favour
of the whole establishment. With the men and women servants his rank and agreeable manners made him, as a matter
of course, prime favourite. No standing aloof with him.

"About people of real good birth there is never no nasty low sort of pride," declared the united voice of the servants' hall.

Even the cattle within Mrs. Jubbins' gates evinced a discriminating partiality for so worthy a gentleman.

"They're like children, bless you," he said to Mrs. Jubbins, in kindly explanation. "They know who is fond of them. Why, look at your young folks! (Gad! who'd think you were old enough to be their mother?) They'll leave any of your rich friends, your City magnates rolling in money, to come and stroll about with me, poor as I am. They respect Nicholas Gayre, Banker, but they like Geoffrey Chelston, Beggar—that's about it."

Concerning his wife, Geoffrey Chelston, Beggar, had fairly mystified Mrs. Jubbins. In broken accents he had formerly told how a reconciliation was imminent; how he had been a very bad boy, who meant now to turn over a new leaf—upon his soul he did; how Gayre was the best fellow living; how Margaret could be regarded but as little lower than the angels; what a wretch he had been to the best woman who ever lived; with a great deal more to the same effect, which often caused the widow to wonder if that great trouble which bowed old Mr. Gayre's gray head, and left Sir Geoffrey's little daughter motherless, had been all a dream.

In their first shame and misery the Gayres were unable to hide the sorrow which had fallen on them within their own breasts; but now, to hear Sir Geoffrey, any one might have thought all the sin and scandal were of his own making.

"He is certainly most magnanimous," said the widow to Mr. Gayre.

"*Most* magnanimous!" agreed the banker, with an irony perfectly unintelligible to Mrs. Jubbins. "He is quite willing to let bygones be bygones; so is Margaret, and so am I."

"I think it may prove a comfort to the poor girl to have some old friend to whom she can speak," explained the Baronet to his brother-in-law. "The Jubbins is not much, to be sure; but she means well and is faithful, and will serve better at first than nobody. 'Pon my honour, Gayre, I like the widow; for her rank, indeed for any rank, she is a most excellent sort of person."

She was indeed so excellent a sort of person, Sir Geoffrey thought, after his wife's death, he could not do better than confide a few of the many troubles besetting him to her. "And now the poor dear's gone and all that's knocked on the head, and the link which bound Gayre to us is broken, what is to become of Peggy God only knows. As for me it does not matter ; I can make shift anywhere. Great happiness has never come to me, and I needn't expect happiness now. I did look forward to some peace and quietness with Margaret ; but she has gone to that bourne—you have read *Hamlet*, of course, Mrs. Jubbins ?"

Mrs. Jubbins said she had seen it acted, and that she felt very sorry for Ophelia. Upon the whole, the Baronet gathered, she considered Hamlet rather a foolish young man, and his mamma a most dreadful and wicked person.

" Only think of the unprincipled creature marrying again in that way !" she remarked.

" Only think of people marrying again in any way !" capped the Baronet ; " I couldn't, I know. That is a point I have always admired especially about you, Mrs. Jubbins. It is not often one meets a woman young, rich, handsome, calculated to adorn society, resolute as you are to wear the willow, even for the best husband that ever lived."

" Ah, but where would you find so good a husband as mine was ?" sighed the widow.

" Nowhere—nowhere," promptly agreed Sir Geoffrey. " I have heard things from Gayre about your husband that make me lament I did not know him." And then the Baronet, after accepting an invitation to stop for dinner, walked off to find some of his young friends ; while Mrs. Jubbins hastened away to change her dress, considering, as she did so, that poor dear Mr. J. always did like her to " look her best."

But for Sir Geoffrey, the dinner would have passed off very heavily. He, however, proved the life of the party.

" A most agreeable gentleman," said Hoskins, as he descended to the basement, " as I am sure I shall always be the first to admit. Nevertheless—"

" Nevertheless what ?" demanded Mrs. Jubbins' own maid.

" Things aren't what they was," observed Mr. Hoskins oracularly. " The position is changed, if I may so express myself. The events of the last fortnight has altered the relations of parties. We can't stand still, Miss Lambton."

" That's true enough," agreed the cook. " If wages ain't rising they're falling, which I will maintain to my dying day."

" Well, and if we can't stand still, what then ?" asked Miss Lambton.

Mr. Hoskins closed one eye with decorous solemnity ere answering,

"Least said soonest mended. Though I have a high opinion of a gentleman who shall be nameless, his manners being agreeable, his taste in wine as good as my own, and himself open-handed, I do not altogether know that it is a match to which I could give an unqualified approval. There is wheels within wheels, Miss Lambton; and I have heard a word or two drop which might render caution necessary."

"Get along with you, do!" expostulated the cook. "Missus ain't going to make a fool of herself, though other people may choose to make fools of themselves;" which was a very unkind allusion to the fact that Mr. Hoskins meant, ere long, to take Miss Lambton and a public-house, both for better or worse, and leave "a good place, where he had nobody to trouble him, for a wife who did not know how to cook a potato and a landlord certain to call for his rent regular."

At that very instant the genial Baronet, who during the whole of dinner-time had been on his very best behaviour, was saying to Mrs. Jubbins' sons,

"Look here, my lads! I promised your mother I would not let you sit long over dessert; and, as I don't want to lose any of your agreeable company, why, we'll all make a move. One minute, Gayre," he added, as his brother-in-law, acting on the hint, rose all too willingly; " I have a word for your private ear. Let the young fellows go. We'll be after you immediately."

And then the dining-room door closed; and, literally in the twinkling of an eye, Sir Geoffrey had poured out and swallowed a bumper of sound Madeira.

"It's a sin to put a wine like that on the table when there's no one to drink it but women and boys, who would just as soon have a sweet sherry. But that's not what I kept you back for—it's not, upon my conscience. I wanted to tell you I saw Susan slip into your Bank to-day. Nay, never fire up, man ; surely sight is as free as the street; and, indeed, I was glad to see the poor little soul had turned to you in her trouble. I meant to tell her she'd nothing to do in this case but ask and have ; but the chance did not offer. So, as I was saying, I saw her pop up your steps just like a hunted hare. But Mum's the word as regards me ; and, were I in your place, Mum should be the word too."

"I have not a notion what you are driving at," exclaimed

Mr. Gayre testily. "Why can't you say what you have got to say in plain English, and be done with it?"

"O! hang me, that's too good!" laughed the Baronet. at the same time, as if in very excess of mirth, jocundly seizing the Madeira decanter, and filling out another bumper. "Do you know, Gayre," he went on, "I have heard some fool advance the opinion that the more a man drinks the less he understands about wine. Did you ever hear such rubbish? Why, the more a man drinks, of course the better judge he becomes. Practice makes perfect. I don't suppose even you grasped the whole science and mystery of money-changing at the first intention."

" That is a matter into which I really must decline to enter at present. Mrs. Jubbins will be wondering what is detaining us."

"I'll explain that I had to speak to you on a matter of business—and so I have. Don't you talk about Susan or Susan's affairs to the widow. She's an excellent person. no doubt—I'm sure I have no cause to say one word against her; but in all these City folks there's a deuced hard kernel; and she wouldn't approve, and she'd launch out on poor dear Susan, and she'd advise and preach and talk against Dane; and then they'd quarrel, and Susan would close another door between herself and her friends. She's just in the humour to fight anybody for the sake of Dane; and, Lord, what use is it? By the way, why *don't* you marry her?"

"What do you mean? Marry whom?"

"The widow, to be sure."

"You might as well ask me why I don't fly to the moon; the one inquiry is about as reasonable as the other."

"Don't think so. In the first place, you don't want to fly to the moon; in the next, you couldn't fly there if you wished ever so much. Now, you could marry the widow, and you have led her to believe you meant to do so."

"I utterly deny it."

"That is all very well; but she expects you to ask her, and so do her friends. As far as I am a judge, they are only waiting for the word."

"Surely I am not answerable for their expectations."

"Yes, you are—to a great extent, at any rate. Unless a man means business he has no right to fool around a house in which there is an eligible woman, as you have been circling about The Warren. Gad! if I'd been her brother, I'd have had something definite out of you long ago. And when all that is settled, why the deuce shouldn't you marry her? She is as well born as you—both of you are the children of respectable citizens. If her father did go wrong, your father might have gone wrong. Heavens! which of us has a right to throw stones? I don't know how rich you may be, but she is rich enough in all conscience even for a lord to marry; and if you took a house in some neighbourhood away from that vile City connection, and gradually got rid of the young fry—perhaps put one of the sons in the bank—and made a quite fresh start in the country. I feel confident you might get amongst the best county people. It's never too late to mend! and if I were you I'd try to have some value for my money even at the eleventh hour— I would, upon my soul! The widow is certainly both personable and presentable. I've seen worse driving to a Drawing-room. Besides—"

"It is really exceedingly kind of you to take such an unselfish interest in my affairs, but—" Mr. Gayre tried to interrupt.

"Unselfish! Not a bit of it, as you'll know when you let me finish what I was going to say. There's Peggy, now. If you married the widow, see what a home there would be for her—that is, if you liked to ask her to the house."

"She and Mrs. Jubbins don't exactly hit matters off," observed Mr. Gayre maliciously.

"That's true at the present moment; but if Mrs. Jubbins were Mrs. Gayre, you'd see she'd take even to Peg to please Peg's uncle. 'Pon my soul, Gayre, the woman worships you— that's the plain state of the case; and why, for very gratitude's sake, you don't make her your wife passes my comprehension. It's not as if there were anybody else."

"No. it is not as though there were anybody else," agreed Mr. Gayre. in a spirit of the bitterest sarcasm.

"And then think of all the good you may do. Why, to go no further, you'd be able to offer poor Susan a rest for the sole of her foot—"

"Better at once start an Asylum for the Fatherless and Afflicted," suggested the banker.

"You might do worse," said Sir Geoffrey, who had by this time emptied the decanter. "What greater happiness can a man desire than the welfare of his fellow-creatures? That is a point you rich fellows are somewhat apt to overlook; and yet what is the use of money unless you can do some good with it?

For my own part, if I were well off—which, of course, I never expect to be now—I'd at once begin to consider how I could best spend part of my wealth as a sort of thank-offering—you understand."

"If you have quite finished your remarks, as you have the Madeira," said Mr. Gayre, "I should wish to make one observation."

"One, my dear fellow! A dozen, if you like; I am in no hurry."

" But I am," retorted Sir Geoffrey's "dear fellow." "What I wish to say is this : I have not, and I never had, the smallest intention of marrying Mrs. Jubbins."

"Honour bright ?"

"And what is more," persisted Mr. Gayre, ignoring the implied form of asseveration. "I don't mean you to marry her either."

"I wonder what you take me for !" cried the Baronet, in indignant expostulation —"with my heart still bleeding for the loss of my poor darling! Ah, Gayre, how can you say such things? Why, the flowers on Margaret's coffin must still be fresh."

"If that is a question pressing upon your mind, you may be very sure they are as dead as she is," answered Mr. Gayre; "and for the rest, remember what I say—you shall *not* marry Mrs. Jubbins."

"Well, if ever there was a dog in the manger !" muttered Sir Geoffrey, as he followed his brother-in-law along the corridor.

CHAPTER XXIV

LACKING the many admirable qualities which—if the Baronet's own report of himself might be relied on as correct—rendered Sir Geoffrey such an exemplar and benefactor to his fellow-men, Mr. Gayre was never unduly anxious to part with money, even when he saw a chance of getting a good return. It would have been difficult, however, before a month was over, to name any sum within reason he would have refused to pay, if by doing so he could have rid himself of that dreadful Old Man of the Sea, Oliver Dane. The petition was on his mind the last thing at night, and woke him long before dawn. It strolled by his side to the Bank, went to luncheon and returned to dinner; though it failed to eat itself, and effectually deprived him of all appetite, it sat at the table as long as he did, and only rose when he made a move, in the vain hope of ridding himself of its company.

Life was not worth living with that petition locked away in his safe. It would have required a great reward to compensate him for the humiliations heaped on his head in the matter of Mr. Colvend's defaulting clerk ; and there were times when Mr. Gayre believed he should get no reward whatever. Though he saw Susan often, though the most intimate and friendly relations were established between them, the banker could not blind himself to the fact that it was Oliver Dane, and Oliver Dane only, the girl considered : Oliver Dane lying for six months at Millbank ; Oliver Dane soon going to Portland ; Oliver Dane, convicted thief and forger ; Oliver Dane, in whose behalf he, Mr. Gayre, was compassing heaven and earth in order to obtain signatures he did not know what he should do with when he had got them ; Oliver Dane, whom he hated with a detestation rare even amongst bosom friends ; in whose guilt he had always believed, and whom he certainly did not imagine he was ever likely to consider innocent.

He felt weary to death of the man, the case, and the petition. He would have liked to argue out the matter at considerable length with Susan, and try to convince her how erroneous were all her plans and projects in connection with the great Oliver Dane question, but for the certainty that their first conversation on the subject would be their last.

"It's just 'take it or leave it,' with Susan now," declared Sir Geoffrey. "Never saw a girl so changed in all my life. Faith, I always thought there was something stiff about that short upper lip of hers, but I little imagined my lady would develop so hard a mouth. Gad! except as a sign to bolt, she minds the bit no more than a silken thread. Why, she was nearly having a spar with me the other evening because I said I was afraid the pardon would have to be sent down to Portland after all. What progress are you making, Gayre?"

But Mr. Gayre utterly declined to say what progress he was making, or whether he was making any. In answer to the Baronet's question he used some strong language, and expressed his heartfelt regret he had ever meddled in the business.

"For, supposing the sentence should be commuted—and I for one do not see the slightest likelihood of anything of the sort happening—Miss Drummond's very first act, I foresee, will be to make our interesting convict marry her."

"O, hang it! Dane's not such a cad as to do that."

"I fancy he is a cad; but, in any case, you'll find she'll have the license and everything ready for his appearance. It is pleasant to see a girl in earnest; but I really cannot think that your young friend will find life agreeable under the circumstances I have indicated."

"I tell you I know Dane, and even for gratitude's sake he would not let Susan throw herself away on him."

"And I tell you I know something of women, and I declare to you that she will marry him (even if he does not want to marry her) for sentiment's sake."

"Then had you not better drop that petition business altogether?"

"I should have done so long ago, if I had not, in an evil hour prompted by some demon—you, I believe—promised to do my best for this eligible lover."

"Surely it would be doing your very best to let him stay where he is. What could any rational being want more? Fed, lodged, clothed at the expense of his country; large airy house; regular hours, resident chaplain, medical attendance, free of charge! Better let Dane enjoy these advantages till Susan is married, at any rate. Afterwards something might be done— he can't be in any hurry for a year or two ; and if a free pardon were got, the lad could then be slipped out of the country. Perhaps you yourself might not grudge a trifle to set him up in some decent trade at the Antipodes."

Mr. Gayre turned and looked at his brother-in-law steadily, as if trying to read his thoughts.

Sir Geoffrey, on his side, returned this scrutiny with an expression of calm and satisfied innocence, which Mr. Gayre seemed to find hard to contemplate, for he said at last, with angry decision,

"I have promised, and it is not my practice to keep a promise to the ear and break it to the heart."

"Most creditable, I am sure," answered Sir Geoffrey, drawl- ing out the last word so as to make almost three syllables of it.

"Whether creditable or not, such is the fact."

"I never suggested otherwise. All I mean is I trust you may have a better gaol deliverance than I fear Dane is likely to meet with. The whole thing seems to chafe you terribly, Gayre."

Which was indeed the fact. Never in all his life before had the banker gone through such an experience. Hitherto, when he asked a favour, friends and strangers alike had seemed only too pleased to grant it. To do anything, no matter how slight, for Mr. Gayre, was once in the City esteemed both an honour and a pleasure ; but now, words could scarcely describe the change that all in a moment had come over popular opinion. A cold wave of amazement and disapproval flowed steadily from every commercial quarter towards Gayres. Why should a man in the banker's position interest himself about so flag- rant a case ? The culprit was no kith or kin or friend of his. His acquaintance with him had been no closer than that he presumably maintained with the favoured clerk of any other old and valued customer. The young fellow could not for a moment be supposed innocent. He had deceived an employer who never missed an opportunity of doing him a kindness. He had been found guilty after a long and fair trial. If the sen- tence were heavy it was not too severe. Forgery and embez- zlement were crimes which could only be put down with a strong hand ; other clerks would hear and tremble ; young fellows tottering on the brink of temptation would step back in time ; employers feeling their interests were considered might take heart and resume some little of their wonted con-

fidence. What the deuce—what the —— did Gayre mean by
trying to upset justice, and get up a false sympathy for a most
deceitful and unprincipled young man who, having deeply
sinned, was now most justly suffering?

"Not so long ago he'd have swung for it, sir," remarked
one City magnate to his fellow ; "and I'm not at all sure but
the old way was the best way too. The gallows and a little
quicklime were an effectual way of stopping this sickly sort of
sentiment. Once a man begins stealing he'll go on stealing—
can't help it ; and Gayre ought to know this as well as anybody. Sign the petition ! Did *I* sign it, do you say? Not I.
'You really must excuse me,' I observed to Gayre, 'but it's a
thing I wouldn't do for any consideration whatever. Why, it's
subverting the whole constitution of Great Britain. No, I am
very sorry to refuse the son of my valued friend any favour ;
but you see this is not a matter of time or money. It is a
question of *principle*. I have a duty to discharge to my brother
merchants. How should I be able to look them in the face
if I espoused the cause of a felon against his employer? Why,
the case might have been my own or yours. How on earth
could you ever prosecute one of your people, after doing your
utmost to defeat the ends of justice as you are doing?' "

Wretched Mr. Gayre had thought this difficulty, and indeed
all other difficulties connected with the matter, out alone with
his own heart. He knew that attempting to play the part of
Good Samaritan towards a clerk would be regarded as an act
of wicked quixotism by the collective wisdom of Mark Lane
and Capel Court. Many things might be forgiven a man in
his position, but interference with vested rights was not one of
them. He had done himself incalculable harm, and he had
not done Oliver Dane any good. The chances of the "unfortunate nobleman then languishing in prison " for a mitiga-
tion of sentence seemed quite as good as those of Mr. Colvend's ex-clerk. Mr. Gayre felt very weary and worn. He
had done a great many things he would much rather not have
done, and yet Susan remained as far from him as ever. He
knew he was losing instead of gaining ground. The long
talks, the confidential conversations, the hours spent in fruit-
less discussion, and still more useless retrospection, were full
of nothing but Oliver Dane. The air might be different, but
the words were ever the same—Oliver, Oliver, Oliver ! Susan
had once held her peace concerning her lover till she deluded
Mr. Gayre into the belief that thought of man born had never

agitated her gentle breast. But now the string of her tongue was loosed she spoke of little else. The volume of life for her contained but one name ; all interests, all hopes, all fears, were bound together with a single clasp, upon which was graven the story of one man's sorrows. All this did not recommend itself to Mr. Gayre. He would not have cared so much had he discerned one sign of love or even liking. Gratitude there was, but it seemed rather anticipatory gratitude for some favour to come than appreciative understanding of the enormous trouble the banker had already given himself. With that intuition which so rarely deceives women, Susan had long before discovered her friend neither liked nor believed in her lover ; whilst upon Mr. Gayre's mind there was gradually opening that vast field of speculative observation filled by the selfishness of an unselfish woman.

In those days Susan had no more thought to spare for any one free to come and go, to laugh and be merry, than a mother nursing her sick child has for some healthy waif, stout of limb and sound of lung. The prison containing Oliver Dane was to her the whole miserable world ; the man pent within those cruel walls the entire human race. Susan could think of nothing, talk of nothing, except him and his trouble. It was but an aggravation of the trial that she should be at large whilst he was in confinement. If her lover had not been a rival Mr. Gayre must have found the constant iteration of his name, and the eternal harping on one subject, wearisome ; but, as matters stood, he felt he was fast reaching the limits of his patience.

To jest openly with a power like Gayre's seemed, at the first blush, little short of profanity. Nevertheless, the banker found himself exposed to broad hints and sly allusions, which greatly tried his equanimity.

"I understand there's a pretty face in the question, eh ?" said one ex-Lord Mayor, who thought his twelve months of office had conferred grace to his manners and a pleasing elegance to his diction. It was even whispered in City circles the air of the Mansion House had so affected his brain that, finding sober prose inadequate to express lofty imaginings, he broke into verse, and indited a ditty. entitled "The Aged Beggar : an Idyl of Threadneedle Street."

He was a dreadful person, who, if he once got hold of even a faint similitude to a joke, worried and played with it as a puppy worries and plays with some useless rag. When his

friends hoped he had forgotten the wretched thing he went off
at score and dug it up again. Even in an ordinary way Mr.
Gayre avoided him as he would the plague; but now avoid-
ance was impossible. His late lordship, as City wags faceti-
ously dubbed him, which title they often exchanged for "The
Aged Beggar," would not be denied. When from afar Mr.
Gayre saw his portly form looming in the distance he igno-
miniously tried to avoid the encounter by turning down some
convenient court; but such cowardly tactics usually proved
useless. The former chief magistrate's knowledge of the City
was at least as exhaustive as the banker's; and he found no
difficulty in executing a flank movement of considerable ingenuity, and appearing at the supreme moment from an apparently blind alley or deceptive doorway. He had signed the
petition, and therefore felt himself free to make merry at Mr.
Gayre's expense.

"I'd advise you to be on your guard." he said one day in a
stage-whisper, meeting the ex-officer in Copthall Court. "They
do say *she* was the widow;" and then, with a fat laugh, which
set his sides shaking, he passed on before Mr. Gayre could
resent his remark.

Godless and graceless young stockbrokers, too, who had
not the fear of Gayres' before their eyes, were in the habit of
offering to append their names to any paper—not a bill-stamp
—if Mr. Gayre would procure them a sight of Dane's "young
woman." Altogether it was horrible. Oftentimes the banker
felt beside himself with anger. His very clerks he fancied
were laughing at him in their sleeves. He was a mere butt
for cockney wit; and through some horrible fatality, Susan's
name had cropped out, and become a very shuttlecock for
men, who could not comprehend the purity and grandness of
her self-imposed task, to toss from lip to lip.

By almost imperceptible degrees, also, a doubt as to the
correctness of his own opinions on the Dane question was
stealing across Mr. Gayre's mind. By a slow process of reasoning he was arriving at the conclusion Susan had long before
grasped instinctively, that an enemy's hand might be traced
in the transaction. Things had happened since the trial inexplicable on any other ground. Proved guilty and punished,
the man and his sin would, in an ordinary way, have been forgotten; but for Oliver Dane there seemed, indeed, no rest.
Stories were circulated about him which Mr. Gayre's common
sense resented as untrue. Mr. Surlees' utterances concerning

their former clerk were characterised by a stinging bitterness that seemed to the banker hard to explain. Mr. Colvend's attachment to, and sorrow for, the young man could, according to Mr. Surlees, only be regarded as evidences of a weakened intellect; whilst Susan herself was stigmatised as a sort of adventuress, who, "I feel no doubt whatever, was Dane's accomplice in the matter. So far as I am concerned, I regret that we did not proceed against her as well."

This was awful. Mr. Gayre remained speechless with indignation; and it was not till Mr. Surlees went on to say, "I advise you to be careful what you are about. Take my word for it, this Miss Drummond is a most dangerous and unprincipled person," that his anger found vent in words.

How he expressed the rage burning within him he never subsequently could remember. All he knew was he and Mr. Surlees parted in hot anger; and when, during the course of the same afternoon, Mr. Colvend called to try to make peace, his well-meant efforts resulted in signal failure.

Altogether, nothing but humiliation and irritation resulted from his attempt to "subvert the British Constitution, and defeat the ends of justice."

It was discovered a clerk had been ingeniously robbing the bank for some considerable time, but Mr. Gayre felt literally afraid to prosecute. He had never loved the City, but now he grew to hate it. The pavements of Lombard Street, and the purlieus of the Exchange, were mere haunts of terror. He dreaded the sight of his fellow-men, if those fellow-men had offices within sound of Bow Bells; whilst for Susan—the labour of Sisyphus was not more discouraging than the endeavour to win smiles from a woman who refused to smile, whose faith in her lover never swerved, and whom absence only made fonder!

So far as the petition went, Mr. Gayre felt he had got all the signatures he was ever likely to obtain. Some great names were appended, but the longer he contemplated the paper, the less hopeful he felt on the subject of ultimate success. He stood, indeed, between Scylla and Charybdis; if he failed, Susan would blame him in her heart; and, on the other hand, he did not wish to succeed. No prospect, indeed, could have seemed less pleasant to him than the idea of Oliver Dane's reappearance in the world of free men.

"I had better have given up all thoughts of the girl the moment I found out she was fond of the fellow," he considered irritably. "Somehow I have botched the whole thing, and every step I take only seems to lead me further into the mire. Supposing I could prove him innocent to-morrow, how would that better my position? I am not working for Oliver Dane, but for Nicholas Gayre; and I am as far from my object—farther, indeed—than I was the first day. I think I shall keep away from Islington for a week, and try the effect; she will long to talk to some one, and must miss me, even for that reason. Yes, I shall stay away."

It was the last evening of that week, a Sunday night. He had not seen Susan for one hundred and sixty-eight endless hours. He had refrained from writing or calling; and having just returned from church, whither he had gone to kill time, he sat beside his hearth, thinking about the man who was now at Portland—considering what he was doing, how he felt, how any human being could face the prospect of seven years of penal servitude and—live.

"It is awful," he said, almost aloud. "And suppose, after all, the fellow *should* be innocent!"

He rose uneasily from his seat, and began to pace the room with slow and measured steps.

His hands were loosely clasped behind his back, his head was bent a little forward, his whole attitude, his whole expression, that of a man engaged in deep and unpleasant thought.

He was, in fact, reviewing the whole matter from the commencement, and facing the question of what he should feel to be his duty supposing he were once really persuaded of the prisoner's innocence.

"If the matter rested with me now, for instance," he thought —"if I had the proofs in my hands, how should I act? That is a question I might once have answered without any hesitation; but now— However, he is not innocent, and I have no proofs. Who can that be?" he added, as the sound of a modest double rap broke the stillness of the quiet house; "not Sir Geoffrey, I hope."

A minute elapsed. There seemed parleying in the hall; then his servant entered the room bearing a card.

"'The gentleman'" (there was just the slightest touch of hesitation in the way he spoke this word) "says he wishes to see you on business of importance. He will not detain you long, Colonel."

"Samuel Fife?" said Mr. Gayre, reading the name printed on the card; "I wonder who Samuel Fife may be?"

" He says you know him, sir."

" Does he? I wonder if I do. Show him up into the drawing-room; I will be with him directly."

" The name seems somehow familiar, and yet I cannot associate it with any one," he added to himself. " Fife— Fife!" and then he opened the drawing-room door, and entered.

Under the chandelier stood a short, stiffly-built, middle-aged man. He was dressed in his Sunday clothes—a rough top-coat, dark trousers and waistcoat, thick serviceable boots. He held his hat in his hand, and looked up somewhat nervously as Mr. Gayre appeared.

" Good-evening," began the banker. " To what am I to— Why, it is you, is it?" he added, in a tone of intense surprise. " What do you want with me—why do you come here?"

" I wrote to you a while ago, and you took no notice of my letters."

" I never heard from you in my life, so far as I am aware."

" O yes, you did. I wrote to you three times, signing myself ' Justice.' "

" You are ' Justice,' then. I see."

" Why did you not send me any reply?"

" Why should I reply? Why should I take any notice whatsoever of anonymous communications ?"

" It was true what I said, though, Mr. Gayre."

" That Dane was innocent, and you could prove him to be so?"

" Yes."

" In that case why did you not speak before?"

" I should not speak now if I had been properly treated."

" Have you not been properly treated?"

" No."

" Will you not sit down, Mr. Fife? If we are to talk— and it is unlikely you would have come here unless you intended to talk—you had better do so."

" Do you recollect what I said in my first letter?" asked Mr. Fife, as he sat down on the corner of a sofa, glancing at Mr. Gayre, who had flung himself into an easy-chair.

" I recollect you said in all your letters you wanted money. It is not an uncommon want ; you are not singular, Mr. Fife. Many persons desire money ; but there are not many who get it."

" Will you give me what I asked for?"

"That is not a question I can answer off-hand. Upon the whole, however, I think I may say I do not think I shall give you any money."

"If you are sure of that I will go to Miss Drummond."

"Why did you not go to her first—supposing always you have not been to her?"

"I thought I could go to her after I had tried you. I knew it would be useless coming to you after I had been to her."

"Really, Mr. Fife, your candour is quite refreshing."

"I am glad you think so."

"I do think so; though I cannot in the least imagine why you come to me—"

"I come to you," interrupted Mr. Fife, with startling directness, "because you are in love with Miss Drummond—because you can make her marry you if you prove Dane innocent—because it will be worth your while to pay me *well* for the card I can place in your hand."

"I do not know which I admire most—your frankness or your impudence."

"It is not impudence, Mr. Gayre; and you are as well aware of the fact as I am. As you have asked me to sit down I presume you mean to entertain the matter. In a word, I have something to sell; will you buy it? You know my price; does it suit you?" and, shifting his position, he took possession of a music-stool which chanced to be close to the chair in which Mr. Gayre lay back, his legs stretched out, and the tips of his fingers idly touching each other.

THERE ensued an awkward silence. The one man did not want to speak—the other would not.

At length the spell was broken by Mr. Gayre, who said, without looking at his visitor, and as if his words were merely the outcome of a long course of exhaustive reasoning,

"You see, some one must criminate himself."

Mr. Fife laughed. "You don't trap me that way," he answered.

"Believe me, I had no intention of trapping you. I was only stating a fact."

"O, of course. I quite understand that !"

"If we are to discuss the matter at all, Mr. Fife, permit me to suggest you must do so in a different spirit."

"I don't know," answered Mr. Fife, "that I feel disposed to discuss the matter further. In effect, there is nothing to discuss. I have told you plainly, Dane is innocent, and that I can prove his innocence. I have told you I want to be paid for my information, and the price I expect from *some one*. It does not much signify to *me* who pays that money, but I should imagine it signified a great deal to *you*."

Mr. Gayre winced. The man's tone, the man's manner, seemed terrible to him. He had never been spoken to with such offensive familiarity before, even by his equals ; and as he shot a glance aside at Mr. Fife, and remembered the former cringing deference of his address, it came home to his mind more fully than ever that he was wading through very dirty water indeed, and that he had better get out of it as soon as possible.

"I think," he said, "I would rather wash my hands of the whole business."

"Just as you like. I suppose, however, you have fully considered what washing your hands, as you call it, exactly means ?"

" I fear I scarcely follow you."

Mr. Gayre's voice was freezing in its cold respectability.

"I don't believe you do. Now listen. No, you needn't look so indignant. I mean no offence. Remember you are not in Lombard Street now ; and if you were, I want nothing out of your strong-room except a sum of money, for which I am willing and anxious to give you full value. We're man and man at this minute, sir. I'm not Samuel Fife, manager at Colvend and Surlees' ; and you're not Nicholas Gayre, banker. We're equals, that's what we are—equals. If there is any disparity in our respective positions, the turn of the scale is in my favour, for I have something you want to buy, and that you can't buy from anybody but me."

During the delivery of this address, Mr. Gayre faced the speaker in amazement. As he did so, it dawned upon him that though Mr. Fife was not drunk, he had, according to his own simple vocabulary, been " priming himself."

Had Sir Geoffrey been present, he would have read the " abandoned miscreant" a lecture concerning the wickedness of persons imbibing who " could not carry their liquor decently ;" but Mr. Gayre, though utterly abstemious, did not feel himself such a saint that he dare adventure upon any argument concerning the sinfulness of Mr. Samuel Fife.

Instead of entering into that question, he remarked,

"I do not know that I want to buy anything."

" Well," said Mr. Fife, nowise disconcerted by a statement meant to be crushing, " you had better know whether you do or not during the course of the next fifteen minutes. Time is getting on. It now"—and Mr. Fife produced a whitefaced silver watch—" wants exactly five minutes to nine o'clock. If by ten minutes past nine o'clock you, Miss Drummond's *friend*, have failed to decide what you are going to do, I shall not trouble you further. There," added Messrs. Colvend and Surlees' manager, in beautiful continuation, at the same moment laying his silver watch and steel chain on a table at Mr. Gayre's elbow, " is the time—Post-office."

"In the name of Heaven," cried poor baited Mr. Gayre, " why should you suppose all this concerns me ?"

" Better invoke the name of the Deity, sir," suggested his unwelcome visitor, with bibulous solemnity : " in that case I should answer, with no beating about the bush, I suppose ' all this ' concerns you greatly. You're in love with the girl— that's what it comes to. If you can lay your hand on your

heart and say honestly you are not, why the sooner I go to
Miss Drummond the better. She'll pay me my price, I know."

" If you are so sure of that, why do you trouble me? Why
did you not go to her direct?"

"There are wheels within wheels," replied Mr. Fife loftily.
"I have my reasons, which I do not intend to tell you—not
yet, at all events—perhaps never. Now, Mr. Gayre, are you
making up your mind, because I am determined to settle the
matter one way or other before I sleep?"

" I have made up my mind on one point," said the gentleman so peremptorily addressed, " namely, that I will not pay
one sixpence till you furnish me with some proof you really do
possess the knowledge you profess."

" That is fair enough ; but on the other part, I do not
show my hand without something binding on your side. Give
me the merest scrap of writing as evidence of your *bona-fides,*
and I'll tell you what I know."

" But what you know, or think you know, may turn out
practically valueless."

" Upon my soul, I believe you do not want the fellow
proved innocent. I think if his release rested with you he
might stop in gaol for ever—rot there before you would lift a
finger to get him out !"

"I trust you wrong me, Mr. Fife. At any rate, you must
allow me to observe your own anxiety on the subject is not so
disinterested you have any right to attribute such ungenerous
feelings to me."

" Pooh !" retorted Mr. Fife ; "that is all very fine, but we
both know more of the world than to believe much in generosity or disinterestedness, or any such humbug. What you
are afraid of now is, that when Dane appears once more on
the scene. Miss Drummond won't marry you. Neither she
will, if *I* tell her. She will marry Dane, —— him ! But make
a fair bargain with me, and the game is in your own hands.
'Take me,' you can say, ' when I obtain your lover's release ;
refuse me, and my gentleman remains at Portland for the term
to which he was sentenced.'"

" What a scoundrel you are, Mr. Fife !"

" I am not a hypocrite, at any rate. And why should the
girl not marry you? She will have everything money can buy,
except a conceited empty-headed puppy without a sixpence to
bless himself with. And she deserves a better fate ; for, though
I don't care much for that style myself, she is good-looking,

and has as nice manners—I'll say that for her—as any woman I ever spoke to."

"Have you spoken to her?" The amazement in Mr. Gayre's tone was not complimentary.

"Rather! I lodge in the same house: if I take a thing in hand I do it thoroughly; and I wanted to make sure of my ground before I came to you. There has been nothing more than 'Good-morning,' or 'Good-evening,' or 'It's cloudy,' or 'What a wet day we have had!' but it was enough. Her voice is soft, and her ways sweet. She'll make you a very suitable wife; and though, to be sure, you are not young, I daresay you'll make her a very good husband."

"Mr. Fife, you shall hold no further communication with this most faithful and unfortunate lady!" declared Mr. Gayre, rising in hot wrath. "If only to save her from the degradation of hearing you mention her lover's name in her presence, I will pay the exorbitant sum you exact as the price of your shameful secret."

"Come, that's to the point at last. Hard words break no bones, and it is perfectly immaterial to me why you find the money, so long as you do find it. If you have a piece of paper handy, just write that, upon my proving the fact of Oliver Dane's innocence to your satisfaction—"

"You must do more than that," interrupted Mr. Gayre.

"Well, word it any way in reason you like. I'll give you the key, but you must do the rest yourself, remember. Say, when Samuel Fife has given you the means of proving Oliver Dane's innocence to the satisfaction of Messrs. Colvend and Surlees, you will hand him over an open cheque—"

"I will give you a bank-note; I wouldn't write your name on a cheque."

"Dear me! but it is of no consequence; a note will do just as well. Now, if you put that into form, and sign it (I'll not ask for a witness—I don't believe you will try to shuffle out of your bargain), we can get to business—"

"I almost wish I had not passed my word."

"Ah! but you have, you know: and besides, though you may choose to break your promise, I sha'n't break mine. Make any further objections, and I see Miss Drummond before I sleep."

Chafing with anger, more thoroughly furious perhaps than he had ever felt before in his life, yet supported by the determination to do a right and unselfish action, Mr. Gayre intimated that writing materials being in his study, an adjournment had better be made to that apartment.

"It does not matter to me where the thing is written, so long as it is written," said Mr. Fife, with easy impudence. "I have made up my mind for this throw, and I do not want to waste any more time before making a clean breast. You have a very fine house here," he added, as he descended the stairs; "but it needs one other piece of furniture, a handsome wife. You'll have that before long, though, no doubt; and I know whom you ought to thank for it;" and he laughed as he turned his head and looked at Mr. Gayre, who had much ado to refrain from kicking him to the bottom of the flight.

Something of this feeling must have shown in his face, for Mr. Fife proceeded to make a sort of apology.

"Don't mind me to-night," he remarked. "I'm mad; that's what I am. I'm going to cut my own throat. I mean to do that which will force me to leave Colvend's. Perhaps you would like to know why? Wait a little. That's in the story as well."

"I do not feel at all sure that I am doing right in entering into any compromise with you," said Mr. Gayre, as, after carefully closing the library-door, he motioned Mr. Fife to a seat, and, taking a chair himself, began to write.

"That is a pity," commented Mr. Fife, with a smile.

"Are you aware you have made no stipulation with regard to your own safety?" asked Mr. Gayre.

"Yes, I am aware of that;" and his smile grew broader.

"I thought I would just mention the fact," said the banker.

"Very kind of you. In common gratitude, I think I ought to give you a hint: don't let your young lady get an inkling of how you are going to help her lover till you have made everything safe as regards your own marriage. If you do, she'll find a way to slip out of her agreement. They're all alike: so long as a man can give or get them something they want, they'll purr round him, and be pleasant and winning as a child looking out for sweets; but the moment he has served their turn, it's 'Thanks, so many;' and the pace isn't known, quick enough to their fancy to take him out of their sight."

Mr. Gayre ceased writing, and contemplated the speaker in astonishment.

"Your knowledge of the sex seems almost exhaustive, Mr. Fife," he observed.

"I can't tell whether you are chaffing me or not; and I

don't care," answered that gentleman. "'There is one thing, however, I will say—that, let you know women as you may, I know them better."

"The usual thing," remarked Mr. Gayre. "You generalise concerning the sex from one example."

"Never mind what I do, but remember what I say. If you don't, you'll repent it."

"Before I sign this paper, there is one question I fear I must ask."

"What is it?"

"There are no other defalcations?"

"So far as I am aware—none."

"Do you object to my embodying that statement?"

"Not in the least;" and Mr. Fife laughed outright.

"Will this do?" inquired the banker, wondering what Mr. Fife had found so amusing in his question.

"Yes, that will do; a lawyer, I daresay, could pick a few holes in it; but friends ought not to be too particular. With your good leave, I'll just put it in my pocket-book—so. That's done," he added, drawing a breath of relief; "and now for my part of the pact. You conclude I forged that signature, Mr. Gayre?"

"I should not have ventured exactly to make such a suggestion, but, as you are kind enough to do so, I hope you will excuse my frankness when I answer ' Yes.'"

"Beyond annexing a cheque I had nothing to do with the matter."

"Indeed!"

"Truth, I assure you—gospel."

"Then perhaps you will tell me who did write the name of the firm?"

"Certainly; there shall be no reservations on my part. The party—or, to speak more accurately, the lady—was christened Theodora Alberta Colvend; but she is usually called 'Dossie' by a fond and foolish parent."

"Good Heavens!" exclaimed Mr. Gayre. "Good Heavens!"

"And 'Good Heavens!' again, if you like," said Mr. Fife; "my information seems to surprise you, sir. If you remember, I more than hinted my knowledge of women was greater than yours."

"But why should she? Why should any woman do such a wickedness?"

"Name the devil that eggs women on to commit any and every sin. You can't. Well, what do you say to jealousy? Miss Dossie was madly jealous of your pink and white beauty, and, as she was afraid to throw vitriol in her face, she decided to put Mr. Oliver Dane out of the way of matrimonial temptation for some time."

"And you helped her?"

"I helped her."

"And what possible motive could *you* have?"

"Ditto to Miss Dossie's. Scarcely that, however; for though I did, and do, hate Mr. Oliver Dane, he might still have been walking the streets a free man so far as my enmity was concerned."

"You wanted, then—"

"I see you are beginning to understand. I wanted Miss Dossie—that was the bargain. She promised to marry me, and like a fool, I believed her—yes, I believed her." And Mr. Fife broke off with a muttered oath, and something between a gulp and a gasping choking sob.

"Surely she is not worth that." said the banker, regarding him with quite a new interest. It seemed strange that an exterior such as Mr. Fife's should cover joys, sorrows, hates, loves precisely the same—save only, perhaps, that they were more intense—as those, for example, which dwelt within the breast of Nicholas Gayre.

"You're right enough; she's not worth it—she's not worth *that!*" and Mr. Fife snapped his fingers—"not worth one thought of an honest man; and before God, Mr. Gayre, I was honest in word, thought, and deed till she laid her fiendish spells upon me. However, all this has nothing to do with you; only I want you to think of me hereafter as not quite an outcast. I'll be bound now you fancy I'm going to take all that money as the mere price of what I know?"

"You ask awkward questions, Mr. Fife."

"Never mind that; answer me truthfully, if you don't object."

"As you press me so strongly, I am afraid I must confess the idea you have suggested has crossed my mind," said Mr. Gayre delicately.

"Wrong again!" laughed Mr. Fife. "Had I seen my way to earning even a hundred a year, once Colvends gave me marching orders, I'd have told you the whole story long ago, with the greatest pleasure; but a man can't starve, can he?"

Feeling many better men than his visitor had starved, and fearing lest even so general a statement might commit him, Mr. Gayre decided that, both in the interests of courtesy and prudence, he would be wise to hold his tongue.

"I'm taking your money on the principle of self-preservation, which, as you know, is the first law of Nature," proceeded Mr. Fife, taking silence for consent.

"And mean to go abroad with it, no doubt?" suggested Mr. Gayre.

"I don't mean to tell either man or woman where I'm going," answered Mr. Fife, in a sudden access of caution. "I think I may safely say you'll see me no more; and that is about all you'll get out of me concerning my future movements."

"Certainly I had no right to make any inquiry as to your intentions; and I beg your pardon for having done so."

"O, no offence; I'm not at all a touchy fellow. What was I talking about? O, that young jade, Miss Theodora. If you only knew—if you could only imagine—how she led me on and on and on; upon my soul, Mr. Gayre, there was a time when you might have thought she liked the ground I walked on. It was not easy to get me to do what she wanted; but there are words, looks, and tones no man with blood in his veins can resist: I could not, at any rate;" and Mr. Fife started from his chair, and took a couple of turns up and down the room before he resumed his narration.

"I am a fool," he said—"I was a fool; for though I never in my heart believed she cared for me, or for any created being except herself and Oliver Dane—and for him only because he would have nothing to do with her—I let myself be led by the nose till she had got her turn served."

"Other men have been treated in the same way," said Mr. Gayre. "The story is as old almost as creation."

"And when I claimed my reward," went on Mr. Fife, unheeding this interruption, "she laughed in my face. Since, I have wondered often I did not kill her. I wish now I had struck her down where she stood, with a mocking devil in her eyes and a sneer on her lips. 'Marry you!' she said, 'marry you! That is an honour I really must decline.' And she wasn't afraid, though we were alone on Wimbledon Common, and there was not a human being but ourselves within hail. You've seen her, Mr. Gayre?"

The banker nodded.

"Well, you know she looks as if a breath would blow her

away. You might span her waist; I believe she is so light I could hold her on my palm stretched out like that;" and Mr. Fife thrust across the table a hand of which a prize-fighter need not have been ashamed. "Often and often I've watched her coaxing and making much of the old man, till any one might have thought there was not such an affectionate, tender soul on earth. 'My poor Dossie!' he would say, 'my dear, tender, little Dossie; she's such a clinging, timid darling.' Clinging! timid!" repeated Mr. Fife, with wild scorn; "I never saw the thing she was afraid of yet, except of not getting what she wanted."

"It is strange she was not afraid of *you*," observed Mr. Gayre.

"When I found she would not give me anything for love, I tried the other tack with her; but I might as well have held my peace. I said I would tell her father. 'He won't believe you,' was her answer. 'I'll show him your letters.' 'The person who could forge the name of the firm could write any number of letters.' 'But I did *not* forge the name of the firm.' 'Ah, that you'd have to prove,' she said. 'Mr. Surlees would believe me even if your father did not.' 'He might; but you won't try to make him believe you.' 'Why won't I?' 'Because you would lose your situation; you would not be permitted to retain it an hour.'"

"The weak point, then, in your evidence is that if Miss Colvend choose to deny the statement *in toto*, you have no means of proving her complicity."

"I hadn't; I have now. The cheque, if you remember, was presented by a woman."

"Not Miss Colvend?"

"No; her maid. She had a situation ready for the girl to drop into. The very next day she went out to India as attendant upon a lady who was going to join her husband. Miss Colvend sold a quantity of jewelry to make things square with Adela."

"Adela will have to be found, then, I suppose; and when she is found perhaps she may deny the whole story."

"O no, she won't. She is back in London. At the Cape, news met the lady that her husband was dead; so she took the first vessel home and brought Adela with her. I met the girl quite by chance, and, from a word or two, I know she would be glad enough to get the matter off her conscience, if only she could be sure of not being thrown on the world."

"How did the notes get to Dane's lodgings?"

"I do not know; but I fancy Miss Colvend herself slipped them into the letter-box."

There ensued a pause—longer even than that which had prefaced the gist of the conversation. Mr. Gayre, in his turn, rose and paced the room, while Mr. Fife watched him anxiously. No greater change could be imagined than that which had taken place in the manager's look and bearing. He was not anxious now concerning money, for he knew whatever course Mr. Gayre elected to pursue the slip of paper in his pocket-book represented money's worth. But he was playing for another stake as well. And if the banker decided to take no action in the matter, he would, he felt, rise from the game a loser after all.

He grew weary with following the tall erect figure, of hearing that leisurely measured tread, of trying to gain from the banker's inscrutable face some vague idea of what was passing through his mind, ere Mr. Gayre, pausing suddenly, said,

"I do not see my way at all."

"No?"

"The whole story is such an improbable one."

"It is true, though."

"I am not impugning your word. Still, you yourself must admit the tale you have told me has not exactly the ring of true metal."

"That depends on whether you wish to believe the gold sterling or not. If you don't, Mr. Gayre, I will give you back your paper and go straight to Miss Drummond. Even supposing she should have gone to bed, I know she will get up to hear what I propose to say to her."

"Why should I wish to disbelieve you?" asked Mr. Gayre, looking Mr. Fife sternly and steadily in the eyes.

"Because," replied the other, with a resumption of his former boldness—"because you are afraid to think Dane innocent. You are afraid of yourself; you want to fancy you would 'do right, let come what may,' as the French say (I daresay I can read French as well as you, Mr. Gayre), and you know you won't do right. Why should you? The girl will be a thousand times happier if she marries you than as Dane's wife. He is a rackety chap; he can make the money spin. I don't mean to say there is much vice about him; but, upon my conscience, he can go a pace. So far as I know, he was never in the habit of frequenting races; but he had something on every one—

Derby, Oaks, Ascot, Goodwood, St. Leger, and plenty more. He, and that Hilderton fellow too, did go to some very queer places—places I wouldn't be seen in. Of course you'll do as you please; but were I in your shoes, I wouldn't get a waster out of prison only to marry him to a young woman in whom I took an interest. In my opinion it would be sinful; but, without doubt, you know best."

"Your feeling towards Mr. Dane seems something malignant," observed the banker. "Without meaning any impertinence, I really should be glad to know how he has injured you. Even according to your own showing, he paid no attentions to Miss Colvend, neither did he in any way encourage her fancy for him."

"A true bill on both counts," answered Mr. Fife. "And I don't much mind answering your question. I suppose you wouldn't call me a handsome man, now, would you?"

"I am scarcely a judge. I feel no doubt, however, there are many ladies in whose eyes you would find much favour."

"That's chaffing."

"I assure you nothing was further from my intention than chaff of any kind."

"Well, at any rate, I am not handsome, and you know it. *She* said I was like Quilp, or the Black Dwarf, or that other ugly fellow in Victor Hugo's *Notre Dame.*"

"I think Miss Colvend was wrong in fact as well as in taste."

"Thank you. I don't believe I am quite so bad as she made out. I pleased her well enough so long as she was making a tool of me; but, however, that's not the question now. You want to know why I dislike Oliver Dane. I'm short, and broad, and plain. I haven't a good feature in my face. I'm a common-looking fellow, according to Miss Dossie; and for once, most likely, she spoke the truth. He, on the contrary, is the right height for a man; not too tall—he is some inches shorter than you—yet tall enough. He has a straight nose—thank Heaven, that has been brought to the grindstone; he has dark-blue eyes; he has brown hair cropped close—it is cropped closer now; he has the 'sweetest' moustache—curse him! he has hands white and soft as a lady's— a use he never expected has been found for them lately; he is ten years younger than I am; he can dance; he can sing; he can ride; he can row; he can shoot; he can do anything, in a word; yet he has not half my brains or any of my steadiness.

He is a mere popinjay; but he was preferred before me. I
have served Mr. Colvend faithfully since I entered his house;
yet I was left out in the cold, while Dane was petted and
pampered and done well by. Miss Dossie would have blacked
his shoes if she could have won a smile from him. Not a soul
came into the office but I knew went out of it thinking, 'What
a delightful manner that young Dane has!' If there were any
halfpence going, he got them; but the kicks were all given to
me. It was hard measure, and you can't deny it."

"As you put the matter, perhaps so; yet I do not suppose
you would have been in much better plight had such a person
as Oliver Dane never existed."

"I am not so sure of that. If Mr. Colvend did not love,
certainly, once upon a time, he valued me. In those days it
was 'Fife, I wish you could call there,' or 'Fife, if you can
spare time, just run along and see to this!' But, bless your
soul, once Mr. Dane, with his soft hands and well-kept nails
and hair parted down the middle (I hope the Portland barber
has altered that parting) and white teeth, came into the house,
times were changed for your obedient. And he wasn't the
making of a business man; he hadn't it in him. I swear to
you, Mr. Gayre, if I were a merchant and wanted a clerk, I
wouldn't give him a hundred a year. It was only that plausible
manner of his drew men to him, as aniseed will rats. I don't
much like the smell of aniseed myself, and I never took to
Mr. Dane's manner."

Mr. Gayre smiled, with a cynical relish of this frank revelation of human weakness. He could afford to smile, believing,
as he did, himself above all human weakness.

"Give me three days," he said, "and I will tell you my
decision."

"Great Heavens!" exclaimed Mr. Fife, striking his clenched
fist on the table so vehemently that everything upon it trembled, "do you mean to tell me you need three days, or one,
or an hour, to decide what you intend to do now the game is
in your own hands?"

"I cannot see that it is. In the first place, it may be difficult to convince Mr. Colvend of the truth of your statement."

"Then try Mr. Surlees," advised Mr. Fife, with an unpleasant grin.

"And in the next place," went on the banker, as suavely
as though this advice had not been tendered, "it is possible I
may not care to stir in the matter at all."

"That is very likely. By ——! that's what I thought from the first. You fancy you will yet be able to win the girl, if you only keep her and her lover apart long enough; but you're wrong. Time won't make her forget him. Faith, were I a woman," he added maliciously, "I don't know that I should forget his handsome face in a hurry myself! Make your bargain. You'll be doing the girl a real kindness, and you'll be doing Dane himself a good turn, by giving him his liberty. Don't you be afraid the young woman won't marry you. She'd marry *me* on the terms; and if she had a little more money, that is a view of the question I should certainly entertain."

"Thank Heaven, she has not more money, then!" exclaimed Mr. Gayre, almost involuntarily.

"So you may; you see it leaves the field open for you," retorted Mr. Fife, wilfully misinterpreting the banker's remark.

"At the end of three days—say Wednesday night—you shall have my answer," repeated Mr. Gayre, meanly taking refuge in simple assertion, and declining further contest with an adversary able to hit out so straight from the shoulder and hit so mercilessly.

"I feel very much disposed to cut the knot by going to Miss Drummond to-night."

"You would have taken that course at first if, for some reason best known to yourself, it had not seemed more desirable to deal with me."

"There is considerable truth in that statement," was the cool reply. "Well, I will give you till Wednesday; only understand one thing, Mr. Gayre—I'm not going to take your money and hold my tongue. Either you tell all I have told you to Colvend and Co., or I shall do so."

"Evidently you take me to be such another as yourself," said the banker, more angry than he would have cared to confess, spite of the chivalrous resolution he had formed.

"I take you for a man," answered Mr. Fife, lifting his shabby hat and putting it on defiantly; then, as he left the room, he turned to Mr. Gayre, who was promptly ringing the bell, and said with jeering insolence:

"If you don't ask me to the wedding, I hope you will send me a good slice of the cake."

"Thank God!" ejaculated Mr. Gayre, drawing a long breath, as the door slammed behind his unwelcome visitor, and looking round the room rid at last of Mr. Fife's presence.

Then he sat down, and, his head supported on both hands,

T

remained for quite half an hour buried in profound thought. All at once he rose, and, like one in some violent hurry, went into the hall, took down his top-coat, put on his hat as determinedly as Mr. Fife had done, and was marching straight into the night, when his servant, hastily appearing, said :

'You are surely not going out, Colonel; it is pouring in torrents !"

The "Colonel" never answered, but, flinging wide the door, passed out upon the doorstep, where he was met by a fierce gust of wind and a perfect deluge of rain.

"Shall I try to get a cab, sir? You will be wet through before you get twenty yards."

Again Mr. Gayre did not answer. He looked up and down the street, then at the black vault above his head, and the pelting storm.

"It would be madness," he muttered. "I could not ask to see her, soaked to the skin. I must defer the matter till to-morrow;" and re-entering the house, he passed into the library, which he paced till the night was far spent.

CHAPTER XXVI

IF the woman who deliberates is lost, the man who hesitates does not lag far behind her on the downward path. When Mr. Gayre put on his coat he meant to go straight to Susan, and tell her what he had heard. Casting temptation behind him, he resolved to do the right, "let come what would."

Money, time, influence, all—all should be spent in unlocking the door of Oliver Dane's prison. He would not palter with his own conscience—he would not tell specious lies to his own soul, and profess to be thinking of the girl's happiness whilst he was really seeking to compass his own selfish ends.

He would not give with one hand and take with the other. In honour and honesty there was but one course to pursue. At the price he would have to pay for her, even Susan Drummond must be considered too dear. That which was proposed to him seemed worse than any crime; it would be more cruel than seething the kid in its mother's milk to sacrifice that tender heart in the fire of its devoted affection.

If he was base enough to insist upon the condition suggested to him, how could he ever again look in those trustful brown eyes—red with weeping, dim with tears—touch the hand which had once lain close in that of her lover, kiss the lips he had seen quiver when she spoke of the ruin one day's work had wrought in his life? Such a sin might not be done —by him. Another—a different man, perhaps—but there he stopped in his mental sentence. The very strength of the temptation, the very determination he had to call up to resist that temptation, warned him he was in mortal peril. He was fighting for more than life—for right, for self-respect, for everything valuable to a human being, save that which he felt to be a part of his soul, and which might never, never now be aught to him—never for ever. Till that moment he had only faintly grasped what Susan was to him. Daily, hourly, the vision of her married to another, after the first terrible moment of grim revelation, grew less and less distinct, till it seemed a mere shadowy memory of some troubled dream. Even supposing his endeavours to obtain a commutation of Dane's sentence were crowned with success—and in the whole world nothing appeared less likely—how could any one with such a stain on his name, without character or money, or friends willing and able to assist him, marry and support a wife? If he were not wholly worthless he would refuse to accept the gift Susan was sure to offer; he would go away, and leave her free—he would not suffer the girl to mate with him. But now—now— one hour, and the world itself seemed changed to Mr. Gayre; the blackness of despair closed around him as he thought of the glorious hope he could carry to that lonely girl sitting in a solitude worse than widowhood. For her the dawn, the sunrise, the glad sights and sounds of early day, the songs of happy birds, the light breeze of morning; for him the darkness and ever-deepening gloom of a long, cold, cheerless winter's night.

This was the point he had mentally reached when, rushing from temptation and fully prepared to put the affair beyond the power of retractation, he was driven back by the pelting rain, which swept down upon him in its wild fury and lashed his face, cutting him almost like the sting of a whip.

Then the whole trouble had to be gone over again. For hours, as his weary restless feet fell silently on the Turkey carpet, he went on telling the same story to himself, repeating the same arguments, wandering along the road he already seemed to have been travelling for years. At such a crisis thought is worse than useless; it becomes the mere drudgery of a horse going round and round in a mill, making, so far as its own benefit or satisfaction goes, no progress, returning every few minutes to the point it has but just left, and growing at length well-nigh giddy and stupid from the constantly-recurring sight of objects which have grown familiar to distraction.

Mr. Gayre had arrived at this pass mentally before he went to bed. Not a fresh thought or useful idea occurred to him. Everything Right could find to say was said during the first ten minutes after Mr. Fife's departure. On the other hand, while the pleadings of Wrong were unduly protracted, they were not one half so convincing; had an impartial judge chanced to be on the bench, Wrong would have been ordered out of court at once. Still, that side which a man wishes to espouse must always make itself heard; and accordingly temptation, though often driven back, again came stealing up, and laid its soft hand on the banker, and tried to lead him by almost imperceptible degrees from the path there is no mistaking into that which conducts to wilds and mazes we once should have recoiled in horror from the thought of being compelled to traverse. Nevertheless, during the watches of that lonely night, Mr. Gayre's purpose never really faltered. He did not shrink from the wrong, most earnestly he desired to cleave to the right; but he felt that the impulse which had so nearly driven him to see Susan before he slept, and put the matter for ever beyond all power of recall, was past. He would not now be precipitate. Even for her own sake he would not offer a cup of happiness which might next moment be dashed to the ground. How was it competent for him to tell what of truth or of falsehood lay folded within Mr. Fife's extraordinary story? So many things had to be thought of; there was so much to consider. No; most certainly he should not speak to Susan yet; with a safe conscience he might for a brief span longer maintain that sweet fancy which he openly confessed to his own soul was a delusion—that marriage between Oliver Dane and herself could only be regarded as impossible.

And then he wondered for the hundredth time whether he could be generous as well as just. Whether he could ever forget he had been her lover, and really enact the part of friend; help Dane, for example, along the rough road of life, visit at their house, listen to Susan while she talked about how everything her husband touched prospered. But the last part he felt was impossible.

" I might as well," he considered bitterly, " propose myself standing godfather to their first child, and presenting the best silver mug and fork and spoon, and coral and bells, money could buy. No; I *may* be able to rise to such a pitch of magnanimity as to give him a leg if he can't mount the good steed Fortune by himself, but all else is beyond me. Some day I *must* tell Susan how I loved her, and never see her again. She will then think of me with far deeper interest; her thoughts will often stray to me; whether he is near or far off, she will have one sad corner in the garden of existence *he* will never be asked to visit. She will wonder what the man who, with her for wife, might have climbed so high, but who, lacking her, did nothing, is making of existence; and if what Fife says is true, the time may even come when she might think—Good God! what a villain I am! Were I in my senses to-night, I know I would not, for the sake of holding her in my arms, have her for one moment, even in thought, false to the man she loves." Having attained to which moral state of mind, Mr. Gayre at length repaired to bed.

Both interviews—the short talk with Mr. Fife and the much longer talk with his own soul—had taken a great deal out of the gentleman some persons casually referred to as "our slow friend the Old Tortoise in Lombard Street;" for which reason it was no doubt that when at length exhausted nature sought some repose he slept soundly.

The next morning he did not revert to his idea of rushing off to Islington. Quite the contrary. Light and air and sunshine but confirmed his determination to proceed in the matter slowly and cautiously, to make very sure he stood safely on one step before ascending to another, and to be hampered in his actions by the fads and whims of no woman living.

"I should know no rest," considered Mr. Gayre, "if once she were aware how matters stood."

Possibly he was right. Yet still it would have been better had she been aware.

The weary day went by—such a day as the banker humbly trusted he might never spend again—and at length the hour came when he meant to ask Susan for that cup of tea of which he had not partaken in her company for seven long days.

"I am so thankful to see you." This was her greeting. "I felt so afraid you were ill. I should have written, but I did not like to be troublesome."

And all the time her face wore a tender anxious smile, and her eyes, out of which the sunlight of happiness faded one summer's morning at Enfield Highway, looked with inquiring solicitude into his. And she did not withdraw the hand he held, but let it lie in his strong warm grasp as though he had a right to keep it, as though in the whole wide world there were no Oliver Dane for whose sake she deemed the love of all other men valueless.

She did not know; but he knew—knew that it was impossible he could give her up, with his own lips pronounce his death-warrant, and, while opening the gate of freedom for Oliver Dane, kill every goodly hope, the tendrils of which had grown around his heart and entwined their roots with his very being.

"I have been well," he answered; "but a rather annoying affair has vexed me. However—" He broke off to say, "I will not harass you with my worries. And you? You are ill, I fear. What is it—what is wrong?"

"Only the old story," she answered sadly. "Waiting is such heart-breaking work. Time goes on, and nothing seems to advance. It is more than six months now, Mr. Gayre. He went to Portland last week."

The banker had forgotten this fact. As she spoke, however, he remembered: and it was with a sharp twinge of conscience he saw the girl's eyes were full of unshed tears; that the trouble—her lover's trouble—was indeed sapping away her great courage.

"It has been so difficult to get the signatures," he remarked, more because he could think of no other words to speak than for any comfort or novelty contained in them. They—he and she—had gone over the same ground so often, the same things had been repeated so constantly, that they were both weary of the subject, which to him had been one long course of annoyance and humiliation, while to her it represented but hope deferred and cruel disappointment.

Now the signatures were procured, what was to be done with them? To Mr. Gayre it had always seemed a mere waste of time, this stringing of influential names together; while Susan, tossed about by the advice of friends—counselled to do this by one, to take some quite different course by another, and "get out of the whole affair" by a third—was growing utterly hopeless and discouraged.

The week too spent without seeing or hearing from Mr. Gayre had tried and spent her even more sorely than that gentleman intended it should.

As she poured out his tea he noticed how thin and transparent her hands looked, how hollow her cheeks were getting, how fragile her figure had become. With one sentence he could have caused her face to flush with hope, and given movement to those listless hands; but that one sentence he did not mean to speak—not, at all events, while it was capable of giving her unalloyed happiness.

"Lal Hilderton says," began Susan, after a pause, "that it is a case we should get ventilated by the press. Do you know any one connected with the press, Mr. Gayre?"

Mr. Gayre, thus appealed to, thought for a moment, and then could not call to recollection that he did.

"It seems to me," he went on, "that the time is past for that. A chance might have existed while the severity of the sentence was fresh in the public mind; but now—"

"Lal thinks there may be a chance even now."

"There may," said Mr. Gayre, but his tone was not hopeful.

"Ah me!" murmured Susan softly; and then for a moment she covered her face and kept silence.

"Does not Mr. Hilderton know any newspaper men?" asked Mr. Gayre, merely for the sake of saying something.

"No one possessed of any influence," answered the girl; and then she looked at him with all her heart in her eyes. What her look meant was, "Cannot you get to know some person of influence able and willing to bring Oliver's wrongs before the public, or Parliament, or the Queen, or anybody competent to set him free?"

How he did it, with Mr. Fife's story fresh in his mind, Mr. Gayre never afterwards could imagine; but he looked straight back at the girl and shook his head.

"O!" she cried, "do not think me wearisome, but is there *nothing* to be done? Must I sit here with my hands folded, whilst he is dragging out such a life as that? You do not know him—really, I mean. If you did, you would understand what I feel. He never could bear restraint of any sort. It was only for me—for my sake—he came to London at all. He hated London, and business, and—and—" Her voice shook so much that she could not finish her sentence.

"There is the memorial, remember," suggested Mr. Gayre, feeling himself the worst of criminals.

"But Lal says he is sure that won't produce the slightest effect."

"It is a pity," observed the banker irritably, "you and he did not arrive at that conclusion a little earlier. If you remember, from the first I felt doubts concerning the expediency of moving heaven and earth to obtain signatures from people who knew practically nothing of the case."

She sat with bowed head, her hands clasped tightly together, the while slow hot tears dropped heavily from her downcast eyes.

"I did—not—mean—to vex you," she said at last, with a mighty effort; "but the delay, the hopelessness of the whole thing, is killing me. I can't sleep, I can't eat, food chokes me; the horror of night, the thought of him lying all in the dark, eating his heart out, with those endless years stretching away in the distance, seem more than I can bear. And my feeling is not selfish—God knows it is not! If I could purchase freedom for him to-morrow, I would die—cheerfully, thankfully—if I only could think of him able to go where he liked and do what he liked, even though I never were to see him again, I could be content. I am a great trouble to you, I know, Mr. Gayre. You must be sick and tired of us both; but if you could only think of any plan, or any person, likely to help him in this awful strait, I would do anything you told me. I would follow your advice implicitly. I would listen to no one else—Lal or anybody. Won't you think, Mr. Gayre? Forgive me for troubling you so much; but it is just like saving a man from drowning, and you would do that, I know, at the risk of losing your own life. O, you will think; I see you will! How can I ever thank you?"

He could have told her, but he did not. Once more he was fighting that demon of temptation, and silently swearing he would not let his better self be conquered, all the landmarks of his higher nature he removed, because of a love he had always instinctively felt was not for the good of his soul.

How should she know? Heaven grant, he thought, she might never know the forces of evil beleaguering the citadel of his humanity at that moment! They came in serried ranks, rushing onwards with almost resistless power, and at last he understood fully what the temptation a man has to war against means, the awful battle he has to wage when once he lets himself be drawn into such a conflict. At that juncture he intended to do right. Self-abnegation seemed grand to him. Again a sweeping sea of chivalric feeling brought a great opportunity to his feet; but while he was stretching down his feeble hands to seize it, the waves ebbed, and bore the chance back into that ocean where so many things, once fair and beautiful and of good repute, lie engulfed.

"Yes, I will think," was all he could say, in a tone which conveyed far, far more than he intended.

In a second she had risen from her chair, and taken a step towards him. He never knew what purpose was in her mind, for she stopped suddenly, while a painful colour dyed her cheeks and forehead, and even her throat.

"I was forgetting something I wanted to say," she remarked, after an embarrassed pause. "It is probable I shall be leaving here soon."

"Why?" Mr. Gayre was so astonished he could only utter one word.

"I have been told I ought not—that is to say, I have been advised—I should not live all alone here, as I am doing. Perhaps you, too, think I have done wrong; but I had no intention. I never thought of that side of the question."

"It was one of your own sex, I presume, who asked you to consider it," hazarded Mr. Gayre, to whom, even at so supreme a moment, the idea of Susan and conventionality being associated suggested a conjuncture so absurd he could scarcely refrain from smiling.

"Yes; though I do not exactly know how you came to that conclusion," and once again the girl coloured. "There was a time," she went on earnestly, "I should not have cared. I should have said, 'Let people think what they like;' but I could not say that now. I have never before been quite by myself. I have always had some other person's wishes to consult, and judgment to lean on; but now my whole life is altered—"

"And?" inquired Mr. Gayre.

"And I suppose I must make a change of some sort. If Oliver were in London—that is, where he was able to know what I was doing—it would not matter. He could, in that case, take care of me, and himself too. Now, I have got him to think of—him as well as myself."

"That is very true," said Mr. Gayre, with a ring of bitterness she did not detect.

"So I have come to the conclusion," Susan continued, more readily, "that I will take a little cottage somewhere near London. I don't care if it be no better than a labourer's. My old nurse would come up and live with me. Indeed, I have written to ask her to do so."

"O, you have written, have you?"

This time it was Susan's turn to look astonished.

"Yes. I would have consulted you, only I could not tell when I might see you next."

"I fancy it would have been impossible for any one to give better advice than that you have already asked and followed."

"You really think so? I am very thankful. For other reasons, too, I want to leave here. I could live cheaper—in— in the labourer's cottage, and I most anxiously desire to save every penny I can. If, some morning, when Oliver comes back, I had not enough to enable him to make a fresh start, I should never forgive myself; but what a far, far cry it is to Loch Awe! Will he ever come back to me? Shall I ever see him on this earth again?"

Within a somewhat wide margin, Mr. Gayre could have answered this question had he liked; but he did not like, and so contented himself with uttering a certain number of regulation forms of comfort, which sounded so cold and unreal, Susan shrank from the consolation they offered.

"He does not believe in Oliver's innocence," she considered after Mr. Gayre's departure. "How am I ever to persuade this the only man who could really help him, of how incapable my darling is of crime?" And because she saw no way of compassing this, she cried herself into a troubled slumber, unwitting the banker felt as certain of Mr. Dane's being guiltless as he did of his own existence, and that over her head there slept a person who could have told her the name of "a conceited puppy's" enemy.

Meanwhile Mr. Gayre's loneliness had been enlivened by a visit from his straitlaced brother-in-law.

"Gad," began that worthy, "what a time it is since I have seen you! Why, you look as washed-out as an old muslin gown! What is the matter? Bilious, eh?"

"I have got a confounded headache," returned the banker, with that lack of ceremonious politeness only warranted by relationship.

"Bad—very bad," returned Sir Geoffrey, with a sympathetic shake, as one who had exhausted the whole run of human ailments, and found nothing so hard to bear as a headache. "'All work and no play,' you remember, 'makes Jack'—far worse than a dull boy; a sick one. Now, look here, my friend, you know I am not a man to recommend stimulants when they can be avoided. I wish to heaven my constitution did not require them! If you think the matter over quietly, Gayre, it really is an awful thing to have a constitution that eternally wants 'picking up.' Mine does, worse luck; if it didn't, I should indeed be thankful. But, however, what I want to say is this: for a headache like yours, you know, there is nothing so good as brandy-and-soda. I think I have mentioned the fact before, but I may as well give you the recipe again. I wouldn't take much—say a glass of brandy and a split of soda—your man might finish the soda; it would not be wasted, pity to waste anything. Try my prescription, Gayre; 'pon my soul, you'll find yourself a new man after it."

"Thank you greatly for *all* your suggestions, but I do not mean to take anything, except some sleep."

"Balmy Nature's, et-cetera," said the Baronet. "Well, I'll not prevent your swallowing that medicine, so I'll be off. O, I forgot what I came to say. Peggy's back."

"When were father and daughter reunited?"

"I wouldn't sneer, Gayre, were I you; I wouldn't, upon my soul; it doesn't suit you, and it's not the thing to make a fellow exactly loved and respected. But, to answer your question, Peg and I were rejoined in filial bonds—no, that's not it; how the deuce does the thing go? However, the dear girl returned to the paternal roof (for paternal read Moreby, thanks to the Jews) a week ago, looking lovelier than ever. We must marry her, Gayre; we really must, you know."

"Marry her if you like, she's not my daughter."

"For which little circumstance you may be very thankful, if you knew all, I can tell you."

"I don't want you to tell me. I want to go to bed."

"I'll not hinder you. She went over to see Susan the very day after she came back."

"Did she really! How *very* good of her!"

"Wasn't it? And she found the poor little woman altogether out of sorts. I am afraid she made a great mistake going and engaging herself to a wild sort of chap like Dane. Something quiet and sensible and domestic I should have thought much more the figure; but there, you never can tell anything about what suits girls. When I think of your poor sister—tut, what am I talking about? Just tell your man, Gayre, to fetch you one bottle of soda and a thimbleful of brandy. Acts like a charm. I know it does with me. No? then I won't keep you up! Good-night—*good*-night!" And the Baronet was gone.

CHAPTER XXVII

" HOW MUCH ARE YOU SORRY?"

PURPOSELY Mr. Fife deferred keeping his appointment on the Wednesday, when Mr. Gayre was to give a final answer, till the last possible moment.

" I thought you had perhaps changed your mind, and were not coming," said the banker.

" It seemed to me only fair to let you have as long as possible," answered Mr. Fife; "although when a man fails to make up his mind at first I generally notice he experiences considerable difficulty in making it up at last. Well, how is it to be?"

" I have decided to go on with the matter."

" Come, that is more to the point. Have you spoken to Miss Drummond?"

" Not yet."

" When will you do so?"

" I cannot tell; probably not until I am able to say, 'Mr. Dane has been proved innocent. He will be at liberty in a few days.'"

"Good Heavens!" ejaculated Mr. Fife. " Is this Bedlam, and are you one of the patients?"

" I should be mad indeed, Mr. Fife, if I pursued any other course."

" It does not make much difference to me. I suppose you know your own business best; but I confess I was not prepared to find Mr. Nicholas Gayre, of the sign of the Tortoise. Lombard Street, so romantic a gentleman. All that remains now for you to do in the way of self-renunciation and chivalry is to give the bride away, take Dane into partnership, and entreat both husband and wife always to regard you as a devoted friend. They won't know how to express their gratitude sufficiently for a while, and then they'll begin to say, 'How intolerable it is to have a stranger coming in and out at all hours ! He takes good care we shall never forget that kindness he did us,' or else Mr. and Mrs. Dane will begin to wrangle about you. He will observe he should have preferred to work out his time rather than lie under an eternal obligation ; and she will remark. she wishes he had never been let out of prison."

Mr. Gayre looked across at his tormentor, but spoke no word—indeed, he had no word ready to speak.

" When are you going to Colvend ?" asked Mr. Fife.

" I have not made up my mind."

" O !" and Mr. Fife laughed ironically.

" May I ask what you mean by your extremely offensive manner?" inquired Mr. Gayre.

" Not much. but enough," was the calm reply. " When do you suppose you will make up your mind ? There is no time to be lost, you know."

" I do not mean to be dictated to by you." declared Mr. Gayre, trembling with passion.

" Pardon me, I fancy I must dictate to you a very little. Just give me an idea, will you, as to the outside period within which it may suit you to open proceedings ?"

" If it is money you want—"

" I want money ; but I can do without it for a short time. And now, as you can't, or won't, give a straightforward answer to a plain question, listen to me. I am not going to wait your convenience. A wrong has been done. and it must be righted," added Mr. Fife, with a nasty jeer. " That nice young man ought to be set up on his pedestal again. He needs comfort ; and we know who will console him. It really is a shame that an innocent person should remain under such a cloud merely because you are unable to decide what you will do."

" I quite agree with you, and you had better see Mr. Colvend yourself."

" Softly—softly ; it is Miss Drummond I shall see first."

" See Miss Drummond, then."

" But I thought you were going to spare her the crowning humiliation of an interview with my unworthy self."

" I meant to do so ; but as you cannot refrain from insolence when addressing *me*, I feel it impossible to carry negotiations further with *you*."

" The insolence, as you call it, has, I fancy, been more on your side than mine. I came here to do you a good turn, and at the same time benefit myself. How was I received ? And now, when all I want is some definite answer from you as to the length of time you purpose to wait before seeing Mr. Colvend, you turn round and advise me to go to my principals, or Miss Drummond, or anybody likely to make a beautiful mess of the whole business, in preference to yourself, who have posed as Oliver Dane's best friend. Friend, indeed? If you could keep him in penal servitude for life I believe you would do it."

"For Heaven's sake take the matter into your hands, and leave me in peace! I will still stand to what I said as regards money, but I should prefer, in other respects, to be out of the affair."

"Meaning, I presume, you would rather some other person hung you, than put the noose round your own neck and kick the stool away."

It was really appalling! Mental analysis, the comprehension of hidden motives, knowledge of the weakness and wickedness of human nature, Mr. Gayre had always previously considered matters appertaining to the higher culture. He felt shocked to find a low fellow like Mr. Fife—a man he would not have shaken hands with on any consideration—a humdrum routine creature as he had seemed, could lay his finger with unerring certainty on a festering sore, and by the aid of instinct, or some equally unaccountable natural gift, jump to the comprehension of motives understood but dimly even by the person they influenced.

It is a shock to any one who thinks himself acquainted with the world to find that his knowledge is of the narrowest description, and Mr. Fife's remark affected Mr. Gayre like a cold douche.

"I fear I scarcely follow you," he said.

"O yes, you do," was the uncompromising retort. "In your class of life your remark is merely, I suppose, a polite hint for me to amend or retract my words; but it is only because I remember my rank is not yours I have refrained from using plainer and stronger language. By appointment— your own appointment, remember—I came here to-night, as I understood, finally to arrange details: and first you tell me what I knew before, that you had decided to go on with the matter; and second, because something I say does not quite please your mightiness, that I had better go through with it myself. The whole fact is you want to 'trim,' and you do not exactly see how to do it. You do not like to tell Miss Drummond her lover is innocent, and trust to her generosity, because you know as well as I do women have no generosity, and no gratitude either, if you come to that. You are averse to going

to Colvend because you feel the first sentence you speak will
put the girl beyond your reach for ever; and you object to
adopt the plan I suggested because you desire to keep up the
character of being something more than human. That is how
the case stands, and accordingly you wish to drift for a bit, to
see if anything turns up. The captain in the old song 'Told
them he would marry, but he never said when,' and in like
manner you may keep on 'intending' to go to Colvend's till
the Millennium, or till the term of Oliver Dane's sentence has
nearly expired."

"If you have quite finished, Mr. Fife, perhaps you will
kindly return me the paper I was foolish enough to sign, and
leave my house."

"As to leaving, I shall go in a minute; as to giving up the
paper, I'm not such a flat. As to the rest—this is Wednesday
—if by Saturday, you have not spoken to Mr. Colvend, I shall
take the liberty of asking a private audience with your young
lady on Sunday."

"Why delay? Why not tell her all you know—if you do
know it—to-morrow?"

"I said before, I had my reasons. I say again, I have my
reasons; but even they won't allow me to postpone action in-
definitely. Oliver Dane is ill; next we hear of him he may be
dying. If he should die—and he is just the sort of chap to
break his proud heart—what becomes of both of us then?
You would have to whistle for your young wife a long time
before you could get her, I am afraid; and I should have to
whistle for my money and something else—"

"How do you know that Dane is ill?"

"What does that matter? I know as all men who are
their own detectives always do know. Yes; and if you had
not been so confoundedly high and mighty with me, I should
tell you something else it might be your interest to hear. As
matters stand, I mean to keep my information to myself for
the present."

"Believe me, I would rather remain in ignorance for ever
than be enlightened by you."

"That is courtesy, I suppose, and good breeding, and all
the rest of it. However, he laughs best who laughs last. Now
I am going. Saturday, remember, is the latest, and I shall
not come here again. Good-night, Mr. Gayre. You think
yourself a very wise man; I will not shock your refined nerves
by telling you my opinion on that point."

He was gone. As he closed the library door with a bang, Mr. Gayre understood the Dane complication had entered on a new phase. After ninety-six hours it could be no longer in his power to speak or to refrain. That halting steed, himself, would—unless he made good use of the short time still at his disposal—be altogether out of the running.

There might be racing hot and swift—hope, despair, falsehood, asseveration, exultation, disappointment; but his share in the excitement, the rush, the prize, would be *nil*. Not even as a friend might he hope to participate in the gladness of the day of triumph, for he understood perfectly that if he failed before night on that fatal Saturday to decide, nothing but renunciation was possible. Mr. Fife, in telling the story, would make Susan clearly understand how he had hesitated between good and evil and failed to do what was right, though he lacked courage actually to commit a wrong.

"Yes; that is the way this brute"—so he mentally styled Mr. Fife—"would put the case." After all there is but a right, there is but a wrong; and would Mr. Fife have been totally inaccurate in describing the banker's conduct as cowardly? Perhaps the courage or the temperament which enables a man to plunge headlong into sin may upon occasion give him strength to perform some act of enormous self-abnegation—sacrifice his own life to save some other life to all appearance perfectly worthless, smilingly wave farewell to happiness for the sake of one who, to our poor human thought, does not deserve to be especially happy.

It is a great mystery. The tendency of our modern life is to wipe all strong emotions, all supreme passions, off the society slate; and yet in a book it has of late become somewhat bad form to study, but which will survive, as it has survived, many changes of fashion and creeds of morals, we are specially warned against being neither hot nor cold.

Perhaps as Mr. Gayre beheld the face of that devil which skulks within the heart of every man and woman, he felt it might have been better had he chanced to be weaned on some different creed than one ignoring our humanity and the temptations which assail it.

Seven times were the walls of Jericho compassed ere they fell; but at the sound of the final trumpet Jericho was an entrenched city no longer, because its foundations were rotten and accursed. If a tree have no root, how can it produce leaf and bud and fruit? The earth, which is gracious even to its meanest child, may give it for a short time some poor show of vitality and greenness, but it is not strong enough to drink in a sap which shall support even during the few short days of springtime; and so it withers away, and is cut down because it " cumbereth the ground."

In the day of his trial, Mr. Gayre found himself wanting; in the hour when he should have been strong to bring forth the best fruit of a man's life, he was barren. At last he knew it is not enough to decide that we will resist temptation—we should flee it. Those who are wise will not let even its shadow fall across their path.

If that night—that first night—he had allowed his better angel to have her way, and lead him through storm and darkness to a land of safety, whence return to the wave-beaten rock where he sat so long considering was impossible, this terrible struggle need never have rent his bosom; but now he could not with his own hand sign the death-warrant—with his own lips he could not speak the words which should give to Oliver Dane his liberty, to Susan Drummond her lover.

He could have done great things for Susan—he could have died for her; but it seemed absolutely impossible he could live without her. He had allowed the grandest opportunity of his life to slip by. What would she not have thought of him! How she would have loved him! And now he had lost all chance even of gratitude.

Mr. Fife would open the ball; and some day, no doubt, tell Susan and the world how he offered Mr. Gayre the choice of being first spokesman, and how that gentleman refused to speak. He might come to be a common jeer, a mere laughing-stock. Mr. Gayre rose in a fury and paced his room. He had still time left. It was still not quite the eleventh hour, though near it. Thursday was gone. Friday wanted but few hours of being garnered into the great eternity. Should he still go to Susan? No; he felt the task beyond his strength. She should be led to meet her lover, but not by him; the delicate rose-tints should once again blossom on her cheek; but when that lovely portrait of tender affection—of perfect happiness— was finished another artist than Nicholas Gayre would add after his name the word "pinxit."

No, he could not do it. He might that first night, in the mad rush and hurry of his soul, have battled through the wind and rain, and, drenched and buffeted, told her all the story; how he had loved, how he had been tempted, how he had resisted, how he had come to bring her peace ; and then once again taking his lonely life in his hand, passed out into the darkness, away from her for ever. Desolate though such an ending of the sweet love-dream might seem, it would have been a thousand times better than the wreck of honour and honesty suggested by Mr. Fife. Then the absolute cowardice of the middle course he was treading ! Was this what years of idleness and prosperity had done for him ?—years of sleeping soft and eating regularly, of conforming to the world's code of conventional propriety, of holding aloof from sinners, and consorting only with those who had balances at their bankers', and were mighty reputable and respectable men and women ?

Yes, it *was* this. Ever since he had left the army, and striven to shape the pattern of his life to that of those amongst whom his lot was cast, he knew each day, as it came and went, found and left him more and more truly a Pharisee thanking God for something which probably was not in the least degree pleasing to the Almighty. He had grown to like and respect money—or at least the things money can buy ; the deadly canker of riches and conventionality had eaten into his very soul, and gnawed away the graces of impulsive generosity and noble chivalry which once undoubtedly were rooted there. He was not the same man. Yon poor publican, who durst not as much as lift his eyes to heaven, would go down to his house justified, rather than Nicholas Gayre, banker, who would gladly have given all he possessed in exchange for strength to do an act of the most ordinary justice. But he could not do it. Just as a drunkard will drain some fiery draught to the last drop, even while loathing the smell and detesting the taste, so this man, whose breath had once come shorter when hearing of great deeds, while recalling wild achievements, lacked courage to cut the rope binding him to the thought of wrong, though honour lay in doing so, and shame abode in that from which he refused to cast himself adrift.

"To-morrow will end it all," he thought, looking forward as a criminal on the eve of execution may think of the following noon when he shall have been hours in eternity.

He would not lift a finger to retard or to expedite events. It seemed to him as though during the course of five days and nights he had lived a lifetime, and he knew at the end of that time one thing he had never known before—namely, that passive resistance is no victory, that a man may lose far more in the course of even a short siege than during a battle.

The library clock first chimed the quarters and then struck nine. But three hours, and then midnight. Mr. Gayre stood still in the centre of the apartment. It was not yet too late; should he still go to Susan?

Irresolutely he turned towards the door, and took a hesitating step in the direction of honour and safety, then—

" Sir Geoffrey Chelston and a lady are in the drawing-room, Colonel. Sir Geoffrey would like to see you immediately."

Mr. Gayre stared at the man.

"Lady!" he repeated. "What lady? Miss Chelston?"

" No, Colonel, not Miss Chelston."

" Good Heavens, perhaps the Baronet has got hold of Miss Colvend!" was the idea that flashed across Mr. Gayre's mind. "What a lunatic I am!" he next decided; "the world contains a few other people and things besides Oliver Dane and his interests."

He went slowly up-stairs; for the second time, as it seemed, Fate had interposed between him and his purpose. He was making yet another most reluctant move towards the right when the mysterious shadow we may feel, but can never see, laid her hand upon and held him back.

Harlequin-like assuming the gay presence of Sir Geoffrey Chelston too! Mr. Gayre smiled as he stood on the landing, considering the remarkable shape it had pleased his deterrent angel to assume. A man possessed by the almost sardonic sense of humour nature (or circumstances) had given him ought to have been able to steer clear of moral pitfalls. But we are all imperfect; and, in his hour of need, Mr. Gayre certainly found his sense of humour a mere snare and delusion.

It had not delivered him from temptation; it had not proved that friend in need which is the friend indeed; quite the contrary. Now the Philistines were on him in reality, his perception of the ridiculous, which had so often come to the rescue when, as regards mercantile non-success, envy, hatred, and all uncharitableness might otherwise have taken possession of his heart, left him with the power to gibe indeed, but the inability to fight. He could see the absurdity of forty-five thinking of mating with twenty-one; but he could not give up his fancy for all that. Susan was none the less fair because the summers of her life had been so few; he was all the more in love for the very reason that he had heard so often the joyous rustling made by Nature when the first touch of spring sunshine awakens her from long winter sleep.

No; it was as well Sir Geoffrey had come. For almost the first time in his life Mr. Gayre felt glad to know the Baronet was close at hand.

He opened the drawing-room door and entered. In the centre of the apartment directly under the chandelier stood the once owner of Chelston; his legs as usual a little bowed; his white hat, which he held in his left hand, ornamented by a broad mourning band; his whole unique person serving unintentionally to screen a lady who, with averted face buried in her hands, sat in an armchair close behind.

"How do, Gayre?" It was the Baronet who spoke. "Knew you'd forgive me. I've brought a poor little broken-hearted soul to you for comfort. I said, 'If Gayre can't help you nobody can. Never met with such a fellow for helping other people.' Susan, Susan, my girl, look up; don't go on crying like that! Here's Gayre. Lord bless you, he'll find some way out of the trouble." And Sir Geoffrey, who was not given to the melting mood, broke off with a very suspicious tremor in his voice, merely to add next moment: "For God's sake, Gayre, think what we can do! I'd take a petition to the Queen myself, only I'm afraid she wouldn't read it!"

"What has happened? What is the matter?" asked Mr. Gayre, feeling literally stunned by the turn affairs had unexpectedly taken.

"There, Susan; there, my dear! What did Papa Geoff tell you? Your own old Papa Geoff;" and the engaging Baronet stroked his favourite down, as if she had been a horse. Mr. Gayre forgave him though; the wretched sinner's genuine love for so pure a creature covered—in his brother-in-law's eyes—a multitude of faults. "Didn't I say to you as we came along, 'Beyond all things, Gayre is practical; he has always his wits about him; he'll make something out of this bother. There's a silver lining, you know, and gad! if there's any silver to be got Gayre's the man to get it.'"

Having concluded which complimentary speech, Sir Geoffrey reined in, and left either jockey who pleased to do the rest of the running.

"Miss Drummond, what *is* the matter?" asked Mr. Gayre.

He had walked across the room, and was standing close beside her, so when, for answer, she held out a piece of folded paper, he could take it from her hand without the intervention of Sir Geoffrey.

"Do you wish me to read this?" he said.

Just for a second she turned towards him a tear-stained face, out of which all the beauty had temporarily been washed by vehement weeping, and murmured,

"Yes."

"I had no notion of it. It was the last thing I should have thought of, 'pon my soul it was," murmured Sir Geoffrey in a stage aside. It was the last thing also Mr. Gayre could have thought of, and yet the most natural in the world. Finding he made no move, already Mr. Fife had commenced to open the ground for himself.

Thus ran the note, which had neither prefix nor signature :

"Oliver Dane is very ill; removed to infirmary. If his friends mean to come forward, they must do so NOW OR NEVER."

After he had read, Mr. Gayre stood silent, clutching the paper in his hand. At last he thoroughly realised the position. Oliver Dane, innocent, buried as a felon; Susan broken-hearted —Susan removed as far from him as heaven itself. Another man, and that man Samuel Fife, would step in, perhaps almost too late to undo the evil intensified by Mr. Gayre's want of decision. But what could Mr. Fife or Susan, or any one who lacked money and influence, effect without tedious and possibly fatal delay? No; it should not be. Mr. Fife's action determined him; all hesitation was over. One surging wave removed in an instant all the landmarks of his life. Good and evil, right and wrong, meant nothing to him then. He would save the man, but he must sacrifice the woman. With his own vacillation he had destroyed the will to choose. Only a single word escaped him at that crisis, "God!" but it was no cry for help, only an utterance of despair, as he turned him to the darksome way that leadeth to destruction.

There ensued a silence which though brief seemed to Susan endless. Twice Mr. Gayre tried to speak, and twice his parched lips refused their office; but at last he managed to say, in a tone harsh by reason of the strong effort required to make himself audible, and the still stronger constraint he placed upon his words,

"I do not see, Miss Drummond, why you should distress yourself so much."

Once again she lifted her tear-stained face, this time to look at him with amazement, while she mutely pointed to the paper in his hand.

"No person who knows anything of the world," went on

Mr. Gayre, "attaches the slightest importance to an anonymous letter."

She rose and stood erect before him—stood encircled by the indefinable charm which was her birthright—stood in her youth and sorrow the better to say fully what was in her mind.

"That letter is true," she gasped ; " I feel it, I know it. I was not thankful enough for my misfortunes. God had been very gracious to me. Though He saw fit to separate us, it was not by the great gulf of death, and yet I murmured ! O, Mr. Gayre, what is to be done? Can't you—won't you—help us? It may seem nothing to you, but it means life to Oliver." And in an access of grief, this girl-woman, with the marvellous eyes and hair, such as the Venetian painters dreamed of but rarely saw, and a tender heart and a nature grand and strong as ever was held within a lissom binding, flung herself on the floor, and held out her clasped hands in an attitude of agonised entreaty to the man Sir Geoffrey had taught her to regard as well-nigh omnipotent.

"For Heaven's sake don't kneel to me!" entreated that man, recoiling a little ; for he was still sufficiently master of himself to know he dared not lift the prostrate figure, lest he should strain it to his heart.

"Gently, gently, does it, old lady," said the Baronet, as, without the smallest desire to take her to *his* heart, he raised the one human being he loved with an unselfish attachment, and placed her again in her chair. "Don't frighten my brother-in-law. He's very slow, but he is indeed very sure. He'll find a way out of the mess, or my name's not Geoffrey Chelston ; and, as I feel I am totally in the way, I'll just—to put the matter colloquially—walk my chalks. You and Gayre will hit on some plan ; I know you will. In sorrow, as in love, two are company, you remember, but a third is a confounded nuisance. And look here, Gayre, this room may be all very fine, but it is beastly cold. Don't you see Susan is shivering like an aspen? Haven't you got a fire somewhere? and can't you manage a cup of tea or coffee, or—or anything for her while you are talking over what is to be done ? Come along, Sue ; come down-stairs with me, and cheer up, my beauty ! Gayre will find a way out of this trouble. Don't cry your eyes out. What would Papa Geoff do if he never saw the sunshine dancing in them again, eh ?"

Discoursing which innocent and childlike prattle, Sir Geoffrey guided the girl from step to step and led her into the library, where he wheeled up the easiest chair to the fire, placed her " where you'll get thawed," patted her on the shoulder, said "ta-ta," and left her to "come to," while he walked into the hall, followed by Mr. Gayre, to whom he made a sign, intimating he wished to speak to him alone.

By, of course, the merest accident Sir Geoffrey turned into the dining-room, and, without waiting to be asked whether he would have anything to "pick him up," in the merest absence of mind laid hold of a decanter and poured out a beaker.

"'Pon my soul," he said, " I don't know how women manage to get through their troubles on tea; but then, to be sure, look at the state they reduce themselves to."

"You have at least the consolation of feeling an undue use of tea has not destroyed your nerves," observed Mr. Gayre.

"No, faith; and I take very good care it never has the chance. Now just look at Susan, poor Susan! She's all to bits. Girl, too, who used not to know the meaning of the word 'fear.' Why, she'd have gone at anything in the old days; and here she is to-night all of a tremble because she is told her lover is sick. And that reminds me she'll need a very light hand, Gayre—she will indeed; she'll not stand much. You'll have to be very cautious. Let her think she's having her head. I don't suppose we can do anything, really; but there's no need to tell her that. In my opinion it would be a capital ending to the whole business if Dane did die; but of course it isn't natural that she should take that view. And now I'll be off. Well, thank you, I may as well have a thimbleful more. Don't trouble, I'll help myself. As I was going to say, when you have finished your talk, bring her up to North Bank. She must not be alone in those lodgings. Peggy's gone to the play with Mrs. Wookes, and is to stop the night; but that makes no odds. Mrs. Lavender will make Susan comfortable. Excellent woman, Mrs. Lavender, though she is so confoundedly ugly. No; I can't stop another minute, really; besides, I'm only keeping you, when I know you are longing to speak comfort to my poor girl. Good-night, good-night. Bless you, Gayre;" and Gayre was left alone.

CHAPTER XXVIII.

HIS PRICE.

WHEN Mr. Gayre re-entered the library, Susan was not sitting by the fire, as Sir Geoffrey had left her, but standing in the middle of the room, with a dazed hunted look on her changed face.

"I think I had better go," she said. "I know you can do nothing for me; if you could, you would have done it ere this. Sir Geoffrey made me come. He thought amongst your friends —but I told him—"

"Do sit down," entreated Mr. Gayre; and he led her to the hearth, where she almost fell into a chair, and sat staring with unseeing eyes at the leaping firelight.

"How do people go through such misery as mine and keep silent?" she murmured at last. "I am sorry to be so trouble-some; but O, if you knew—if you could imagine—" and she broke once again into passionate and uncontrollable weeping.

"Do try to compose yourself, Miss Drummond," entreated Mr. Gayre; "you distress me intensely."

"I can't help it," sobbed the girl, "though my tears won't give him life or liberty. If I could only do something—go to some one! Is there no human being, Mr. Gayre, who could help us? Think of him lying ill—dying, perhaps, in that dreadful place! If it were your own brother, or your friend— but I am talking folly! I will go now. I must not occupy your time any longer."

"You must not think of going yet," he answered. "I have ordered some tea for you;" and even as he spoke tea appeared. "You will have a cup, will you not?"

"It would choke me," said Susan, shaking her head. "I feel as if I never should eat or sleep again."

Mr. Gayre stood before the fire, looking down upon the drooping figure, the bowed head. At that moment his soul was not a battle-field, where good and evil were waging an almost equal war. No; the fight had ended, and he remained silent only because he was waiting for words in which to express his meaning.

All at once he spoke.

"If a man were to say to you to-night, this moment, 'I will strive to set your lover free—there is one way in which I *might* be able to obtain his release,' what would you do for that man? You spoke the other night as though no price which could be asked would seem to you too great."

"Nor would it!" she cried, lifting her swollen eyes, lit with a sudden gleam of almost despairing hope. "Do you know such a man? What would I *not* do for him? Every sixpence I own in the world he should have. I would be his servant—his slave—"

"Would you be his *wife?*"

She did not say anything; she only looked at him in bewilderment.

"Would you be *my* wife?"

It was done. If he lived a thousand years he could never recall that utterance. Till his dying day the expression of incredulous horror that came into her face will never quite fade from his memory.

"You—you—are jesting!" she gasped.

"Am I?"

"I did—not—think you would have jested at such a time; but—"

"Do I look as if I were jesting?" he asked.

If she had lifted her eyes she would have seen a man with the whole fashion of his countenance altered; his lips compressed, his cheeks pale, his gaze bent on her with a terrible concentration; but she did not lift her eyes. She shrank a little into herself, mentally cowering under the weight and horror of the blow he had dealt.

"You never thought of this?" was his next question.

"No; never once."

"Did no idea of anything of the sort ever cross your mind?"

"No; never once."

"You supposed my care for and interest in you arose from the extreme amiability of my disposition?"

"I thought you were my friend."

"There is no such thing as friendship, there can be no such thing as friendship, between man and woman," he said almost fiercely. "It is either love or indifference, unless, indeed, it may be hate," with bitter emphasis on the word. "Perhaps you hate me now?"

She did not answer; she did not even make a sign of dissent.

"Yes; that is always the way with your sex; they are willing—eager to seize every valuable a man has to give, his love, his life, his money, his time, his thought; and then if he ask for the smallest return, he is thrust out into the cold, to find a path through the lonely darkness of his after existence as best he may."

"There is little I would not have done for you, Mr. Gayre," she answered, and there was no faltering in her voice; "but what you ask is not mine to give; and if it were—"

"Yes; if it were?"

"I should not give it you."

"I have made such a mistake in my mode of asking for it?"

"Yes, you have made a mistake. I was grateful to you; I was indeed. But now—O, how can I ever forget what you said a minute ago?"

"I do not want you to forget it. I want you to remember—No; you must not go yet. As you have heard so much, you must hear more."

"I must not," answered the girl. "I feel as truly Oliver Dane's wife as if I were married to him, and the words which would have insulted me in that case insult me now."

"You are mistaken. I am not insulting you. I am offering you the truest, deepest, most loyal love of which my nature is capable."

"Love!" she murmured softly.

"Yes, a man's love, not a woman's—a love I have felt ever since I first saw your face—which I have struggled with, fought against—that has for months past cursed every hour of my life—that is killing me—that I am glad you at last know has crushed all things noble and honest out of my heart, and made me so base I am capable of driving a bargain with you— you, for whom I would die, if, in dying, I could win one look of love."

She stared at him appalled; the very calmness of his tone and the restraint of his manner lent a greater terror to the passion of his words.

"I never meant to tell you this," he went on. "God is my witness, when you entered my house to-night I had no more intention of letting you catch even a glimpse of the war I have been waging with myself than you have of marrying me. A thousand times I have been on the point of saying something which should part us for ever; but I refrained. All unconsciously you have tempted and tried me as man surely never was tempted and tried before; yet I resisted. But a man cannot go on resisting for ever, and I am glad my resolution has broken at last. Yes, if, after to-night, we never meet again, I shall not feel sorry you know that which, but for your own utter absorption, you would have known long ago."

She sat like one stunned. The tears, which had well-nigh blistered her fair cheeks, were dry. Her eyes felt as if red-hot sparks had been thrown in them; her lips were parched, her tongue stiff; and through all there was a pervading sense of shame and misery—of having lost something of great price—of having looked through an unclean window out on a world which never again for ever could seem just the same to her.

For the moment she forgot even her lover—forgot his trouble; as sometimes, in the worry and turmoil of daily life, we forget for a brief space our dead. Then it all came back to her, and she lifted her head and gazed up at Mr. Gayre with a hunted appealing expression on that face capable of silently saying so much.

"I ask you to forgive me," she said at last, with a great effort. "I have been absorbed—and—I did—not know."

"No, you did not know," he answered, with a sad cadence in his voice which touched her inexpressibly.

"I am very, very sorry."

"Why should you be sorry? You have only wrecked a man's life. What are twenty lost lives to a woman?"

"Good-night, Mr. Gayre." She was standing now. "Don't let us part in bitterness. I will try to think of all this only as a bad dream."

"How very kind you are!" he sneered.

"Good-night."

"Wait a moment. What about Mr. Dane? Is he to stop where he is, or—"

She raised her right hand with a gesture of passionate despair.

"Can you really do anything for him, or were you merely trying me?"

"I cannot say. I would have striven."

"And you will still do it for him, though you think me so ungrateful?"

"No. by Heaven, that will I not!" said Mr. Gayre, a torrent of rage breaking down all the barriers he himself had raised. "You have made your choice—abide by it. I shall not try to influence you further. This night I part company with you and your lover. Do what you can for him without my help. Why should I be the one to give up everything?"

Mournfully she turned a little aside, walked to the table, then stood and faced him with a steady front.

"What is it you could do for Oliver?" she asked.

"I have no intention of doing anything now," he answered.

"What was it, then, you thought you might have done?"

"I regret being rude to a lady, but I must decline to answer that question."

"Do you think you could have done anything?"

"I could have tried."

"But you have always tried."

"Well, yes, that is true. Still, formerly I felt my trying would not effect much, or perhaps I should not have been so eager in the matter. Before you go, it is better for you to understand me thoroughly. I believe there is one chance for your friend, which, properly worked, may unlock his prison-door. Shall I try that chance. or not? It is a question for you to decide. I will not hurry your decision. Take till ten o'clock to-morrow morning, and then give me an answer. On the one hand, liberty for the man you profess to love; on the other, happiness to the man who loves you. For I do love you as Mr. Dane never could. I ask nothing from you unless he walks out a free man. Should that day never come till the term of his sentence has expired, you will remain at perfect liberty to greet him when he returns to you."

"And he is ill—perhaps dying now."

"I know nothing of that; he may or he may not be ill. As I said before, you ought to attach no importance to an anonymous letter."

"But I dreamt last night he was dead."

"I really fear I consider a dream of less importance even than an anonymous letter."

"And if he did die?"

"I should say he would be better dead than alive at Portland."

She did not answer. She looked down at the carpet, then

up at Mr. Gayre, then down at the carpet again before she
said,

"I will go now.   I am sorry to have given so much
trouble."

"You will return to North Bank?"

She shrank at the sound of the name, and said,

"O, no—no!"

"As you wish, of course.   You must allow me to see you
to Islington."

"Don't, please don't!" she entreated, with a fervour which
was far from complimentary.

"Just as you like.   My servant shall go with you.   I will
send him for a cab."

"I would much rather walk."

"As this will most likely be the last time on which you
may ever be harassed by my advice, I must entreat of you to
do what I counsel now.   You are in no state to walk, even
were such a course fitting.   I will not intrude further upon
you till Rawlings has procured a conveyance."

He did not trust himself to stay longer with her.   He knew
he had spoken roughly, barbarously, yet he felt that the words
uttered were as nothing in comparison with those he had kept
back, and enough of manly instinct still remained to make
him dread a prolongation of the interview.   Had she gone on
crying and breaking her heart, had she pleaded to him for help
and mercy, he might have at least kept the devil, that was
tearing him sore, out of sight; but the horrible disappointment
of finding she would not even entertain a thought of buying
her lover's liberty on the terms proposed was more than he
could bear.

"Let her try what she can do, even with Fife's help," he
thought bitterly; "and if Dane die while the affair has been
messed up and muddled, she will at least have the consolation of knowing she remained true to her sex, if not to
her lover.   Yet I was a brute.   What other answer could I
expect?"

Had he only been able to obtain a glimpse of Susan's
mind, he would have found the very abruptness of his declaration, the suddenness by which she was made aware of the
nature of his feelings, had produced an effect on the girl's
imagination years of gentle wooing must have failed to do.

She felt horror-stricken as he laid bare before her the passion of his soul, and her strongest sentiment, next to what

Oliver was to do, proved an absorbing pity for the man who loved her vainly, and a deep reproach towards herself.

" I ought to have known," she thought, as she sat looking into the depths of the blazing fire, that seemed no fiercer than the heart the secret of which she had been allowed to see. " I have been all wrong. This was what Margaret was insinuating the other day. If we live in the world there are things we must not blind ourselves to," and she covered her face, though there was no one but herself, to hide the shamed blushes crimsoning her cheeks as the full nature of the position in which she had placed herself was, in its nakedness, revealed.

" Your cab is at the door, ma'am," said Rawlings, just as she reached this culminating point of utter misery.

Instinctively she drew down her veil ere passing out into the hall, where Mr. Gayre stood waiting for her. Gravely he offered his arm, which she just touched with the tips of her fingers. Rawlings opened the cab door, and, at a sign from his master, mounted the box beside the driver, while Mr. Gayre, standing bareheaded on the pavement, said in a low voice,

" Shall I come for your answer to-morrow, or should you like me to send for it?"

She paused a second. His question put the whole of the issue at stake into a concrete form before her.

" I will write," she at last murmured.

" Remember that after to-morrow *I* can do nothing."

" Nothing?"

" Nothing whatever. And now, in case we never meet again (whether we do or not rests wholly with yourself), let me say good-bye and God bless you !"

He was gone. Before she had time to speak, almost before she was able to draw back the hand she had half stretched forth to lay on his, she saw him pass out of the darkness of night into the solitude of his desolate home. The door closed behind him, and she was driving with her own memories and fears, for bitter company, through the streets.

There are assuredly times in life when we are incapable of sustained thought. At such periods the mind drifts like a dead thing over the ocean of being; it is tossed by the waves and buffeted by the currents and driven by the wind ; but, till it awakens in a different hereafter, it knows next to nothing of the tempest it has ridden through, the incongruous points it has touched, the abysses it has swept over.

Mr. Gayre had reached that state. Thought was out of the question. Impulse and passion had urged him on till, among billows of temptation, the better life was beaten wellnigh into insensibility. He paced the room till he was weary, but when, exhausted, he flung himself into his chair, he could not rest. Once again, driven by the fiends within him, he was forced to resume that ceaseless march, up and down—up and down, till he had walked miles over those few yards of carpet.

His servant was a long time absent. Islington might, to his irritable fancy, have been in Africa, judging from the period occupied in covering the distance.

Three times had he rung to inquire if Rawlings were back, and he was just about to ring again, when the man entered with a note.

" I was detained, Colonel," he said apologetically; " the lady kept me over an hour while she wrote this letter. You have been wanting me, sir ?"

" Yes—no—it does not matter, now," answered his master, scarcely waiting till the door closed ere tearing open Susan's missive.

" I cannot stop till morning," these were the words it contained, " to tell you that I have made up my mind—*I agree.*"

She had added a line after this, and then blotted it out. Despite his earnest endeavour, Mr. Gayre failed to gather what she had written and deleted; but there stood forth, as if in letters of fire, the sentence he once never expected to read—*I agree.* She did not trouble him with the reasons which had caused so extraordinary a change, she made no prayer, put forward no excuse; the paper was not stained with tears, the caligraphy was clear as usual. In the travail of her soul such a decision could only have been born, yet there was no hint of agony in the cold decision of her resolve.

" I AGREE !" After hope was dead, at a moment when despair was holding high carnival in his soul, he had got what he wanted. Success was his at last; and success had come thus.

After a time, when the first astonishment was over, and his scattered senses began slowly to return to their owner, he sat down and wrote Susan a long letter.

What he said he never afterwards could clearly remember;

but it calmed and comforted him. After the fret and turmoil of the week he felt indeed strangely tranquil, when, in the early morning, he went out to drop his letter in a pillar-box near at hand.

"I will call," he had written. "about nine to-morrow to see you;" and behold it was to-morrow already, and he had but time to snatch a few hours' sleep ere Rawlings roused him with the words,

"Seven o'clock, Colonel!'

LONG ere Rawlings awoke his master out of that sound sleep which can only be induced by utter mental or physical exhaustion, Susan Drummond was about her business. She had made up her mind on the previous night what she meant to do, and starting from fitful slumbers she rose before a streak of dawn tinged the darkness, to begin a work out of which all hope and happiness was eaten.

But even in the first anguish of her self-abnegation she was not miserable. She had given up everything to try to save her lover, and she did not mean now to make her own task harder and his life wretched by looking idly back on a past which seemed more remote as well as more beautiful than those far-away hours of childhood when she first knew Oliver Dane.

If she were able to save him, if by any sacrifice she could give him life and freedom, what did her personal sacrifices matter?

She had always hoped and prayed that if a great trouble came to her she should be given strength to bear it bravely. The fretting of uncertainty was what had broken her health and bruised her spirit. Now there could be no more uncertainty. She had cast all on one great die in a game, the stake for which was Oliver Dane's liberty. She had done all she could, and she felt content. For the first time since the trial, since that desperate cry of " I AM INNOCENT !" rent the silence of the court, she could think of her lover without hot tears rising to her eyes—without feeling a wild sick desire to rush off and tear the very walls of his prison-house with her poor impotent fingers, so that she might be doing something to lessen the barrier between him and God's free earth.

In her anguish she had cried aloud in the night-time. When there was scarce a star to be seen, when the moonbeams cast lines of mournful silver light on floor and walls, and threw masses of chequered and changing brilliancy into the darkness of her chamber, she rose and paced the apartment's narrow limits, and wondered whether those cold sorrowful rays were piercing the gloom of Oliver's cell; whether his heart was breaking at the thought of the time when they together, hand locked in hand, looked up into the heaven of the tender summer night, their happy souls too full for speech.

But now all that was over; to that great unrest had succeeded a period of almost unnatural repose. She would have given her life for him, but as no one wanted her life, she had sacrificed something which she felt to be more valuable—her future. Yet not sacrificed; for she flung the gift thankfully and with rejoicing at the feet of a man who would never know the price she had paid for his freedom.

It was a changed Susan who went down-stairs at the appointed hour to meet Mr. Gayre.

He looked at the girl with wonder. Where were the tears, the passion of grief, the sorrowful scorn of his own meanness he had witnessed only the previous night? The tears were spent, the passion was over; the girl Susan had departed into that shadowy land of memory, from out of which, any more than from the grave, no friend who once vanishes into it may return to smile upon or greet us save in mournful recollection, and in her place stood a woman who would never again laugh with the gladness, or weep with the passion, or mourn with the despair, he remembered so well.

She gave him her hand, but it lay cold and still in his, like a dead thing; in her sweet eyes he saw deep depths of sorrow, but no light of welcome; the very tone of her voice was different. A swift wave of remorse swept over Mr. Gayre as he looked on the change wrought by a single night. Had he killed her, he could scarce have felt more a murderer than in that first moment of remorse; but the emotion rested on his soul no longer than a passing shadow. The woman seemed dearer to him than the girl had ever been; her beauty greater; the grave dignity of her manner, the unutterably sad cadence in her tone, proved more captivating to his middle age than the young charm and gay grace of the Susan Drummond he should never see again.

Always he had felt there was a chord in Susan touched as yet by no one; and now he understood the nature of its harmony, there arose an evil rejoicing that his had been the hand to awaken the full deep swell a human heart never gives forth till, having eaten of the tree, it becomes as a god, knowing good and evil.

Yes, he had done this, and so become a part and parcel of her life for ever. Let her forget what else she might, it would be impossible for her to forget him. The lore he had taught her was more subtle and mysterious than love, for it showed her the sin love is capable of begetting, told her something of the terror of passion; whereas hitherto she had tasted only its sweetness.

In one night she had grown afraid of him, too; afraid of the wrong a man will do, not merely *though* he loves a woman, but *because* he does so. Already she had graduated in a school many of her sex—maids, wives, and mothers—never enter; nay, of the very existence of which some remain in ignorance.

She dreaded both his power and his will. Once she thought of him but as an ordinary friend; now she recognised him for an enemy. If he had not seen the change in her face, Mr. Gayre would have known from the first words she spoke that, since they parted on the previous evening, she had thought more about him than during all the preceding months of their acquaintance.

" I received your letter," she began. " Thank you for writing it; but we need not talk about what you said in it, need we ?"

" If *you* see no need," he answered, " we will not discuss the matter. I think, however—"

" At all events we need not talk about it *yet*," she interrupted. " Perhaps," she added, looking at him, as if trying to read his very soul, " we might never have to discuss it."

" You mean in the event of my efforts proving abortive?"

" Partly that ;" and her eyes fell under a gaze steadier than her own.

" It is better you should understand me clearly," he said, and the change in her voice was not more marked than that in his " *Remember, I shall hold you to your promise!* I know if you chose to cheat me you could; but I am sure you would not cheat me."

" No," she replied slowly ; " you know I would not cheat you."

" Neither will I delude you—do not imagine I shall release you from your bargain—it was optional with you to make it. There is time even yet to cancel it—do you wish to cancel it?"

" Not unless I could save Oliver by other means."

" It is still doubtful, remember, whether he can be saved by any—"

" So you told me in your letter."

" And as it was optional with you to enter into such an agreement, so it will be optional with me whether I hold you to it or not. I *shall.* It is only fair to tell you this, to warn you to expect nothing either from my weakness or my generosity. And do not say to yourself ' If he loved me, he would not exact such a price,' for you would be wrong. It is precisely because I do love as only men like myself who have passed their youth can love, that I swear if any human being can compass Mr. Dane's liberty he shall walk out free. Then you must marry me. I leave it all to your honour, you see. Were I wise, perhaps I should stipulate for my price first ; but I trust you implicitly—I, who once thought never to trust a woman again."

" You may trust me."

" And some day you will love me. Do not shake your head ; no woman marries her first lover ; indeed, I do not believe the woman lives that could tell who her first lover was. I have no doubt Oliver Dane was not yours."

" I have loved him all my life."

" And no one else ?"

" No one else !"

" Then I shall have only one rival !" he remarked.

" I want to say something to you, Mr. Gayre."

" What is it ? '

" *He* must never know."

" I do not understand you."

She twisted her white fingers nervously together.

" Never know why I did it. Let him think me fickle, false, wicked. I would rather he supposed me the worst girl ever breathed than that he came to understand I had done what you ask for his sake. Liberty would not be sweet ; he would fancy the very air tainted, if he knew the price I had paid to set him free."

" Are you not mistaken ? Is not Mr. Oliver Dane a gentleman who would prize liberty on any terms ?"

" No. And it is you who are mistaken. Mr. Gayre, why is it you hate him so much—he, who never injured you ?"

" You love him," was the answer. and a dead silence supervened.

" There is another thing I must tell you."

" If it be of the same nature. it might be well to defer the communication till we meet again."

"It cannot be deferred.   I had another letter last night."

"From whom?"

"I do not know; but in the same handwriting as that I showed you."

"And—"

"It said, 'No time should be lost if anything were to be done for Oliver Dane.   Some word of hope ought at least to be sent to him at once.'   Can any word of that sort be sent him?"

"I do not know; my acquaintance with prison rules is, unfortunately, of the slightest."

"But you will ascertain?"

"Yes, I will ascertain.   For my own sake I do not desire that any harm should happen to Mr. Dane."

"Sorrow enough will meet him.   O, Mr. Gayre, how can you?   If you were fond of any one, I would not try to take you from her—not if I cared for you as much as—"

"You do not," he finished.

"That was scarcely what I was about to say; but—"

"It will serve, and is perhaps a shade more courteous than the form you had in your mind.   Again, believe me you are mistaken, or else you are an exception to every rule of your charming sisterhood.   I have seen—great Heavens! what have I not seen done by women!   No trick has been too cruel, no artifice too mean, to sever lovers, to entice a man's heart. Ay, and I have known worse than that.   I have known a woman set out with the deliberate intention of winning affections she meant to fling away, and did fling away, as a child casts aside a broken toy.   I have known the best years of a man's life ruined because he found himself jilted by such a woman—his faith destroyed, his hopes blasted, his belief in purity, goodness, honour, ay, even common honesty, shaken to its foundations."

She could not answer him.   Because she had no knowledge of how such things affected a man, was it competent for her to deny their reality?

Further, she grasped he was talking of himself—that in the background of his life's picture there lurked just such a woman as he had indicated—smiling, fair, false.

"No," he went on less vehemently, "believe me, nor man nor woman can tell the evil that 'desperately wicked' thing the heart is capable of conceiving and executing till it is placed where its power for sin has a full and fair chance of develop-

ment. You have no right to say what you would or would not
do. How can you know? You have no experience to fall
back upon ; you are like one walking in darkness who thinks
he sees. Yesterday morning nothing would have seemed
more incredible to you than that you should promise to marry
me. Who can predict what a day will bring forth? Who dare
say temptation shall not tempt, wrong shall not conquer me?"

"I cannot tell," she said, answering his thoughts rather
than his words. "All I know is that, whether right or wrong,
what I have done has been done for Oliver. If it be a sin, I
cannot help it. There seems no other way in which it is possible for me to serve him. It may be I ought not to commit
so great a wrong to you, myself, and him ; but I cannot think
of him ill, dying, perhaps, and remain firm while there remains
even a chance of saving him. I am only a woman after all."

"If you were only a woman you would consider yourself
first and your lover last. It is because you are what you are—"

"Do not go on, please," she entreated ; and he stopped
suddenly, knowing what she meant—namely, that it was outside their contract to speak about love till his portion of the
compact was fulfilled.

"What are you doing about Oliver?" she asked after a pause,
during which she had sat listening to the howling of the wind
—it was a boisterous morning—and fancying what words her
lover traced in its sound.

"I have done nothing yet. I am going to-day to see a
person I think may do something."

"Then why—"

"Do I not go about the business at once? I could tell
you, but I do not like. Yet I will tell you. I stayed here
because I am mad—because I could not help saying and doing
and looking that which makes you hate me. But I will leave
you now, and not come again till I am able to say either I have
some hope of obtaining his release or that I shall never be able
to obtain it ;" and without word or touch or glance of farewell
he was gone, leaving Susan more utterly alone than she had
ever felt before. He had been her friend, and he could be
her friend no more. The only news it was ever likely he
should bring her would be death to all hope for her lover, or
the tidings that the date of her own execution was nigh at hand.

"Can I go through with it?" she thought, with a sickening
horror ; and then the courage which had carried so many a
Drummond high above all considerations of danger and sup-

ported him in death rose strong and great within her. "It is for Oliver," she whispered, and clasped the talisman of her lover's name closer to her loyal heart.

Meanwhile Mr. Gayre was hurrying Citywards, as if pursued by a thousand demons. He had done the things he ought not to have done, and left undone those he ought to have done. He had sneered at Susan, whose tender nature was vulnerable to all his shafts. He had twitted her with love for her lover, as if a woman should not believe her lover without peer. He had failed to comfort—nay, rather he had torn her. He had been—good Heavens! what had he not been?

"But at least," he thought, while slackening his pace as he drew near Prince's Street, "she shall find no half-heartedness with me in the matter of Oliver Dane. The sooner he is released the better I shall be pleased;" and before repairing to his own place of business he turned into the office of Messrs. Colvend and Surlees, which was close to Lothbury.

"Mr. Colvend in?" he asked a porter.

"No, sir. Mr. Colvend has gone to Brighton."

"Can I see Mr. Surlees?"

"Mr. Surlees is out, sir. He will not be back to-day. I think he is going down to Brighton also this afternoon."

Since his first glimpse of Susan Drummond, some check had always interposed between Mr. Gayre and whatever purpose he might have in view; but he meant to take no check now. Less civilly than usual, because hitherto he had always striven to be courteous towards persons in the City. even though his heart was not one with them. the banker remarked:

"I suppose, however, there is some person in charge to whom I can speak on business?"

"Certainly, sir—Mr. Fife, sir. Perhaps you will walk into Mr. Colvend's room, and sit down for a moment. I will tell Mr. Fife you are here."

Mr. Fife, in the character of chief clerk in the old-established and steady-going firm of Colvend and Surlees, seemed a very different person from the insolent individual who in his own had bullied and taunted Mr. Gayre in Wimpole Street. The atmosphere of the City, and the consciousness he was only a person in the receipt of salary, had so impregnated the manner of his working hours that it was at first quite a deferential and cringing Samuel who, in a couple of minutes, entered Mr. Colvend's private room, and said,

"I hope I have not kept you waiting, sir."

Troubled as he was, Mr. Gayre could have laughed out-right. The famous story of those bankers in Newcastle, who, when the great hair movement first made a stir, intimated to their clerks that "though out of business hours they should not presume to dictate what their *employés* were to wear, yet within those limits they must request the absence of moustaches," recurred to him.

Drink, however, unlike a man's own hair, can have its times and seasons; and during business hours Mr. Fife never indulged in any wilder carouse than half a pint of bitter.

"I am sorry to find Mr. Colvend absent," said Mr. Gayre; "I wished to speak to him."

"On a private matter, or on business connected with the firm?"

"On a private matter."

"O! Can I be of any assistance to you?"

"You can give me Mr. Colvend's address."

"And so the cat ate up the blackbird, and things went on as usual," commented Mr. Fife; and he took a rapid turn up and down the room.

"I have no doubt there is profound wisdom underlying your remark; but wanting the key——"

"Being eaten up meant a good deal to the blackbird, but nobody else was much concerned by the catastrophe. Heaven and earth are likely to crash together in the Colvend establishment; but in Lombard Street people will try to overdraw their balances just as usual. And I don't suppose any difference in the Bank-rate will be reported to-morrow."

"If you will kindly give me Mr. Colvend's address, I need not detain you longer."

Mr. Fife did not answer. He took another turn over the Turkey carpet ere he said,

"Man and boy, I've been in this office a matter of—— But that does not signify. What I was thinking is, I'll have to clear out now."

"It certainly does not seem likely that you will be entreated to remain," commented Mr. Gayre.

"I wonder if I have been a great fool!"

"That is a point on which no one can possibly arrive at so accurate an opinion as yourself."

"Anyhow, I'm not going to draw back now. That young minx sha'n't have everything her own way. When were you thinking of going down, Mr. Gayre?"

"By the next train."

"Better not. Stop till after five o'clock, and I'll go too.
You will want me, you know."

"H—m," remarked Mr. Gayre doubtfully. "Well yes—
perhaps I shall."

"You won't find it all plain sailing," said Mr. Fife. "Miss
Dossie can lie through a deal board, and make her father
believe her. You must see him and Mr. Surlees together, and
I ought to be one of the happy party."

"I have no particular objection. But how are we to insure
the presence of Mr. Surlees?"

"How? He will be there, of course: where your treasure
is—you remember."

"I have not an idea what you mean."

"Why, that he is going to marry that simple, innocent,
fragile, timid darling, Miss Dossie, —— her!" and Mr. Fife
turned white with rage, and tramped up and down the room,
as though he were treading over Miss Dossie's body.

"She has cursed my life," he said; "but she'll find she
has met with her match. I'll stop the publication of those
banns, anyhow."

"I hope and trust you will be able to prove your story. It
would be exceedingly awkward if—"

"I know that," interrupted Mr. Fife; "and I tell you
fairly, we'll have a lot of bother both with the old man and the
young lady. That is one reason why I want to go down with
you. I can say what you can't say. I'll not let either father
or daughter humbug *me*."

"Do you think, then, that they could humbug me?"

"They would try," said Mr. Fife, in a tone which suggested he considered the attempt might not be wholly unsuc-
cessful.

"In that case we will go to Sussex Square together," said
Mr. Gayre, glancing at the slip of paper on which the manager
had written Mr. Colvend's address.

"Not nice weather for a trip to the seaside, is it?" suggested Mr. Fife; and then he opened the door for the banker
to pass out, and deferentially attended him through the outer
office.

At that moment the same idea crossed the minds of both
men.

"I sha'n't cross this floor many more times," thought Mr.
Fife.

"He has paid tolerably dear for *his* whistle," considered Mr. Gayre.

As the express rushed down to Brighton that evening the wind howled and tore around the train, and seemed to be trying races with it. It had been a wild day, and a wilder night was coming on. There was scarcely a creature about on the Marine Parade when Mr. Gayre and his companion walked in the direction of Kemp Town; but at almost the loneliest part of the road there stood a female, wrapped in a long cloak, looking out seaward, into the black and dreary night. Neither man noticed her. Mr. Fife was speaking, and Mr. Gayre's head was turned towards him.

"I suppose you have squared matters with Miss Drummond," the manager said; "because if not—" and the remainder of his sentence was lost in a sudden gust of wind.

The woman turned and stared after the retreating figures. It was Susan Drummond.

She had that day fled from London with her nurse, leaving a note for Mr. Gayre, stating she felt she must get away for a short time, and promising to send her address when settled.

A terrible unrest had again taken possession of her, but it was physical rather than mental. She could not remain still. The stormy blast was no fiercer than the fever coursing through her veins; invisible hands seemed drawing her into the night; voices, audible but to herself, cried to her from the sea; the darkness was filled with fantastic shapes; everything appeared different from what was actually the case. A moment after Mr. Gayre had passed she began to doubt whether she had really seen him, whether the words were not a delusion of her own brain.

"I wonder what is the matter with me?" she thought. "I suppose I ought to go home."

She did not, however, make any effort to do so. She remained, with the wind buffeting her, with the sea moaning and lamenting below, with the night getting wilder, and the gloom growing denser, till a hand was laid on her arm, and the old servant, who had been anxiously seeking her, said:

"My dear, what are you doing? You will catch your death of cold."

"I do not know what I have been doing," she answered. "Where am I? O, nurse, take me somewhere—anywhere away from all these dreadful people and this horrible noise!"

"What have you done with Susan. Gayre?" asked Sir Geoffrey Chelston, walking one morning into the dining-room at Wimpole Street, where his brother-in-law sat at breakfast. "Now that I have caught you I mean to get an explicit answer. I call here, and I call at the bank, and you are never to be found. I write to you, and for reply I receive something to the effect that if *I* could tell *you* where Miss Drummond is, you would be much obliged to me. I can hear neither tale nor tidings of the girl. Her aunt does not know where she is, or her cousin, or Lal Hilderton, or Mrs. Jubbins. And *I* don't know; and I may just as well tell you, I consider the whole affair deucedly strange. I left Susan in this house, and I've never set eyes on her since."

"Do you suppose she is in this house still?" asked Mr. Gayre, buttering a piece of toast with great deliberation.

"I do not know what to suppose. One way and another, I feel distracted. I half suspect Sudlow wants to cry off. And now there's Susan. If you do not know where she is, you ought to know. Gayre; that is my candid opinion."

"Miss Drummond is at Brighton."

"Brighton! What on earth took her there?"

"To get ill, I suppose; at any rate she has been ill."

"And why could you not have told me all this long ago?"

"Because I have only been acquainted with her address since eight o'clock this morning. She has had fever or something of the sort, and was unable to write. She is getting better now."

"I feel a load taken off my mind," cried the Baronet. "'Pon my soul, I have been madly anxious about the poor girl. Best girl in the whole world; and to think of her being laid up all alone at Brighton."

"She isn't alone; she has some former servant with her. Won't you have some breakfast, Sir Geoffrey?"

"Not a morsel, thank you—must be off. And yet, now I think of it, if you could just let your man bring me a glass of beer. I fancy I might manage a slice of that cold beef—second thoughts, you know, eh, Gayre?"

Mr. Gayre rose and rang the bell. As he returned to his seat the Baronet eyed him critically.

"I say," he cried, "what's up? What have you been doing to yourself? Why, you are losing all your flesh; and you are not half the man you were a month ago! No panic in the City, I hope?"

"If there were, I do not suppose it could affect me much. A house which does not go in for great gains cannot afford to incur the risk of heavy losses. No, I have been worried to death about that Dane business. I had better have gone and hanged myself before meddling in the matter."

"Ah, by the bye," said Sir Geoffrey, with guileless innocence, "what is this I hear about Dane?"

"I don't know what you may have heard about him."

"Why, that he is not guilty, and all the rest of it."

"Who says he is not guilty?"

"That is beyond me to tell you. There was a paragraph about him in the *Chelston Banner*, a vile, low Radical broadsheet. Wookes sent it up to me marked. The London Correspondent stated he had good reason to believe the whole case would be reopened; that it was whispered one of the parties engaged in what seemed to be a most nefarious plot against the young man's reputation was about to give himself up to justice; that a thorough investigation had been solicited; that extraordinary facts had already come to light, and further startling revelations might be expected; that a gentleman in the City, possessed of wealth and influence, had gone into the matter heart and soul; and that it was chiefly owing to his exertions the whole villanous conspiracy was exposed. Several romantic circumstances were connected with the case, and the name of a young lady freely whispered as having taken a somewhat active part in the affair."

During the course of this recital Mr. Gayre's face was a study. His colour changed from white to red and from red to white once more; he compressed his lips, an angry light shone in his eyes, and he struck the table passionately as he said,

"That scoundrel will make a nice mess of the whole matter."

"Dear me! Then there is something in it! Poor, poor

Susan, I am so glad! If you remember, Gayre, I always said
Dane was innocent. When you were hardest upon him, I
maintained no young fellow, born and brought up as he was,
could have sunk into a common thief."

"You did no such thing," retorted Mr. Gayre. "You said
he was guilty, and complained he would not make a clean
breast of the matter."

"No, excuse me, Gayre, it was you."

"Excuse *me*, Sir Geoffrey, no man could have spoken
more strongly than yourself—"

"Of course, in his behalf! When all the world was against
him I raised my voice, and—"

With a muttered oath Mr. Gayre pushed back his chair and
rose from the table.

"I know of old," he said, "it is of no use trying to pin
you down to any statement, or expecting you to remember
anything except what suits your own convenience; but I tell
you fairly I am not in any mood to stand much more of this
fooling. Would to Heaven I had died before I ever heard the
name of Oliver Dane; and I wish I could go to some part of
the earth where I should never hear it again!"

After which expression of opinion, Mr. Gayre left Sir Geoffrey to his meditations.

The Baronet shook his head.

"Poor fellow!" he said, in audible soliloquy, "he's harder
hit than I thought; shouldn't mind betting something now his
chances are not worth a brass farthing. or half the money.
Pity, too! Well, I did all in *my* power. It was a match I
should have liked vastly. Lord, who'd have thought of things
taking the turn they have! Daresay Dane will get a lot of
damages out of those rich beggars. Hope he'll chance on a
good solicitor—some sharp lawyer up to his work; that's what
I've wanted all my life. Must talk to Susan about it." And
Sir Geoffrey went to the sideboard, and poured himself out
another tumbler of beer; having drunk which, and casually
remarked to vacancy that his throat was as dry as a whistle,
he went off about his business, whatever that might be.

Meantime, in hot rage, Mr. Gayre had chartered a hansom,
and drove down to the Borough, in a street off which thorough-
fare Mr. Fife had hired a "second-floor front," large enough
to contain himself and all his worldly possessions. His first
interview with Mr. Colvend on the great Dane question proved
his last. He was not permitted to remain long enough in the

office, even to balance his petty cash; and had there been anything wrong in his accounts, things would have gone badly with him. Usually the mildest of human beings, Mr. Colvend's indignation against the ex-manager knew no bounds; and when Mr. Fife insisted upon being brought face to face with the fragile Dossie, he absolutely refused to produce his daughter till Mr. Surlees said, in common justice, that young lady should hear the charge made against her.

That young lady denied everything. She clung to her father; she asked how he or any one else could believe such dreadful stories about her; she declared she had never written a letter to Mr. Fife or spoken to him, except in her father's office, in her life. She looked at Mr. Surlees with great appealing eyes shining through a mist of tears, and said, "Surely you won't desert me;" she called Mr. Fife a "bad, wicked man;" she ran up and down the gamut of all her little arts and graces, and finally bursting into a torrent of passionate tears, rushed from the room, Mr. Gayre, with deadly courtesy, opening the door for her.

Mr. Colvend followed his daughter with feeble and tottering steps; already he looked an old and broken man.

When he was left alone with Mr. Gayre and the manager, Mr. Surlees rose, walked to the hearth, and standing with his back to the fire, and hands deep in his pockets, remarked,

"Here's a nice kettle of fish."

It was so nice a kettle of fish that not only had Miss Colvend lost her husband who was to have been, but a dissolution of partnership between Mr. Colvend and Mr. Surlees became imminent.

"And whenever," remarked Mr. Fife to Mr. Gayre, "two men fight, if you notice some dog gets a kick. I'm the dog that has got kicked this time."

"And serve you right," thought Mr. Gayre, but he did not say so.

Amongst the various persons concerned somehow or other, Mr. Dane's little affair had come to a deadlock. Mr. Colvend pooh-poohed the idea of taking action in the matter: Mr. Surlees would not. Mr. Gayre was at a loss to know how to proceed. Time drifted on, and an innocent man lay at Portland, fighting with disease and eating his heart out.

"Cannot you get a message conveyed to him somehow?" Mr. Gayre asked Mr. Fife, who inquired what good that would do, unless some one meant really to push the matter ahead.

"*I* don't intend to let Miss Dossie and her papa walk over the course," said Mr. Fife, a little later. "*I'll* find a way of forcing their hand, or my name's not Samuel."

"This, then, was Mr. Fife's notable scheme," considered Mr. Gayre, as the hansom swirled round corners and dashed along crowded thoroughfares.

"It was you put that notice in the Chelston paper," he said, entering Mr. Fife's room, where he found him busy smoking a pipe.

"Even so—it was I."

"And what object could you hope to compass by putting in such a rigmarole of nonsense?"

"It is not nonsense."

"Why, who in the world is going to give himself up?"

"I am, if things are not soon put on some different footing. I have got a friend—as clever a chap as you'd wish to meet—and he told me that was the best and only way to checkmate them and benefit myself."

"I think it might be checkmate to you. So you have been taking advice about this business, Mr. Fife, have you?"

"Only in a general sort of way. I'm not a man likely to make confidants, unless I see my interest in doing so. I can keep my own counsel till I find it pays to open my mouth. By the way, Mr. Gayre, have you ever been to Tooting?"

"No; why do you ask?"

"O, only out of curiosity. To revert to the Dane question: is it likely, do you suppose, that Messrs. Colvend and Surlees mean to stir in this matter at all?"

"Not if they can avoid doing so."

"And they consider themselves honest and honourable men, I suppose?"

"Mr. Colvend does not believe your story."

"None so blind as those that won't see."

"And Mr. Surlees' notion is, Mr. Dane's friends are as well able to take up the matter as he. What I gather from his reluctant remarks is, that he knows he must have a great deal of trouble about the matter, but he wants to have as little trouble as possible. He means, I see, to put no obstacle in the way, and is willing to facilitate any steps which may be adopted to obtain Mr. Dane's release. You can judge, therefore, the annoyance I feel at the unwise step you have taken."

"I am not so sure it was a mistake," said Mr. Fife, with a nasty leer.

"No?" questioned Mr. Gayre. "While I am here, Mr. Fife," he added, "pray oblige me by putting out that pipe. I don't want to go about the City reeking of tobacco."

"I have no wish to offend you," returned Mr. Fife, at once complying with the banker's request. "Upon my soul, I'd rather work for than against you, if only I could make you understand it's of no manner of use trying to gammon me. You see, I was not brought up to the genteel humbug sort of business, and I had to see so much and do so much of it at Colvend's that I'm more than a bit tired of trying to act the saint when I feel myself a sinner. Now to tell you what you came here in such haste to know. Do I think that little paragraph in the paper will stir up Colvend and Surlees? No, I don't—except to bitter wrath."

"Then what made you put it in?"

"Well, you see, there are a few other persons on earth besides Colvend and Surlees."

"Meaning—"

"Meaning in this especial connection Mr. Oliver Dane's friends."

"I am afraid Mr. Oliver Dane has no friends except Miss Drummond."

"Not even you?" And at this juncture Mr. Fife took up his pipe once more, but immediately laid it down again.

"I have tried to do what I could—I hope I always shall continue to do what I can—for Mr. Dane—not, however, on his own account; I never laid claim to being a friend of his."

"Suppose we drop all disguise, Mr. Gayre, and talk as if we were—I really don't exactly know what; because were I a partner, say, in Glyn's house, likely as not I should put a gloss on for you; and supposing—ah, that's it—supposing you were such as myself, what would you say to me, and I to you, eh?"

"Really, Mr. Fife, I do not know; much the same, however, I imagine, as I am saying to you now, and you are saying to me."

"Not a bit of it!" exclaimed Mr. Fife. "What I should say is this: 'I meant to make one person speak, and that person's surname is Gayre, Christian name Nicholas. He has been trying to drift on with Miss Drummond, and now he knows he must speak if he does not want somebody else to forestall him; and as he dislikes having his cattle hurried, he is furious with Samuel Fife for spurring them on a little.'"

"Your knowledge of me and my motives seems exhaustive," observed Mr. Gayre.

"I am very glad you think so, because that is precisely my own opinion. I have given a good deal of thought and attention to you, one time and another. Long before this question about Dane arose I used to wonder—wonder like the deuce—how any man in his sober senses could let a business such as yours go to the dogs."

"Is the manner in which I conduct my business any concern of yours?"

"No; I only wish it were. People would soon see some changes in Lombard Street that might surprise them. I know what is passing through your mind—'bachelor's wives and old maid's children;' but a bachelor can surely tell when a man's wife is going wrong, and an old maid need scarcely be a Solomon to know her neighbour's boys are a set of unruly brats."

"If my affairs have given you any amusement, Mr. Fife, I am sure I ought to feel gratified. As to Miss Drummond, even had I been disposed to repeat to her the story of Miss Colvend's evil-doings, no opportunity has presented itself for doing so. I have not seen Miss Drummond for nearly a month."

"Why, what's the cause of that?"

"Illness, from which she is only now recovering."

"Whew!" whistled Mr. Fife. "That's a bad job. I wish I had known. If I had, I wouldn't have trumped your ace just yet."

"It can't be helped," said Mr. Gayre, accepting his own defeat and Mr. Fife's concession with an air of lofty magnanimity. "I confess I did desire a little time in which to prepare Miss Drummond's mind for the fact that it might be possible to prove Mr. Dane innocent. Now, however, thanks to you, matters have reached a point which compels me to go straight from here to my solicitors."

"All right," answered Mr. Fife; "and if they tell you there is only one way to clear Dane, I'll stand to what I said, and give myself up. Ask your solicitors whether they think I'd get clear off, and if not, the term for which I should be sentenced. I want to know, for more reasons than one."

"Very well, I will ask them," agreed Mr. Gayre, wishing more than ever, as he made his way down the narrow staircase of a house let out in "apartments," he had never heard the name of Oliver Dane.

IT is somewhat humiliating to consider how much sickness and how little sorrow affects our personal appearance. A bad bilious attack will pull a man down more than the death of his wife; toothache keeps a sufferer on whom it has fastened its fangs wide awake, though heartache often fails to do so.

All her mental anguish—and there could be no question but that, since the previous summer, the girl had passed through a season of intense and continuous agony—had failed to work the change in Susan Drummond a few weeks of serious illness sufficed to do.

Mr. Gayre felt unutterably shocked when, ushered into the room where she sat in an easy-chair propped up with pillows, he saw the havoc so short a time had wrought.

Pale, wan, emaciated—a mere shadow of her former self—her eyes dull and weary, her listless hands thin and nerveless, her whole tired attitude that of one who had just returned worn out from so long a journey into the Dreadful Valley—it seemed almost as though she might better have gone on to the end of her awful pilgrimage, and entered a land from whence no tone returns to earth, no echo even of a sigh.

Could this really be Sir Geoffrey's Susan, with whom he had ever associated the idea of strong health and almost superabundant vitality?

"Miss Drummond," he said—and those were the only words he could speak, as he tenderly took her wasted fingers in his own strong clasp—and looked mournfully at the woman he loved.

"Won't you sit down?" she asked feebly—the while she smiled a wan, sad smile, which smote him to the heart.

"Why did you not send to some of your friends?" he asked; "it was cruel to leave us in ignorance of where you were, in such uncertainty as to what could have become of you."

"No one knew where to send," she answered. "I wrote as soon as I could."

"I wanted to write to you," said Mr. Gayre, "but having no address—"

"Yes— about what? Oliver?" and for the first time she hesitated a little over his name, and coloured painfully.

"Yes, about Mr. Dane."

"Is he—free?"

"Not yet, but—" as she turned her head aside with a faint gesture of sorrowful disappointment, "pray do not look so wretched, Miss Drummond. I have every reason to hope his imprisonment will not continue much longer."

"You are only saying that to comfort me. Perhaps he is *dead*. I have been ill such a time. Tell me the worst! O, if he is dead, I wish, I wish, I had died too."

"He is not dead. Upon my word of honour, as far as I can know anything I have not actually seen, I believe him to be well again, or at the worst, very much better. A message, I understand, has also in some manner been conveyed to him, so that he knows friends are at work who soon hope to compass his release."

"But friends have always been at work—and hitherto no good has resulted—and I don't think any good is likely to come from their efforts. O, what shall I do—O, my darling, what can I do? If only—only you were able to tell me,"— and as she finished this last apostrophe, which was not in the least degree addressed to Mr. Gayre, great tears rolled down her cheeks—tears she was too weak to wipe away.

"For Heaven's sake do not cry," entreated Mr. Gayre, "I bring you nothing but good news. There may be delay; there always, in such cases, must be delay, for though it seems to be easy enough to get a man into prison, getting him out is a difficult matter. Circumstances, however, have come to my knowledge that make me feel sure ere long Mr. Dane *must* be liberated. I mean to spare no effort in the matter. I have instructed my solicitors, and they are taking all necessary steps. I assure you I feel it cannot be long before Mr. Dane is once again a free man."

"And on what ground are you asking for his release now?" she inquired, "because he is so ill?"

"No—because he is innocent," answered Mr. Gayre, flushing up to his very temples, yet nevertheless looking straight at Susan.

"But he was always innocent—I always knew that."

"Yes, only the difficulty is, you see, to get other people

to be of this opinion. There was a time when I myself fully believed him guilty. There remains no doubt on my mind now but that he is innocent, yet I see the greatest trouble ahead before we can prove him to be so. My solicitors seem to think, however, that if we are only patient for a short time, they will be able to find a way to persuade the Home Secretary to order a searching inquiry into the whole matter, or grant him a free pardon at once."

"A free pardon for what?" asked Susan, indignation endowing her for a moment with sufficient strength to grasp the arms of her chair and sit up, the while the colour of old dyed her cheeks, and her eyes grew dark with the intensity of her passion, "for a crime he never committed."

"I seem not to be able to speak to-day without distressing you," said Mr. Gayre, almost at his wit's end. "The words are a mere form, and what can the form signify in such a case? You want to get Mr. Dane away from Portland; do not quarrel with the means likely to compass that object most speedily."

"I will not—I forgot. Liberty for him on *any* terms— *any*," and she laid her head wearily back on the pillow, "yet I can't think Oliver would care for freedom as a favour, which ought to be given to him as a right. He must know nothing about it till he is out again. Were I a man—" and she stopped and made a sign for Mr. Gayre to give her water.

It was sweet to do even this much for her, but it was dreadful to feel how she shrank from contact with him as he held her up, and see the way her feeble hand shook, and hear the glass tinkle against her teeth, because he who once would have been denied no privilege of staunch and kindly friendship, had passed the border line and mentioned love.

Putting a strong constraint on himself, as a father might have done, he withdrew his arm, and took the water from her lips, and crossed the warm covering over her panting breast. Then he said, moved by what demon he could never afterwards imagine,

"Were you a man you would feel like a man, and the man does not live who, after a few months—ay, days—of penal servitude, would not take his liberty on *any* terms."

She did not answer him for a minute. Restlessly she moved her averted head, as though struggling with some great emotion. Before turning her face again towards him, she said, in a feeble voice, yet with the greatest decision,

"Had Oliver been the poor creature you think him, I should never have promised to be his wife. Though that is all gone and past, you must *never* say anything against him to me. For even in spite of all his faults—and he has faults—I shall think of him as the one perfect man I ever knew. A man could not be perfect who was more than human."

"It is something," said Mr. Gayre, "to know how to avoid your displeasure. I only wish you would tell me how I could win your favour."

"I am so tired," she moaned, "I wish you would go. No, I did not mean to say that; only I feel weary—weary—"

"I am going," he answered. "I will not intrude longer; but before I go tell me what I can do to please you."

She could not speak the words that trembled on her lips, but she looked at him with that piteous look of dumb entreaty we sometimes see in the eyes of an animal utterly at our cruel mercy, then—

"Be just to Oliver," and hid her face, whilst giving him her hand.

Yes, this was all he could ever expect from Susan Drummond. If his name never passed her lips, it would be "Oliver," "Oliver," "Oliver," in her heart for ever.

Mr. Gayre had some time to wait before a train started for town, and he employed the interval in walking along the Rottingdean Road till he found a point whence he could reach the shore.

The tide was out far as tide at Brighton ever is, and while he stumbled back over the great stones and shingle, he took a savage satisfaction in telling himself the mess he had made of a life that once promised a brilliant future.

"First Love, then Money, then Love again. Accursed be both love and money," he muttered, regarding that horrible waste of long and unpicturesque sea which is seen to such advantage from the East End of Brighton.

"When she marries me—and she will marry me, because such as she cannot give a promise and take it back—the same loyalty which has kept her true to a man under a heavy cloud will keep her faithful to her husband. I shall have to dread no rival save the never-to-be-forgotten and perfect— And yet, my God," he added, turning quite unconsciously seaward, as though he felt somewhere—somewhere beyond the low horizon running in an expanse of dull gray water—the God in whom he believed—our God who sits above the water-clouds would hear the cry of one of His creatures, who in no great or grand fashion had drifted so hopelessly wrong—" I would rather try conclusions with *any* rival than contempt—any man than repugnance."

" What have I done," he thought, walking slowly along the beach, with head bowed and hands clasped idly behind his back, "that twice I should have loved women who had no look or smile for me? I—" And then memory, taking him gently by the hand, gave him back the shy glances, the faltering tones of those who, in the days of the dead gone by, which could be his no more, would have been glad to take him for better, and equally ready to leave him if worse ever came.

" It's all a mystery," he thought, as some time or other we have most of us thought, when trying to solve the great problem of lives mismatched, or worse than mismatched; and then he went back to town, and in the stir and bustle of London forgot the lesson of which, by the mournful sea, he had caught a mere glimpse, but which there was nothing surer than that, in some form or other, he would have to learn the last word ere he understood Nicholas Gayre.

Once again time went on, the days flew by. Two or three afternoons a week, occasionally more frequently, the banker ran down to Brighton, but he made no progress with Susan. In fact, he made as little progress with her as his solicitors seemed to do with the Oliver Dane conspiracy.

At last there came an hour when Susan spoke plainly. She was getting strong again; she could walk a short distance; the far-away look he had come to know so well lay constantly folded within the deep brown depths of her tender eyes. The roses which go on blooming, even over the grave of human hope and happiness, had begun to tint her cheeks once more; her figure gave promise of again being rounded. The Susan he once knew had gone like the last year's snow; but a fairer, nobler, more worthy Susan paced the Marine Parade, rejecting the supporting arm he would have wished her to lean on for life.

Once again spring had come upon the earth—spring, early spring, that year filling the world with gladness—gay with flowers, bright with sunshine. All through the land hawthorn was blooming, and birds were singing, and wild flowers decking the fields and river-banks and copses.

The sea looked blue and glittering, as it lay calm under the azure sky; but Susan had no thought to spare for sea or sky,

or white-winged vessel. Still Oliver Dane remained at Portland, breaking his heart or eating it out, according to whether
despair or frenzy was at the moment in the ascendency.

"I mean to leave Brighton, Mr. Gayre," she said at length,
"and return to London."

"You prefer London?" This was interrogative.

"I think I may be able to do something for Oliver, there—
and I know I am doing nothing here."

Mr. Gayre bit his lip, but made no reply. They walked on
a little further, and then Susan, pausing and looking over the
parapet down at the shore beneath, went on,

"And I have been also thinking that when I do go back to
town it might be better if you did not call so frequently."

"May I ask your reason?"

He knew his wisest policy would have been silence, but the
question rose to his lips, and he had no power to restrain its
utterance.

"You know," she said, "our arrangement was conditional—"

"Yes; but we mentioned no special time in which those
conditions were to be fulfilled. It is not from any lack of
endeavour on my part that—"

"I am quite willing to believe you," she interrupted; "it
would be terrible to think, really, you had *not* done all in your
power; nevertheless—"

"It is a matter which cannot be hurried—"

"I mean to try if I cannot hurry it; and if through *my*
exertions Oliver should be set at liberty—"

"Our contract is to be considered at an end; is that what
you want to say?"

"I feel it had better be at an end. You see," she went
on more firmly, now the first step had been taken, "if Oliver's
release cannot be procured *soon*, it may as well never be procured."

"You think so?"

"Yes, I do; a few months more, and he will have been in
prison for a year. You cannot tell me now, certainly, that at
the end of another year he will be free. It may be all very
well for us—standing here, able to go and come as we like;
but for him—" and she broke with a little passionate cry for
help to the God she sometimes thought—she could not avoid
thinking—had deserted her.

"If"—and her voice was calm and steady once more—"if,

though innocent, I cannot prove his innocence—if there is no justice or mercy to be hoped for—we must bear our burden of sorrow as best we can. He has lived somehow through this awful time. If I can do nothing, I must live too, that I may meet him when he is once more free. I have made up my mind, Mr. Gayre. It was for Oliver I said I would marry you if you obtained his release. It is for Oliver I say that, as you seem able to do nothing to help him, we must part. No woman cares less for the world's opinion than I, but I am bound to consider the man whose wife I mean some day to be. Though he has lost everything else, he shall find he has not lost me."

Mr. Gayre did not answer immediately—he felt stunned. That she could arrive at such a decision was an idea which had never occurred to him. Something lay beneath the surface. Could Mr. Fife—could any one—have sent her that cutting from the Chelston paper? No, he scarcely thought that; but—

"I presume you do not mean to sit down and abandon Mr. Dane to his fate without making some further attempt in his behalf."

"No. I told you I thought I could help him, and I intend to try."

"And may I not be permitted to assist?"

"Well, you see, Mr. Gayre, so far your assistance hitherto has been of but little use, and—"

"I have asked such a price for it," he finished.

"I would have been willing to pay that price for it; I would have paid *any* price almost, before my illness, to set Oliver free, and ever since, till quite recently, no thought of refusing to act up to the letter of our bond occurred to me. But you have not fulfilled your part. Oliver is still in prison; time goes on, and nothing is done on his behalf. His innocence is not proved; even that free pardon of which you spoke is not obtained. Why should I remain in servitude when no good results to him? If nothing can be done by man, I must ask God to give Oliver and myself strength to bear our burden with submission, and live as cheaply as possible, so that when he comes out he may have a home to receive him, and money enough to take us both abroad should he wish to leave England."

"In other words, Miss Drummond, you have thought of some scheme by which you may obtain his release irrespective of help from me."

"Yes, I have thought of a plan; but I daresay it would never have occurred to me, had your help promised to be of the slightest use."

"May one inquire what your plan is? If it be a secret," he added, seeing she hesitated, "pray do not feel yourself under any compulsion to tell me."

"There is no reason why I should not tell you," Susan answered. "Before I left London, if you remember, I received two anonymous letters."

"Yes, I recollect."

"Well, I think the writer meant kindly by Oliver and me."

"Possibly."

"And what has occurred to me to do is this: Advertise and entreat the writer of those letters to come and see me. I have thought the matter over, and it seems to me there is hope in the plan, even if only a forlorn hope."

"There may be."

"You do not seem to think much good likely to result from my scheme?"

"My own have not hitherto borne so much fruit I dare venture to disparage yours."

Her heart dropped down like lead at his words. Had he opposed her she would not have felt half so much discouraged.

"It may do no good, I can but try."

"And if you fail, Miss Drummond, do I clearly understand that I am to make no future attempt?"

"Not unless—"

"Unless what?"

"Unless there seems a likelihood of something being done for Oliver immediately."

"What do you call immediately?—a day, or week, or month? Give me some idea of the time you mean."

She paused a moment, then said: "Suppose we fix a period of not more than three months."

"And if within that time I can procure Mr. Dane's release, you will marry me?"

She paused again before she answered,

"Yes, I will marry you if, meantime, I fail to set him free through my own exertions."

"I see."

"And, Mr. Gayre, during the period you must not come to me."

"Or write?"

"I should like to know what you are doing."

"The plain English of which is, you wish me to write."

"I wish to hear about Oliver."

"And if I have nothing to tell you about him. I am to send you no letter."

"I would much rather you did not."

"You are very plain spoken."

She made no reply to this—only walked a little way, before she said, "I think I should like to go back now."

Without a word he faced round and they slowly returned the way they had come. Mr. Gayre's spirit was very bitter within him. He knew, at any moment, some circumstance might occur to make the Dane affair plain sailing. Over and over he had told himself it was impossible no means could be found to liberate an innocent man. His solicitors, though slow, were sure; but if Susan took the helm she would do one of two things. either run her vessel on the rock, or else, by dint of sheer determination. get the case brought so prominently before the public that Mr. Colvend, by the mere force of popular opinion. would be compelled to urge his daughter to confession.

Further. he distrusted Mr. Fife. He could not understand the expression with which the ex-manager occasionally regarded him. He had no reason to suppose the man meant to play him false, yet that some scheme was maturing in his busy brain, he felt it impossible to doubt. He knew him to be needy, unscrupulous. desperate ; so far he had been living on the money Mr. Gayre paid him, but from time to time he threw out hints which implied his views of the future were large, and that it was not his intention to render those dreams realities by dint of hard work.

"Had enough of it for dog's pay." he explained ; "whatever halfpence might be going Dane got—I had the kicks for my share."

Likely as not the moment Susan's advertisement appeared he would go to her, get money from her, and tell her the whole story.

"No, I'll stop that," thought the banker, looking askance at his companion, who, with eyes bent down. seemed trying to solve some knotty problem, "and you *shall* marry me yet. You will find you have not to deal with a boy, or even Oliver Dane,"—having arrived at which conclusion he said aloud,

"'Though I am not to write to you, you will write to me, if

you think I can be of any service—and you will not go away
and hide yourself without leaving even an address where a
letter might find you."

"I did not do so before, intentionally," she answered.
"You know I was so ill, so very ill. Just when you spoke I
was thinking about the night when I came down here. It
seems a long time ago, but perhaps you remember what a
stormy day it was."

Yes, Mr. Gayre did remember—he was never indeed likely
to forget that journey from London, with the wind howling
round the carriage—and rain dashing itself at intervals against
the glass.

"It was a wretched day," he agreed, "and a more wretched
evening."

"Well, do you know I could not rest in the lodgings, but
came out here, where we are now, alone in the wild weather.
I must have been mad to do such a thing—and am going to
tell you the oddest fancy. As I stood here—just about here—
I felt sure I saw you pass. A strange idea, was it not?"

It was not half so strange and inexplicable as the tell-tale
colour which rushed up into Mr. Gayre's face. He could not
help it, he could not command his features.

"*Were* you here—really?" asked Susan, astonished. "I
always thought it must have been a fancy of mine—but—"

"It was no fancy," said Mr. Gayre; "I came down here on
the Oliver Dane business. I hoped to have settled it that night."

"And there was some one with you."

The banker made a gesture of assent. He could not have
spoken then to save his life.

"And he said—ah!" and Susan pulled herself up in the
middle of her speech, as we sometimes start in the middle of a
dream.

They did not exchange another word till they reached the
lodgings. Mr. Gayre, though uninvited to do so, followed the
girl in. Susan did not sit down, and so he could not.

"I am to go, then," he said, "and never return unless I
bring you good news—it is rather hard for me, is it not?"

"It is better," she murmured.

"Yes, for you, perhaps. I wonder, though, if my absence
will make you as much happier as you suppose—whether you
won't miss me a little. Before we part, can't you find one kind
word, Susan, to say to a man who loves you as he never loved
any creature before?"

It was the first time he had called her by her Christian name, but she did not take any notice that he had done so. Lifting her eyes she looked him strait in the face, and said:

"I will try and forgive you, Mr. Gayre."

"Forgive me for what?" he asked.

"For hating Oliver, for seeking fee or reward in this matter, for doing so little to help him in his strait. I know you would not have done anything if you could have helped. Had the cases been reversed, he would not have acted as you have done. He would have moved heaven and earth to compass your freedom ; he would not have tried to take your promised wife from you ; he would not have insisted on a woman marrying a man she could never love nor respect, as the price of her lover's freedom."

"Good-bye," he said, holding out his hand ; "do not let us part in anger ; you will be sorry, after I go, to think you could speak such cruel words. I asked for a blessing, and you give me instead something akin to a curse. I wanted some pleasant memory to carry away with me into the world, and you impute the worst possible motives to me, whose only sin has been loving you too well and faithfully. No, you need not tell me to go, I am going. Why are you so angry with me, that you will not give me even your hand? What is the reason of this extraordinary change ; why will you not speak? Well, I had better go, I suppose. Good-bye, Susan. Good-bye, my darling."

"Good-bye," she anwered coldly.

He took a few steps towards the door, then, moved by some sudden madness, turned, and before she could have the slightest idea of his purpose, had clasped her in his arms, and kissed her over and over again.

She did not struggle, she did not speak a word, only when he released her, which he did as suddenly as he had caught her to him, she stood for a second, looking with eyes full of wonder and reproach, and then, still in silence, walked out of the room.

Mr. Gayre was not, perhaps, in the happiest state of mind for seeking an interview with Mr. Fife, yet it was to that individual's lodgings he repaired immediately he arrived in London.

Before he slept he felt he must know the course Mr. Fife would adopt. If Susan advertised for the writer of those letters would he go to her? that was the question Mr. Gayre put plainly to Messrs. Colvend and Surlees' late manager.

" *I* sha'n't take a morsel of notice," declared Mr. Fife. " What's the reason of this new move? She's not satisfied, I suppose."

" Very much the reverse."

" What's the matter with her? Rome wasn't built in a day, or a night either, and it's not so easy to get a man out of gaol, as anybody might suppose till he tried the experiment. Besides, what does she want? Her young man running loose about the world, no doubt! If she could only realise the fact, he is far safer where he is; and when all that is settled, why doesn't she marry you? I thought the matter was finally arranged."

Mr. Gayre shook his head. " We will not discuss Miss Drummond any further if you please," he remarked; and on Mr. Fife saying " All right " very cheerfully, the conversation would have ended, had not the ex-manager suddenly put this question:

" By the bye, Mr. Gayre, *have* you ever been to Tooting?"

" You asked me that same question some time ago," said the banker. " Is it a conundrum, or have you any special reason for referring to the place?"

" Well, yes, I have. Look here, Mr. Gayre, should you like me to put you in the way of making a lot of money?"

" Money is always useful. Is there a gold-mine anywhere in the Tooting direction?"

" There is a quagmire, at any rate, where a fortune is in the way of being lost. When I used the word making I ought to have said saving. I can prevent your being a good bit out of pocket, or I am much mistaken."

" Prevent my being out of pocket! What do you mean?"

" Precisely what I say. I believe I can be of use to you, Mr. Gayre; but I do not want a sum of money this time—I want a commission. Will you give me ten per cent on any loss I am able to put you in the way of avoiding?"

" I have no objection to make such a promise, if I see that the loss without your interposition would have been certain."

" Will you stick to that?"

" Yes, subject to the condition mentioned."

" The commission is too heavy. Look here, let us say five per cent certain, and I will leave the rest to your generosity, or rather to your justice, for I don't believe you are generous."

" You ought to be honest, Mr. Fife, for you do not flatter."

" You would not give me sixpence more if I did flatter you. Now before we engage on this other matter, I should like to understand exactly how you and Miss Drummond stand. She wants to see me, and you do not want me to see her. What's up?"

"I have told you. She thinks she can find some means to obtain Dane's release."

"And supposing she did—what then? O, you don't want to tell me that; come, you had better. There was once a lion, you know, and there was likewise a mouse. Two heads are better than one, remember, particularly when the second head is mine. What was the nature of the arrangement you made with her?"

Mr. Gayre stood silent. Even to this man, who had been his evil genius, he could not tell the nature of the bargain he had made.

"Shall I guess for myself?" said Mr. Fife, with a nasty laugh. "The arrangement was conditional—speak if I am wrong—and the lady now wants to back out of it. I could have told you exactly how it would be. They are all alike. The very best of them can't bear to wait a minute for anything. If you are unable to hand the article they ask for across the counter they will have none of it. You ought to have married her first—made her fulfil her part of the contract. She will never marry you now. If the truth were known, I daresay she is tired of Dane too—perhaps seen somebody else she fancies better than either of you."

"No, *that* she has not!" exclaimed Mr. Gayre vehemently, finding voice at last. "I wish to heaven she had! She speaks of nothing, cares for nothing, thinks of nothing, but Oliver Dane. I can see she is now gradually making up her mind to wait for him. She has done a rule-of-three sum. One year has nearly gone by: seven years will in the same way pass somehow for both of them. Once she relinquishes all hope of getting the sentence reversed, she will put down the number of days before he can walk out a free man, and every night, after she says her prayers, strike one off the list."

"Do you mean to say, then, matters are quite at an end between you? I thought, from your wanting me to keep quiet, you had not quite played out all your own cards. Tell me the real state of the case. After to-night you will not be able to devote much time to Dane's affairs, and you will need my help there too, or I am greatly mistaken."

Though still not easy to talk of the matter, Mr. Gayre found it easier to say he had still three months, during the course of which, if Dane could be set free, Susan would marry him.

"It's not long," observed Mr. Fife, rubbing his chin, when, after a considerable amount of hesitation on the banker's part, he found himself in possession of the girl's expressed determination, "but we must see what can be done. It is getting dusk now, Mr. Gayre; if you will kindly put on your hat, we will make the best of our way to Tooting. If you do not care to be seen travelling with me—and, indeed, it is as well we should not seem acquainted—we can behave like total strangers on our journey."

"I leave the whole matter to you," said the banker carelessly; though, indeed, there was nothing he less desired than to be going about the world in the character of Mr. Fife's bosom friend.

Long before they reached their destination it was quite dark, but by the aid of a lamp close at hand, Mr. Gayre was able to take in most of the details connected with a fine old house, to which his companion silently directed attention.

It stood well back from the road, and was approached by a gravelled sweep, which enclosed a circular grass-plot. There were trees and shrubs of old growth about the place, and an air of stability and repose marked the house and its surroundings.

"You would not say that establishment could be kept up on a few hundreds a year," suggested Mr. Fife, as they stood together looking over one of the entrance gates. "There is a stable at the rear, and one very good horse in it. There is a coach-house and a natty brougham in it. There is a garden which requires two men to keep in order; and there is a presiding deity in the shape of a lady, who cannot get through the day without being waited on by a butler, a maid, a housemaid, and a cook. Just a quiet, modest, steady-going, respectable establishment; no show, no ostentation; nevertheless, one that must require some small amount of money to keep going. Don't you agree in my opinion?"

"Certainly," said Mr. Gayre, sorely puzzled.

"The lady," proceeded Mr. Fife, "who resides in that house is supposed to be a widow, possessed of a fair fortune. Her reputed name is Stanley. She is not very young—over thirty, at any rate—but she is handsome. You have taken in as many of the details of the place as is possible, unless we could get inside, which we can't. We must not stand here any longer. I want to call on a friend in the neighbourhood for five minutes; so if you will charter a cab and drive home to

Wimpole Street, and give your servants orders to admit me when I appear, I will follow you as quickly as possible."

"You intend to tell me something you think I ought to know?"

"Yes; for Mrs. Stanley is not a widow, was never married, and has not a sixpence of her own."

"Then who—" began Mr. Gayre.

"What I mean to tell you when I get to Wimpole Street is the name of the man who supplies the sinews of war necessary to carry on that campaign."

CHAPTER XXXII.

AWAKENING.

MORE than an hour elapsed after Mr. Gayre's return to Wimpole Street, before Rawlings, opening the library door, announced Mr. Fife. Contrary to his evening custom, that gentleman was perfectly sober; and as he deferentially took a seat opposite the banker, he looked once again a model clerk—a man who had not a thought, hope, wish, beyond the counting-house and his employer's interests.

He was paler than usual, and seemed fagged, which fact he accounted for by remarking,

" It's a long pull from Tooting here."

" Surely you have not walked !" said Mr. Gayre.

" O no, I haven't walked; but take it any way you like it's a long pull." Then he sat silent for a while, contemplating the candlesticks as if he were appraising them.

" I am going," he at last began, speaking slowly, and never removing his steady gaze from the candlesticks, " to tell you the name of the man who keeps up the establishment we were looking at this evening. He is called Nicholas Gayre."

" Are you mad ?" asked the banker. " I never was at Tooting in my life before. I never knew there was such a house as that you took me to see, and I never heard there was such a person on earth as the Mrs. Stanley, who, you say, lives there, till you mentioned it."

" That may all be—indeed, I know it all is. Nevertheless, it is you and no other who rent the house, pay the wages, settle with the tradespeople, and spend Heaven only knows how much on madam—"

" You will perhaps presently kindly explain the enigma."

" Presently—yes. I suppose "—and at this point Mr. Fife turned his eyes towards Mr. Gayre—" you will not dispute the fact that a business cannot stand still ?"

" I should have thought it possible."

" Should you ? Well, it can't; nothing under heaven can stand still; it must be always advancing or retrogressing.

When your great-grandfather died he left a fine business behind him. When your grandfather died the business was a fine one still, but the diminishing process had begun. The world was going on, the business was being left behind. When your father died comparatively Gayres' had dwindled to quite a small concern; when you die—"

"Pray proceed; do not allow any feeling of delicacy to stop you," urged the person whose end was so plainly alluded to. "When I die—"

"There will be no Gayres' if you do not meantime either attend to your business yourself, or see that somebody else attends to your business for you."

"May I ask the connection between all this and the house at Tooting?"

"Certainly; I am getting on to that. When your father died he left you, amongst other things, a safe business, if a small one."

"You are quite accurate, Mr. Fife."

"And a perfectly honest staff of clerks?"

"I believe so. Till quite recently I never had any reason to suspect the honesty of any one in the establishment."

"And in that case it was not *you* discovered there had been peculation; it was your manager, Mr. Pengrove."

"It was his duty to discover if anything of the sort was going on."

"Exactly. And whose duty is it to discover if anything is going wrong with Mr. Pengrove?"

"With Pengrove! O, that is too absurd!"

"Is it? I suppose Mr. Pengrove's salary does not exceed eight hundred a year; in fact, I know it does not."

"I do not know where or how you obtain your information, Mr. Fife, but in this instance it is correct."

"While up to the year 1866 he had but five hundred. During the crisis of that summer he proved himself so able and trustworthy that your father advanced his salary to six hundred."

"Again you are right."

"Since that period you gave him another advance of a hundred; and last year finding personal attention to business more and more irksome, and the society of your brother-in-law more and more fascinating, and your manager more and more trustworthy, you finally raised his honorarium—that is the word, is it not?—to eight hundred."

"Though of course delighted to find how thoroughly acquainted with the details of my business you are, I must confess to some surprise as to how you have mastered them."

"I could tell you that, too; but it is a matter quite beside the question, and would only detain us from the point we have to consider. Mr. Pengrove, then, till about the end of the year 1871, had nothing except six hundred a year on which to support a wife, educate his children, and what is called 'maintain his position.'"

"Mrs. Pengrove was an heiress."

"Heiress to what? No money, certainly. To ill-health, I admit, and a tendency, not uncommon amongst ladies, of rendering home somewhat unpleasant to her husband."

"Do you know for a fact she did not bring Mr. Pengrove a fortune?"

"For a fact. Mrs. Pengrove was a Miss Garley, the daughter of a gentleman out at Homerton, who amused himself by preaching thunder and lightning sermons on Sunday in a little whitewashed barn, and supported a large family by selling exceedingly bad grocery through the week. Miss Garley had nothing but her face, and that soon faded; she looks now like a very poor portrait in water-colours which has hung for a long time on an exceedingly damp wall. Mr. Pengrove, I presume, told you his wife had a fortune?"

"Merely incidentally. Whether she had or not was, of course, no business of mine."

"O, of course not; no more your business than whether Jane, your housemaid, meets her young man round the corner."

"Mr. Fife, will you kindly say in so many words how that house at Tooting concerns me?"

"With the greatest pleasure. Mr. Pengrove is Mrs. Stanley's 'trustee.' Mr. Pengrove is constantly at the house on business; and one of these fine days he will marry the lady, and take up his abode at Tooting altogether."

"Bless my soul, the man can't marry her! He has got a wife already, as you are well aware."

"Yes; but that wife can't live long. She has an incurable disease. It is only for 'contrariness' she has not died long ago; and when she does die, you shall see what you shall see if you fail to put a stop to Mr. Pengrove's little game at once."

"And what is his little game?"

"That is for you to find out. I have sketched an outline; you surely can fill in the details. I have no exact means of telling how much you will find yourself to the bad; but I should imagine the deficiency will turn out to be not less than a hundred thousand pounds."

"What?" said Mr. Gayre; and he said no more, for the simple reason that he could not.

"And if you don't want to be utterly ruined," went on Mr. Fife coolly, "you will put your own shoulder to the wheel, and try to get your cart out of the rut."

"But how?" asked Mr. Gayre, at length finding voice— "how could any man rob me to such an extent?"

"I'm sure I cannot tell; you know the position of your own bank better, I should imagine, than anybody else, except your trusty friend and servant, Mr. Pengrove. If you have not money in your strong-room, you have, I suppose, money's worth. Where are you going? No, for Heaven's sake, Mr. Gayre, don't make any disturbance to-night. If you go to Pengrove's house, he'll give you the slip safe as you are alive. Let it be till to-morrow morning. Get to the bank early—*he's* always there early; have him into your private office, and don't let him leave it till you know where every title-deed and bond and mortgage is you may ere long be called upon to make good."

"I will go down to the bank now, and examine the securities. If I find one missing, I shall give him in charge to-night."

"Do; and *I* give *you* not longer than eight-and-forty hours to repent not taking my advice. Why, your bank is not a strong one—you know that; and if at a day's notice the deposits are withdrawn and all securities required, you may as well put up your shutters."

"I would rather do that than—"

"But why should you do anything of the kind? You must make up your mind to lose a lot of money, but you need not lose all. If you must have revenge, well and good; but first count the cost. It's all very well to cut off your nose to spite your chin; but after a while a man must begin to miss his nose. If you only keep a quiet tongue in your head, you may pull through yet; if you don't the Bank of England couldn't save you so far as to enable you to get a living out of Gayres' in the future."

Far into the night Mr. Gayre and Mr. Fife sat talking. According to custom, at a certain early hour the female servants repaired to bed, leaving Rawlings on guard below. He was the most discreet and faithful of butlers; yet even he could not help marvelling what his master could find to say to that low impudent fellow Fife.

"He might just as well ask *me* into the library, and order up a devilled bone and some punch for my supper, as have *him* there," grumbled the man to himself; and then Mr. Gayre's bell tinkled, and Rawlings, quiet and decorous, went up-stairs and waited just inside the door to hear what his master wanted.

"Shut that door," said Mr. Gayre, "and come in."

Rawlings obeyed.

"I am afraid something is wrong in Lombard Street," began his master.

"Truth is," interposed Mr. Fife, fortified by hot brandy-and-water, "I *know* there is a great deal wrong in Lombard Street, have just come round to give your master a hint and—"

"Allow me for a moment, please, Mr. Fife. I shall want your help to-morrow, Rawlings; therefore please see breakfast is ready at eight, and that you are at liberty to leave for the City at half-past. I will give you full directions in the morning."

"Thank you, Colonel," and the man could scarcely refrain from the old military salute, so delighted was he to be taken into confidence, so relieved to find this unaccountable intimacy with Mr. Fife indicated nothing worse than something going wrong in Lombard Street. "Though, indeed," thought Rawlings, "that might mean a good deal to some of us. I wonder if the Colonel would go back into the army? I don't know how I should take to that myself after the time I've had of it here."

"Do you think you can trust him?" asked Mr. Fife, as Rawlings left the room.

"I would trust him with my life," answered Mr. Gayre.

"Ah, but this is not a question of life; it is one of money," said Mr. Fife, with a sarcasm that would not have disgraced the banker himself.

Late though it was before Mr. Gayre went to bed, he never closed his eyes. He had slept after the loss of his self-esteem, but he could not sleep now the loss of money was in question.

At last he realised all the bank had done for him; how little he had done for the bank. What Mr. Fife said was painfully true. As each succeeding Gayre for generations had departed, he left, in proportion to the times, less money behind him. It was pretty nearly the old story of the single talent repeated in Lombard Street. Safety the Gayres had thought of to the exclusion of progress ; and now, as a fitting sequel, the last of the name seemed likely to be not merely shoved up in a corner, but left, in addition, well-nigh destitute.

"And you have no one to thank but yourself," Mr. Fife had most truly observed. "If a man professes to be in business, he should attend to his business. Your father did not ask you to give up the army merely that you might drop into the bank for an hour a day. He could have found a dummy to do everything you latterly professed to do—better."

It was of such utterances as these, and of how certainly he had left things to "take their chance," Mr. Gayre thought as he tossed restlessly from side to side.

Even then Ruin might be keeping watch in Lombard Street, though the outer world were still in ignorance of her presence. Ruin ! worse than ruin ! Value lay, or was supposed to lie, in the strong-room at Gayres' to a larger amount than the whole of the money he owned in the world would cover.

"Nothing had been advanced upon those deeds and mortgages and bonds, and plate and jewels ; but "—and at this point Mr. Gayre started up with the intention of going there and then to Lombard Street to learn the worst—"if these things were not forthcoming, how should he meet man or woman who had confided them to his keeping ?" The Act of God was one thing, the carelessness of man another ; and Mr. Gayre knew, since he relinquished the idea of making Gayres' a big power in the City, that he had been criminally careless both of his own estate and the goods of other people.

"During this last year particularly," conscience hinted, in no uncertain tones, " each day you have been getting worse and worse ; each hour you have been leaving more and more to subordinates."

"A true bill," he murmured. "I have not done any real good since I saw Will Arbery riding Squire Temperley's hunter in the Park. Would to Heaven I had selected any other route that morning, never stopped to speak to Sudlow, never set eyes on my niece, never watched young Arbery managing that horse, never seen Susan Drummond ! Yes," he added vehemently, " I would to God Susan Drummond had never crossed my path !"

It was not the first time he had expressed that wish ; but even when the powers of good and evil were waging war within him, he had never felt it more fervently. To be not only lowered in his own esteem, but to be poor as well, seemed more

than he could bear. Hitherto, if he gained Susan he accounted
the world well lost; but when it came to the test, when he was
called upon to lose much the world accounts of value, Mr.
Gayre could not be quite so certain.

Suppose at that moment Ruin was actually in the cellars of
Gayres', crouching beside The Tortoise, removed from its
proud position by his grandfather, what could Susan avail him?
She did not love him rich; was it in the least degree likely she
would care more for him when poor? How could he humble
himself to tell her that even riches had refused to stop with
him: that his boasted wealth was gone, and his social position
also? She would say, perhaps, they would have to make the
best of matters; say it with that look of half contempt and
whole dislike he had learned to know so well. He never could
make her care for him: while the sun set and the moon rose
while grass grew and water flowed, he never, let him do wha
he would, might win a glance of love or a smile of welcom
from the woman he had treated as a conqueror might a slave.

Over and over and over again, through the watches of tha
dreary night, he conned the words of that song so many d
us, under like circumstances, have set to doleful music of ou
own making, the burden of which is Loss, and the refrain
Despair.

He tried to sleep, but he could not. He strove to chea
himself into the belief Mr. Fife had spoken untruly, but eve
that poor reed broke as he touched it. Mr. Fife's way of talk
ing was not that of a man who desired to delude or conciliate
Quite the contrary—Mr. Fife was terribly plain. He said Mr
Pengrove had stolen, was stealing, would steal; that Mr. Gayre
had no more right to complain of having been robbed than a
shopkeeper who puts his goods out on the pavement for any
thief to walk off with.

"Confidence," he went on, "may be a very fine thing in
theory, but your customers, I fancy, would think caution a vast
deal better in business. You should have kept your keys yourself, Mr. Gayre, and seen the locks were not tampered with."

Long before it was time to go to Lombard Street Mr.
Gayre had finished breakfast.

Having agreed to follow Mr. Fife's advice he could not, as
his inclination prompted, rush down into the City and go
through the contents of Gayres' strong-room without another
moment's delay.

"If once the affair gets wind you may suspend payment,"

Mr. Fife told him. "Follow my counsel, and, unless things are in a very much worse state than I think they have yet had time to get into, you may, with hard work and judicious management, pull through. But remember, you will have to work hard, and bring all your common sense to bear on the matter. Half the bankrupts in London smash up because the moment some bother comes they lose their heads. I am talking of the honest men. Swindlers rarely make a mistake of that sort."

At length the moment arrived when he might make a move, and, like a greyhound let out of leash, Mr. Gayre started for the City.

It was the first time in his experience he had ever wished to go there; and even in the midst of his anxiety he could but smile to consider the reason. "I have let all these years slip by," he thought, "and now in a moment the fear of poverty brings me to my feet, as the hope of gain never could have done."

In Lombard Street he met Mr. Fife, and turned with him for a moment into Change Alley.

"Think you are in command again, Colonel," said the ex-manager very earnestly. "It needs as much courage to face a difficulty like this as to stand fire. I'll be at hand when you want me."

The interview between Mr. Gayre and his manager was not long, but it sufficed to change Mr. Pengrove's whole appearance. When he entered the private room he looked a smug, prosperous, respectable man of business; when he came out he resembled nothing so much as a thrashed hound, longing for a quiet corner in which to lay its aching bones.

But there was to be no quiet corner that day. He had to go on with his work just as if detection were still in the far distance. He was obliged to assist in checking the securities; he had to compel his trembling lips to speak and try to steady his hands, and strive to seem unconscious that even when, for appearance' sake, he went out at one o'clock for his accustomed chop, he was never lost sight of for a moment.

During the whole of that busy day Mr. Gayre's thoughts did not once stray to Susan Drummond. For the first time since their ill-starred meeting, he forgot the fact of her existence. The hours were so full of excitement and anxiety. Love found himself out of court; and when, late at night, the banker returned to Wimpole Street, he saw, almost with indifference, a letter addressed in a handwriting which four-and-twenty hours previously would have stirred his every pulse.

The contents were merely to the effect that Susan had returned to her former lodgings. The note began " Sir," and ended " yours truly."

" I shall have to think about all this later on," he considered, feeling in very truth he was unequal at that moment to think of any subject save whether it would be possible to save his credit.

" You must get money, and that immediately," had been Mr. Fife's last words before he left the bank, where he stopped for hours after every one else—even Mr. Pengrove—was gone ; and it was how to get money without exciting wonder or arousing suspicion which occupied Mr. Gayre's mind as he walked ceaselessly up and down his dining-room.

Able to come to no conclusion, exhausted both in mind and body, feeling his tired brain at last refuse to answer to his call, he went wearily up-stairs to bed, where, perfectly certain he should not close his eyes all night, he fell into a deep and peaceful slumber.

The sun was streaming into his room, when he awoke with a start, and the words some one had spoken to him in a dream still ringing in his ears.

" Mrs. Jubbins will lend you the money—go to her."

Yes, Mrs. Jubbins would lend him the money, but *could* he go to her?

Mr. Gayre thought not, and the close of another anxious day found him in the same mind.

" Have you decided on the best way of quietly raising enough money?" Mr. Fife asked, when once again they parted at the bank. " There is no time to lose."

Mr. Gayre knew that. Nevertheless, he felt he could not possibly ask for help from Mrs. Jubbins.

" If your bank," said Mr. Fife, who really was working heart and soul in the matter, " had been like any other bank, there would be no trouble about the matter ; but no legitimate reason exists why Gayres' should be short of cash. You don't discount, you don't advance ; you run no risks ; you have done nothing like anybody else ; and the consequence is, now you need to borrow, everybody will imagine there is something wrong. Yet money must be got till you are able to turn yourself round. Have you no friend who could and would help you at this pinch?"

Mr. Gayre answered that he had friends, but he did not like to ask them.

" Perhaps you would rather go into the *Gazette?*" suggested Mr. Fife. " I foresee that will be the end of the matter if you delay much longer ; and it would be a thousand pities. Lord, if you only had a few capable men about you, what might not be made of this business even now ! Why don't you go to your solicitors ?"

No, Mr. Gayre thought, he would not go to his solicitors then, at any rate.

" There is one person I feel sure would lend me all I want," he at last explained, with a little natural hesitation.

" Then for Heaven's sake do not lose a minute in seeing him !" cried Mr. Fife. " Any day or any hour some one of these things may be required, and the worst of most of them is that no money could replace them."

" That is too true, unfortunately," answered Mr. Gayre. " I will go now, before I change my purpose."

" That is right," said Mr. Fife ; " and I hope from my soul you may be successful."

MRS. JUBBINS was not in her pleasant drawing-room when Mr. Gayre arrived at The Warren. After a minute or two spent at one of the windows idly trying to catch the only peep of the Knockholt Beeches obtainable from Lady Merioneth's dower house, the while every instinct he possessed was revolting from the errand which had brought him down, Hoskins appeared to say his mistress was in the Wilderness—should he send for her —or would Mr. Gayre prefer to go to Mrs. Jubbins there. Mr. Gayre preferred the latter suggestion, and, making his way into the Wilderness by a walk which led straight from the trim terrace into a grassy hollow, where the trees grew so thick they found it a hard struggle for existence—where bracken and grass and blackberry runners, and hemlock and gorse and wild flowers all mingled in rank and picturesque luxuriance— soon found, by the noise of voices, he must ascend to a higher part of the grounds, left almost as much to the gardening operations of nature as the dell he had plunged into.

It was with a little cry of genuine pleasure and surprise that Mrs. Jubbins, seated on a mossy bank and surrounded by some of her younger children, welcomed his arrival.

"You are *such* a stranger," she began, "but I won't waste a moment in scolding you now you have come. I *am* so glad to see you again," and Mrs. Jubbins really looked delighted as she stood, handsome, prosperous, happy, and middle-aged, with the sunbeams glistening upon her luxuriant hair, her well-developed figure, and her rich yet quiet dress.

"You have not lunched?" was almost her first question.

"Yes, thank you, I have."

"Then what should you like best to do, go indoors, or stop out here, and enjoy this perfect afternoon?"

Mr. Gayre, deciding to enjoy the perfect afternoon, found a seat for himself on a felled tree, and took off his hat with a view, as Mrs. Jubbins decided, of making himself quite at home.

Never, perhaps, on the face of this earth did man feel himself less at home, but he was in for the matter and did not intend his courage should fail him at the last moment.

"Where *have* you been all this time," asked the widow, "out of town?"

"No, not out of town except for a day, now and then; I have been very fully occupied."

"And how is your niece?"

"Very well, I believe—I have not seen her for some time."

"When is she to be married?"

"I really do not know—I have not seen Sir Geoffrey either very lately. Have you?"

"Not since Easter. He does not come here now—"

"O!"—and Mr. Gayre looked at Mrs. Jubbins, and Mrs. Jubbins looked at Mr. Gayre.

"And I am so sorry," added the widow, "for I thought him a most delightful person, so amusing—and original—"

"Happily," interpolated Mr. Gayre.

"But he chose to take offence, and of course I could not beg and entreat of him to come here on a merely friendly footing."

"It was much safer not," said Sir Geoffrey's brother-in-law.

"And how is that dear Miss Drummond?"

"She is getting better."

"Still at Brighton?"

"She was the other day," answered Mr. Gayre, who had his own reasons for not mentioning the fact that Susan was in London.

"What about that wretched man, Dane?"

"I trust he will be at liberty ere long."

"Dear me, I hope not."

"Why do you hope not, Mrs. Jubbins?"

"Because that poor girl will marry him, and there can be nothing but misery for her with so dreadful a creature."

"There are persons who believe he was wrongly convicted."

"That is too shocking—of course, if he had been innocent he would not have been found guilty."

"I do not think that exactly follows."

"O, but it does, you may be quite certain! I was talking to Deputy Pettell about the matter only yesterday, and he assured me there could be no possible doubt upon the subject. Of course he must know, having so much to do with the Lord Mayor, and being constantly at the Mansion House."

"I should not dream of pitting my poor opinion against that of Deputy Pettell."

"Now you must not be naughty, Mr. Gayre. I can't allow it. I really can't. Mr. Deputy is a particular friend of mine, and he is not to be laughed at."

"I was not laughing at him, I assure you. Nothing could possibly be further from my mind than laughter of any sort."

"And I am sure I do not feel inclined to laugh when I think of that sweet Miss Drummond being married to a convict."

"But, my dear Mrs. Jubbins," expostulated Mr. Gayre, "you signed the petition for that convict's release."

"So I did, but I never thought anything would come of it."

Mr. Gayre laughed—though in no mirthful mood, Mrs. Jubbins' answer tickled his fancy.

"You are always making fun of us poor women," said the widow. "It is really the case, though ; I would not have put my name to anything of the sort if I had thought there was the least chance of Mr. Dane being released. I did so hope that poor Miss Drummond would have forgotten him, and married somebody else. I knew Sir Geoffrey hoped the same thing—indeed, he more than once implied he knew a gentleman who was very fond of her, and would make her a most excellent husband."

"He did not mean himself, I suppose," suggested Mr. Gayre.

"O, Mr. Gayre, how can you ?—Why, she is a mere child in comparison with him, and besides—"

"Sir Geoffrey was thinking of some one else !" finished the banker, with a dubious smile.

"I did not mean to imply that," said Mrs. Jubbins, laying a sprig of moss on the back of one white hand, and smoothing it with the other. "It was of Miss Drummond, though, we were talking. If you have any influence over her—and of course I know how *great* your influence is over every person with whom you come in contact—do persuade her to forget that wicked young man."

"It is an unfortunate fact," answered Mr. Gayre, "that I have not the smallest influence over Miss Drummond. I do not think an angel could turn her out of any road she thought would lead to Oliver Dane."

"I am afraid that is too true. The very last time I saw her she told me she should prefer water and dry bread with him, to anything in the way of luxury wealth could furnish without him."

"She will, I fancy, shortly be able to indulge her preferences."

"I do not like to speak hardly about her, but it seems to me infatuation. If we did not know those old spells and things had long been done away with, I should almost say she must be under some possession or fascination."

"So she is—she is in *love*," returned Mr. Gayre.

"But there ought to be some sort of reason in love."

"There ought, but there rarely is," and Mr. Gayre sighed involuntarily, and looked down towards the hollow where Mrs. Jubbins' young fry, tired of the improving conversation between their elders, had betaken themselves. He and the widow were alone. Sunbeams were glistening through the leaves—the wind was gently stirring the boughs, a great peace reigned all around; if he was ever to say what he had come to say he felt he ought not to let this opportunity slip. Mrs. Jubbins was looking at him a little perplexed. He raised his head and looked at her, then plunged into the matter, at that moment nearest to his heart.

"I have come down to-day," he began, "to ask you a favour—a great favour."

"Whatever the favour may be it is granted," she said quickly.

"No," he answered, "you must not bind yourself in any way till you have heard what it is."

The ice was broken, what he had to say seemed easier with every word. If there were one thing Mrs. Jubbins understood better than another, that thing was business. She liked sentimental books, she had a fancy for romantic and melancholy poetry, she adored rank, and would have done aught a woman might to get rid of that dreadful name she had taken for better for worse in St. Pancras Church; but, when all was said and done, her one talent was for business. Even while Mr. Gayre continued speaking she grasped the position, she saw exactly where the difficulty lay, and how it was to be surmounted; no need of tedious explanations or wearisome repetitions with her. Mr. Gayre had to listen to no weak expressions of wonder, or feminine ejaculations concerning the sinfulness of Mr. Pengrove. In fancy, it is true, Mrs. Jubbins saw Gayres' tottering to its foundations, and herself as guardian angel, restoring the stability of the bank with her

money-bags; but, refraining from all gush or effusion, she simply
said,

"You can have as much as you want. Every penny I own,
if necessary. I know the money which I feel I only hold in
trust for my children will be safe with you. I am very grateful
to you for coming to me."

There is nothing like doing things thoroughly. Mr. Gayre
felt almost stunned by such impulsive generosity, such unques-
tioning confidence. He forgot the ideas which annoyed and
the mannerisms that amused him in Mrs. Jubbins, and remembered only the warm-hearted woman who had never once
ceased in her attachment and friendship for himself. He had
not treated her well, he thought; he had not done justice to
the nature his father always declared he could not sufficiently
extol.

Yes, Eliza Jubbins was a thoroughly good creature. To
eyes wearied with looking at possible ruin, she seemed positively beautiful, seated on that mossy bank, tearful yet smiling
—so glad, so very, very glad he had come to her.

"'Thank you for your trust in me," he said. "I will not
abuse it."

"No need to tell me that," she answered, "the very idea!"

It was a delicious afternoon. To Mr. Gayre's fancy, Heaven seemed to have come down to earth on a brief visit. The
utter peace of Nature in her milder moods had never before
appealed so strongly to his soul. There was rest in every sight
that met his eyes, in each sound that came wafted to his ear.
As in a dream he looked at dancing leaves and velvety moss
and opening fronds, at the rich brown of the old ferns that
still littered the ground, at the pine cones and the last autumn's
acorns and oak apples bountifully strewing the ground, at the
tiny wild flowers blooming amongst the short grass, almost too
minute for individual notice, yet spangling the sod with such
beauty as the art of man might strive in vain to equal. There
was a solemn hush about the place also to one accustomed
to the din of London—a hush broken only by some sound of
country life; near at hand a thrush was singing long gushes
and snatches of song; down in the hollow the young folks
were laughing and playing; from further off, softened by distance, came the gruff shout of a wagoner to his horses. The
air was full of the thousand nameless yet subtly exquisite scents
of spring. As a man just rescued from drowning might sur-
vey with languid rapture the aspect of some fair land of safety

to which he had been borne, so Mr. Gayre looked at the sylvan scene surrounding him, listened to the twittering of birds,
the rustling of leaves, the occasional scurry of a rabbit, inhaled
the balmy air and all unconsciously drank in the health-giving
odours of resinous pines.

"How pleasant it is here," he said, "what a delicious spot
to rest in."

"Yes, it is very nice," agreed Mrs. Jubbins, "but I do wish
sometimes it was nearer town. People will not come so far; and
really, after London, one cannot help finding the country dull."

"I daresay any one living in it always might find it dull,
but to me this spot seems perfect."

"You would tire of it if you were here always," declared
Mrs. Jubbins, with decision. "I do not mean The Warren is
not very pretty and all that, but, dear me—I so often wish it
could be transported bodily eight miles nearer the Bank. I
should not so much mind if there were any pleasant neighbours who would drop in of an afternoon or evening in a
pleasant way, but when one has to get one's society, as well
as many other things, down by train, the country becomes a
trial."

"Have you not society in the neighbourhood, then?"

"There is plenty of society if it would be sociable, but it
won't. To be anybody here it is necessary to be *enormously*
rich. In Brunswick Square I used to think I was a person of
some consequence, but amongst all the great people about me
I assure you I feel very small indeed."

Mr. Gayre turned an interested glance upon the lady.
Hitherto it had seemed to him any one with such an income
as was possessed by Mrs. Jubbins might have secured a fair
social position. Beyond a certain point it had not before
occurred to him money was essential to social standing.

He had heard of such things as a pair not associating with
a single brougham, of butlers refusing situations where one
footman at least was not kept, but his own path having led
him out of the way of these nice distinctions of modern rank,
he had always felt inclined to believe stories of the kind must
be the invention of some poor wretch in a garret, striving to
earn an honest penny by gibbeting respectable people, of
whose habits and thoughts and modes of proceeding he knew
literally nothing.

"And at times I really find it very dull," went on Mrs.
Jubbins, who having got her father-confessor in an agreeable

AA

mood seemed determined to improve her opportunity. "Of course there are my children, but they have their pursuits, and indeed, occasionally even for their sakes, I long for something different in the way of friends—greater variety. Of course the people my dear husband knew and esteemed always must be friends of mine, but the world has gone on, and since I came down here I see clearly that what seemed very good society to him and your kind father would not be thought very much of now."

"It was a very safe sort of society, at all events," suggested Mr. Gayre.

"I know that; but look at the sons and daughters of some of the families your father was most intimate with. They are enormously rich, they have had advantages such as I never thought of, they can talk all sorts of languages, they can play and sing and paint like professionals; they mix amongst the aristocracy, there is no line drawn now between the City and the West End if people choose to entertain, and push themselves forward. Things were very different once, and not so long ago either. I am old-fashioned enough to dislike such rapid changes, and to feel that though I am, thank God, so well off and happy, it is a little hurtful to be left out in the cold."

The banker sat silent for a minute, then he said, "I often wondered you have never married again."

"Have you? I do not think you need," she answered.

There ensued an awkward pause—not long—but sufficient for a proposal had he wished to make it. Mrs. Jubbins sat on thorns, till unable to bear the idea that she had in any way committed herself, she added, as if in continuation, "Where should I ever meet with any one who would do full justice to my children? Of course, I might have married, every woman who has money can do that—but—"

He did not make her any reply; he looked at the moss, at the flickering leaves, at the modest wild flowers, while his thoughts raced backward to the time when his father wanted him to ask this woman to be his wife.

He might have done a great deal with her. He might have made much of his life, taken a position in politics, become a landed proprietor, gone on, as Mrs. Jubbins truly said, other people had gone on, doubled the ten talents committed to his charge, beyond all things been spared the awful trial of loving a girl young enough to be his daughter, who would never care for him while seed-time and harvest endured.

It was all a tangled hank, that might once have been woven into something beautiful and useful, but which now— With an impatient gesture he changed his position, and idly clasping his hands, remained with head bent and eyes fixed on the ground, while Mrs. Jubbins watched him, and wondered what he could be thinking of.

"I am sure," she said at last, "you will be kind enough to stay and have some dinner with us. Mr. and Mrs. Gibson have taken a house on the Common, and they are coming over this evening. It would be such a pleasure to me if you could stop and meet them—I know you do not care much for City people, but—"

"You must indeed think me ungrateful if you suppose it is likely I should refuse any request of yours."

"Now," cried Mrs. Jubbins, with an attempt at playfulness which sat a little heavily upon her, "I can't have anything of that sort. It is I, and I alone, who ought to feel grateful—all these years you and your father have been showering kindnesses on me, and hitherto I have not had even a chance of making the slightest return. Then you will stop for dinner. Thank you very, very much."

They strolled back to the house through the Wilderness and the dell, over the grass that stretched down to the hedge dividing The Warren from the high road, up the steps into the garden, and so leisurely back to the house through banks of flowers and across green soft sward.

"It is a lovely place," said Mr. Gayre, with conviction, as he stood within the porch looking at the still peaceful quiet of the scene, and he repeated the same idea to himself as he leaned later on beside one of the windows of a dressing-room built out so as to command a view of tangled greenery and lofty forest trees. The ground at this point sloped sharply away from the house, and he could see down into the hollow, round which were planted beautiful and rare shrubs; rhododendrons grew there in the wildest profusion; variegated hollies lifted their heads on high, the graceful Italian broom and the double gorse clustered together in friendly acquaintance. Nothing which could please the eye, and gratify the taste, and delight the heart seemed absent from that fair little domain. It was an emerald gem encircled by a band of deeper green.

"A human being might be very happy here if he did not bring his own misery down with his furniture," thought Mr. Gayre, as he turned from the window and addressed himself to making such a toilette as was possible under the circumstances.

The bodily fare provided that day at dinner was as good as fare could possibly be, but the mental nourishment appalled the banker. It partook of the nature of mental bran, and though wholesome was scarcely satisfying.

Mr. and Mrs. Gibson had been old and valued friends of the lamented Mr. Jubbins—they had also, though in a distant sort of way, known the elder Mr. Gayre, and their talk was of times gone by, and how things had changed, and the price of property in the neighbourhood of Chislehurst, and the rents of good houses, " good fine houses," in the squares, in the better period of old.

" Ah !" said Mr. Gibson, " there was no necessity then to trouble oneself with keeping carriages and horses—and a lot of fellows in the stables to eat a man out of house and home— one could cover one's friends then with a handkerchief. It was just across the square, or over the way, or up the street, all quiet, and comfortable, and friendly—no hurry to catch trains—no tearing and rushing about the world. Modern improvement may be a very fine thing, but give me the days before steam, sir ; life was worth having then."

" I trust, Mr. Gibson, you find life a little worth having still," Mrs. Jubbins interposed ; and then Mrs. Gibson said it was all talk—that no one appreciated the convenience of railroads more than Mr. Gibson, who could not endure stopping trains. " You know you can't, Charles."

It was all perfectly safe conversation ; no human being could have objected to it on the score of morality, but Mr. Gayre felt as if he were back in the " old days before steam," and should never get out of them again.

Nor when that weary dinner was finished, and Mr. Gibson had drunk as much wine as he thought good for him, did the banker find himself at liberty to depart.

" Mr. Gibson does *so* long for one rubber, Mr. Gayre," pleaded Mrs. Jubbins ; and then of course a table was opened and the inevitable pack of cards produced—and the usual jokes about partners uttered—and then a dead silence settled down, and Mr. Gayre found himself in possession of a series of as bad hands as man could be dealt.

They played for money—Mr. and Mrs. Gibson were partners to Mrs. Jubbins and Mr. Gayre. It was perhaps for this reason the banker's run of ill-luck was regarded by his opponents with such equanimity.

"Never mind, Mr. Gayre," said Mr. Gibson cheerfully, as he pocketed his share of the spoil. "Lucky at cards, you know, unlucky in love." And the old gentleman laughed at his own wit till the tears ran down his cheeks, while Mrs. Gibson said archly, "You ought to be ashamed of yourself, Charles," and Mrs. Jubbins coloured and tried to smile.

Mr. Gayre also made a feint of joining in the merriment, but considering the result of his last encounter with Cupid it may not seem surprising that his well-meant efforts failed to prove signally successful.

The interminable evening wore on, and at length the banker was able to remark that if he wished to get back to London that night he must really say good-bye.

"The best friends must part," remarked Mr. Gibson regretfully, "we have to thank you for a most enjoyable evening; lor, what a time it is, Matilda, since we have had such a game of whist."

"Good-night," said Mrs. Jubbins, giving Mr. Gayre her plump hand, which he held for a second longer than seemed to Mrs. Gibson absolutely necessary. "And I heard her say to him distinctly," mentioned Mr. Gibson, as he and his wife drove home a little later on, "you have made me *so* happy."

Perhaps that was the reason he repeated his joke to Mr. Gayre as that gentleman was searching for his hat.

"There really seems to me," he said, "to be a great deal of truth in the proverb I quoted just now—'Lucky in cards, you know.'"

"What an insufferable old donkey," thought the banker to himself, as he took the short cut through the gardens to the station.

THERE is nothing more true than that misfortunes never come singly. They love company; and when the first of the dreary brood knock for admittance the dwellers in any house selected for so great a distinction may feel tolerably certain that several more unwelcome guests may speedily be expected to follow.

It seemed to Mr. Gayre, as he walked up Wimpole Street, that Fate must be pretty well tired of buffeting him, that she could scarcely hold within her quiver another barbed arrow wherewith to harass his body and lacerate his soul. He felt inclined to regard Mrs. Jubbins' generous compliance with his wishes as a sign the worst was over, and a new and better era about to commence.

Silently he sang a song of thanksgiving; the peril but just escaped was so recent he felt a sense of gratitude stirring within him, to which hitherto he must have been almost a stranger. Once more he breathed freely. He saw he could save the bank, and saving the bank meant saving Nicholas Gayre also.

" I have never been sufficiently thankful," he considered, in which reflection there was, indeed, a much greater amount of truth than the banker imagined; truth is, we remember the perils we have encountered, but take no note of those we escape ; and it is always the good things human beings have lost or lack they clasp tight within their memories, whilst blessings literally showered upon them are forgotten. " Not sufficiently thankful." Why, this unconscious Pharisee had never been thankful at all. He wanted too much out of life; and behold, that he might understand fully the value of the gifts he had despised, he saw his possession of them trembling in the balance.

But all danger was now past, he decided ; no need for him to contemplate the possibility of having to go down into the ranks and painfully strive to work his way up once more into that state of life which had been his only by purchase. He

felt most grateful to Mrs. Jubbins for having relieved him from
the pressure of extreme anxiety, and after a vague sort of
fashion he did thank Providence for having sent him so generous
a friend at such a crisis. If conscience whispered the remark
that he had not treated Mrs. Jubbins exactly well, plausibility,
ready for the emergency, suggested the greater Mrs. Jubbins'
disappointment the greater her merit; had she given with the
one hand and taken with the other the virtues of self-renunciation could scarcely have been attributed to her. It would be
quite competent for him always to think hereafter of Mrs.
Jubbins as his good, his best friend; and the reflection pleased
and soothed him, spite of his positive assertion to Susan Drummond that friendship between a man and a woman is an impossibility. Circumstances alter cases; and as he felt love towards
Mrs. Jubbins to be on his part out of the question, he reverted
to that convenient word which he averred to Susan was nothing
but a delusion and a snare.

"Confound that stupid old owl, with his 'lucky at cards,
unlucky in love,'" he repeated, as he put his key in the lock at
Wimpole Street. "All that sort of thing is such execrable
taste and makes a woman so uncomfortable, too," and then he
stepped across his threshold to meet a fresh misfortune, which
had been patiently awaiting his arrival.

"Mr. Fife left this note for you, Colonel." said Rawlings,
coming across the hall; "he told me to give it to you the
moment you returned. He waited for a long time." and then
the man paused and pretended to be putting his master's
umbrella in the stand, while Mr. Gayre tore open Mr. Fife's
communication and read:

"Pengrove has given us the slip. I was always, if you
remember, doubtful of your friend the detective, who, I imagine,
has been 'squared.' P.'s disappearance means, I am afraid,
that there is something wrong you have not yet discovered.
Quite knocked up and must get some sleep. Better call on
me as you go to the bank to-morrow—does not matter how
early. P. never showed after luncheon to-day."

"Call me at six to-morrow morning, Rawlings." said Mr.
Gayre, after he had read this agreeable communication twice
over. "What is the matter?" he added, for the first time
noticing Rawlings' manner, "any one else been to see me?"

"No, Colonel, no one except Miss Chelston."

"Miss Chelston; Sir Geoffrey, you mean, I suppose?"

"*Miss* Chelston; she came about four o'clock, and Mrs.

Bowcroft had the spare room got ready, and she went to bed an hour ago—she said she felt so tired—"

"My niece in this house," said Mr. Gayre, who really doubted the evidence of his ears.

"Yes, Colonel, I took her luggage up-stairs, and there is a letter in the library, in which, she told me to tell you, Sir Geoffrey had explained everything."

"I suppose I am going to hear some other pleasant piece of news," thought Mr. Gayre, passing into the library and taking up his brother-in-law's epistle.

"Dear Gayre" (it began),—"Peg will take this to you. Poor Peg, I am forced to bundle her out of North Bank at a moment's notice—long expected has come at last! A scoundrelly wine-merchant, whom I may without any vanity say I made, put in an execution yesterday. Just shows what one has to expect from that sort of person. Why, the beggar must have had thousands of orders from fellows who drank his wine at my table. If right were right he ought to be in my debt, instead of its being made out all the other way. However, he can't get sixpence out of me, that's one comfort. This is the solitary advantage of being poor—you can't strip a naked man—not but what, if the law would let them, many of these rascals would like to flay a debtor.

"Of course I had to go down to Moreby's lawyers. They put a man in ostensibly to put the other bailiff out—and they're serving me the pretty trick of keeping him in. They are acting as badly as gentlemen of their kidney know how. Fortunately it does not matter much to me—I would rather leave here, but for Peg—poor little desolate woman, don't be hard on her if you can help it; you are not the Almighty, remember, and there is no necessity for you to visit her father's and mother's sins on the girl. I'll write you again as soon as I know what I am going to do. I shall keep out of the way for a little while, as I know there's a nasty thing now, called contempt of court, whereby any pestilent ruffian of a creditor, when he fails to get his money in meal, can apply to have it in malt, in other words take your body if he fail to pick your purse. Heaven only knows what is to become of me. It is all darkness—I do wish earnestly sometimes Heaven would kindly give us a hint as to its intentions—a lot of time and trouble might be saved, if we only knew the direction in which we were expected to work.

"I can't give you any address, for I don't know myself where I am going. Very likely, however, you would just as soon be without one, as you are near the top of the hill, and I am close to the bottom.

"Don't be hard on Peg.—Yours faithfully,

"GEOFFREY CHELSTON, Infelix.

"By the bye, you had better take Sudlow in hand. He's an awful cad and I can do nothing with him. I always thought that party at Mrs. Jubbins' was a mistake—he ought not to have been disillusioned regarding your social standing. However, that can't be helped now, as he's so old a friend of yours possibly you may be able to bring him to book. Good-bye, if you never see me again, remember, I did my best—but a man who has wind and tide always against him can't do much."

Mr. Gayre's first feeling when he finished Sir Geoffrey's valedictory address was surprise that the Baronet had not thought long previously of so simple and excellent a way of burdening some one else—and that some one himself— with the fair Marguerite. It seemed to him that the young lady might just as easily have been passed on to Wimpole Street months before. If the transference were possible now —and in the face of the evidence before him how could he doubt its possibility?—no reason existed why it should not have taken place then.

Flinging himself into a chair he tried to think the matter out and failed. Strive as earnestly as he would to consider the question of his niece, his mind constantly wandered down to the bank or the securities, all locked or not locked, in the strong-room.

Sleeping and waking the bank was now on his mind. Not more sorrowfully did the five foolish virgins lament that fatal delay in buying their oil which involved such disastrous con- sequences than did Nicholas Gayre mourn concerning the way he had neglected his business, and allowed what remained of a once fine property to drift so far across the sea of loss.

Returning from Chislehurst, it had seemed to him safety and honour were still possible ; but now he began to doubt. What if a further loss were really impending—if some security quite beyond his power to replace had been abstracted? In such case he saw no resource, except to make a full and swift con- fession, give up every sixpence he owned in the world, and middle-aged though he was, try to make some fresh start in life.

Why had all this trouble come upon him, he wondered? Other men had fallen in love with young girls and won them too; other men had trusted to subordinates without being absolutely beggared through over-confidence; other men better born, more highly connected, possessed of friends, mixing in the very first ranks of society, had "gone in" for business and found good in it instead of evil. Dimly he understood the fault lay somewhere in himself, that he had been too sure, too confident of the sagacity and honour and honesty of that excellent person Nicholas Gayre; by slow degrees it was dawning upon him that not merely was he no better than those outer sinners the publicans, whom he had in his heart derided, but that he was a great deal worse. One short year ago had any one said—" You will behave to the girl you love like a cad, you will try to shirk your duty to your neighbour, and strive to skulk by on the other side if you can; you will ask a woman for money you know has always hoped you would marry her, and accept substantial help, though you are well aware you never had a feeling of affection for her; you will almost succumb under the apprehension of loss of money, and let a low vulgar fellow beat you in resource and in promptitude "—he would have answered, " Is thy servant a dog that he should do these things?"—and behold he had done them and more.

There was nothing to set on the other side of the account; the few good actions he had performed were prompted, he was well aware, by any other spirit than that of unselfish benevolence. Could he in future do any better?—he asked himself, as he lay that night between such intervals of unrefreshing sleep as Nature pleased to vouchsafe. He had meant to try, but now he did not know. If anything more than what he was already aware of had really gone astray at the bank, he felt a dead man might as readily offer to make atonement to the living as he. Now he grasped how greatly he had valued money, and once during the darkness he wearily wandered away into sleep, with the words of a long-forgotten text recurring to his memory: " There is he that scattereth, yet increaseth."

Nicholas Gayre had not scattered even a grain of wheat he could avoid, and he had not increased; rather poverty threatened to come "as one that travelleth," and it was with an uneasy sense of the converse of the text being in his own case literally fulfilled that he followed this first suggestion into the mazes of dreamland where he lost it.

Early the next morning, after pencilling a few lines of

reluctant welcome to his niece, who, being fond of her ease, had no fancy for "brushing the dew at early dawn," Mr. Gayre proceeded to Mr. Fife's lodgings.

"There *may* be nothing in my notion, you know," said that gentleman, "but upon the other hand there may. 'Bolting' seems to me an uncommonly bad sign."

"But I have gone through all the securities, and they seem right enough."

"Perhaps. If I were you I'd go over them all again; there is such a thing, you know, as—"

"Forgery," suggested Mr. Gayre.

"Well, I was not thinking exactly of forgery," said Mr. Fife. "My notion is, he has 'substituted.' You see it would be easy enough to get a fresh cover drafted, and I'll be bound, you never took time to examine more than the outside of the deeds you hold in trust."

"Good Heavens, no," exclaimed Mr. Gayre, "practically, therefore, there may be no limit to the extent of his defalcations."

"I shouldn't go so far as that," answered Mr. Fife; "after all, the thing has not been going on very, very long. I knew about the amount of his losses, and though I can't tell how much that little game at Tooting cost, still I have allowed a pretty tidy margin for the expenses there. If you remember, I said I thought you would find yourself a hundred thousand out of pocket. We have not quite touched that sum in our investigations. Suppose the worst comes to the worst, you will find a hundred and fifty thousand amply cover everything. I suppose Gayres' can stand that."

"Not if the bank is to keep open."

"H—m. Well, the best thing we can do is to get to Lombard Street, and find out the exact nature of the leak. We can talk about stopping or sinking afterwards. You've found some one, I hope, to lend you enough money to go on with."

"Yes; but I sha'n't take it unless I see my way clearly to pull through."

"Well, we need not discuss that point now. It may be necessary to apply for a warrant for our friend, but don't do that till later in the day. Let him get as long a start as possible. We don't want him back too soon, if ever. Now, if you walk quietly up to the bank you'll find me at your private door almost as soon as you're ready for me."

During the whole of that day each person who wanted to

see the manager was informed his wife was ill, and he absent
from business. If on receiving this reply any individual adventured to inquire whether Mr. Gayre happened to be in town,
he received for reply the unexpected intelligence that Mr.
Gayre was in town, but so deeply engaged he could not be
interrupted. There never was a truer statement: Mr. Gayre
chanced, indeed, to be engaged! All the forenoon and most
of the afternoon he was busy checking the securities, and he
finally left himself barely time to go round and see his solicitors
and proceed with one of the firm to the Mansion House, where
he applied for a warrant to take the person of Titus Pengrove, on the charge of robbery and of dealing with valuable
securities.

Then he walked to the station and took train for Chislehurst. He had made up his mind he would not take Mrs.
Jubbins' money now he knew it was impossible for him to meet
his liabilities and keep on the bank. He must withdraw capital
from the business, and he could not. even on the Gayre system
of commerce, do that and still manage to keep afloat. Only
the previous night safety seemed possible; less than twenty-
four hours had served to change the whole aspect of his life.

The Chislehurst woods were not less fair, the grass was not
less green, the spring flowers had not closed their petals, the
air was full of the sweet scents that yesterday seemed so fragrant. Nature was the same, but the man who looked upon her
exceeding loveliness had changed totally. His body lacked
strength, his limbs were weary, his forehead burned. his parched
lips made speech painful. his mind was so distracted he took
no notice of distance, save by the measure of physical fatigue;
the hill leading to The Warren, in those few hours since last he
breasted it, appeared to have grown strangely steep, the series
of rustic steps leading up through the garden from the wicket
gate to the house seemed interminable; two or three times he
was forced to pause while ascending them. For him tasselled
larch and silvery birch and burnished copper beech and trembling linden had donned their bravest apparel all in vain. He
was like one blind and deaf wandering through a world of
beauty and delight. As a sick man rejects the most delicate
food. as a broken heart finds discord in the most harmonious
music, as laughter grates on the ear of grief, and mirth increases
the sadness of sorrow; so to Nicholas Gayre all the sweet
sounds and influences of Nature seemed to his dulled senses
and hopeless heart but so many aggravations of his grief. For

others—for the children, for happy lovers, for eager youth and prosperous middle life, and ripe old age contented to sit basking in the sunshine of ease and competence—flower and bud and leaf and bird might add fresh charms to the soft beauty of spring and the glory of summer; but to this man, born and bred amongst those who considered money a necessary essential before the most ordinary happiness could be hoped for, and who now saw the fortune he once fully believed founded on a rock beaten by the rain and shaken by the wind, and engulfed by the flood and levelled with the earth; what thoughts, save those of loss and disaster, could the changing seasons ever in the dark future bring?

The power of riches, the possibility of fame, the hope of love, the wild longings, the noble aspirations of youth, all gone —all vanished like the pageant of a dream—what remained for him to do? Nothing, save to tell Mrs. Jubbins the truth, and release her from a promise given in ignorance of his actual position. And for Susan? Yes, he would do right there too; but he could not think about her just then. For a moment he lingered, looking into the hollow where he had stood beside her on that happy night so long, so long ago, when the sound of the music floated softly down among the ferns and the undergrowth, when, with her hand resting on his arm, she talked about love in a cottage, and looked under the starlight a woman to love on earth, an angel to lead a man to heaven.

And what had he made of that chance? Almost with a groan he put that question aside, and walking on as quickly as his tired limbs permitted, once more found himself at the porch inquiring if Mrs. Jubbins were within.

He found her alone in the smaller drawing-room, engaged, with a humility quite touching when evinced by so rich a woman, in modestly knitting a stocking.

"Well, this is delightful!" she cried. "How do you do, Mr. Gayre—why, what is the matter?" she added; "surely you are not ill?"

"No, I am not ill," he said, "but something has happened;" and then he told her.

They were both standing. She had risen to greet him, and he opened his budget of ill news so suddenly—and it was such awful news—she never asked him to be seated; the ordinary questions of life for the time were completely driven out of mind.

For a minute or two after he ended, she remained perfectly

still, grappling with the difficulty—trying to make the whole matter clear to her comprehension; then, laying her white strong hand upon his arm, she spoke these words :

" We mustn't let the bank go ; whatever we do, we must not let the bank go."

" I can't prevent it going," he answered.

" But *we* can," she persisted ; " if my poor husband were alive now—if your dear father could come back to us—they would both say, 'Don't let the bank go.' Why, it is madness even to think of Gayres' suspending payment. You know the worst now, and between us we can surely weather the storm. Sit down, and let us consider what is best to be done. You say some of my securities have been abstracted ; that does not matter in the least; there are plenty left. O Mr. Gayre, I wonder if it was for this all the money was left in my hands, so that I can do what I like with it, without asking the consent of any human being."

He did not answer—he could not; the revulsion of feeling was too great, too sudden. Ten minutes before he had regarded himself as virtually a beggar, and now—

" But before we get to business you must have something to eat ; I daresay if the truth were known you have not tasted food to-day. No, do not look like that, I cannot bear to see you. Surely—surely you won't object to taking help from an old friend. Besides, as I told you yesterday, hitherto it has been all the other way. I have been the person obliged. It is merely my turn now ; you can't grudge giving me the happiness of helping you a little. If the cases were reversed, I know you would do the same for me, and more."

He knew no such thing, indeed he knew the very opposite ; impulsive generosity, unreasoning friendship, liberality except on undoubted security, had never been failings of the old-established and highly respectable firm of Lombard Street bankers. Mr. Gayre would not have objected to lending Mrs. Jubbins a few thousands, or even to giving her a moderate sum of money had she really stood in need of it; but to act the part towards her, or anybody else, she was proposing to act towards him (and she a clever woman of business, and one who knew the value of capital), would have seemed to him, and perhaps with reason, the height of madness.

She had grown quite earnest in her appeal. The same loyalty of feeling which impelled the Jacobites to exile and the scaffold was stirring in Mrs. Jubbins' warm heart then.

·Gayres' had ever been to her what the Stuarts were to the
Cavaliers. She could not reason about the matter; it seemed
impossible to her that Gayres' should go while she had the
power of saving it. The spice of romance which, hand in hand
with the most practical common sense, had ever walked beside
Eliza Jubbins, *née* Higgs, was at last fully asserting itself. Still
a handsome woman, possessed of a face on which years had as
yet traced very few lines, well preserved, prosperous—for the
moment sentiment and the consciousness of meaning to perform
a kindly action made her actually beautiful.

The evening sunlight fell across hair thick and glossy as
ever; her fine eyes were soft and liquid with emotion, her
mouth was sweet with tender smiles as she pleaded to be
allowed her share in trying to save Gayres'; her hand was unconsciously pressed more heavily on the banker's arm, and yet
he could not speak, only slowly he took that persuasive hand
in his, and held it close while he looked wistfully at his old
playmate.

Before that look her eyes fell; her colour rose, and she
would have released her hand but that it was locked too fast
to be withdrawn without an unseemly struggle.

" You will let me help you," she said, dissembling even to
herself, as women always do at such a juncture.

" If I may keep this hand," he answered, and kissed the
ringed fingers she did not now even strive to withdraw.

It had come at last; after years he had proposed, and in
this fashion.

That morning it never entered his mind he could ask Mrs.
Jubbins to marry him, that morning she could not have conceived it likely that bliss was ever to be hers. She may have
wished it had come at some other time, and in some other
guise, but it was welcome at any time and in any form. The
whole matter did not seem to her strange. Before Mr. Gayre
returned to town she felt as though she had been engaged to
him for years. On both sides it was indeed, as old Mr. Gayre
would have said, "most suitable"—what poor Mr. Jubbins
might have thought was quite a different affair. At parting,
Mrs. Jubbins said, " Now you will promise me to see a doctor
this evening, for I feel sure you are going to be ill," to which
Mr. Gayre replied, " I will see a doctor, but I shall not be ill
now."

Upon the whole it seemed perhaps pleasant to have even
Mrs. Jubbins anxious concerning his health; except so far as

the malady might affect Oliver Dane, Susan would probably not have cared had he been smitten with smallpox! Travelling back to London, Mr. Gayre, reviewing the position at his leisure, found more cause for satisfaction than discontent. He felt very grateful to Mrs. Jubbins, yet he shrank from the idea of marrying her.

When menaced by two dangers, however, it is true wisdom to select the least, and Mr. Gayre decided the widow was by far a lesser ill than beggary. And he meant to act fairly to her and to her children. Perhaps he thought he had given a tangible proof of the *bona-fides* of his intentions by making that tardy offer of his heart and hand.

THOUGH in no gay mood, Mr. Gayre laughed as these words crossed his mind. He recalled his own experience. If ever man had been passionately in love that man was himself, and yet when put in the scales love flew up to the beam, and money weighed down the balance. "It is all very well for young people," he thought, "to talk like that; young folks always expect the wherewithal to feed love will spring up like the grass. Prudent papas, mercenary mammas, who have saved and toiled for their children, are to provide the few items love requires to make itself comfortable. Love—true love, the love of the poets, wants its rent paid, its taxes settled, its tradespeople satisfied, its servants fed, its pocket-money found by somebody else; the moment real Love finds there are a few difficulties in the way, and that bed, board, and lodging must be hardly toiled for by the lover, it has a nasty but wise way of metamorphosing itself. It ceases to have golden locks; it assumes the form of Mammon sometimes in a wig, but always in a carriage, and with a satisfactory income."

All of which tirade merely meant that Nicholas Gayre was trying to reconcile himself to the course he had taken. It was he who felt his love required many other things beside bread and cheese for its maintenance. If we come to that in the days of King Nebuchadnezzar there were but few of the children of Israel found constant to refuse the meat and the wine they considered defiled, and able to remain faithful to the pulse and water which gave them "knowledge and skill in all learning and wisdom, and Daniel understanding all visions and dreams." The heart of man has not changed much since then. In his soul Mr. Gayre knew that even had Susan cared for him he should have preferred the fleshpots of riches to the manna of poverty.

No one finds it exactly pleasant to face the fact of his own worldliness, and the banker found it convenient and almost

BB

pleasant to meet the knowledge of his own unworthiness with
a gibe.

Besides, Susan disliked, and Mrs. Jubbins liked him. If
marriage in his then state of impecuniosity were to be at all, it
had better take place with a woman who brought not merely
money but love into the state " ordained by God."

There could be nothing more certain than that Mr. Gayre
meant to act quite honestly by Mrs. Jubbins. He intended to
pay her back every farthing she had advanced, to promote her
children's interest, to be a father to young people who were
antagonistic to every taste; in a sentence, "to do the right
thing." He felt very grateful to the widow, he liked her better
than he had ever thought to like her. He intended to give
way to her in many things; he purposed being a good steward,
a faithful husband; nevertheless, he loathed and despised himself for having made such a bargain, he who never hesitated
about riding " straight into the jaws of death," who had once
sprung into the saddle more cheerily than bridegroom ever
went forth from his chamber.

He could not even say to himself that he had acted from
impulse. His reason felt satisfied with his conduct, though his
soul recoiled from it. The thing he had done was " after his
kind,"—no use for him even to say he had not followed his
nature. This much there was to be said in extenuation of that
step which could not be retraced. He had proposed not
because he knew he should otherwise fail to get what he
wanted, but merely in grateful recognition of the widow's kindness. Such generosity he felt merited some return, and so he
offered all he had to offer—himself. It was far more than
enough he considered, with a shudder. That one entry reversed
the debit and credit side of their account. He merely meant
to take the use of her money for awhile, and in exchange he
had given her his life. Well, it did not much matter. Hitherto
he had not made so great a use of his opportunities that one
more flung away need break his heart. He would conform to
the world's ideas—he would settle down to business—he would
believe in the greatness of City magnates, he would try to forget
that time which seemed so far away—when the blare of the
trumpets—the call of the bugle, seemed to him the sweetest
music ever heard by mortal ear. He would remember youth
with its illusions was gone—that middle age with its realities
had come—that, worst of all, the autumn and winter of life
were creeping on—that he was growing too old for sentiment,

and that besides Susan Drummond did not love him, while to Eliza Jubbins he had ever seemed a hero of romance !

A great deal of unpleasant work still lay before him. He had to put the bank straight, to arrange many business details with Mrs. Jubbins—see how things stood between his niece and Mr. Sudlow—hurry on his lawyers about the Oliver Dane affair, and last, but certainly not least, end everything for ever between himself and Susan Drummond.

In England a man cannot legally marry two wives. Often he finds one more than enough, and it was evident that now Mr. Gayre was engaged to the widow he must sever all connection with Susan Drummond.

So far Mrs. Jubbins had behaved with the strictest propriety—but her old playfellow had not forgotten those resonant kisses, those fond embraces, which made existence terrible to him in his boyhood. With trembling fingers Mr. Gayre just lifted the veil of the future and peeped behind it. The prospect was awful—most awful—so awful and abhorrent he dropped the curtains incontinently. Nevertheless it was better than ruin and disgrace. Greatly to be preferred, a line in the marriage list to a paragraph in the money article. The Gayres had held themselves so high, and believed they were so secure ! Mr. Jubbins had looked up to them, and lo and behold it was his money made in oil which was now to prove to the Gayres temporal salvation.

Well, it is of no use blinking facts, and the first thing evidently to be done was to release Susan from her agreement. But how to word the case he certainly could not say. "I am going to marry Mrs. Jubbins," or "I have lost my money." How on earth would it be competent for him to put it ? Mr. Gayre felt he could only await the chapter of accidents ; lie low and watch results.

But yet he must in some way indicate the way of the wind to Susan. It was essential he should tell her that ill-starred engagement might be considered at an end; therefore next day, before he showed at the bank, he repaired to her lodgings, where the landlady, who in person answered the door, greeted him with a pleased smile, and said, Miss Drummond was at home.

He waited for her a minute or two, then Susan appeared, and with a stiff bow recognised his presence.

" You wished to see me," she said, laying her hand on the table and speaking as though she had been walking very fast, and found it strangely hard to get her breath.

"Yes, Miss Drummond, if you will kindly sit down I shall perhaps be able to talk a little better."

"About—Oliver?"

"No, singular as it may seem, not about Oliver. Besides that gentleman, there are a few millions of other persons in the world, myself a unit amongst them, you understand that."

"And, Mr. Gayre—?" she said, rising, and looking strangely cold and resolute as she spoke.

Just for a moment he swayed his hat gently to and fro ere he spoke—then—

"I have come to release you from our compact," he said, quite quietly.

She looked at him, startled.

"Do you mean—" she asked, at last.

"Just what I say," he answered, "I bring you liberty; never again need you look at me as one abhorred; never more will it be necessary for you to shrink from my touch; you are perfectly free."

He thought he heard her murmur, "My God, I thank Thee," but the cry of gratitude was merged in the question, "And what about Oliver? O, Mr. Gayre! don't give us both up together."

"No," he answered, "no, I shall never cease striving for his release till you and he meet once more. Good-bye, Miss Drummond—good-bye, my dear. I was mad once, for which I beg your pardon. I am sane now, and really I do not think I need beg your pardon at all."

"But what about Oliver?"

"He must wait a little, his case is being seen to. Gracious Heaven. Miss Drummond, you have heard me just now give up my soul's desire, and yet you never say, thank you; you have no thought or pity save for 'Oliver.' Take him, marry him," added the banker, shaken by a sudden whirlwind of passion. "Only I pray God that, living or dead, I may never hear his name again."

"Mr. Gayre—Mr. Gayre," she cried, rushing to the door after him and laying a detaining hand upon his arm, which he tried in vain to shake off.

"Go," he said—"go. I lament the day I first saw you, the hour I first spoke to you; till that time I respected myself fairly, but ever since I have been acting a mean, cowardly part towards my Maker and my fellows. For the Almighty's sake, do not tempt me to lose my soul and my substance as well. I never was rich, and my love for you has left me bankrupt, not merely in heart, but also well-nigh in pocket. Let me go while I am master of myself; good-bye."

But still she held him, she clasped his arm with both her hands, and her tears fell down like rain as she sobbed, "I can't bear it—I cannot. You shall not leave me till you say you forgive me—that we are friends."

"*Friends!*" he repeated scornfully. "How like a woman—to prate about *friendship* to a man who has loved as I have loved. You have been very cruel to me—you are not really sorry for me now. You do not know what love means when youth is over, when spring has gone, and no fresh sap can ever rise again to nourish one green leaf of hope and promise."

"O, do not say that," she entreated; "there will be a fair springtime yet for you. The day must come when you will meet some one you can love and marry, and—"

"I shall probably marry." he interrupted, "but love again I never can. Besides, who could love me? You have taught me that the whole passion of my soul—the undivided affection of my heart—is incapable of winning one tender smile, one feeling of regard—"

"But O!" she said, looking up at him with swimming eyes full of sorrow and womanly pity, "my love was given long before we met. If it had not been—had I never known Oliver—"

He could bear no more. With a sudden wrench he tore himself away, leaving the girl, who had never come so near loving him before, in an agony of grief. For the moment she forgot even Oliver, the great tide of her faithful affection seemed to ebb out in one huge wave, leaving an arid waste of memory, on which was traced only the image of a broken and despairing man.

Had she known more of his nature, however, she would have understood that paroxysm of ungovernable agony was but the dying struggle of a passion which had torn and tormented him. Even in the first misery of that final parting he felt a sense of relief that all was over. The face of his dead wore as yet no look either calm or beautiful, but at least the misery of suspense would not have to be gone through again for ever. He had suffered, no human being could know how horribly; he had grown hateful to himself; he had been falling lower and lower in his own esteem, till at last self-examination became torture. He had done things of which he could not have believed himself capable ; he had forgotten honour, mercy, justice—all because a woman had sweet, wistful brown eyes, and the fairest face he ever looked upon.

If love fail to purify the waters of a human soul it fouls them, and it is not without reason we pray the best instincts of our nature may produce a blessing. not a curse. It rests with each amongst us to decide which course to pursue. We can climb, blinded it may be into tears and shod with sorrow, to heights illuminated by a sun which never streams across any low or unworthy road mortality elects to tread ; or we may trail our love through the mire of earth, till nothing remains at last but the marred and broken image, from which our anguished hearts shall finally behold the last trace of comeliness fade utterly away.

CHAPTER XXXVI

From the time settlements were first mentioned his most partial friend could not have described Mr. Sudlow as an ardent suitor.

He had tried every means of avoiding making any, and when he found Sir Geoffrey what the Baronet described as " stiff," he began seriously to reconsider the whole question of marriage.

He had learned that money makes any man of value in the matrimonial market, and it occurred to him that he might do a good deal better than Miss Chelston. He might not get a more beautiful wife, but there was no reason why he should not secure one even better born and moving in the best circles. Mr. Sudlow's only weakness chanced to be a craze for good society, and he had not long possessed the privilege of Sir Geoffrey Chelston's friendship before he clearly understood whatever the rank of that gentleman's acquaintances might be, his daughter did not visit at grand houses or receive visits from ladies whose names were ever likely to figure in the *Court Journal*.

Not all the Baronet's finessing and talk about great people could deceive him on this point. For a short time he suffered himself to be deluded into the belief that his adored one could introduce him to those charmed circles where fashion holds high carnival, but this idea was soon dispelled.

As regarded Mr. Gayre also, Sir Geoffrey's notion was right. The banker had ceased to be a hero to his former admirer. There are some persons it is unsafe to admit to a private view of dignity in dressing-gown and slippers, and North Bank and The Warren exactly represented this sort of attire to Mr. Sudlow's artless inexperience. To quote his own mental phrase, he didn't " think much " of the Chelston or Gayre set. He had never met and he was never likely to meet the Canon, and if he had, even that respectable clergyman would scarcely to his

mind have represented a Court card. Sir Geoffrey certainly
did know some persons of title, but then as a rule they were
black sheep, and, whether black or white, took no pains to
conceal that they meant to have nothing whatever to do with
Mr. Sudlow. He was far too careful and model a young man
to find favour in their eyes. He looked many times at a
sovereign before changing it; he would not bet, he did not
drink, he knew nothing about horses, he was not amusing, or
good-natured, or useful; he bored even Miss Chelston to death,
and she certainly was not a peculiarly lively person.

Altogether Mr. Sudlow felt greatly disappointed with the
result of the first love-affair he had adventured upon that could,
with any propriety, be spoken about, and he was steadfastly
purposed if possible to make those settlements a cause for
breaking off the match. It was ridiculous to expect him to
marry a girl who had not a shilling or a settled social position,
who, spite of being a baronet's daughter, was in reality more
thoroughly a nobody than himself. If Mr. Gayre liked to give
his niece a fortune, he would put down an equal amount.
There was no reason why the banker should not do this, yet
Mr. Sudlow scarcely felt brave enough to make the suggestion.

When he received a note, however, from Mr. Gayre, asking
him to call in Lombard Street, he began to think matters might
still take a favourable turn. He knew Miss Chelston was in
Wimpole Street, but he did not know why, and under the
circumstances it was natural enough he should imagine Mr.
Gayre at last meant to "act handsomely" by her.

Walking along the Strand to keep the appointment, he ran
across a man he had met in North Bank. As a rule he passed
Mr. Sudlow with a careless nod, but on this occasion he stopped,
and, with hands plunged deep in his pockets, and hat tilted
back from his forehead, said,

"Heard if Chelston is out of danger?"

"I didn't know he was in any danger."

"Didn't you really? Awful smash; mare bolted with him
the very day after he went down into Yorkshire; he was picked
up for dead, so Graceless tells me. Pity, too! never saw a
finer horseman. Hope they'll save his leg;" and Mr. Helsey,
who was waiting for a friend, leisurely took his cigar out of his
mouth and looked at it with a contemplative cast of countenance.

"I am very sorry," remarked Mr. Sudlow.

"Sure you are; not half a bad fellow, Chelston. No one's

enemy but his own. That was a bit of a bother up at North Bank, wasn't it?"

" I have not heard—"

" Why, bless my soul, you know nothing, and I thought you were hand and glove there, not but what Graceless said long ago he believed you meant to cry off. You are just as safe too, perhaps. Shouldn't care for Chelston for a father-in-law myself ; and though the girl is quiet and demure enough, still where there has been anything with the mother I think it's risky work. *What!* you don't mean to tell me you never knew *that.* I wouldn't have spoken only I made sure you knew all about it. I believe Lady Chelston was as little in fault as a woman ever can be when she goes off with somebody—*not* her husband. It was a hard blow for the Gayres ; the old man never really held up his head after it. Ah, here comes Jennings. Hope Chelston will pull through all right. Ta-ta."

Mr. Sudlow did not pursue his walk eastward ; instead he despatched a curt note to Lombard Street saying he could not call, and giving no hint when it might suit his convenience to do so. The note reached Mr. Gayre before he left the City ; he kept very different hours from what had formerly been his wont, and he decided to take Mr. Sudlow on his way home.

" I have come to have some talk with you, Sudlow," he said, " about my niece."

" Yes, Mr. Gayre."

" I consider matters are in a very unsatisfactory state between you ; and as her father has left her in my charge, I want to come to a thorough understanding with you on the subject."

" What is it you wish to know?"

" First, when the settlements are to be signed ; next, when the marriage is to take place."

Mr. Sudlow hesitated ; he didn't like Mr. Gayre's tone, and he liked the look of Mr. Gayre's clenched hand laid firmly upon the table still less. There was very little of the banker about that hand, and there was a great deal too much of the cavalry officer. At that moment the old Adam was very strong in Mr. Gayre. He had a fierce desire to quarrel with somebody, and he felt he would rather quarrel with Mr. Sudlow than any other human being.

" I am waiting for your answer," he said.

" You are very imperative," Mr. Sudlow replied ; " what is the cause of all this sudden haste?"

"There is nothing sudden about the matter. The affair has been at a standstill for months. On one paltry pretence and another you have managed to put off the signing of these settlements from autumn to spring, and we are no further forward now than we were in the autumn."

"That is true, and I fear we shall never get any further forward."

"What the devil do you mean, sir?" asked Mr. Gayre.

"Just what I say. It is of no use trying to bully me, Mr. Gayre. I don't intend to sign those settlements, and I don't mean to marry your niece."

Mr. Gayre sprang from his chair, and Mr. Sudlow sprang from his. Just for a moment they looked across the table at each other, then—

"Sit down, you coward," said Mr. Gayre, "I am not going to strike you. Now, tell me the plain English of all this? What makes you say you will jilt the girl?"

"I was duped into proposing to her."

"You were *what?*"

"I was misled."

"Who misled you?"

"You must know I had every reason to suppose her father was a very different person from what I find him to be."

"I know no such thing. From the very first, when you would insist on being introduced to my niece, I told you in so many words her father was a blackleg, a scoundrel, and a cheat. If you did not choose to believe me—if you would persist in thinking a baronet could not fail to be a paragon of virtue, the fault was yours, not mine; but you did not think anything of the sort; you have some other reason for wanting to back out of your engagement, and I insist on your telling me what it is."

"I always objected to those settlements."

"Why did you not then refuse to make any? When Sir Geoffrey said you should not have his daughter on any other terms, why did you not tell him fairly you declined to marry her? You have not acted straightforwardly, Mr. Sudlow; you have kept shilly-shallying about the affair till I am tired of hearing it named. But I intend to put matters on a different footing. It was competent for you once to withdraw your offer—but you shall not do so now. I mean you to marry her soon—or else know some excellent reason why you won't."

"It is something outrageous to expect me to make such settlements on a girl utterly destitute of fortune."

"It would be something outrageous if a girl possessed of any fortune were willing to marry *you*."

"Now it is of no use taking that tone with me, Mr. Gayre, I won't stand it."

"You'll have to stand it and a good deal more before you have done with me," retorted Mr. Gayre. "And as we are upon the topic; I tell you fairly that if my niece had not been as selfish, calculating, and worldly as yourself, I should never have thought of letting her marry you. In most respects you will, however, be admirably matched."

"We never shall be matched," interrupted Mr. Sudlow.

"We'll see about that," said Mr. Gayre.

"I should have married Miss Chelston long ago," remarked Mr. Sudlow, "if you would have made some suitable provision for her, but I am now quite determined to break off the affair entirely."

"I know, then, what I shall do," and Mr. Gayre took up his hat.

"I have been kept most shamefully in the dark. It was by the merest chance I heard there had even been a scandal about Lady Chelston—and—"

"O, that's it, is it?" and Mr. Gayre laid down his hat—"you had better think twice about what you purpose doing, my friend. When this matter comes into court, as come into court it shall, it will be pleasant for you to hear counsel state the individual who makes an old story about a woman, who had such excuse as wife living never could urge before, whose husband never brought a charge against her, who condoned her error, who laid her amongst his own people, the pretext for refusing to marry her daughter—is the grandson of a felon, transported for life for robbery and attempted murder."

"How dare you state such an infamous lie?"

"Lie is a nasty word, but we will let that pass. I always knew your grandfather had been a convict, but I did not know the full measure of his crimes till I came the other day upon all the papers connected with the affair. The public will find the story very exciting and entertaining reading. I have nothing more to say now, except that I shall be glad if you will remove your account to-morrow, and transfer your securities to the keeping of some other banker. You objected to employing any solicitor over those settlements—I should advise you to look out for some sharp lawyer now, for you will require one before you have done with me.   Good-evening."

As he walked up Wimpole Street, Mr. Gayre felt conscious that he was extremely tired, and needed a long night's sound rest; but the day's work was not yet over.   He had scarcely sat down to dinner before Rawlings announced that Mr. Colvend wished to see him particularly.

"He will wait, Colonel," said the man.   "He said you were on no account to disturb yourself."

When Mr. Gayre entered his library he found the poor old man sitting in a listless attitude, with head drooped and hands clasped together between his knees.

"You must forgive me for coming so late," he began; "but—" and there he stopped.   Twice he tried to finish his sentence and failed, and then fairly giving way, he covered his face and cried like a child.

"What is the matter—what has happened?" asked Mr. Gayre.

"It is my daughter, my poor Dossie.   She has had brain fever—she has been dreadfully ill," moaned Mr. Colvend, in a series of gasping sobs—"but that is not the worst of it.   O, Mr. Gayre! have pity upon me.   I am afraid what that scoundrel Fife said was too true.   There is no doubt she was fond of Dane, and that the trouble unsettled her reason—my unfortunate girl—my dear, dear little Dossie."

"I am very sorry indeed for you," and Mr. Gayre did feel most truly sorry for the wretched father.

"Yes, it is an awful business," went on Mr. Colvend, wiping his eyes and trying to speak calmly.   "Awful: only to think of that young fellow, and of that poor brave girl who stuck to him through all—I don't know what to do.   How is this wrong ever to be set right?   Though she is my daughter, an innocent man must not continue to suffer for her fault.   Would to God, Surlees had never given Dane in charge!   The prosecution was quite against my wish.   The doctors do not think she will ever recover her reason."

"Under the circumstances, that is perhaps scarcely to be regretted," said Mr. Gayre.

"Just the remark Dr. Foynson made; but O, there is no living creature can tell what this has been to me; ever since the terrible truth was forced upon me, I have thought about that unhappy young man till it seemed as though I should go mad myself."

"I do not imagine if you join with me there can be much difficulty now in procuring his release."

"I will do anything and everything in my power. The cause of this frightful illness was that Fife came to the house and told Dossie, as all other means of clearing Dane seemed unavailable, he meant to give himself up. He frightened the poor little thing to death, said her letters to him would be read in court. When I got home I found her in the most dreadful state of mind; of course I did not believe she was in fault then, any more than I believe Fife's statement that night you came to see me at Brighton; but I can't blind myself any longer; she had never been crossed before, and she lacked strength of mind to bear up under the trouble of knowing Dane was in love with some one else. Why couldn't he have fancied my darling?—I'd have given her to him, poor child! She was all I had—and now—"

"Gone mad, has she?" commented Mr. Fife, when Mr. Gayre subsequently repeated the substance of Mr. Colvend's statement to that individual. "Don't you believe a word of it; she's not the sort to go mad. I daresay she has had a touch of brain fever, but it would puzzle a wiser man than Dr. Foynson to tell where temper ended and fever began. If they mean to get Dane out, though, without any fuss or publicity, I shall be well enough content now; I am going to turn over a new leaf, and I think I would rather not turn it before a magistrate."

"It is a great pity you do not turn over a new leaf," said Mr. Gayre, "for you certainly are exceedingly clever."

"And trustworthy," added Mr. Fife, "that little matter of the cheque, notwithstanding. O, I forgot to mention, Mr. Sudlow was at the bank three times to-day while you were out. He wants you to make an appointment—he left a message he had something very special to say."

"Did he?" said Mr. Gayre, scarcely able to refrain from smiling.

CHAPTER XXXVII

Eight weeks slipped by so fast that, like the seven years Jacob
served for Rachel, it seemed but a day, and Mr. Gayre, seated
one glorious summer's morning in his private room at Lombard Street, was dreamily reviewing the events which had
occurred since the previous July when a letter was brought to
him, directed in Sir Geoffrey's sprawling handwriting. It was
a lengthy epistle that Mr. Gayre cut open, not without some
curiosity as to what the contents might prove.

"Dear Gayre" (began the Baronet),—"Though you never
liked me as much as I liked you, I fancy you will be glad to
know I am at last getting better. Whether my leg will ever be
a good leg, it is difficult to tell. The doctors say not—which
is the reason, I feel inclined to think it will. Lord, what a
lot they are! If I had followed their bidding I'd have been
comfortably tucked up with a spade long and long ago! What
do you suppose they kept me—*me*—on for one blessed fortnight?—you'd never guess—*milk* in some confounded form or
other. Gad, I was so weak and wasted at the end of that time,
when I looked down at my hands I thought they belonged to
somebody else. Remonstrance was not a bit of good. Bless
you, a fellow that used to come and feel my pulse two and
three times a day would have put a navvy on the same diet as
a new-born child! I'd never have picked up again if it had
not been for the landlady, who is as trim and smart an article
in petticoats as you ever set your eyes on. She keeps all the
business of this house going—ostlers, waiters, chambermaids,
and the whole gang of them. Her husband's occupation is
dying as fast as he knows how (the doctors have put *him* on
milk and soda-water—ugh! poor wretch), and the only recrea-
tion he has strength enough left to indulge in is whist. There
are generally some decent fellows stopping at this hotel, so we
manage to make up a party most evenings. While I was

pretty bad we were in the habit of playing on my bed, so you see time has not been spent quite unprofitably after all. However, as I was saying, if it had not been for Mrs. Fitz-Hugh, rather a high-flying sort of name, isn't it? you would never have been troubled more, by yours truly.

" ' For heaven's sake,' I said to her, ' get me something fit for a man to drink—not cat-lap.'

" ' But the doctor, Sir Geoffrey.'

" ' My dear soul,' I expostulated, ' I am not a calf—if I were, I have no doubt I should relish milk greatly; being what I am, if I don't have some brandy soon, I'll not answer for the consequences.' Firmness, Gayre—it was firmness saved me. How Mrs. F.'s father did laugh to be sure, when she told him; his name is Sponner, and it is said he had netted seventy thousand pounds *by always betting against the favourite.* He's a funny old chap, who can scarcely write his name. 'That's a good one,' he roared. ' Sir Geoffrey Chelston, the hardest rider and the heaviest drinker in England, put into training on kettle tea and pap. No—no, my lass, that won't do at any price. We'll find him something better than that, doctor or no doctor.'

" You may imagine I am pretty comfortable here. I don't exactly know who is going to pay the piper, but I rather expect Dashwood will stump up. 'Twas his mare, or rather one he was thinking of buying, took the notion of trying a race with the wind. I never went so fast before, and I suppose I may venture to say I never want to go such a pace again. All's well that ends well, though, as I feel quite sure I could not have dropped into better quarters. I thought I had not much to learn in the matter of horse-flesh, but the old gentleman has given me a wrinkle or two.

" I had no doubt but that you would get Sudlow to terms. It is a sort of thing far more in your line than mine. You don't say how you managed to screw him up, but so long as he is screwed the *modus operandi* signifies little. Yes, you arrange about the wedding as you like. I can't come up for it, but I wrote to the Canon to know if he wouldn't tie the knot? 'You had best let bygones be bygones,' I said, 'peace and goodwill in families is both politic and Christian. My daughter is making a capital match, and it is always prudent to cultivate friendly relations with a niece who is well off. Peggy is a confoundedly handsome girl—a girl any uncle might be proud of with a rich husband at her back,' so to cut a long

story short the Canon will officiate, that is, if you like. I said
I had always kept clear of the family quarrels, water, either
cold or hot, being a thing quite out of my line.

"Now the matter rests between you two brothers; just do
as you please, it makes very little difference to me. Give
Peggy my blessing—I am afraid she won't care for that much,
but I have nothing else to present her with. I certainly think
she and Sudlow will run in harness very well together. A
selfish man ought always to marry a selfish woman. This will
sound like a mistake, but it works well in practice. *Entre nous*,
it would have been a thousand pities to spoil two houses with
such a pair. There is a hard commercial smack about them
both that fills me with astonishment. If Peg had been different she would have sent him to the right-about long ago. If
Sudlow had been different I could have hobbled him last
summer.

"What a splendid girl poor, dear Susan has proved herself.
Fancy her smuggling that picture of Delilah out of Hilderton's
studio.

"The young hound!—what a scandalous thing to paint my
daughter's face in such a connection. He meant to exhibit
the painting somewhere too, and then there would have been
the deuce and all to pay. I am afraid Peg did not act fairly
by the lad. She's an out-and-out flirt—a dangerous flirt—these
quiet demure women always are. However, she's met with
her match in Sudlow. They must arrange matters when they
are man and wife. Meanwhile you and I may thank Heaven
we are well out of the whole business. Directly Peg's matter
is settled I shall present my petition in bankruptcy. Poor
girl, she does not know all her father is going through for her
sake! I had thought of having Peg 'turned off' at Chelston
(the Wookes would have been only too delighted to stand a
wedding spread at the Pleasaunce); but second thoughts are
best, and it seemed to me we should act prudently (one ought
always to keep an eye on the future) to play no triumphal
march while the disgustingly woolly sheep, Sudlow, was led up
for sacrifice.

"Besides, the Wookes are total abstinence folks, and you
know what that means when the success of a marriage feast is
in the balance.

"You have managed splendidly about the settlements. In
confidence I may tell you, if it had been impossible to get
Sudlow up to the starting-post so weighted, I'd have let Peg

take her chance without any settlements at all. After my first London experience of her, I knew she would be a most difficult young woman to 'run,' and I think we both deserve the highest praise for getting her married at all! My letter has been the work of two mornings. Of your charity write often, if you can, to this poor 'Exile of Erin.'

"I don't complain. You know I never complain; still there is no denying the fact that solitary confinement in the height of the London season is rough on

"Yours faithfully,

"GEOFFREY CHELSTON.

"P.S.—One little suggestion. Don't you think it might be well to pay that milliner's bill of Peg's? Of course I want to put it in my schedule; but if I do I'm afraid Madame Rosalie will apply to Sudlow for it, and kick up no end of a row, in the event of his not paying her, and whether he paid her or not he would make things confoundedly unpleasant for the girl.

"If you agree with me I am sure you will do what I can't, namely, settle with Madame R. As you are acting so generously about the bridal rig-out all could be paid under one head, and it will be the last thing you will ever have to do for Peg. Tell Susan, by the time her execution morning comes, I mean to be well enough to act as father.

"I am so glad about Dane. As I always said no better fellow ever breathed, and from the very first I felt sure his innocence would be proved. When you are amongst jewellers, I wish you would choose some pretty trifle and send it with the enclosed to Susan. I'll square that account with you out of the *very first* bit of luck which comes in my way.

"G. C."

Mr. Gayre felt inside the envelope for the enclosure mentioned. It proved to be a slip of paper, on which were written the words, "From Papa Geoff."

For a short time Sir Geoffrey's brother-in-law sat contemplating this epistle with a sort of amazed admiration. There had been a period when it would have maddened him, but that period was past, and he could now regard Sir Geoffrey dispassionately as a person upon whose like it seemed most improbable he should ever look again.

Besides, the letter was almost an epitome of the events

which had occurred within the space of little over a year. Was
it really something less than fifteen months since that day when
he sauntered idly across the grass in Hyde Park, and saw Sudlow leaning over the rails? Why, those months seemed to him
a whole existence. He had nearly lived a life in the time.
What a sermon it all was on the vanity of human hopes, and
on the uselessness of mortal projects. What a satire to be
commissioned by Papa Geoff to buy a wedding gift it was
intended he himself should pay for, to present to the woman he
loved!

"I thought to manage Sir Geoffrey," he considered, "and
Sir Geoffrey has managed me. I wonder if he will outwit his
new friend Mr. Sponner. Nothing more likely. And what
about Mrs. Fitz-Hugh when Mr. Fitz-Hugh goes out of business, and relinquishes whist and leaves her a widow? Humph."
and Mr. Gayre, lighting a match, applied it to the Baronet's
letter and watched the precious missive burn to dust on the
hearth.

Whatever his faults, and he had many, the banker was not
really mean. All his instincts led him to loyalty, for which
reason he did not docket and pigeon-hole his brother-in-law's
epistle and consider "This may prove useful some day."

What he did, however, consider was that he wished he had
not to go to Chislehurst in order to spend a "nice, quiet, comfortable afternoon." He was forced to spend many such afternoons at The Warren, and they filled his soul with a terrible
despair. What should he do when he was married and life became a series of such afternoons? Already Susan was avenged.
Never had she shrunk with greater horror from the idea of
passing existence with him than he recoiled from the notion of
spending the years "few and evil" which might be in store for
him with Mrs. Jubbins.

It was the old Brunswick Square business over again. She
had changed the venue, but the pleadings were the same. He
never for half-an-hour together got out of the Jones, Brown,
and Robinson set. Deputy Pettell and others of that connection literally swarmed upon the carpet. Their houses, their
furniture, their carriages, their servants, their friends, their
parties, their travels, their sayings, their doings—was he never,
till death brought peace, to hear any other sort of conversation?
Talk of moulding Mrs. Jubbins! He might as well have thought
of making her a girl again or of cutting down her goodly proportions to the airy symmetry of a Hebe! Endurance was the

-only thing left for him, and to do Mr. Gayre justice he did bear the eternal flow of talk about nothing with saint-like equanimity. He had sold himself for a mess of pottage and he would have to wear the chains of his captivity, though they galled his flesh and ate into his very soul. Already there had been a few differences of opinion, in all of which Mrs. Jubbins marched off the field with a grand composure in the character of conqueror. She would have felt greatly surprised had any one told her she was or wanted to be a conqueror; she honestly believed she was deferring to Mr. Gayre in all things. It is difficult for a woman whose first husband has made an idol of her, and whose widowhood has proved a long career of doing exactly what she liked, to understand her ways and ideas or even her manners and habits can possibly be uncongenial to any one who wishes to marry her. Mrs. Jubbins had fallen into the not uncommon mistake of imagining that all she did, and all she had, stood far above the vulgar height, where holes could be picked in either her doings or belongings. She had her own notions, and of course those notions were right. She had her possessions, and those possessions in her opinion were precisely the proper possessions. She wished to live in town, and as a natural consequence it was ridiculous to suppose Mr. Gayre could really prefer the country. He knew nothing about the country, and she did; she had lived in it for a whole year and was deadly tired of it; he had not lived in it at all, if he had he would be tired of it too. This was Mrs. Jubbins' mode of reasoning, and it is unnecessary to state that the result of discussing future arrangements with Mr. Gayre invariably ended in his apparent conversion to her views; considering what Mrs. Jubbins had done for him he would have been most ungrateful to insist he had any right to maintain his own opinions, but the banker sometimes thought he should like to know whether he might ever be permitted to have an opinion at all. It was very well for Mrs. Jubbins to say, as she did say continually, "I want to consult you." But it was scarcely so agreeable to find that these consultations meant well-nigh interminable talks about what the lady wanted to do.

Mr. Gayre knew perfectly well no better nor kinder woman than Mrs. Jubbins, so far as her light went, ever existed, but he also knew she would wear, and was indeed wearing him to death.

There were things about her which reminded him constantly of his father. He could not forget the monotonous round of

small interests, petty details, contemptible gossip, and narrow
ideas which made Brunswick Square more irksome to him than
narrow cell ever seemed to prisoner. Then he could not say,
" My mind to me a kingdom is," for he often felt his mind was
stultifying while he listened to the even flow of babble that did
duty for conversation in Mrs. Jubbins' house.

Could he face the prospect of being cooped up in a town
house with that eternal trickle of twaddle always running
through his ears ; with the Pettells, and the Jones, and others
of the same ilk, for his only home society ; with his old friends
banished to his club—for he could not—no, he felt he *could
not*—invite men whose ideas were cosmopolitan, who had
travelled, and thought, and read, and seen life, understanding
the phrase in its best and widest sense. to come and listen to
discussions concerning the amount Mr. Robinson's "mansion"
at Walton had cost to build, or the questionable taste of Mrs.
Brown, who having been taken up by a "grand High Church
set." had so far forgotten what her poor papa's ideas of Popery
were, as to go to early service and walk about the West End
clad in hodden gray, and wearing a close bonnet made of brown
straw, just as if she were the wife of a clerk in the receipt of
thirty shillings a week.

Further, he could not disguise the fact that antagonistic as
Mrs. Jubbins might be to him, she was beginning to feel him
even more antagonistic to her.

Honestly, he meant to make her an excellent husband ; but
he had no intention of being a foolish one ! At the first offset
it was clearly understood marriage should not be thought of till
sufficient time had elapsed to enable him to release his own
capital, and finally put matters between him and his future wife
on some business and tangible footing. For a time this arrangement worked admirably, but it could not last for ever, and with
dismay Mr. Gayre found himself expected to play the part of
lover to a lady he had known ever since she wore short frocks,
and blue sashes—and whom he should certainly have thought
old enough to know better. Something of the awe she formerly
felt for him still remained ; but it was wearing away. No later
than the occasion of his last visit to Chislehurst, she entered
through the open window near which he was seated in order to
ask him some question, and in the most simple and natural
manner came behind his chair, put a hand on each shoulder and
called him "*dear*."

Mr. Gayre thought of this experience with a shudder. He

recalled the sudden chill her action had sent through him, and earnestly trusted the good, generous soul felt nothing of the deadly tremor which for a moment turned his strength into weakness.

He could not draw back now. In honour, in common honesty, he was forced to go on. As long as he could make the woman who trusted him happy and content, what did it signify how wretched he felt? He had been placed in a sore strait—on the one side lay the Scylla of poverty, on the other the Charybdis of an uncongenial marriage.

Matrimony was the only interest Mrs. Jubbins would have accepted and that he could have offered for the use of her fortune. Yes, looking back he could see no other course possible for him to pursue. Given that he dared not face bankruptcy, no resource remained but to marry the relict of Mr. Jubbins. The position did not bear thinking about, so deciding not to think about it Mr. Gayre put aside his papers and started for Chislehurst.

He found Mrs. Jubbins arrayed in a very pretty summer dress, which did not become her in the least. Susan or his niece would have looked lovely in it ; but the soft flow of the light material, and the cunning interlacing of delicate colours, were death to Mrs. Jubbins' mature charms. Nevertheless, he had to say something about her attire, and he spoke a few words of compliment with such grace as he could assume. That was the first event of an afternoon he will never forget as long as he keeps his memory. From the first moment things went on steadily chafing his spirit and finally inducing such a state of irritability, that finally addressing one of Mrs. Jubbins' young people in a tone of sharp decision, he said, "Don't be so rude, sir." Mrs. Jubbins' offspring were, as a rule, extremely rude—but no one had ever ventured to tell them so before, and the lad stared at the banker ere, turning on his heel, he walked out of the room, whistling defiantly.

Mrs. Jubbins looked at Mr. Gayre, and Mr. Gayre looked at Mrs. Jubbins—but neither spoke. The boy had been offensively impertinent ; even a mother's partiality couldn't deny that fact. Mr. Gayre regretted his hasty speech, but felt he ought not to apologise. He waited for Mrs. Jubbins to make some remark, but to his surprise and relief she took no verbal notice of what had occurred.

Instead, she began to talk of The Warren, and her wish to return to town.

"I have been thinking," she said, "that I should like to take a house somewhere in the Kensington direction. I do not care much for Palace Gardens, though the houses there are good, and of course it is nice to look out on the Park. I prefer Campden Hill. I really do not think I should object to Campden Hill."

"You have quite decided, then, not to return to Brunswick Square?"

"Quite—the neighbourhood, you see, has so altered its character. Besides, the lease has not long to run, and I feel sure Mr. Motten would be glad to take it for the remainder of my term."

"And I had a letter this morning from an old Indian friend, who is coming home on leave for eighteen months, asking me to look out a place for him within twelve miles of town. The Warren would, I know, suit him exactly."

"I am so glad. I have taken it on for another year, and I should not like to be under two rents."

"That is a thing to be avoided, certainly," and then there ensued another silence. Mr. Gayre felt he was spending a very quiet afternoon indeed.

"Shall we take a turn through the grounds?" asked Mrs. Jubbins, "the gardens are looking beautiful. As Mrs. Gibson was saying only yesterday, they do Holditch very great credit indeed."

As he had observed, a score of times before, Mr. Gayre again observed there could be no doubt but that Holditch understood his business.

"I must just get a parasol, so we may as well go through the hall," and accordingly they passed through the hall, where Mr. Gayre had seen Susan sitting amongst the flowers on that night which seemed so long and long ago.

As though she had known of what he was thinking, Mrs. Jubbins, directly they got upon the gravelled walk leading down the hill-side on which the gardens lay, began,

"That dear Miss Drummond was here the other day; she came to say good-bye."

"Why, where is she going?" asked Mr. Gayre.

"To her cousin's, to the place where she spent her girlhood. She is to be married from there; did you not know?"

"I did know something of it, but I had forgotten. How is she looking?"

"*Radiantly* happy; poor thing, I *am* so sorry for her!"

"Sorry! Why?"

"O, because she *will* marry that young man, and what *can* be in store for her but misery? Nobody will ever believe in his innocence, and even supposing he had been innocent when he was sent to that dreadful place, how can he be fit for any nice woman to associate with after living among thieves and murderers and, as Deputy Pettell calls them, the very scum of the population?"

"I do not think we need discuss that question again," suggested Mr. Gayre, who had heard it discussed till he was tired.

"Then they have so little money; nothing, I assure you, but the trifle she has left out of her own small fortune."

"They have a great deal of love, though."

"But, good gracious, people can't live entirely on love! and, after all, I am afraid, though I did not say so to her, there is much more love on the one side than on the other. I shall never feel quite satisfied about that business of Miss Colvend. If he had not paid attentions to the young lady, of course she would never have thought of getting so violently fond of him."

"You must understand such matters better than I," said Mr. Gayre humbly.

"And I have not patience with his folly in refusing to accept compensation from Mr. Colvend. He says it would look as if he were being bought off—like taking hush money. So ridiculous! 'He ought to take all he can for your sake, my dear,' I told her, but she wouldn't see it. Her cousin means to try and get him an appointment, but I suppose he can only expect some paltry salary."

"I rejoice to hear she is looking well and happy."

"Yes, but I am afraid that won't last. She spoke very gratefully about you, though not *so* gratefully as I consider she ought, considering the *enormous* trouble you gave yourself over Mr. Dane's affair."

"I only wish I had been able to do more, and do it sooner," he answered. "Ah! there goes Joshua! Did you see how he turned back the moment he saw us? He hasn't forgiven me yet for telling him not to be rude."

"No, poor boy; you see my children have never been spoken to in that way."

"If you really think I went beyond the limit of what I ought to have said I suppose I ought to apologise."

"No, no, don't think of such a thing," said Mrs. Jubbins hurriedly : "you did not mean to vex me, only—only—you scarcely understand—you have not been accustomed to young people, and, besides—"

He looked at her inquiringly, as she paused and coloured violently. " I fear I have annoyed you even more than I thought," he said. " Believe me, I had not the slightest idea my remark would wound you in any way. I am very rry. so You know if there be one person in the world whose feelings I should consider more than another, that person is yourself."

She made a little sign to ask him to stop ; then, all of a sudden turning and beginning to retrace her steps, she murmured in a voice so low he could scarcely catch her tones,

" I want to speak to you. Let us go and sit under the ash-trees ; we shall not be interrupted there."

Mr. Gayre assented, wondering greatly. He had not understood an inexplicable change in her manner, which he noticed from the first moment she greeted him. What could she be going to say ? He racked his brain to imagine what had happened.

Afterwards he remembered each detail of that interview, could recall the way the sunbeams lay athwart the road ; could see the trembling of the leaves, feel again the touch of the gentle wind which lightly swayed the branches ; but just at that moment all sense of observation seemed swallowed up in amazement.

" It is no use beating about the bush," she began, and her voice was not quite steady. " I will tell you at once what I have been thinking. We must never marry—our engagement must end."

" Why ?" he aked.

" The last two months have been very pleasant to me," she went on, unheeding his question ; " one week out of them I may say was the happiest in all my life. When I look back I can never remember a time when I did not care for you ; when I was a girl you were the hero of my imagination, the ideal man of all my girlish dreams."

He was about to speak, but she laid her hand on his, as a token she did not want him to do so.

" When I was left a widow and my mother told me your father wished you and me to marry I felt life almost too happy ; I forgot my dead husband and all he had done for me and mine, and thought of you and you only. I am not ashamed to tell you this now," she proceeded, after the slightest break ; " because it's all past and done with; we will, I hope, be good friends for ever; but I have thought matters over, and know it is best we should be nothing more."

" May I again ask you why—I shall not try to influence your decision, but if not disagreeable, I wish you would tell me the causes which have induced you to arrive at it."

" I will tell you as well as I can. First of all, the conviction has been growing upon me, for a long time, that we were unfitted for each other—it is no sudden fancy of mine—that we should never be quite happy together. You have your notions and I have mine, and we could not make them agree. Even in upholstery, the things I like you don't like—and it is the same in other matters. That we might get over though ; but what I never could get reconciled to is that you do not care for me—really. If you ever had cared for me you would have said so, years ago."

" Passionate attachment," he urged, " can perhaps scarcely be expected from a man of my age—but—"

" Yes, I understand all that," she interrupted, " but I should not feel satisfied. I know now, why, at times, lately I have been so unsettled and miserable—yes, miserable—even while I believed myself happy—but there is more still. I have yet another reason."

" I must indeed be a heinous criminal," he remarked, with a faint smile.

" No," she said, " you are not to blame at all, the fault is entirely my own. I have no right to marry—anybody. My husband left me in charge of a great trust, and I ought to try to be worthy of it. How could I do justice to his children and to you? I never thought of marrying anybody but you— and I shall never think of marrying again. I mean to live for my sons and my daughters, and to be what your father once said I was—a faithful steward."

" It is perhaps quite as well, then, that I spoke to Joshua as I did to-day ; otherwise, you might not have found out your duty till it was too late," said Mr. Gayre.

" Yes, I should. I had found it out, and what do you think showed it to me?"

" I would really rather not hazard any conjecture."

" Miss Drummond."

" Why, what did she say ?"

" She said nothing, except two words. I'll tell you how it

happened. When we were talking together, and she was speaking about how happy she was, I could not help telling her I was very happy too. I forgot, for the moment, you and I had agreed to let no one know how affairs stood for the present—and I went on—'I am going to marry a man I have loved all my life; your friend, Mr. Gayre.' I assure you, it slipped out quite accidentally."

"Yes, and then—"

"She repeated '*Mr. Gayre*,' just like that, in an incredulous sort of tone—yet still as if she was shocked—and I shall never forget the look in her face, like some one who could scarcely believe her ears. Then she recovered herself and said, prettily, she wished us all sorts of happiness—but the way she cried out Mr. Gayre, and her startled expression, have haunted me ever since. I could not close my eyes last night, I felt so wretched, and then when you spoke to Joshua as you did, I knew it was best we should consider everything at an end. As for the money, don't trouble yourself about that— keep it as long as you like—I always knew you would not wrong me or my children of a penny—but lending money is one thing and marrying another; and now say you are not angry with me, and that we shall never cease to be friends?"

"Mrs. Jubbins, I never respected or admired you so much as I do at this moment—and I shall always be your devoted friend," said Mr. Gayre—and it is only right to add he spoke from his heart.

"Relief!" Was that any word to express the load taken from his heart? As he returned to town that night he felt very humble, very penitent, very thankful. "Heaven has been more merciful to me than I deserve," he thought, and who can deny but that there was a considerable amount of truth in the observation?

CHAPTER XXXVIII.

CONCLUSION.

WHITSUNTIDE 1877. May once again, for the third time, since that morning when Mr. Gayre stood beside the railings in Hyde Park, and watched Margaret Chelston's meeting with the " fairest of fair women."

London was virtually deserted. On the previous Saturday London had despatched her hundreds, and tens of hundreds, her millions, indeed, into the quiet country, to the seashore, and the Continent. On Monday morning there was not a street situated in as low and poor neighbourhood a district visitor could name, but found means to raise enough money to charter some sort of conveyance and proceed behind wretched horses that must long previously have learned to curse the sound of a cornopean, to such places of resort as represent fun and fashion to the excursionist mind. The great Metropolis was like a city of the dead. Round and about the Royal Exchange many commercial corpses lay awaiting burial, but the ceremony being compulsorily delayed till after Bank Holiday. the men whose cheques and bills had been dishonoured were waiting in suburban villas and great West End mansions, for some miracle to happen in the interval which should enable them to begin the struggle of business life afresh on the Tuesday following Pentecost.

In the streets scarcely a human being was to be met with —cabmen recognising a possible fare afar off hailed him with effusion; a few country cousins wandered four abreast along the pavements without getting "shouldered" for their pains; lads who had no pennies wherewith to pay train or tram fares, tied white woollen scarves tightly round their throats, and started to walk for the nearest places where sticklebacks could be fished for, or the pleasing sport of seeing starved donkeys being thrashed by brutes armed with heavy sticks witnessed. Scarce a soul was abroad. The better classes who were forced to remain in town kept close within doors;

on the railways all distinctions of class were virtually abolished; it was possible to walk from Temple Bar to Ludgate Circus down the middle of the horse-road; the West End conveyed a pleasing impression of rustic seclusion; men walked to their clubs as if a large balance of the seventy allotted years remained in which to stroll along the shady side of the street; in the home counties rhododendrons and early roses, hawthorn, laburnum, lilac, a thousand wild flowers—yellow buttercups, meek-eyed daisies, springing grass—girt London round with a natural belt of emerald green, gemmed by a thousand stars of divine hues, such as no astronomer, no jeweller, ever, out of his own consciousness, could have imagined.

In the hedgerows, by the wayside, flowers were springing, blooming, dying. It was an early year, and in London a May sun positively beamed upon its inhabitants. There were not many belonging to the better condition of life remaining to be beamed on; still one man, well considered and reputed to be wealthy, was walking down Duke Street, St. James', on his way to Victoria Station.

The quietest of quiet pedestrians, the sedatest of sedate gentlemen! Certainly not very young, presumably not very old, a clean-cut, closely-shaved, military-looking sort of person, who might have been anybody, from peer to poet, but who happened to belong neither to the Upper Ten nor to the dear Bohemia.

Suddenly the silence of the West End street was rent with, "Gayre, Gayre! Hillo! Hillo!" and Gayre, for so the gentleman was named, turning round, beheld a figure on the opposite side of the way, making frantic signs for him to stop.

"Ah! you remember me," this individual said, as they shook hands in the middle of the horse-road. "Gad, you are looking well. Years, I vow, run by and leave you younger."

"Why, Sir Geoffrey, I did not expect to meet you here."

"And, by Jove, I did not expect to meet you. Just see here, Gayre," and the Baronet affectionately passed his arm through that of his brother-in-law, as if they were the dearest of dear friends, "I swear it is like water in a thirsty land to look on your pleasant face again. I am glad to have even this glimpse of you. I called at Sudlow's, but, faith, I found such cold welcome there I was glad to return to mine inn."

"They are not a very genial pair, certainly."

"No, but you remember what I always said. I mayn't be a very sharp fellow, but I'm the very deuce in the way of prophecy. I always knew they would suit each other to a T. Lord, how she did go on about my marriage.

"'You hold your tongue, my girl,' I said, 'there was trouble enough to get *you* married.' That shut *her* up."

"And how is your wife?" asked Mr. Gayre. For answer his brother-in-law pulled a newspaper from his pocket—smoothed it carefully over his knee—turned to the first page, folded it up so as to leave the "births" outside, and pointed out one especial paragraph for perusal.

The paragraph ran thus—

"At Brockborough, near Doncaster, the wife of Sir Geoffrey Chelston, Baronet, of a son and heir."

"It is all their own composition," explained the happy father. "Gad, I wish they'd make me an heir, but I'm nobody now, of course. I came up to town to be clear of the fuss. Old Sponner is just out of his senses with delight at being grandfather to an embryo baronet."

"I am sure I congratulate you all very heartily."

"It's more than Peggy did. I said, 'It's of no use your turning up your nose; you'd better by far be civil to the young stranger. He is born with a silver spoon in his mouth. He'll have lots of money when he comes of age. Old Sponner swears he shall have all his money, and his mother says *she'll* see I have no chance of touching it. By the bye, I stopped a night at Susan's on my way up. She's got a jolly little girl, and she is prettier than ever—and as for Dane, he's fairly crazy about her. You'd think no man ever owned a wife before. She's just the same as she used to be, only a little quieter. I think she can't quite forget all that trouble. She is the best creature! She persuaded Lal Hilderton to leave London, and he lives in a cottage on the estate, with Sue's old nurse to cook his meals and mend his socks. He's doing real good work, I hear—don't profess to care for that sort of thing myself! Weren't you surprised to hear Dane had got his grandfather's property? Good job the miserly old sinner could never make up his mind to sign a will. Well, they are a very happy pair—as happy a pair as you'd wish to see. I often wonder you never married, Gayre, but perhaps you're as well as you are—women as a rule are a confounded lot of trouble."

"I am sorry you think so, for I have asked one to take care of me."

"Who is it—Mrs. Jubbins?"

" Mrs. Jubbins will never marry anybody. No. this is the daughter of a man who was my superior officer when I first entered the army. She is a charming girl, or rather woman, for she is nearly thirty, and I hope and believe we are exactly suited to each other. Her father leaves for India before the end of the summer, and then we shall take up our residence permanently at The Warren. You recollect Mrs. Jubbins' party there ?"

" Rather," said Sir Geoffrey. " Well, I'm heartily glad to hear this, my boy—and whenever you're ready, only let me know, and I'll come and look you up. Gad, you've decided on a sweet place. I am more pleased than I can tell you to think you are going to live at The Warren—always thought that dear good creature, Mrs. Jubbins, was the wrong thing in the right place there. Money's not everything—that's what I say a dozen times a week ; but I can't get the set I've got mixed up with to believe me."

" You have quite recovered from your accident ?"

" Yes, quite, thank you ; leg's a bit stiff still, but I can ride as well as ever, Heaven be praised ; don't know what would become of me if I couldn't. By the bye, I was deucedly glad to hear you are allowing interest on balances now. I can send you lots of accounts, and I don't want a penny of commission. Yes, indeed, it was quite a surprise to me to hear some fellows saying the other day that the old Tortoise might chance to outstrip some new hares yet. There's Graceless ! I must be off. Hi, Gayre ! just one thing more. Mark my words, you'll see that youngster won't be able to drink a drop of anything stronger than water. I know he'll turn out a regular milksop. Shouldn't wonder if they make a parson of him. The Reverend Sir Ferdinand Chelston, Baronet. You'll find that's what it will be. Ferdinand is his mother's selection. Well, good-bye ; don't quite forget me."

The banker stood looking after Sir Geoffrey's retreating figure for a few minutes ; his legs were a little more bowed and his hat a little more on one side than usual, but otherwise there was no change in his appearance.

" Forget you," thought Mr. Gayre, as he turned away— " never !"

THE END.